THE FAMILY MAN

Tim J. Lebbon is a New York Times-bestselling writer with over thirty novels published to date, as well as dozens of novellas and hundreds of short stories. He has won four British Fantasy Awards, a Bram Stoker Award and a Scribe Award, and been shortlisted for the World Fantasy and Shirley Jackson awards. A movie of his story *Pay the Ghost*, starring Nicolas Cage, will be released soon, and several other projects are in development. He lives in the Monmouthshire countryside with his wife Tracey, children Ellie and Dan, and his dog Blu. He enjoys running and biking in the hills, and sometimes he imagines he's being chased.

Follow Tim on Twitter @timlebbon

By the same author:

THE HUNT

To find out more visit **www.timlebbon.net**

T.J. LEBBON

The Family Man

avon

AVON

A division of HarperCollins*Publishers*
1 London Bridge Street,
London SE1 9GF

www.harpercollins.co.uk

A Paperback Original 2016

1

Copyright © Tim Lebbon 2016

Tim Lebbon asserts the moral right to
be identified as the author of this work

A catalogue record for this book is
available from the British Library

ISBN-13: 9780008122911

Set in Minion 11/14.46 pt by Palimpsest Book Production Limited,
Falkirk, Stirlingshire

Printed and bound in Great Britain by
Clays Ltd, St Ives plc

MIX
Paper from
responsible sources
FSC˚ C007454

FSC
www.fsc.org

FSC™ is a non-profit international organisation established to promote
the responsible management of the world's forests. Products carrying the
FSC label are independently certified to assure consumers that they come
from forests that are managed to meet the social, economic and
ecological needs of present and future generations,
and other controlled sources.

Find out more about HarperCollins and the environment at
www.harpercollins.co.uk/green

For Pic

Author's Note: Some of the towns and locations in this novel exist in real life. In fact, I live very close to Usk and Abergavenny and they're both very beautiful places. I have also visited Brusvily in France many times, and it is equally lovely. But I've taken the monstrous liberty of changing things about these places to suit the novel – layout, landscape, the names of shops and pubs. It's a terrible indulgence, and I beg your forgiveness.

'The battle line between good and evil runs through the heart of every man.'
– Alexander Solzhenitsyn

Chapter One

The Space Between Breaths

When it regained consciousness, he had already glued its mouth shut.

This excited him. It was like locking the life inside, not letting it bleed out. Usually there was some sort of leakage as something died beneath his hands – blood, breath, tears. This already felt different. He decided that he would use the glue again.

He turned away as it started to twist and moan. The bindings were tight, and he knew that there was no chance of it working its way free. Not in the short time it had left. But for a moment he wanted to observe unseen, not meet its gaze. He liked the power this gave him.

Circling around behind the chair, he paused to watch. Perhaps it could smell him. It could certainly hear him, because his breathing was deep and heavy, calm. But now that it could no longer see him, the panic was deeper, the desperation more divine.

He watched for a while, coughing once, uttering a long, low whistle, excited at how these sounds affected its behaviour – a pause, and then more frantic efforts to break free.

1

He glanced around the room. The house was old and abandoned, everything neat and ordered but layered with years of dust, perhaps the home of a dead person with no relatives. It was out of time, and he was confident that he would not be interrupted. The traditional life represented here by a bulky TV, a table for dinner, and family photographs, was not *his* life.

Far from it.

A loud snort drew his attention back to his victim. Blood and mucus shot from its broken nose, and then it breathed more easily.

He closed slowly from behind, and then pounced.

Moving with confidence, he pulled its head back against the high-backed chair, pressed the tube's nozzle into one nostril, and squirted the superglue inside.

Then he dropped the tube and squeezed its nose shut.

As it squirmed and tensed, attempting to writhe from side to side against the ropes, its strength surprised him. He had to pull back hard, tipping the chair onto its two rear legs. But it didn't take long.

After a minute he let the chair drop back onto all fours. The impact on the hardwood floor had the sound of finality. Retrieving the tube of glue, he moved around to face it for the last time.

Its right nostril was closed, deformed. Its eyes were wide and desperate, issuing pleas that it knew would not be answered.

He could see that realisation in its eyes – there was no hope, and the only future remaining was the space between this breath and its last. That pleased him. Its panic was his fuel.

Pressing its head back against the chair, he heard the sudden inhalation that would feed those final few seconds.

He squirted glue into its open nostril. Squeezed the nose shut. Looked into its eyes.

'Shhh,' he said.

But even then, he did not smile.

Chapter Two

One Thing

It was the downhills that scared Dom the most.

He'd once read that cycling defines the man, and as he mounted the brow of the hill and followed Andy down into the first curve of the big descent, he couldn't help but agree.

Andy was hunched low, hands on drop bars, head down, arse up, and he was already moving noticeably ahead.

Dom's hands were feathering the brakes. They'd ridden this descent together several times before, and it was always at this point that the fear bit in.

The garish pink house flitted by on the left, big dog barking from the raised deck and old man sitting in his garden rocker as usual, a bemused expression on his face.

On the right was a low hedge guarding an incredible view across the Monmouthshire countryside, shimmering and hazed in the growing heat of yet another scorching day. And then the road curved around to the left and grew steeper, and there was no going back.

The breeze blasting past his ears carried a distorted 'Yeaaahaaaa!' from Andy, and Dom grinned and hunkered down over his handlebars. As the road straightened into the long, steep descent, Andy was speeding away from him.

Dom always thought about what could go wrong. He knew the route pretty well, and so could swerve around the two portions that were rough and holed. But he'd once seen a squirrel dart across the road just feet from Andy's spinning wheels. If that happened to him, he'd either strike it and spill, or panic and grasp the brakes, which would probably result in a skid and crash.

There was one area of road halfway down that had slumped, kerb bowing down the hillside and road surface cracked and dipped where it was starting to collapse. Trees shaded the road for the last mile of descent, and in those shadows it was harder to see the surface. He might get a bee trapped in his helmet or, worse, behind one lens of his glasses. A puncture at over forty miles per hour could be catastrophic.

At the bottom of the descent was another bend, not too severe, but at those speeds he'd have to steer on trust: trust that there was no car coming the other way in the middle of the road; no cows crossing; no crows feeding on the slick remains of a crushed badger, or—

But as he switched his hands to the drop bars and the wind rushed past his ears, Dom realised that today felt different. Maybe it was the three straight weeks of record-breaking heat and cloudless skies. It could have been the thrill of being out so early, enjoying almost traffic-free roads for the first hour of their ride.

Or perhaps it was because he and his wife, Emma, had made love on their patio the night before. He'd been worried about being seen, even though the garden of their modest detached home was hardly overlooked. She'd soon seen away his fears.

As his speed increased and he reminded himself to be loose and relaxed, he yelled in delight.

Andy still beat him to the bottom, disappearing around the bend twenty seconds before Dom.

Dom moved into the centre of the road and raised himself slightly, trying to see through the trees and shadows and make out whether anything was coming in the opposite direction. He swept around the corner and drifted back towards the left, and as his momentum decreased he switched down a few awkward gears and started pedalling. He'd have to get his gearing sorted before the descents. One more thing he should work on.

Andy was waiting for him half a mile further on. He straddled his bike in the village hall car park, gulping down a drink and looking cool in his expensive shades. Dom came to a stop beside his friend, breathing hard, not from exertion but from the thrill of the descent.

'Fifty-one!' Andy said.

Dom checked his bike computer. 'Forty-eight. Fastest I've done down there. Felt good today.'

'Do one thing every day that scares you.' Andy was fond of the Eleanor Roosevelt quotation, and it always made Dom smile. On these long rides with Andy, he'd usually manage two or three things, at least.

'Christ, it's scorching already,' Dom said. Now that he'd stopped the sweat ran down his face and soaked his jersey, even speckling the hairs on his legs. Andy looked sweaty too, but it seemed to suit him more. His T-shirt was tight and clingy, but whereas Dom's jersey showed his pudgy waistline and lanky arms, Andy's clung to his flat stomach and broad shoulders.

'You'll beat me down one day,' Andy said.

'Doubt that.'

'Should do. You have a distinct weight advantage.'

'Yeah, yeah, thanks.'

Andy grinned. 'So, cake and coffee with the Moody Cow?'

'Damn right.'

Moody Cow was not the name of their favourite pit stop on this particular route, nor the woman who ran the cafe. That was the Blue Door and Sue respectively. But she'd given them enough stern looks to invite the name which had become permanent.

Andy reckoned she fancied him and was playing hard to get. Dom thought it quite likely. Over the two years he'd known Andy, Emma had called him grizzled, rough, and lived-in, and his string of casual girlfriends attested to his effect on the opposite sex.

'Race you!' Andy said. He caged his drink bottle, clipped in and moved off without looking back.

Dom followed. He was pretty good at sprints on the flat, and had been working hard on his turbo trainer over the previous winter to improve his power. Nevertheless, it took the whole two miles to the village of Upper Mill for him to catch Andy, and even then he had the weird feeling his friend let him win.

'Pipped me,' Andy said outside the Moody Cow. 'Coffee and cake on me.' He leaned his bike against the fence and opened the big blue door.

Dom watched him go, leaning on his handlebars. He was exhausted, breath heavy and burning in his chest, legs shaking. Sweat ran behind his biking glasses and misted them, and he had to take them off. Andy had hardly seemed out of breath.

'Bloody hell, fat bastard,' he muttered, taking deep breaths and feeling his galloping heartbeat beginning to settle. In truth, he wasn't fat at all. Compared to most men in their early forties he was way above average when it came to fitness, even though he carried a few pounds extra. But Andy wasn't most men, and Dom really wished he could stop comparing himself to his friend. They were good mates, but their lifestyles were chalk and cheese, and he wouldn't change a thing.

Leaving the bikes against the timber fencing that surrounded the cafe's front garden, he chose a table in the shade.

There were a couple of elderly couples having their morning coffee, and at the garden's far end a group of businessmen nattered over fluttering sheets and a laptop.

There was also a couple of women, maybe in their early thirties, dressed in tight shorts and vest tops. They'd obviously been for a run, water bottles discarded on the table in favour of tall fruit smoothies. One of them caught his eye. He smiled; she glanced back to her friend.

Dom unzipped his jersey halfway, self-consciously turning his back on the women. As he sat down and kicked off his bike shoes, one of them laughed softly. It was nothing to do with him. It can't have been.

He took the phone from his jersey's back pocket and slipped it from its pouch. There were no missed calls or texts, but he took a selfie with the cafe behind him and sent it to Emma. *Refuelling stop*, he typed with the picture.

Andy appeared and scraped a seat across into the sunlight before slumping in it. 'The coffee stop of kings,' he said. 'Our lovely hostess will bring our morning repast forthwith.'

'Nice.'

'Ahh, this is the life.' Andy stretched like a cat. 'Nice spot, this.'

'Sue should start giving us regulars' discount.'

'Right, I'll let you ask her.'

Dom smiled.

'So what's next week got in store for you?' Andy asked.

'New kitchen fit-out up in Monmouth.'

Today, Dom had given himself a rare day off from work. He ran his own small electrical firm, just himself and an apprentice who'd been with him for three years. Davey was a good worker and a pleasant lad, and Dom was pretty sure he'd soon be making a break to set up on his own. He didn't mind that so much. It was bound to happen, and he couldn't expect the lad to stay working for him forever.

Andy chuckled. 'Oh, Mr Electrician, have you come to rewire my plugs?'

'Yeah, like that's ever happened.'

'Sure it has.'

'Not all manual labourers have lives resembling the plots of pornos, you know.'

'No?'

'That's just you.'

'Sure, the sordid life of a freelance technical writer.'

'So how is the gorgeous Claudette?' Dom asked.

Andy had been on–off dating a French doctor spending a year on a work exchange at the hospital in Abergavenny. Early-thirties and beautiful, Dom had only met her once.

Andy leaned over. 'Porn star,' he whispered, grinning.

Dom rolled his eyes, and when he looked at his friend again, Andy was staring across the road.

'Take a look at that,' he said.

Dom followed his gaze. He was expecting to see the two women jogging away, or another attractive woman perhaps walking her dog. So at first he couldn't quite make out what Andy had been staring at.

'What?'

'Security guy.'

A security van was pulled up across the square, and a man was carrying a heavy black case into the local post office.

Dom had never been in there, but it was obviously a typical village post office, doubling as a newsagent and grocer. It had a selection of wooden garden furniture for sale out front, windows half-filled with flyers for local jumble sales and amateur dramatic presentations, and a homemade display wall of bird tables and feeders.

He'd seen people going in and out, and often they'd stop and chat on the wide pavement in front of the shop. This village was far smaller than Usk where he lived, and everyone seemed to know everyone else. The Blue Door cafe probably only thrived because of the main road that ran through the place. That, and the entertaining sourness of its owner.

'So?' Dom asked.

'Doesn't have his helmet on.'

'It's hot.'

'And he's left the van's driver's door open.'

'It's *really* hot. So, what, you're casing the joint?'

Sue arrived then, placing a tray on their table and giving them their drinks and cake. She knew whose was whose.

'Busy day?' Dom asked.

'Rushed off my feet.' She left them and cleared a couple of tables before going back inside.

'Wow. Positively chatty today,' Dom said, but Andy was still staring across the street and didn't respond. 'What now?'

Andy stuffed some flapjack into his mouth and took a swig of coffee. Then he nodded across the small square again. 'Just asking to be ripped off.'

The security man was standing outside the post office talking to a large, middle-aged woman. Dom had seen her before, and he guessed she was the postmistress. They were standing in front of the display window, shielding their eyes against the sun as they chatted. The woman threw her head back and laughed. The man waved his free hand as if to illustrate a point more clearly. He still carried the case.

'How much do you reckon's in there?' Andy asked.

'No idea.'

'Just standing there.'

Dom started on his chocolate shortbread, balancing the guilt against the promise of a thirty-mile ride back home.

Andy ate silently, then drank more coffee.

It wasn't like him to be so quiet, Dom thought. Usually he'd be joshing, making quips about some of the other patrons, talking about the ride they'd had and the route to take back home.

'Suppose it's pretty safe around here,' Dom said, more to break the silence than anything else.

Andy shrugged.

'Just take one daring person, though.' He licked his finger and picked up crumbs from his plate, looked into his empty cup, obviously contemplating another coffee.

'Or two,' Dom said. He chuckled. '"And no one ever suspected the two innocent cyclists", the papers'll say.'

Andy glanced up at him, and the moment paused.

Dom still heard chatter from the women and businessmen, and even the distant mumble of voices from across by the post office. But the air between him and his friend seemed to stop for a moment, movement ceased, and Andy's eyes grew painted and still.

Then he sat back in his chair and stretched, interlocking his fingers and cracking his knuckles above his head.

'Gonna be a hot ride,' he said. 'Get back to Usk two-ish. How about I carry on home and change, then get back down for a couple of early evening ones at the Ship?'

'Friday cider weather,' Dom said.

'Damn right.'

They stood and headed back to their bikes.

On the way through the small garden area they passed the two joggers. 'Morning, ladies,' Andy said. He got a smile from one of them, and a lingering stare from the other.

Dom sighed. It was a hilly ride home. He'd be following in Andy's wake.

Chapter Three

Dangerous

Later that evening the Ship was full, customers spilling across the gardens and down onto the riverbank. Dom was enjoying the familiar post-exercise glow, a tiredness that felt earned, knowing that his aching muscles the next day would soon fade away. Three pints in, his potential aching head was another matter.

'Another?' Andy asked.

'You're driving home. You're already over the limit.'

'I'll drink lemonade. Doesn't mean you can't have another pint of dirty.' The Ship served a local scrumpy that they'd nicknamed dirty, an acquired taste but seemingly brewed especially for scorching summer evenings like this. After a bike ride. With canoes on the river and half the village sprawled around the pub.

Dom held out his glass. 'Hit me, baby, one more time.'

Andy headed for the pub, leaving Dom sitting on the grassy riverbank staring at the water moving lazily by. He knew plenty of people here to chat to, but he was enjoying this moment of peace and calm reflection.

He'd always considered himself blessed. He and Emma

made a good team. Their daughter, Daisy, was almost eleven years old, bright and fun, growing towards her teens with grace and intelligence. Some of their other friends were having trouble with their teenaged kids, ranging from strops and long bouts of sulky we-know-better moods, to full on boozing, and in one case being hooked up with a guy ten years their senior. At twenty that wasn't so bad. At fifteen it was an issue.

But Dom did not fear Daisy growing up. She already seemed to have her head screwed on right, and had a great sense of humour that he put down to her confidence amongst adults. Sometimes he looked at her and loved her so much it ached.

He blinked and smiled softly. Booze getting to his head. He'd changed a lot upon becoming a father. Softened up, so Emma said, and when he found himself sobbing watching certain programmes on TV, he couldn't argue. But as well as softening up, becoming a father had rounded him out. Occasionally Andy's shenanigans sounded attractive – the women, the bachelor pad, the impulsive trips abroad to climb some mountain, or kayak along a bloody river somewhere – but he couldn't imagine being without his family.

He and Emma had their troubled moments, but what married couple didn't? They were comfortable, at least to the extent that they didn't really worry about the day-to-day things. More money would always be nice. Working less would be good, too, both for him and Emma. He didn't want to be grafting like this into his late fifties and sixties, that was for sure. But overall they were blessed.

So he wondered just how that seed planted by Andy had taken root.

Every time he blinked, he saw the postmistress standing outside her shop, leaning back and laughing at the sky.

'Here you go, pisshead.' Andy handed him a pint and sat next to him. He had a pint of lemonade and a couple of bags of nuts. 'They never should have banned swimming in the river.'

'It was dangerous. Young Sammy Parks almost drowned.'

'Yeah, and spoiled my view.'

'Not all women in bikinis are parading for your delectation.'

Andy stared at him hard. 'Of course they are.'

They laughed. Drank. Two friends with an easy, undemanding friendship. Andy got on well with Daisy and Emma. He flirted with Dom's wife, but he'd flirt with an oak tree if it wore a skirt. Or probably more so if it didn't. Harmless fun, friendly banter.

Andy was the impulsive one. The dangerous one, Emma had said more than once, which Dom didn't try to take as her saying *he* should be more impulsive or dangerous.

'That post office,' Dom said.

'Yeah.' Andy turned suddenly serious, speaking quieter and looking around. Kids played and laughed, music rode the steamy evening air from somewhere. No one was paying them any attention. 'We should do it.'

'Huh?'

'As you said, no one would suspect us.' Andy swigged his lemonade. He'd had three pints of cider beforehand, but Dom had rarely seen him drunk. Alcohol didn't seem to affect his friend's opinions or judgement. It barely seemed to touch him at all.

'Yeah,' he agreed. 'Me, an electrician. Primary school governor. I've even got a Labrador. Mr Average, Mr Boring.'

'You're not boring.'

Dom looked at Andy. 'I'm not the one who jets off to climb glaciers.' One of Andy's recent trips had taken him to Iceland. He'd been gone for two weeks.

Andy shrugged. He had a strange expression, similar to what Dom had seen at the Blue Door earlier that day. A blankness to his eyes, like he was suddenly someone else.

'And you,' Dom said. 'Technical writer. Lots of cash. Bit of a cock, true, but never been in trouble.'

'Bury the cash for a while,' Andy said. 'Carry on normally.'

'Just one job,' Dom said, chuckling at the cliché, then falling quiet again. It was a weird subject to be talking about in such a place of sunlight and laughter.

'So let's plan!' Andy said. 'It'll be a laugh.'

It took on the air of a joke, and with that lightness came a rush of ideas from them both. It was a throwaway conversation, one they'd have both forgotten by the time they got home, just one of many conversations that filled the times they spent drinking together. Emma would often ask, 'So what did you talk about all evening?' Dom's response was invariably, 'Can't really remember.' Four hours with barely a pause for breath, and he often recalled none of it.

This was like that. Except their conversation had an air of danger about it, and a sense that they were discussing forbidden things, secrets that could never be shared. It was a private, almost intimate thing between them, and it made Dom feel good.

'We'd have to steal a car,' he said.

'Or just blank the number plates with mud. Use yours. Everyone's got a Focus.'

'Right, thanks.'

'Just that stealing a car changes it from one job to two.'

'Fair point. So . . . weapons?'

16

'Don't need them,' Andy said.

'And we couldn't get them even if we did,' Dom said.

Andy didn't really answer. 'These postmasters don't give a shit about the money in their safe; it's not theirs, it's insured, and they won't lose a thing if it's nicked.'

'You're sure about that?' Dom asked.

'Just guessing.' Andy drained his lemonade. 'It's afterwards that matters. The job takes ten minutes, but it's the days and weeks afterwards when we could give ourselves away.'

'We'd still have to ride out that way!' Dom said. It was almost exciting. 'Sit outside the Blue Door as usual.'

'Everything as normal,' Andy agreed.

'Then we'd be seen on crime scene photos by the investigators, like perps returning to the scene of their crime.'

'What, Dom, you after infamy?'

'I'm after nothing,' Dom said. It sounded awkward, too serious. 'Just buckets full of cold, hard cash.'

'Probably won't get buckets from a little provincial place like that.'

'How much do you reckon?'

'Dunno.' Andy shrugged. 'Hit it at the right time, maybe forty grand?'

'Nice little nest egg.'

'Not bad for ten minutes' work,' Andy agreed. He looked around and smiled. 'Wonder what everyone would think if they knew what we were talking about.'

Dom glanced around at the full pub garden and bustling riverbank. Men with sun reddened torsos smiled wider than usual, alcohol soothing their worries. Women sported summer hats and sleeveless dresses. Kids darted here and there, a few people in canoes fought against the river's flow, and a couple of hundred metres along the bank, youths were jumping ten feet into the water from an old wooden mooring. A boy and girl crouched near the bank with phones, trying to get the best shots.

'No one would believe us,' Dom said. Andy grasped his arm and leaned in close.

'That's why we really should do it.'

'Don't be soft.'

'Why not? It's not hurting anyone. Your worst criminal record is a speeding fine. I don't even have that. We're the last people the law would turn to. In, out, done. And like you say, a nest egg for the future.'

Dom swigged some more cider. It was going to his head now, swilling confusion behind his eyes, freeing inhibitions. Emma always said he was a man made free after a couple of pints, as if alcohol could snip off the constraints he'd imposed upon himself to get by in society and life.

'Sure,' he said. 'After another pint.'

'Pisshead.'

'Sure.'

Dom swayed a little as he walked across the pub garden, nodding at the people he knew, pausing to chat a couple of times.

Inside he dumped the empties on a table and went for a leak. Leaning his head against the wall, watching his piss swill down the urinal, he tried to make light of the post office idea.

But he couldn't. Though it was something he knew he could never really do, just thinking about it was exciting, and talking it through with Andy gave it that edge. That sheen of reality. Andy had a way of making the dangerous seem possible.

Dom knew he should stop drinking, but it didn't feel like a normal day. Still buzzing from the long ride, the blazing sunlight and unusual heat, and the weird sense of danger pervading their conversation, he bought one more pint.

On the way back to Andy on the riverbank he was thinking about disguises.

'One last glass?' Mandy asked.

She and Emma had already polished off one bottle of Prosecco between them, and were halfway through the second. But it was that sort of day. Gorgeous weather, a nice couple of hours that afternoon with Dom in the garden after his bike ride, Daisy at a camping sleepover with friends.

Mandy had turned up at their house unannounced, complaining that her boyfriend, Paul, had fucked off on a football weekend without her again, and it had turned into one of those long, impromptu boozy evenings that were always the best kind.

'Be rude to leave it in the bottle,' Emma said.

'Rude,' Mandy agreed, giggling. She couldn't hold her drink very well, but she drank the most out of all Emma's friends. It wasn't *quite* a problem, Emma usually thought. Not yet.

Conversation had moved rapidly on from character assassinating Mandy's absent boyfriend. They'd gossiped about others in the village, the housing estate being built on the outskirts, the new headmistress in Daisy's primary school, and a dozen other things she could hardly remember. It had been a fun couple of hours. But now there was a slight chill on the evening air, and as Mandy poured, Emma stood to fetch blankets for them.

'You're lucky,' Mandy said.

'How so?' Emma leaned against the back door jamb.

'Dominic. He's so dependable.'

'Yeah, he is.' Emma nodded and smiled, glancing at the ground.

'Oh, really,' Mandy said, shaking her head and almost tumbling herself from the patio chair. 'Come on, Em, there's no way you can deny it.'

'I don't deny his dependability. Never have.'

'But . . .' Mandy said. 'Sheesh.' She shook her head and took a big swig of Prosecco.

They'd had this conversation a thousand times before, and Emma was angry at Mandy for bringing it up again. She'd done it on purpose, barely mentioning Dom before launching into judgemental mode.

'We're fine,' Emma said.

'Yeah, but he's "boring".' She made speech marks with her fingers.

'I've never said that.'

'You've never had to.' Mandy tapped her glass. She wore rings on every finger apart from her wedding ring finger. 'Got a good business, worships you and Daisy, not bad looking. Good in bed.'

Emma waved her hand from side to side, trying to lighten up the conversation. She really should tell Mandy to stop, go home, sober up. Her boyfriend would be home in a couple of days and she could take it out on him.

'You should be happy. You're lucky.'

'I *am* happy,' Emma said. She ignored the inner niggle casting doubts on that thought. She always did.

'Dunno what's good for you,' Mandy muttered.

'I'm going to get those blankets.' Emma entered the house

and stood in the kitchen for a while, pouring a glass of water from the fridge and relishing its cool tickle down her throat.

She moved past feeling angry at Mandy. They'd been friends for a long time, but Mandy was sometimes a mess, and she was never averse to projecting her own unhappiness onto her friends. Some of it was self-pity, some jealousy. She was definitely jealous of Emma.

She glanced at the clock. Dom would be home soon. She smiled, because there was nothing wrong with dependable. Perhaps compared to what she'd known in her younger years, he *was* boring. But boring was better than imprisoned, boring was better than dead. She had friends from her twenties who were both.

'Bloody freezing out here!' she heard Mandy shout from outside.

Emma went through to the living room and swept up a couple of throws from the sofa.

'So when do you and Paul go to Menorca?' she asked when she returned outside, determined to take control of the conversation.

Mandy smiled, then frowned, then started crying. Yeah. It really was time for her to go home.

'I remember when a first class stamp used to be eighteen pence,' Andy said. 'What is it now? Fifty? Sixty? I've lost touch. It goes up so often I'm confused. That's not inflation, that's Royal Mail screwing us for as much cash as they can because they're a monopoly.'

'There're other delivery firms,' Dom said.

'Like who?' Andy took another chip from the polystyrene tray between them. It was such a nice evening that they'd decided to sit in the small park opposite the chip shop to eat.

'Little old grannies,' Dom said. 'It'd hurt them. Stealing pension money that an old granny needs to buy her food.'

'Wrong,' Andy said, his voice sing-song. He had a way of doing that, sometimes. Announcing Dom's mistake with a flourish, almost revelling in his wrongness. 'I told you, they're insured.'

Dom sighed and held his head, elbows rested on the wooden park table. He didn't feel drunk any more. He felt tired, a little hungover, and the heat had gone from pleasant to claustrophobic. With darkness fallen, the humidity persisted like a ghost of the day just gone. *I really need to go home*, Dom thought. *Emma. Bed. Normality.*

Instead, they were talking about robbery.

Dom still couldn't quite put his finger on when things had changed. Even at the Ship, their discussion had been conducted with the air of an adventure, an almost child-like game of *what-if?* As fresh pints of dirty stole his balance and slurred his voice, Dom had found himself giggling as they'd discussed what sort of disguises they could use, what to call each other, and how it would actually work out.

I want to be Mr Black.

Does Emma wear stockings or tights? Can you steal some?

That was Tim Roth. Wasn't it?

Or Muppet T-shirts, with holes for eyes.

Maybe it was Harvey Keitel.

'No one will lose out, apart from the Royal Mail,' Andy said. He was a shadowy silhouette, silvered by moonlight, a stranger who Dom hardly knew. 'And do you know what effect a forty grand loss will have on them?'

'What?' Dom asked.

'None at all.'

'I'm going home,' Dom said.

'Sleep on it.'

'No.' Dom snorted, standing from the small park bench. '*No*. I'm not sleeping on it. You might think I'm pissed, but I'm really not any more. To be honest, it worries me that I can't tell whether you're joking or not.'

Still seated, Andy smiled up at him and ate some more chips. He looked smug, confident, strong. Superior. Dom hated the way his friend sometimes made him feel.

'You're just taking the piss,' Dom said. 'I'll walk home.'

'Don't always be a loser,' Andy muttered.

'What?' Dom wasn't quite sure what he'd just heard.

'Huh?' Andy asked, eyebrows raised. 'Nothing. Thanks for a good night, mate. See you soon.'

'Yeah,' Dom said. 'Soon.' He walked through the children's park to the gate, doing his best not to sway or swerve, head pounding with the promise of tomorrow's hangover. With every step he felt Andy's gaze upon him.

No one will lose out . . . no one will ever suspect us.

At the gate he glanced back, but Andy had already left.

At first Emma thought that Dom had gone to sleep.

She knew that he'd drunk more than usual, and he'd come through the back gate and thrown his arms around her, as if she was his one safe place. He'd kissed her and smelled her hair, and they'd hugged with an unusual strength. Usually it was an affectionate kiss before work or a fly-by hugging while they were busy around the house. But this was an embrace with need.

She'd wondered what had happened that evening. What he and Andy had been talking about. But when she'd asked his response had been, *This and that. Can't really remember.*

He was breathing heavily, snoring very softly, lying on his back. They were both naked on top of the bed covers. If Daisy had been here they'd have covered up. But it was still swelteringly hot inside, even though it was almost midnight. Their house was a detached dormer bungalow, so essentially they slept in the roof. They'd talked for some time about buying an air conditioning unit for the upstairs, but it had remained just talk. The ceiling fan did little to alleviate the humid discomfort, but at that moment she didn't mind being hot.

She was often the one to initiate sex. Especially after they'd had a drink, when Dom inevitably lasted longer, and inhibitions melted away. She lay on her side and stared at the shadow of him, listening to him breathing. Mandy was wrong. She didn't think Dom was boring, she thought he was safe. Although sometimes, just sometimes, that might mean the same thing.

She reached across and rested her hand on his thigh. He was slick with sweat. He always perspired more after a few pints.

Emma closed her eyes. Her breathing came deeper. She was far from drunk, but she was tired and contented. The *swish swish* of the ceiling fan was soporific, and at last she was starting to feel a cooling chill where the shifting air passed across her own damp skin.

She dwelled in that nebulous dreamland between consciousness and sleep. Dom passed by her on a bike, chasing Andy but never catching up. They were on a desert road. The distant hills were snowcapped, the plain harsh and flaming here and there from the relentless sun. Even though he was way in the lead, Andy kept passing by where she sat at the roadside, grinning at her each time. *He's in the bath*, she said every time he whipped past, dust roiling in his wake. But she spoke in his words, because it had been him who'd actually muttered them. Far across the plain a band played, their music silent but its anger painting the landscape around them red. From this distance she couldn't see for sure whether it was Genghis Cant, the band she'd hung out with when she was in her early twenties, but she was quite certain it was. There was no other reason she'd feel the way she did.

Andy's bike whipped past again and again, faster and faster, and the lead singer of Genghis Cant, Max Mort, suddenly screamed his most infamous song into her face, exhorting her to snort the heroin of life from the thighs of the dead.

Emma experienced a moment of dislocation as she snapped awake, but it quickly faded. Dom had rolled across and taken her in his arms. The safe night enveloped her and she sighed in comfort, and relief, and an overwhelming desire for the man who had been her husband for so long.

They kissed passionately, saying nothing. Their skin was slick where their bodies pressed together. She reached between them and grabbed him, slowly stroking. His right hand explored her body, moving across her stomach and down between her thighs. He breathed heavily into her mouth and then kissed her cheek. He smelled of alcohol and sweat, but it was a clean, honest smell.

He gently bit her neck just beneath her left ear. Emma gasped, and a shiver went through her. He might have been drunk, but he knew what she liked.

'Let's go outside,' Dom said. 'Do it in the garden again.'

'Really?' She wished he hadn't spoken. It broke the moment. And he'd paused, his passion held back even though their bodies were entwined, hands no longer working at each other, only holding.

'Do one thing every day that scares you,' he said, propping up so he could stare down at her in the weak moonlight.

'You sound like Andy,' she said, chuckling.

Dom stiffened, then pushed himself off, flopping down on his back. The loss of contact was a shock, and Emma felt suddenly cold.

'Why would you mention him?' Dom asked.

'I was only . . . I didn't mean anything.'

'But why bring him up, now, when we're doing this?'

'Dom, you're being silly. Okay, we'll go outside.'

'Forget it. Don't bother.'

'Dom.' He got like this sometimes after a drink. Horny and passionate, but angry too. Alcohol loosened him in many ways.

'I don't feel like it anyway.'

She rolled across and grabbed him, squeezing. 'Part of you feels like it.'

'Maybe in the morning.' He sighed heavily and turned onto his side, back to her.

'What the hell?' she asked. But Dom didn't reply. His breathing was heavier, but she knew he wasn't asleep. They knew each other so well. 'Dom?'

''Night,' he said.

'Yeah.' She sighed heavily and pulled a single sheet up to cover herself. She wished she hadn't mentioned Andy. In a darkness suddenly made uncomfortable, she remembered that one awkward moment between them a year before.

Neither of them had mentioned it since, and it had grown into nothing more.

Emma fell asleep unfulfilled, dreaming of more dangerous times.

Chapter Four

Not You

Angry at himself, at Emma, and most of all at Andy, Dom wanted to make things right. But he was stubborn. Alcohol increased that stubbornness, and though he so wanted to roll over and apologise to Emma, he couldn't shake what she'd said.

You sound like Andy.

Why say that? When they're lying together, naked and familiar, his hand between her legs and hers around his hard-on? Why was that an acceptable time to tell him he sounded like his fitter, better-looking friend?

He could hear Emma's breathing, slow and even, and he guessed that she'd already fallen asleep. She would not appreciate being woken now.

Don't always be a loser.

He wasn't sure if he'd truly heard that from Andy. But the truth didn't really matter. He *thought* he'd heard his friend muttering those words, so in reality it was Dom saying it to himself.

Don't always be a loser.

'Fuck's sake,' he whispered into the humid, dark bedroom.

He needed a drink of water. He couldn't decide whether he was more drunk than he'd believed, or dehydrated from the heat. If he moved he might wake Emma. He also needed to piss.

He lay there for some time, drifting in and out of a troubled doze. The day felt unfinished, still primed with wasted opportunities for lovemaking with Emma, and adventure with Andy. Settled sleep evaded him. Eventually the need to urinate forced him towards the en suite.

Emma stirred and rolled from her back onto her left side, groaning in her sleep, a deeply sexual sound. ' . . . in the bath,' she muttered.

Dom heard her even breathing and smiled. Maybe the next day he'd ask her about her dreams.

But dreams were the last thing on his mind when he woke the next morning.

He slept in, partly because it was Saturday, partly from the effects of the previous evening's cider. Jazz woke him. She licked his face, and as he shoved her away the phone rang. It was one of his customers, Mrs Fletcher. Her electricity kept tripping, and she was desperate for Dom to come and sort the problem.

Emma was already up and dressed, ready to go and collect Daisy from the friend she'd stayed with the night before.

Dom was pouring coffee and waiting for toast to pop from the toaster when Emma said, 'I was hoping we could go together.'

'I really can't say no to Mrs Fletcher.'

'No. Sure. What about later?'

'Later?'

Emma stared at him for a few seconds, and Dom didn't like what he saw in her expression. It was like a stranger's. She was someone he didn't know assessing him, not the wife he adored. He felt a moment of frank appraisal, so intense that it made him feel uncomfortable.

Emma sighed lightly and looked aside, running a hand through her hair. As if she'd looked him over and found him lacking.

'Lucy's party.'

'Oh, of course, I'll be there. What time?'

'Two.'

'Right. Play centre, yeah?'

'Thirty kids shouting and screaming in a ball pit,' Emma said. 'The joy of parenthood.'

They orbited each other in the kitchen for a few more minutes, then Emma left first. She gave him a perfunctory peck on the cheek.

He wanted to say something about the previous evening. But the day was gathering velocity, things were moving on, and he was already thinking about Mrs Fletcher's electrical problem.

That, and something else. Sober, yesterday's discussions with Andy did not feel quite as he'd first experienced them. His friend had been probing, rather than plotting. Behind every 'No one will suffer' comment had been a deeper, blander thought – *Boring fuck. Stuck with the same woman for years. Drifting through life on the tails of those really living it.*

As Dom drove through Usk towards Mrs Fletcher's old cottage, he thought of Andy powering downhill ahead of him on his bike. Seeing the future first. Filling his face with the wind, daring fate, while Dom tweaked his brakes, preferring the climb because it was more tempered, slower, predictable and safe.

By the time he'd reached Mrs Fletcher's, he'd already decided to text Andy.

Got time for a coffee?

And it was as if Andy was waiting for him, because his reply was almost instant.

Sure. Where you at?

Dom told him, named a time and a place, then grabbed his toolbox and went to work.

'I'm talking, you're listening,' Dom said.

He sat opposite Andy. They were in the outdoor area of the garden centre cafe, two coffees and a selection of cake slices already on the table. Andy had arrived twenty minutes before him, and Dom had taken childish pleasure in making his friend wait.

Andy held his hands up, then drew one across his lips.

Dom glanced around and sat down. The cafe was busy with the usual Saturday morning crowd of squabbling families, elderly couples, and a group of local kids drinking hot chocolate. A couple of dogs tugged on their leads and snapped thrown treats from the air. Tame sparrows and a robin hopped from table to table, causing squawks of delight from children and smiles from parents.

No one was paying them any attention.

'No weapons,' Dom said.

Andy raised his eyebrows.

'No one gets hurt. We don't lay our hands on anyone.'

'Right,' Andy said, nodding. 'Of course.'

'We hide whatever we take, leave it for a year.'

'At least a year.'

'Any inkling that we might get caught, any reason why it's not as easy as you seem to think it'll be, then we're out.'

'Sure. But it *is* easy.'

'Right, yeah,' Dom said. 'But any sign that it won't be, and it's off. I have a beautiful family that I love very much. I won't do anything that's a risk to them or me.'

'You do have a lovely family,' Andy said. 'You're lucky. They're why you're doing this.'

Dom nodded. Yes, because of them. But as he drank some of his coffee, slowly, savouring the taste, he knew that wasn't quite true.

This was all for him.

'I'll think it all through properly today,' Andy said. 'Get back to you tomorrow. A call, not a text. You spend the weekend with your family, all very normal.'

Dom's heart was beating too fast. He was sweating. He was also excited, and pleased at his friend's surprise. *He never believed I'd really do it*, he thought. But he would not say that out loud.

'When should we go?'

'No more for now,' Andy said. 'Cake. Coffee. Check her out, over there.' He nodded behind Dom.

Dom turned to look over his shoulder and caught the eye of an attractive young woman in shorts and T-shirt, just as she was looking their way. He glanced away, embarrassed, and Andy laughed.

'Bastard.'

'You know it. She's giving me the eye, though.'

'Jesus.'

'I'll be whoever she wants me to be.'

They chatted some more, but Dom's mind was on one thing. He felt like he'd made a commitment, even though the deed itself still seemed distant and unlikely. He felt lighter.

His horizons had been opened to a new beginning, and it was time to start living.

'Monday,' Andy said.

'Really? That soon?'

'Why wait?'

'So . . . how?'

'Bike ride tomorrow? We can chat then.'

'Sure.'

'I'll be at yours about ten o'clock.'

'Yeah.'

'Have a nice evening, mate. Say hi to Emma for me.'

That Saturday evening, Dom played with Daisy in the garden while Emma cooked some chicken for a warm salad.

The weather was scorching, and Daisy wanted to play Scrabble. Usually that bored Dom. Most games bored him, and he'd often feel more inclined to watch some TV with her, or perhaps encourage her to get some sketching paper out and keep herself occupied.

That evening, however, he felt different.

Later, with Daisy in bed, he brought out a bottle of Emma's favourite wine. She liked dry white straight from the fridge, so cold that it sometimes gave him brain freeze. They sat in the garden together and drank the bottle, then when they went inside around 10 p.m. he made them mojitos.

'A less suspicious woman would think you were after something,' Emma said.

'Innocent me?' Dom asked.

They made love on the sofa, moving to the living room

floor when they became more energetic and the leather made too much noise. Jazz barked at them, and Dom had to jump up and shut her in the kitchen. Then he returned to his wife, and the heat didn't matter, the uncomfortable rug bothered neither of them. They came together.

Dom knew it was one of those evenings that would stay with him forever. A perfect time.

'I like today,' Emma said later when they were snuggled in bed. It was hot, but they both enjoyed the contact. 'It's a very not-like-you day.'

'Oh, thanks,' he said. But he was not offended. He liked her thinking that.

Soon they disentangled themselves and Emma fell asleep.

Dom took a lot longer to drift off. He spent a long time staring at the ceiling, thinking, and feeling not quite himself.

Chapter Five

Loony Tunes

'Mad dogs and Englishmen,' Dom said.

'Huh?'

'Go out in the midday sun.'

'What the hell are you on about?' Andy was in the driver's seat. It was Dom's car, but Dom had not wanted to drive. He'd muddied up his own number plates and stuck colourful sun blinds in the back to distract attention.

Andy had just switched off the engine and left the keys in the ignition. They'd discussed that. It was to aid a quick getaway.

'It's a saying. A song, I think.'

'Dom, you're not flipping out on me, are you?'

'Nah. I'm good.' But Dom really couldn't decide whether he was good or not. His body wouldn't let him. He felt sick, his stomach rolled like he wanted a shit, he had a headache, sweat soaked his T-shirt and shorts, slick against the car's upholstery. It was due to be the hottest day of the year so far, with a forecast that records would be broken. Even this early, sunlight scorched the air so that he could see everything with a crisp, awful clarity.

'Because this is your last chance,' Andy said. 'Last time either of us can back out. You know that, right? I explained? Once we get out of this car suited and booted, it's on. No going back.'

'Yeah, Andy, I'm fine. Honestly. Just nervous.'

'Nervous is good. It'll keep us alert. But you look petrified.'

Dom closed his eyes and took several deep breaths. Andy let him, and he was grateful for that. Somewhere in the distance he heard the trilling of a kid's bicycle bell, and it took him back thirty-five years to a childhood summer – playing cards taped between his Chipper bike's spokes; TV footage of empty reservoirs with cracked beds; the smell of calamine lotion as his mother tended his sunburn. He took in a deep breath and the smell of sweat and latex snapped him back to the present.

'So, you ready?' Andy asked.

Dom looked past his friend, across the small square at the Blue Door cafe. This early in the morning there were only a couple of people there – an old man reading a broadsheet newspaper over breakfast, and a young mum with a pushchair. The table where the two of them had sat just three days before was deserted, and he imagined the ghosts of themselves there, watching in silent disbelief at what was about to occur.

'Dom! You ready?'

'I can't believe . . .'

'Okay.' Andy touched the car keys, but didn't turn them. 'This isn't happening. Let's go.'

Something panicked Dom. A sense of failure he didn't want, the idea that this ridiculous, otherworldly moment of his life might suddenly be over. Confusion skewed his sense of self, so much so that he glanced in the mirror to make sure he was still there.

Don't always be a loser. Those words sat with him, heavy, echoing. As did, *It's a very not-like-you day.*

'Wait,' Dom said. He picked up the child's Hulk mask in his lap and slipped it on. It took a couple of seconds to place the eyes properly. His breathing sounded close and intimate, and he'd never been so aware of its sound. Too fast, too light. He breathed deeply again. Then Andy slapped his leg as he opened the driver's door.

Dom opened his own door and stepped from the car, and from one breath to the next he changed his future.

The road was quiet, the small square still. The air outside was heavy, and only slightly cooler than inside the vehicle. He could smell cooking bacon, coffee, and dust, and the sun singed the already reddened skin of his forearms.

After a quick, nervous ride the previous day with Andy – including a roadside stop to discuss their plans – he'd spent the rest of the day in the garden with Emma and Daisy. They'd cut the lawn, dead-headed some rose bushes, and eaten a salad on the decking. He'd wanted it to be a normal Sunday. And it would have been, if today hadn't been at the back of his mind. 'Silly,' Emma had said as she watched him moisturising his arms that evening. He'd forgotten sun cream.

At least he'd had heat and sunburn as an excuse for not being able to sleep.

No one seemed to have noticed them. The post office had only been open for an hour, and only a few of the display items were outside. The postmistress had been occupied accepting a delivery from the security van. The shop door was already blocked open in an attempt to keep the inside cool, and Dom heard tuneless whistling coming from the shadowy interior, and something else. The sibilant rhythms of a radio, song unidentifiable.

'Two minutes,' Andy said from behind his Iron Man mask. He went first, taking several confident strides and passing through the door. As he did so he lifted the carrier bag in his right hand, pointing its contents ahead of him.

Dom followed, drawing the smaller bag from his shorts pocket. It contained a chunk of wood, but it could have been anything. He entered just behind Andy, in time to see the postmistress standing behind the shop counter, eyes wide, lips still pursed in a silent whistle. The tune had died on her lips.

The radio still sounded from somewhere behind the shop. It sounded like Radio One, the sort of music Daisy listened to but which Dom thought of as noise pollution. He couldn't imagine that this woman would choose that.

'This is all going to be very easy and painless,' Andy said. He held the carrier bag across his chest in both hands, like a soldier would nurse a rifle. 'You understand?'

The woman nodded, glancing nervously back and forth between Iron Man and the Hulk.

The enclosed, glazed post office area was to the left, "Closed" sign still propped across the metal money tray beneath the glass screen.

'Fuse board?' Dom asked. The woman pointed above the greeting card display. Dom glanced at the fuse board and noted the incoming phone line junction box next to it. Perfect. He nodded at Andy, then turned his back on him and the woman.

He felt sick. He held the bag away from his body so she would see it, then peered through the window between advertising cards and posters. He wondered whether he should close the door, couldn't remember what they'd decided about that. Had they decided anything? Door open or closed? He started breathing heavier again, balls tingling, head pulsing.

Outside, everything looked fine. Across in the Blue Door's garden the man turned a page of his newspaper, and the young mother had the child on her lap. Neither of them were looking his way.

A car passed by, a man in shirt and tie driving, jacket hanging in the back. He was talking into a mobile phone. *Stupid*, Dom thought. *He'll cause an accident.* He tried to smile but it would not come.

'We're here for money, that's all,' Andy said behind him. 'It's not yours. You won't be hurt, and you'll even find a bit of fame from this. Being robbed by Iron Man and the Hulk. You can sell your story.'

'What have you . . .?' the woman asked. Her voice was high, shaking with fear. Dom closed his eyes briefly, flushed with shame.

'I have a sawn-off shotgun,' Andy said. 'My friend has a grenade. We're not using them. Just carrying them. That's all. Now, no panic buttons. No shouts. Just open the safe and we'll be on our way.'

'Okay,' the woman said.

'How much are you holding?'

'Sorry?'

'Money.'

'Oh . . . thirty-eight thousand.'

There was a pause, a silent moment with no movement or talking. Dom almost glanced back, but he kept watching the road and square, as they'd agreed. *You have to keep watch,*

Andy had said. *That's the most important job. Anyone looks like they've seen us, anything out of the ordinary, and we're gone.*

'Who's up there?' Andy asked.

'My granddaughter. Teacher training day at school, so she's here with me. Having breakfast in her room, listening to music. I tell her to turn it down but . . . she's only young.'

'We'll be gone before she knows we're here. Now hurry.'

Dom felt suddenly, irrationally hungry. He hadn't been able to eat breakfast, had told Emma that he'd grab something on his way to the builder's merchants. And in half an hour he'd actually be there, buying some supplies and equipment for the kitchen rewire he was doing in Monmouth. Davey was already at the job, stripping old wires and first fixing. They'd been working there for two days the previous week, and the couple they worked for were nice. They gave them a steady supply of biscuits and tea.

The smell of cooked bacon and coffee made his stomach rumble.

'Hulk!' Andy said, impatient, as if he'd already called his friend's name.

'All quiet,' Dom said.

He heard the rattle of keys, the creak of an un-oiled door. Movement as Andy crossed to the post office area. Dom glanced at his friend's back. Beyond, behind the glass screen, the woman was opening the safe. Andy had the carrier bag containing his lump of wood resting on the shop counter, angled through the doorway into the post office area.

One Direction started harmonising from elsewhere in the building. A young girl's voice joined in, unaware that anyone other than her grandmother was listening. Dom smiled, but the smile fell into a frown.

'Hurry!' he said. It would be bad enough knowing what her grandmother had been through. Last thing he wanted was the girl coming down and seeing it. There was no knowing how she'd react. If she ran screaming into the street . . .

Then they'd have to flee. That was all. No one was getting hurt.

'Pile it into the post bag,' he heard Andy say. 'Yeah, coins too.'

Across the square, Sue had emerged from the Blue Door cafe, carrying a tray of cups and food. She deposited it on the paper-reading man's table, then chatted to him for a while. She even laughed at something he said. Dom felt offended. She was always so brusque with him and Andy. Maybe she really did hate cyclists.

He laughed, short and loud.

'What?' Andy snapped.

'Nothing, nothing. It's just Sue—'

'Hulk, shut the fuck up!' It was like a slap. His eyes stung like a berated child's. Then he realised what he'd said, and why Andy's reaction had been so harsh. 'Out of there, now,' Andy said to the postmistress.

Across the square, Sue went back into the cafe. The man stirred his coffee and picked up a sandwich, studying it before taking a bite. Dom wished he was sitting there now with Andy, talking bullshit and anticipating their ride back home. Not here. Robbing a fucking post office.

'Okay, Hulk, we're good.'

Dom pocketed the bagged chunk of wood and drew a pair of wire snippers from his other pocket. He had to stretch to reach the fuse board. One snip cut the phone line. It was probably pointless in this age of mobiles, especially with a teenaged girl in the house who was probably glued to hers.

41

But for the sake of a second it was worth it. Then he opened the misted cover to the fuse board, flipped the switch that cut power to the building, and dug beneath the switch and snipped the wires within.

One Direction fell silent.

'Nan!' a girl called.

'Okay,' Dom said. The post office probably had a direct panic line to the local police station, but that was five miles away in the nearest small town. At least the postmistress now wouldn't be able to activate the local alarm the second they left.

Andy shoved gently at his back and they exited into the blinding sunlight. Dom walked quickly around the front of the car. He had never felt so exposed, so scrutinised.

A Range Rover turned into the square and came towards them. Sunlight reflected from the windscreen, hiding whoever was inside. It slowed as it approached, then accelerated quickly away, swerving across the road and striking the kerb. It made a sudden left turn around the square and stopped outside the Blue Door.

'Don't worry, get in!' Andy said. He was already opening the rear door, dropping the heavy bag onto the back seat. Dom opened the passenger door, glancing back over his shoulder.

The Range Rover's door was open and a tall, grey-haired man stood beside it, shielding his eyes as he looked across the square at them. He was only thirty yards away, and Dom could hear the deep timbre of his voice as he shouted at Sue and the patrons of the Blue Door. The young mother was standing also, holding her toddler, half-turned as if to shield him or her from danger. The breakfasting man stood and dashed into the cafe so quickly that he knocked over a chair and spilled his coffee pot. It hit the ground with a loud metallic clang.

'Hulk!' Andy said.

Dom laughed at the ridiculousness of it all. 'Don't make me angry!' he shouted across the square, almost hysterical.

'Mate,' Andy said, surprised. 'Come on.'

Dom dropped into the car and slammed the door, panting, hands sweaty as they clasped for the seatbelt. 'We did it?'

'Yeah,' Andy said. He sat motionless for a beat, then ripped off his Iron Man mask. That wasn't part of the plan.

'Andy?'

No response. No movement.

'Andy, what's—'

'Yeah, we did it,' Andy said. He started the engine, slipped into gear and pulled away.

A white transit van entered the square ahead of them, screeching around the corner and veering across the road. Two figures sat in the front.

Bugs Bunny and Daffy Duck.

'Oh, fuck,' Andy said. His voice sounded flat.

What? Dom thought. Maybe he even spoke it. He wasn't sure.

Dom braced himself against the dashboard as Andy turned to the left, hitting the kerb so that one front wheel mounted the square's small lawned area. The van nudged the car's rear wing on the driver's side, a glancing blow.

Another vehicle had skidded around the corner, close behind the transit van. A silver BMW. It passed so close to them that wing mirrors kissed.

Andy pressed on the gas. The Focus bounced down onto the road again and accelerated towards the corner around which the van and BMW had appeared.

'What the hell?' Dom shouted. 'Andy, what the fuck?' He twisted and looked through the rear window.

The van had halted in front of the post office, slewed across the road. The passenger door opened and Bugs Bunny jumped out. He held a gun. Dom had no idea what kind, but it was big and ugly, and looked very real.

'Andy . . .' he said.

'I know.'

The BMW had stopped behind the van. Its driver's window was down, and Roadrunner stared after them.

'Andy, what's happening?'

Andy stared back at the car and van. Then he said, 'We're getting out of here.'

Daffy Duck jumped from the van's driver's side and stood watching them go. Bugs Bunny was already through the doorway and into the post office. The van's rear door opened and Jerry the cat appeared, also staring after the car. Jerry gestured, shouting, and Roadrunner's head turned.

Then they were around the corner and the square was out of sight, and Andy accelerated away from the small village, heading towards the climb into the hills that Dom was so nervous of descending on his bike.

Dom shook. He needed to piss. He tried to take his mask off but his fingers felt numb, he couldn't get them beneath the damp, stinking latex. He was suffocating.

'Deep breaths,' Andy said.

'Deep fucking breaths?' he shouted, voice muffled in the green mask. He worked his thumbs beneath the edge at last and tugged it from his head, edges pulling his hair and raking against his skin. 'What was that?'

'Trouble,' Andy said.

'They had guns, they were there to—'

44

'Trouble coming our way.' Andy was glancing back and forth between road and rear-view mirror, and Dom twisted in his seat.

The silver BMW was tearing along the road towards them.

'Oh, shit,' Dom said.

'You need to work with me, Dom. Got it?'

'Work with you?'

'You saw the guns. Whoever they are, they're serious. You've lived here all your life, you know these roads better than me, so think how we can lose him.'

Andy knocked down a gear and pressed on the gas. The road was narrow and twisting.

'Andy, maybe we should stop.'

'Seriously?' his friend said, risking a glance across at Dom. 'You're serious?'

Dom shook his head. He didn't know. He couldn't quite fathom what was happening, his brain could make no sense of things.

'Dom! Nothing changes. We lose him then we're away, we're good, and we've got a bag full of money. We follow the plan. Understand?'

'How can we?'

'How can we not?' Andy said. 'It's done, mate. We've done it. No going back.' He grimaced as he slammed on the brakes. Tyres screamed as they took a bend too fast.

Dom held his breath. Nothing was coming the other way.

The road started to rise into the hills.

'Closer,' Andy muttered.

Dom looked back. The BMW was so close that he could no longer see its number plate and grille. They must have been doing sixty, and the silver car was just feet from their rear.

Roadrunner's madcap smile was fixed on him. The driver held up a phone, camera pointed their way.

I took my mask off, Dom thought. But it was too late now.

'Dom, we've got two or three miles to lose him or stop him. After that we're over the hill, out of the woods and we hit the main road. Once that happens, we're screwed. Law will be coming. Helicopter pursuit, the works. What do you think, the tight bend at the top?'

'What do you mean?' Dom asked. He didn't recognise this Andy, but he shouldn't have been surprised. They were in a car chase. His friend was keeping it together.

'This is our future,' Andy said.

'Yeah,' Dom said, and he thought of Emma and Daisy. *His* future.

'So, that bend? We know it, he doesn't. Maybe if I take it fast enough he'll lose control?'

'Better idea,' Dom said. 'Just after that there's a turn right, hundred metres before the pink house, narrow lane, looks more like a field gateway. It heads up into the woods. I used to mountain bike up there before I started on the roads.'

'You're sure?' Andy asked. He dropped down a gear again as the slope increased, then swept around the bend that opened onto the long, straight climb. He pressed on the gas and edged into the middle of the road.

Dom looked back. The BMW was so close that he expected an impact at any minute. He wasn't sure what model it was, didn't know enough about cars to know whether his Focus could outrun it, or at least stay ahead.

'Dom, hundred metres before the house? More? Less?'

'Bit more,' he said.

'Right. Bend's coming up in a minute. When I say, goad the hell out of him.'

'This is crazy,' Dom said.

'It's happening,' Andy said.

The engines roared. The BMW pressed in closer, surging forward. Andy drifted the Focus to the right, blocking the road.

'Okay,' Andy said.

Dom froze for a moment, feeling the unreality of things pressing in close. Then he gave Roadrunner the finger.

Andy swerved them around the bend, wheel juddering in his hand. Dom turned forward again and pressed back into his seat, holding onto the seatbelt.

'There, see it?'

Andy didn't reply. He was concentrating. He slammed on the brakes, and the BMW hit their rear end, shoving them forward. Tyres screamed. The BMW fell back a little, and Andy flipped the steering wheel to the right.

The Focus's nose drifted perfectly into the narrow lane's mouth, and Andy immediately dropped two gears and floored it. Unable to make the turn, the BMW slammed into the raised bank behind them, missing them by inches. As they powered away, Dom saw steam burst from the silver car's front end, its wing crumpled, windscreen hazed.

They soon rounded a bend and the pursuing car was lost from sight.

Andy let out a held breath, gasping a few times. 'Result,' he whispered. 'You okay?'

Dom could not speak. He turned away, watching the hedgerows passing by. With a sick feeling in his stomach he realised that he'd have to go straight to Monmouth now, to work, chatting with Davey and talking about how best to get these wires here, those there, lifting floorboards and drinking tea and eating biscuits.

'My car's bumped,' he said.

'We'll sort that. Leave it to me. You okay, Dom?'

'Yeah. No. Who were they?'

'Looney Tunes.' Andy laughed. Dom joined in, high and hysterical and sounding like someone he didn't know.

Chapter Six

Pillbox

For a moment everything was as it should have been.

Dom surfaced from dreams and dragged some of them with him, balancing them momentarily with reality. Awareness started to build – who he was, where he lived, everything that made him Dominic. The dreams withered and receded. He groaned and stretched, eyes still closed, joints clicking to remind him of his age.

Then he remembered the day before and wished he could fall back asleep. He groaned again, this one more like a deep sigh. *What have I done?*

Daisy screamed.

Dom sprang upright, sitting in bed swaying and dizzied. 'It wakes!' Emma said beside him.

'Daisy!' He threw the duvet off and sat on the edge of the bed. Everything felt wrong. Music pulsed from Daisy's room, when he rubbed sleep from his eyes he saw Roadrunner with a human body, and downstairs their dog, Jazz, was whining.

'Ease up, action man. She's only singing.'

He glanced back at Emma. She was sitting back against her propped pillows, phone in hand, hair sleep-tousled, corner of her mouth raised in amusement. Daisy's voice rose again, and Dom slumped back into his pillow.

'You call that singing?'

'She's got Muse's new album. Trying to match that singer's warble.'

'He does *not* warble,' Dom said, feigning hurt. It was a conversation they'd had many times before. He welcomed its familiarity.

'Like a dog with its bollocks trapped in a gate.' She muttered this, swiping something on her phone and attention already elsewhere.

'He's a rock god,' Dom said. 'Classically trained. Not my fault you have no taste in music, and your daughter has.'

From Daisy's room the track ended and she fell silent. Jazz continued whining from the kitchen below them, eager to see them all. They were familiar morning sounds that made Dom feel almost comfortable.

Sunlight cast across him through a chink in the curtains, and when he relaxed back onto the bed and closed his eyes he saw that white van and silver BMW, cartoon characters hefting guns.

'Feeling better this morning?' Emma asked.

'Yeah, think so.' He answered without opening his eyes, scared that she'd see straight through him. She usually did. He'd told her he had a bad headache the previous evening, needing something to cover up the way he was acting. Weird, twitchy, unsettled. He'd even cancelled his usual Monday evening squash match with Andy, much to his friend's disapproval. *We need to be normal!* Andy had said to him down the phone. *I just feel a bit rough,* he'd replied, unable to say more because Emma had been sitting on the other end of the sofa.

They'd stuck to their plan. After driving back from Upper Mill to Usk they headed into the hills just before the small town, parking off a barely used lane. Dom had left a shovel there the day before on his way home from work. Distant sirens, source unseen, had been the only sign of police.

The old pillbox was almost subsumed by ivy and brambles, hidden in a small woodland that had likely not even been there during the war. They pushed their way inside, careful to disturb as little of the undergrowth as possible. The shadowy interior stank musty and old, as if the war years had hung around. A pile of rusted drinks cans in one corner, the body of a mattress almost completely rotted into the ground, a black bag burst and spilling decayed cloth insides, all paid testament to its last occupant from some time ago. There were no signs of recent use.

Andy had used his phone as a torch while Dom dug. Then they swapped over. It only took half an hour. As Andy dumped the heavy post bag into the hole, Dom realised that they hadn't even checked how much was there. They shoved the soil back over and patted it down, kicking the remaining turned soil into the corners. Dom used the shovel to drag the black bag across the floor. It came apart and spilled shreds of old clothing, and the stink as he dumped it on the covered hole made him gag. Things crawled away in the darkness, rustling dried leaves. He wanted to get out of there.

He'd dropped Andy at a bus stop and then headed to Monmouth. He was only an hour late for work, and he told Davey that he'd swung by the merchant's to pick up some new tools. He had them ready in the car boot.

Their clients had made him a mug of tea and brought a plate of biscuits, and he and Davey had sat and chatted about things he could no longer remember. Then he'd worked.

Then he'd come home. Dinner with Emma and Daisy, driving Daisy to her usual evening scout meeting, watching an episode of *Breaking Bad* with Emma instead of his usual Monday squash match. A hug in bed and then, after a long time, some troubled sleep.

And today was the first day of the rest of his life.

'I'll get the car looked at today,' he said.

'Should have called the police,' Emma mumbled, still distracted by her phone.

'It was a bump in a car park. Last thing they're interested in.' He'd been pleased to discover that damage to his car was minimal. The rear bumper had absorbed the force of the shunt, and where the van had touched them there was a scrape in the paintwork, nothing more. The wing mirror displayed no signs of any impact. It could have been so much worse.

'Still. Ignorant bastard, whoever did it.'

Dom opened his eyes and stared at the ceiling, because with them closed he saw Roadrunner's leering face.

'Bloody hell,' Emma said. He felt her stiffen in bed beside him. From across the landing Muse started again, the same song, Daisy's enthusiastic but imperfect voice singing along. 'Did you see this?' Emma asked.

'See what?'

'Upper Mill post office.'

Dom's blood ran cold. But of course it would be news. Locally, at least, if not nationally.

'What about it?'

'It was robbed yesterday morning. Whoever did it killed the postmistress and her granddaughter. How horrible. God, it's only thirty miles from here.'

'Killed them?' Dom sat up again, but this time it was much harder than before. Everything felt slow, his body

52

heavy, an ice-cold shock around his heart giving way to hot lead running through his veins. Sweat prickled his brow.

'Yeah. Awful. Hope they catch the bastards.'

Dom couldn't stop blinking. His eyes stung, and perhaps between blinks he could reset things, put things right. He already knew that they'd crossed a line. Now, that line had been painted blood-red.

'Dom? Babe?' He felt Emma's hand on his arm and he leaned into her, kissing her cheek before standing from the bed.

'Bladder's going to explode.'

'Dom, what is it?'

He stood at their open door, looking out across the landing at Daisy's closed bedroom door. He'd heard the postmistress's granddaughter singing. She'd sounded happy, carefree, like young kids should.

'I'm okay. Just a shock, that's all. Andy and I sat across the square from that place a few days ago.' He remembered the laughing woman. 'Might even have seen the post office owner.' He looked back at his wife, terrified that the truth of things would be painted across his expression, in his eyes.

'Yeah, it's horrible,' Emma said. She was scanning her phone again, scrolling slowly through the rest of the day's news, already moving on.

And what will she see? he wondered.

The Hulk and Iron Man made off in a red Ford Focus just as their accomplices arrived, and soon after that the gunshots were heard.

The white van hit the red car.

It's possible that two separate gangs were involved.

The Hulk and Iron Man were carrying weapons hidden in carrier bags.

'We didn't have weapons,' he whispered as he stood in their bathroom trying to piss. His bladder wouldn't let go. It was as if someone was standing behind him staring intently at the back of his neck, and he even glanced back over his shoulder.

'Daisy, turn that down!' Emma shouted. Daisy had turned up her iPod dock. Muse were rocking out.

Dom sobbed, once, and turned it into a cough.

'Put the kettle on, babe,' Emma called.

'Yeah.' He started to piss, but still felt eyes on him. That poor woman. Her poor grandkid.

He needed to speak to Andy.

'Of course I've seen the news.'

'We need to go to the police.'

'And tell them what?'

'What we saw.'

Andy didn't reply for a few seconds. Dom could hear him breathing lightly, slowly, sounding in control. 'Really, Dom?'

'I dunno. It's just . . . they *shot* them, Andy.'

'You haven't actually read the news, then.'

'No. Emma told me. Why?'

'They made the kid watch while they smashed the woman's skull with something heavy. Then they glued the girl's nostrils and lips shut with superglue.'

Dom felt the world spinning, or he was spiralling while everything else was motionless. He felt sick. 'Jesus fucking Christ.'

'So you really want to go to the police, and tell them we robbed the post office then saw these other bad guys appear to finish them off?'

'We didn't kill them.'

'I know that, Dom! But we're the bad guys too.'

'Not that bad.'

'They'd never believe there wasn't a link! We admit it, they don't find the others, we're guilty of murder.'

'No,' Dom said. 'Nobody gets hurt. That's what we said.'

'Yeah, I know, mate.'

'That poor girl.'

Andy sighed. The phone line crackled. 'Hardly bears thinking about,' Andy said. Dom stared through his windscreen across the car park. There weren't many cars here this early in the morning, and soon he'd go to the local shop to buy his lunch for the day. But he was suddenly all too aware of the damage to his car's rear wing. It was superficial, little more than a few scratches. He'd already cleaned the mud from his number plates and disposed of the brightly coloured window blinds. But even though he could see no one else around, he felt eyes on him, sizing up the car and taking notes, ready to connect it to the robbery.

And then the white van hit the red car, Officer, and I've just seen it in Usk, I even know the guy who drives it, he's an electrician and a governor at his daughter's school and I'd have never expected that of him, not robbery, and definitely not murder.

He always seemed so quiet.

Such a nice family.

Nothing like that happens here.

'Got to get my car done,' Dom said. 'I don't believe we were stupid enough to use it.'

'It wasn't stupid. We weren't stupid. It was just bad luck.'

'Bad luck that'll get us—'

'I know a guy who'll do the car, up in Shropshire. I've already spoken to him, there and back in a day.'

'I can't drive to Shropshire, I have to work!'

'Which is why I'll do it.'

Dom frowned, thinking things through. His mind was a fog. He couldn't get anything straight, and if he tried to concentrate on one problem, all the others started battering at the edges of his consciousness.

'I just can't think straight,' he said.

'You don't need to. That's why I'm here. Get to work, go home tonight and hug Daisy. Have some wine, shag your missus. Everything's going to be fine.'

'Andy. Do you think if we hadn't done it, those others might have left them alive?'

Andy sighed heavily, and fell silent for so long that Dom thought the line had been cut.

'Andy?'

'That wasn't just murder. They enjoyed what they did to that girl. So I doubt it. No, they wouldn't have been left alive. We had no influence over what happened to them. Understand?'

'Yeah.'

'Sure?'

'Yeah. Andy? What if they come looking for us?'

'They'll be long gone by now.'

'How do you know?' Dom asked.

'Because I would be. Now what time can you get here?'

Chapter Seven

A Quiet Life

She was Jane Smith, the do-over woman, and upon waking every morning her new life built itself from scratch.

She relished those briefest of moments between sleep and full consciousness, when all she knew was the lonely warmth of the French gîte's bedroom, the landscape of bare grey stone walls, the roof light affording a view of the clearest blue sky, and the scents of summer drifting through windows left open all night. For that shortest of times she was free and carefree.

But reality always rushed in, as if she would suffocate and die without it. Her life was constructed around her and she pulled it on like a costume. Her name, her history, why she was here and where she had been before. It no longer needed learning and repeating, this new existence, because she knew it so well. She was experienced at living a lie.

Fragments of her old, real life always hung around, like stains from the past. But she did her best to restrict them to dreams, and nightmares.

She stretched beneath the single sheet. Her body was thin, lithe and strong, limbs corded with muscles. She enjoyed the feeling of being fit. There were hurdles to fitness, buffers against which she shoved again and again, but she enjoyed fighting them. She knew that the more years went by, the harder it would be to deny the wounds and injuries. But for now they acted as badges of honour. Scars formed a map of her past, a constant reminder of her old life that made-up names and histories could not erase.

A spider was crawling high across the stone gable wall close to the sloping ceiling. It was big, body the size of her thumbnail, legs an inch long. She'd seen it before, usually on the mornings when she woke earlier than normal. It probably patrolled her room at night, secretive and silent and known only to her. She imagined it exploring familiar ground in search of prey, and perhaps it sometimes crawled across her skin, pausing on her pillow to sense her breath, her dreams.

It scurried, paused, scurried again, eventually disappearing into its hole until the sun went down. She liked the idea of it spending daylight out of sight. Its sole purpose was existence and survival. There was something pure about that.

She sat on the edge of the bed, stretched again, then walked naked down the curving timber staircase and into the bathroom.

She'd been living in the gîte in Brittany for a little over three months, and she knew its nooks and crannies probably better than the French owners.

In a slit in the bed mattress was a Glock 17 pistol. Tucked behind a stone in the stairwell wall was a Leatherneck knife. A loose floorboard in the bathroom hid a sawn-off shotgun and an M67 grenade, and downstairs on the ground floor, beneath a flagstone in the kitchen, was a small weapons cache containing another pistol, a combat shotgun, and several more grenades.

Though aware of everything around her, Jane Smith did not think of these things now. Her life was as quiet and peaceful as she had ever believed possible. But none of this made her feel safe.

There was no such thing as safe.

She used the toilet, then went down the second flight of stairs to the kitchen. Kettle on, coffee ground, she watched from the kitchen window as the new day was birthed from the dregs of night.

Leaving the coffee to brew, she opened the wide glazed doors that led onto the gravelled terrace. Several rabbits sat across the lawned area beyond. One of them pricked up its ears and froze, but it did not run. Birds sang and swooped across the lawn, picking off flies flitting in the soft morning mist.

The sun would burn the mist away very soon, but for now it formed a pale haze across the landscape. The large lawned garden that sloped down to the woodland, the fields beyond, and past them the wide lake and the steadily rolling hills, were all silent but for the sounds of nature. She did nothing to disturb the peace.

Still, she would not step from the door without dressing. The chance of anyone watching was small. But if a local had walked through the woods this early, and had strayed from the public paths to the edge of the gîte's large property, she did not want to draw undue attention to herself. The quiet Englishwoman could have been anyone. The naked Englishwoman would draw second glances, and discussion in the village bar-tabac, and a form of notoriety.

Jane Smith was well versed in keeping herself unnoticed.

She took her coffee upstairs, showered and dressed. Then she locked the house and cycled her old bike up to the small village of Brusvily. The patisserie was already open, and she smiled and exchanged a few words with the owner in her broken French. She was getting better, and she knew that the locals appreciated her efforts. They were used to British holidaymakers assuming that everyone spoke English, and she made a point of only conversing in French when she was away from the gîte. Just another way to try and fit in.

She bought croissants for breakfast, and bread rolls, ham and cheese for lunch. That afternoon she planned a run down through the woods to the lake, a long swim in its cool waters, then a hike along its shore to the nearest town. She'd eat dinner there, then perhaps run back the same way, depending on how stiff her hip was. If it was giving her grief, she'd walk.

Back at the gîte she brewed more coffee and sat beneath the pergola on the terrace, eating the croissants with strawberry preserve, drawing in the sights and sounds of summer. This had been a long, hot one, and the lawns were scorched dry by the sun and lack of rain.

Her son, Alex, comes crying to her with a grazed knee, grass stains surrounding the scratches.

Jane Smith paused only for a moment, last chunk of croissant halfway to her mouth. Her coffee steamed. A breeze sang through the corn crops in the neighbouring field and stirred the wild poppies speckling its edges like beads of blood on an abraded land.

She finished eating her breakfast and drinking her coffee, licking her fingers and picking up pastry crumbs from the plate. The memory was already gone. But every such memory was also always there.

This life was a thin veneer. Routine gave it substance, and repetition made it almost like being free.

But Jane Smith was more than one person. After brewing her third cup of strong coffee of the day, and still before nine in the morning, she picked up her iPad.

First she accessed Twitter. Her current account was under one of many pseudonyms, but it was time to change, so she opened a new account under a new name. A few quick posts about apple pie recipes, pictures of cakes, and a couple of funny cat memes, then she searched some cookery hashtags and friended a handful of random people. That done, she accessed five accounts that she liked to keep track of and friended those, too. These people were in her past, and though she'd made a promise to the few she liked, most would never want to see her again. She might have helped them, but in many cases she had corrupted and cursed them, too. Salvation came at a price.

She knew that more than most.

There were no messages there for her, secretive or otherwise, and nothing to raise her concern. She was glad.

She was *always* glad.

Leaving Twitter running in the background, she surfed other social media sites from a variety of fake ISP accounts. No name was her own, and none were those she had used in real life. Her net activity left no trail, and every relevant page or search was bookended with several random surfs.

Everything was quiet. That was how she liked it. She could have lived like this for the rest of her life, if her sense of morality allowed. It wasn't that she was always out for vengeance. She wasn't sure what it was.

It's all I can do, she'd think when she mused on things. And considering what she had been, and who she'd had, that was the most depressing thing of all.

When she started scrolling through the news sites and saw the item, and scanned the first paragraph, everything changed. Her stomach dropped, and she felt the familiar sense of change settling around her.

The calm reality of her life at the gîte became a facade. Ever since becoming the person she now was, she'd had the sense of the world beyond her horizons conspiring to draw her out and cut her down.

There were plans, conspiracies, machinations, and sometimes she even imagined vast machines working secretly beyond the hills and past the curvature of the Earth, great steam-driven things that drilled and burrowed through the hollows she could not see, the places she did not yet know. They would connect like massive spider webs, drawing tighter and closer until there she was. Caught. Trapped by circumstance, and unable to look away.

All the horrors she had witnessed and experienced, and the terrors she had perpetuated herself, made looking away impossible.

'Now here we are,' she said. She read the whole article, picked up the phone, dialled. After four rings she disconnected, then she dialled again. He picked up after three. That way they both knew that things were well.

But not for long.

'Have you seen the news?' she asked.

'I try to avoid it. Too depressing.'

'There was a double murder in South Wales. A girl had her lips and nostrils glued shut.'

Silence from the other end.

'Post office job gone wrong.'

'So?'

She frowned. It was strange having this conversation in

such calm, beautiful surroundings. *Over the hills*, she thought. *Past the trees. Machines turning and steaming, vast cogs grinding, dripping oil, casting lines to hook into my flesh.*

'Don't you care?' she asked.

'No.'

'But you've been waiting for something like this for years. Don't you want to . . .' She trailed off. He always steered these conversations even if she started them.

'Take revenge? And how did that work for you?'

A slew of images flashed across her mind. None of them were nice. Her hip ached where she'd been shot in Wales three years before, stalking and killing the people of the Trail, the shady organisation responsible for her family's deaths. Her arm was stiff, muscles knotted and hard from another bullet impact. They'd shot her, but she had survived. Perhaps she'd even triumphed. But she didn't feel like a winner.

'It's a lovely morning,' she said.

'Beautiful. Anything else?'

She'd tried to get close to Holt over the past couple of years. He'd pulled her out of her alcoholism following the murders of her family, then he'd trained her, preparing her for vengeance. Even so, she knew that he'd shown her only a small part of what he had learned and experienced over the years. His history was deep, and bathed in blood and grief.

And all the time, every moment they were together or apart, Holt seemed totally in charge.

She hung up without saying any more. It was her own attempt to take control of the conversation.

Jane Smith, real name Rose, glanced at her watch and decided it was time for another coffee.

*

Rose ran.

She had never been a runner. It still felt like a new thing for her. But since that time in the Welsh hills with Chris Sheen three years before, and the Trail, and the violence and pain that had resulted, it had become therapeutic. The Trail had selected Chris for a human trophy hunt, holding his family hostage to ensure he played ball. If he was caught and killed by the hunters, his family went free. If he escaped, they died.

It was the same terrible dilemma that Rose herself had once faced at their hand. She had escaped. Her family had not.

Chris had shown how running could keep you alive, and not just because you stayed ahead of those who meant you harm. It cleared the mind, flushed the veins, worked your systems. It was like a detox of the brain, gasping away accumulated ideas that were growing staid and stale. It drained thoughts that might do you harm. It was a form of freedom and serenity, when Rose rarely felt free, and to be serene was a state she had forgotten years before.

After leaving Wales, she had started with a few miles. She quickly became obsessed. When it was just her and her route, she might have been free. Now, she often ran eighty miles each week, but she never seemed to get anywhere she wanted to go.

Every step she took jolted up through her damaged hip. *Take revenge? And how did that work for you?*

Holt knew how it had worked for her. Not at all. Killing the people who had murdered her family had done nothing to lessen the hollowness their loss had carved out inside her.

The grief was not tempered, the rage not calmed. It was

something she'd had to do, and he had been partly responsible for her achieving and surviving the task. But so many deaths by her hand had done nothing to make the past more bearable, nor the future more certain.

She dreamed of them less now, at least. Her husband and three children, slaughtered in that basement by the Trail, gone forever without any of them having a chance to say goodbye. But maybe that lessening of dreams was more down to the passage of time than anything she had done.

Sometimes, she wondered whether her killing spree had achieved anything at all.

Rose pounded down the sloping woodland trails towards the lake. There were public footpaths through here, but they were rarely trodden, and she let herself run free. She wore shorts and a vest, knobbly trail shoes, and brambles and nettles scratched and stung her legs, tree branches lashed at her bare arms and shoulders. She welcomed the pain. She never actively hurt herself, but whenever pain came she relished it. It was one thing she'd never talked about to Holt. Partly because it frightened her, but she was also terrified that he would nod, understand, and tell her that she was now just like him.

She didn't want to be like that. She didn't want to descend so far, become so lost. They had worked together several times since the hunt in Wales. She took jobs for people who needed her help, innocents who were suffering or naive people pulled into difficult situations. She liked to think she still had morals, and that her sense of injustice drove her to do the things she did.

It was more complex than that, of course. Rose knew that well enough, but analysing too deeply scared her.

With Holt it was . . . fun. He didn't need the money, and she could not even convince herself that he did those things to be closer to her, or to protect and help her.

She truly believed he enjoyed it.

By the time she reached the lake she was sweating heavily, panting, and her legs were burning. She turned left and followed the path along the shore, leaping a fallen tree, skirting around an area where the bank had collapsed into the water, arriving eventually at the small silt beach. The ground here was hard, the water having receded several feet due to the blazing hot summer they were still experiencing. Dropping onto the compacted sand, she kicked off her trainers and stared across the lake.

The other side was two hundred metres away, heavily wooded and rising beyond into a series of low hills. She'd circled the lake a dozen times before, a tough eight mile run that necessitated passing through several private properties. She was never seen or heard. Now, a group of kids larked on the shore and in the water directly across from her. Music was playing, a sibilant hiss, and they were jumping in from a tree that stretched out across the lake. Their laughter and delighted screams seemed to come from so far away.

Rose waded into the water, still in shorts and vest, and felt the slick bed closing around her feet. She jumped forward and went under, and after surfacing she turned on her back and floated. With her ears below the surface the world was silent, cool, consisting of nothing but a burning sky. She drifted there for a while. Hardly moved. Listened to her breathing, the gentle pop of water in her ears, her world for now so close around her that nothing else seemed to exist.

Molly, her sweet daughter, jumps into the pool, laughing as she surfaces, splashing Rose where she sits reading a book.

Rose rolled onto her front and started swimming. She breathed every three strokes, keeping her eyes closed underwater. Swimming was her least favourite exercise, partly because of the pain in her right arm, but mainly because she did not feel totally in control. She never went far. Fifteen minutes of hard swimming and she left the lake, enjoying the coolness across her skin as the sun dried the water. Even before she was fully dry she slipped her trainers on and started running again, heading along the shore towards the eastern tip of the lake, and the small footbridge that crossed the narrow river that fed it.

She'd already decided what she had to do. It was too easy for Holt to dismiss her on the phone, and it had been six weeks since they'd seen each other face to face.

It took another hour to complete her run and return.

She showered quickly, and as she was crossing the spare room where she kept her clothing and kit, she caught sight of herself in the wardrobe mirror. Even now she sometimes surprised herself. She paused and stared at the stranger staring back. Thinner than she'd ever been, leaner, stronger, she was also so far removed from the mother and wife who had let grief suck her into a well of alcoholic despair. Not a single drop of alcohol had passed her lips for over five years. Sometimes, the despair remained.

Even her dead husband, Adam, would have difficulty recognising her now. Her hair was shorter than it had ever been, spiked and dyed blonde. She wore green-tinted contact lenses. Her face was drawn, cheeks hollowed, and she'd lost every ounce of the fat that had given her what he'd called cherub cheeks. Laughter lines remained at the corners of her mouth and eyes, the scars of old smiles. Her left ear was pierced three times, and she wore a stud in her nose.

It was a diamond. She thought such luxury amusing.

She still carried the tattoo on her thigh. She'd had it because the woman who'd killed her family had it, visiting the same tattooist to glean what information she could. Laser treatment had never occurred to her. It was small, and would only be seen by those looking closely enough. Since her husband Adam, no one had.

She dressed in her cycling kit, locked up, and hit the road.

An hour later, approaching the small caravan that Holt had taken for himself, she was struck once again by how deserted it seemed. Holt fostered such an image, but she braked and paused by the small gate into the field, shielding her eyes and scanning the caravan and its surroundings. There were no signs of life.

She carried her bike across the ridged field. Its crop had already been harvested, leaving only sharp stubble.

'It's me!' she called. It was unnecessary. He'd already know who was there.

The door was locked. She knocked, using their code. Two knocks, five, one. No answer.

'John?' He was John Williams. She was Jane Smith. In public, on the phone, anywhere.

Convinced that she was alone, she took out her bike's toolkit and flicked open the small knife. It took fifty seconds to pick the caravan's lock. She was out of practice. It was something she'd feared when they decided to settle for a few months, that they would become rusty, complacent, soft.

Door unlocked, she opened it a crack and peered through. The failsafe he used when he was inside was disconnected. Anyone breaking in when he was in residence would take a shotgun blast to the face.

Inside, she could already see that he'd left in a rush. Anger coursed through her. He wouldn't have changed his mind so quickly, that was for sure, and even as she'd called him he must have been packing and preparing to leave.

'Holt, you bloody prick!' she muttered. Whenever she thought she was getting close to knowing him, she realised he was more of an enigma than ever.

She couldn't help feeling hurt. He'd seen the reports and chosen to go on his own, not with her. They'd never really been a team, but she liked to think they had become friends, working together a few times since taking down the Trail's UK cell. She trusted him as much as she would ever trust anyone again. She believed in him.

He'd lied to her, left without her, and that smarted.

A small note was propped on the table, beside an empty water bottle. *Changed my mind*, it said.

'Yeah. Right. Bastard.' She sighed and sat outside the caravan, looking across the fields at the farmstead in the distance, and the sweeping patterns the breeze made in dozens of acres of crops.

It took only a couple of minutes to convince herself that she had to follow.

Chapter Eight

Manson Eyes

For the final few normal hours of her life, Emma followed a familiar routine.

'Hurry up, you'll be late for school!'

'Okay, Mum.'

She stood at the bottom of the stairs, listening to Daisy humming along to something on her iPod. Every school morning was the same, and every morning her daughter was out of the door with seconds to spare. It was only her second week back in school following the summer holidays, but it seemed that this final year in primary school would be the same.

'Come on! I've got to get ready myself, yet.'

'Chill pill, Mum.' Daisy appeared at the top of the stairs. Short and slight like Emma, but also possessing her mother's athletic build and love of sports, Dom always said that Daisy was going to be a heartbreaker.

'What?' Daisy asked as she hurried downstairs.

'You're gorgeous.'

'Like a princess?'

'Gorgeouser.'

'That's not a word.'

'It is. I'm your mummy and I say so.'

'Mu-um!' Daisy rolled her eyes. She hardly ever called Emma "mummy" any more, another milestone that had drifted by without them really noticing.

'Got your homework and stuff for your art project?'

'Yep.'

'And you'll walk straight home from school.'

'No, I'll go to town and go to the pub then go to the nightclub.'

'And where's my invitation?'

Daisy rolled her big blue eyes again. 'Mu-um!'

'Love you.' Emma kissed her, opened the door, and watched the most precious thing in her world leave. She often watched Daisy down the driveway and along the street, knew she was embarrassed by it, but guessed that deep inside she also quite liked it.

Even so young, Daisy was quickly becoming her own person. She was growing into someone who made her parents intensely proud, but that couldn't camouflage the sense that she was already leaving them.

Sometimes when Emma watched Daisy walking away, her heart ached.

She closed the front door and sighed. The house was suddenly silent, with no blaring music, hassled husband or singing daughter to stir the air. Emma didn't really like the house this quiet. It sang with the ghosts of children unknown.

She had always wanted more than one child. It had taken three years of trying before Daisy was conceived, after being told by doctors that she would probably never have babies. They'd tried for another without success, and now in their early forties she and Dom were still leaving things to chance. But she felt her clock rapidly ticking, and she was resigned to their daughter being an only child.

Secretly, she was sure that Dom blamed her, probably because in her darkest moments she blamed herself. She hadn't even known Dom in those wild few years she'd spent with Genghis Cant and Max Mort. He had been the steady rock further downstream in her future.

At the age of eighteen she'd fallen so easily into that life, attracted by the glamour of a touring band, the charisma of its lead singer, the carefree atmosphere and sense of freedom that came from being in a different town every week and a different country every couple of months. They'd never been huge, but they'd built a large enough fan base to enable them to tour constantly, make reasonable money from their regular albums, and buy and maintain a small tour bus.

This had been in a time before music was so easy to download for free, and album sales had been much healthier. Genghis Cant had played regular festivals in Germany, Holland and Denmark, and their touring had taken them as far afield as Greece.

Their bus had been called Valhalla. It became the centre of her life. She'd shared one of its bunks with Max for two years which she could now barely remember, and he had been more than willing to share his drink and drugs.

She'd once asked her doctor whether such intense substance abuse could have damaged her chances of mother-hood. The doctor had only stared at her. She'd wanted to strike him, curse at him, because she didn't believe it was his place to judge, however silently. He couldn't acknowledge the way she'd pulled herself back up and out of that life. As quickly as she'd fallen she had risen again, hauled back home by her parents and then saved by Dom.

Those years were a blur now, a poor copy of a movie of someone else's life. She still caught occasional glimpses, and sometimes in dreams she was there again, although viewed from the perspective of comfortable middle-age those times were more nightmarish than daring and revelatory.

She was happy to leave them as little more than vague memories. While she acknowledged that she was a product of her experiences, there were plenty she preferred not to dwell upon.

One thing she hadn't lost, however, was her taste for guitar music.

After Dom left for work around seven thirty and Daisy was out of the door by eight fifteen she always had half an hour to herself to get ready for work. Today she chose Pearl Jam, washing and dressing to the evocative strains of Eddie Vedder. It was at these times, when she was alone listening to music, that she came closest to missing those old wild times.

After she locked the back door and went out to her car, she saw a Jeep blocking the end of the driveway. It was several years old, a Cherokee, white and mud-spattered, tinted windows. She didn't recognise it, and she stared for a while, passing her keys from hand to hand and wondering what to do.

She pressed the button that unlocked her car. She could get in and reverse down the driveway, hoping that the driver would see and move aside. Or perhaps she should walk to the Jeep and knock on the window.

The tinted glass made it difficult to tell whether there was even anyone inside. The vehicle hadn't been there when

Daisy had left for school, so it must have pulled up while she was showering and dressing.

I left the back door unlocked, she thought, mildly troubled.

As she started striding along the driveway, the Jeep pulled smoothly away. Emma frowned, shrugged, jumped in her car and reversed out onto the road.

She waved to a couple of people she knew in the village as she passed by, then hit the main road. The radio news came on, and she was shocked once more by the post office slayings headline. Police were appealing for witnesses. A silver BMW had been found several miles away, but they were still searching for a white van and a red Ford. *Narrows it down to about a million vehicles*, she thought.

By the time Emma reached the college ten minutes later she'd forgotten all about the Jeep.

Emma enjoyed her job. It wasn't a traditional career choice, and when some people heard what she did they occasionally frowned, as if wondering why anyone would actually *want* to be a Student Welfare Officer. But she loved people. She interacted with dozens each day, and she was well liked by the college staff and pupil population alike.

She had her own office with a small desk, a laptop, and a comfortable and informal area for when students wanted a heart-to-heart. She spent most of her time whilst in the office seated here, whether with a student or on her own. She even got to choose the furniture herself.

Dom earned more then her. But he worked far longer hours, and some days it was just him and Davey. He was a nice enough kid, but hardly a conversationalist.

Sometimes that suited Dom, because he was at home with his own company, but to Emma that was the idea of a nightmare. She was a sociable creature. Added to that the pressure exerted on Dom from running his own business – the invoicing, estimating, and other admin tasks that went with it – and her job was a breeze.

Emma spent that morning speaking with a couple of students who'd fallen heavily for each other and had an accident. Got carried away, forgot a condom. The boy seemed more embarrassed than the girl, but Emma had shrugged and said, *That can happen to anyone.* She was good at putting students at ease, however difficult the situation they brought to her, and her conversational manner always put them on the same level.

They'd left in a better frame of mind, with instructions to go to the doctor's for a morning after pill, and after promising to ensure they used protection in future.

After that, an older student came for a chat about work-load, and Emma listened while he talked. There wasn't much she could offer, but he smiled and said that she'd helped a lot. He had long dreadlocks and piercings, and reminded her of Dog Bolton, the guitarist from Genghis Cant.

She decided to drive out to a local garden centre for lunch. The Hanging Garden had a fantastic cafe attached, and their quiche was legendary. She had no afternoon appointments, so she took her laptop, intending to spend a couple of hours after lunch catching up on some work emails and form-filling. The sun was blazing, they had a garden with shaded tables and several water fountains, and she was prepared for a warm, relaxing afternoon's work.

Stepping out of the main college building, the heat really hit her. It was a true Indian summer.

She paused outside the revolving doors and took in a few breaths. Sweat prickled beneath her summery dress and across her nose. She squinted into the light, waiting for her eyes to become accustomed. She loved this weather much more than Dom, but after spending several hours indoors it always came as a shock.

Heat haze shimmered across the expansive college car park, blurring some of the vehicles parked in the distance. It rose from metal chassis as if every car had only just parked. Her car was halfway across in one of the staff areas, and as she neared it she saw the Jeep.

It was parked on the access road, idling, exhaust fumes hanging low and dense in the heavy air. Its nose was pointed towards the exit, rear end facing her. Sun glinted from its raised windows. Whoever was inside was taking advantage of the air conditioning.

She shielded her eyes, tried to make a point of standing still and looking. Was it the same vehicle? It was white, and she *thought* it was a Cherokee, but the heat haze made the air between them fluid, confusing shape and distorting sharp edges. It must have been a hundred metres away.

Emma walked a couple of steps and the Jeep crept ahead, very slowly.

She stopped. It stopped.

Shock pulsed through her chest. *What is this?* More disturbed than she wanted to let on, she turned her back on the Jeep and jumped into her own car. Starting quickly, she reversed and aimed in the opposite direction before glancing in the mirror. It was still there, still idling. She dropped into gear and moved away, heading for a maintenance exit at the far corner of the car park. It was a rough lane and not really for casual use, but some of the staff used it at busier times.

'Stupid,' she muttered, opening every window in an attempt to swish away some of the baked air inside. By the time the air conditioning fired up she'd be at The Hanging Garden, so she resigned herself to getting sweat-sticky.

Once out on the road, she found herself glancing in the mirror more than usual. She considered just why someone might be following her. She came up with nothing.

Occasionally a student became fixated on a teacher or other staff member, and once or twice she'd been involved in one of these cases in her professional capacity. But no one had been coming to see her more than usual; she'd noticed no undue attention. She was pretty sure none of the students who drove to college used an expensive vehicle like that. It was a few years old, but probably still worth twenty grand

'*Fucking* stupid,' she said, and talking to herself was a sign that the Jeep had truly unsettled her.

She drove faster than usual back into Usk, then through the town and out along the river. The roads were lunchtime-busy, but there was no sign of the Jeep. She considered calling Dom, but they rarely chatted during the day. A few texts sometimes, but casual chat was kept to a minimum. They were both busy, and there were no regular break times to catch up. Besides, what would she say to him?

Half a mile from the garden centre there were traffic lights. An area of road had been coned off and excavated, curls of blue pipework piled on the verge. No workmen were present. She stopped at the red light as cars passed from the opposite direction.

A supermarket delivery van pulled up behind her. The driver was singing, bobbing his head and performing as if no one else could see him. In her side mirror she could see back along the road, and a couple of other cars slowed behind them. Then a flash of white and the Jeep was there.

'Shit,' she muttered. This was crazy. Dom preparing to show her a new car he'd bought as a treat? No, that was unlikely, and throwing a surprise like this wasn't like him. Besides, he'd had to leave early to get the dinked Focus fixed.

It was someone from the college coming for lunch, that was all. Usk was full of cafes and restaurants, but The Hanging Garden was picturesque and had great food, and was a firm favourite.

'Different car,' she said. 'Get real, Jayne Bond.' Sitting there in her idling car, the heat felt more oppressive than ever.

The lights turned green. She dropped into gear, and from behind she heard the heavy, angry roar of a vehicle accelerating. She'd pulled across the white line by the time the Jeep flashed past, missing her wing by inches.

'Prick!' She stamped on her brakes, jarring to a halt and readying for a crunch as the supermarket truck hit her from behind. There was no impact. The Jeep roared past the roadworks, then its brakes glared and smoke breathed from its wheels as it slewed across the road. Its back end slid around, almost embedding in the hedge. It rocked to a standstill.

Emma was panting. She glanced in her mirror at the cars behind.

The Jeep's driver's window powered down.

The man was staring right at her. He rested his left hand on the steering wheel, right elbow on the windowsill. He was expressionless, and even from this far away his eyes seemed to pierce to the heart of her. He was anywhere between forty and sixty, with masses of wild, curly, unkempt hair streaked with grey, and a big beard that filled his face and almost reached his chest. One finger of his left hand tapped the wheel, and she wondered what music he was listening to.

Emma rarely judged by appearances. The people she'd mixed with during her tumultuous early years had left her very open-minded, and in her day job she often met caring, sensitive and intelligent students with more art on their skin than a gallery, more metal in their faces than a robot. It was what existed on the inside that mattered.

This man scared her. He looked truly wild, but it was also in the way he stared. At her. There was nothing in his eyes, no expression on his face. No glimmer or hint of what he was thinking. *Charles Manson eyes,* she thought, no idea where the image came from.

He didn't even appear to blink.

'Motherfucker,' Emma muttered. It was her favourite extreme curse-word. She drove forward, aimed directly at the Jeep fifty metres ahead. She had no intention of ramming it. She wasn't really sure what she intended, but the man's stare felt like an assault, and her aggressive reaction was pure instinct.

The Jeep straightened and powered away. The driver's expression hadn't changed at all as he looked away, and a second later he was out of sight. The Jeep was much faster than her car. Even so she followed faster than she should have, watching its tail end moving quickly ahead until it disappeared around a bend.

She slowed as she approached the bend a few seconds later, breathing a sigh of relief when she cleared it and there was no sign of the white vehicle.

Two minutes later, parking in The Hanging Garden's car park and switching off the engine, she gripped the steering wheel and took several deep breaths. Her sweating wasn't only due to the heat.

'Just some nutter,' she said. Then she shivered. *Someone walked over my grave.* It was a weird saying her mother used to use, and it had always spooked the hell out of her.

She pulled out her phone and called Dom.

Chapter Nine

Soft Bitch

Dom made several mistakes in work that day.

The worst was when he sliced his thumb with a Stanley knife. He bled all over his client's new kitchen floor, dabbing up blood with a dust cloth as he held his wounded hand over the sink. He swilled the cut and examined it. He probably needed a stitch or two. Instead, he waited a while, then wound a handkerchief tightly around his thumb, held in place with several loops of insulating tape.

The house they were working on was on the side of a hill above Monmouth town, a big, sprawling place that had been extended several times. The owners kept out of their way, other than the frequent tea and biscuit supplies, leaving him and Davey to get on with things.

Dom liked that. Because the job was quite spread out he'd spent most of the day on his own. His phone being without reception was an added bonus.

He'd needed time to think.

He left just before four in the afternoon, taking the van to pick up supplies for the next day. It would be their final day on the job, and Davey wanted to stay later that evening to get things close to finished. It would mean more overtime payments, but Dom was happy with that. Even more so when Davey said his girlfriend would pick him up when he was done.

Heading along the winding driveway, out into the lanes, and down the hill towards the town splayed across the river plain below, his phone started to chime and beep. He'd have expected three or four notifications, but the frantic flurry of sounds communicated real urgency.

He stopped in the next field gateway and left the engine running. He was already soaked in sweat from the van's sauna-like interior, but seeing the notifications on the screen caused a chill. Four missed calls from Emma, three from Daisy and one from Andy.

His heart jarred in his chest, causing him to cough. He suffered from mild palpitations sometimes, nothing to worry about his doctor had said, ease back on the caffeine and stress. He gripped the wheel and coughed again, and when his heart had settled into a worried gallop he called Andy.

'What's happened?' he asked as soon as his friend answered.

'Car's fixed,' Andy said.

'Nothing else?'

'Like what? I'm on the way back, just stopped for a drink. It's like Death Valley out there.'

'Emma and Daisy have been trying to call, I've been out of service.'

'So have you called them back?'

'No. Only you. I thought something . . .' He trailed off, closing his eyes and trying to calm down. Sweat trickled down his temple. When he opened his eyes again, they stung.

'Dom, you need to call your family. See what they want. Then go home and get pissed in your garden. Just . . . chill.'

'Chill,' Dom said, chuckling.

'I can drop your car down this evening, if you like.'

'I'll pick it up from yours. I'll park the van in the town car park, get Davey to collect it in the morning.'

'It was three hundred quid.'

Dom was stunned silent.

'Joking,' Andy said. 'Text me later, mate. Fucking hot, isn't it?'

'Steaming. Thanks, Andy.' Dom signed off, then dialled Emma's phone. He was almost calming, almost breathing normally, on the verge of enjoying the heavy summer heat and the buzzing of bees, the stunning views down over the town and river, and the idea of sitting in the garden polishing off a bottle of Pinot that evening.

'Where the hell have you been?' Emma shouted as soon as she picked up.

'Babe?'

'Why haven't you been answering—?'

'No reception. You know my phone's dodgy at this place.'

'You should have phoned! You should have . . .' She was so angry it sounded like she was crying. Emma hardly ever cried. 'Should have given me their landline number, Dom.'

'What's happened? Slow down and tell me.'

'Nothing, nothing really.' She sighed heavily, anger settling as quickly as it had exploded. But a cool hand was clutched around Dom's spine, twisting and turning so that the world around him swayed with it.

'Emma, what's wrong? Daisy tried calling me too.'

'I'm in You For Coffee with her now.'

'I thought she was going to Lauren's after school?'

83

'She did, then Lauren and her mum came into Abergavenny with Daisy. Daisy called me to come and pick her up, she said she'd wait in the park for me. Lauren's mother bought her an ice cream.'

'She left her alone in Abergavenny? She's only eleven!'

'Dom, she's been to town before, and waited until I picked her up.'

'Right. So what's wrong?'

'Daisy was on her phone. A woman walked up to her, like directly to her across the grass. Daisy says she looked up to see what she wanted, and the woman just stood there staring straight at her. Then she said, "Soft bitch," and walked away.'

'What? What woman? Why?'

'I don't bloody know!'

Dom heard Daisy say something in the background. She and Emma mumbled something, then there was a scratching sound and her daughter came on the line. 'Dad?'

'Honey, you okay?'

'Yeah, I'm fine. But that woman was scary. Really grinned a lot, almost laughing. Like Mum just told you, she said "Soft bitch," and then walked away. Really slow. She wasn't worried about anything, you know? Didn't think I'd stand up to her or anything.'

'Did you know her?'

'Never seen her before. She smelled of sweat, though. Real stinky.'

'So what did you do?'

'Left the park, tried to phone you, rang Mum and then came to the coffee shop. Do you think she knows the man in the Jeep?'

'What man? What Jeep?'

'Oh, hang on, Mum hasn't . . .' She trailed off and Dom was left with a quiet phone, more rustling in the background, distant voices.

'Emma? Daisy?' His voice was raised, almost shouting, and the car's interior suddenly felt claustrophobic. When he drew in the humid air was it was devoid of oxygen. Throwing the door open, he almost fell out onto the road. The tarmac was hot and sticky. The air was so still that even the birds seemed too lethargic to sing. The landscape held its breath, and through the phone jammed against his ear he heard only the background sounds.

'Emma!' he shouted again, and then she was there.

'Some guy in a Jeep. I think he's been following me.'

Dom closed his eyes. The Loony Tunes had been in a van and a BMW, not a Jeep. The crashed BMW had been found, but not the van. And they were proper criminals, armed and dangerous, so of course they wouldn't use their own vehicles to do the robbery.

They weren't that fucking stupid.

'Are you okay?' he asked.

'Yeah, just rattled. I'll take Daisy home and—'

'Okay, I'll meet you there. Be half an hour. Get me a cappuccino take-out?' He struggled to sound calm.

'Dom?' In only his name she asked a hundred questions. They knew each other so well. *What do you know, what's happening, who is he, why haven't you asked more?*

'Have you called the police?' he asked, and even the word police felt laden with despair.

'No. No, he didn't actually . . . Do you think I should?'

Yes, he thought. 'Not yet,' he said.

'What's happening?' Emma asked, but it was more an instruction than a question. *Tell me what the fuck is going on!*

85

'Might be some guy to do with work.'

'What guy?'

'He owes me money and I threatened to take him to small claims.' The words rolled easily from his tongue, and once they started the lies forming behind them pushed them out with ease. It felt bad lying to Emma. But far better than telling the dreadful truth.

'You didn't tell me about this.'

'It's only a couple of grand. What did he look like?'

'Lots of hair, big beard. Weird eyes, just staring.'

'Yeah, that's him. Don't worry, he's harmless. Grumpy old farmer.'

'Scared the hell out of me,' Emma said, and in the deserted lane, Dom leaned against the van and closed his eyes. He wanted to tell everything, but nothing could make things well. 'So what about the woman and Daisy?'

'Some random nutter,' Dom said. 'Few homeless people been sleeping in that park, apparently.'

'Just because they're homeless doesn't mean they're nutters,' Emma said.

'You know what I mean. We won't let her into town on her own again.'

'We can't say—'

'Just for now,' Dom said.

'Okay. I'll see you at home.' He knew her tone of voice. She wanted him to come and tell them exactly what was going on.

And he had half an hour in which to find out.

'Don't worry, I'll call him now and sort this out. Love you.'

'You too,' his wife said, distracted. He often told her that when they went to bed, but rarely on the phone.

Dom hung up before she could say any more. He stared at the phone. It couldn't be a coincidence. His daughter, his wife . . .

What the hell had he done?

He wanted to shout and rage at himself, take everything back. Travel back to that drink and cake outside the Blue Door and tell Andy he was stupid, that doing a post office over was the most ludicrous idea ever. Move on from there, cycle home, hug his wife and continue their comfortable, boring life. Sometimes she signed up for something mad, like a parachute jump or a forty-mile hike across the Mendips. Sometimes she sighed when he said no to doing those things with her.

He didn't want to do one thing every day that scared him. He wanted his wife and daughter safe, not being followed and spooked. He wanted to feel secretly, quietly, jealous of Andy when he went on one of his foreign adventure trips, or got laid, or when they showered together after squash and Dom saw his friend's fitter body, fuller head of hair. He wanted that jealousy because it meant he was comfortable and safe.

'Fuck's sake,' he muttered, drawing his left hand across his face. He was slick with sweat.

He dialled Andy again, and after three rings he picked up.

'Andy,' he said. 'Emma and Daisy have been threatened.'

Andy was quiet. Dom could hear his friend breathing, hear the sounds of traffic. He must have been driving again, hands-free.

'What have you told them, Dom?' he asked at last.

'Nothing! Are you crazy?'

'Who threatened them?'

'A woman intimidated Daisy in the park. A guy in a Jeep followed Emma. Lots of hair, big beard.'

'What did they say?'

'The woman called Daisy a soft bitch.'

'So they weren't threatened.'

'They were followed! Daisy's not quite eleven, Andy. She was scared half to death!'

Andy's silence again. Dom wanted to reach through the phone line and grab him, shake him.

'Andy, we've got to go to the police.'

'No,' Andy said. 'Your place. I'll meet you there. I'll be there before you. And when you get there, I do the talking. Got it?'

'Is it them?'

'You pissed off anyone else lately?'

'Andy, they're murderers!'

'I know them.'

'What do you mean, you know them?'

'Their type. I know their type. We don't want to fuck around here, Dom.'

'How do you know their type?'

'No police. Just be as quick as you can.' Andy rang off. Dom tried to call him again, but it went straight to voicemail.

'Shit!'

A motor sounded in the distance, coming closer. A car appeared around a bend in the lane, and Dom tensed, wondering who he would see and what they would threaten him with. It was an elderly couple. The man sat in the passenger seat, a small dog in his lap. They both looked at him, and Dom tried on a smile. Neither of them smiled back.

As the car passed he slumped into the van, tried Andy one more time, then placed the phone on the seat beside him. He stared at it. 999, that's all it would take, three easy numbers and a few sentences of explanation. And then his whole life, and that of his family, would be forever changed.

Ruined.

Emma and Daisy would be ostracised in the village. Daisy would have to move school and lose her friends, in the year before her important change to comprehensive school. Emma would lose her job, because they couldn't have the wife of an armed robber working with vulnerable teens. He'd go to prison.

Prison. A place for criminals, not for him. And with that idea came their reason one more time, the factor that had persuaded both him and Andy that they could do this and get away with it: no one would ever suspect them.

I know their type, Andy had said. The realisation that Dom had never truly known his friend pressed in hard.

His thoughts tumbled over each other. He tried to take in a calming breath, but the hot air was stifling and he couldn't think straight. Too much had happened too quickly. It was like a dream, something that made perfect sense when asleep but which was chaotic and surreal in real life. Perhaps he'd already thrown his real life away.

Dom picked up the phone and dialled two 9s before dropping it again. Half an hour home. After that, everything could be resolved.

He drove the van faster than he should, the phone nestled between his thighs and turned up high. It remained silent all the way home.

Chapter Ten

Attenshun

Written in blood, the message said, *Now we have your attenshun.*

Daisy struggled to go to Jazz. She tugged and pulled, trying to break free of her mother's grasp. But Emma had protected this girl since before she was born, and her first instinct now was to hug her tight, smother her with her arms and love, and keep her away from whatever danger had befallen them.

This was more than just a dispute over an electrical contract and a bit of owed money. Dom must think she was stupid.

'Jazz,' Daisy said, her voice sharp with shock and broken with tears.

Their dog was dead. She'd been stabbed many times, and her bloodied hulk was prone on their large patio. Flies buzzed. That offended Emma more than the open meat of her, the gashed flesh, the clotted fur and pale pink of bloodied bone showing through here and there.

Emma moved, disturbing the flies. They took off in a haze, some of them spiralling away, others landing on the bloody words painted across their white rendered wall between back door and dining room patio doors. The writer had cut off Jazz's tail to use as a brush.

Now we have your attenshun.

'We stay together,' Emma said. She eased Daisy around the mess of their dead, beloved pet, trying to shield her daughter's eyes, failing. Daisy was mature for her age, and strong with it. She wouldn't want to not see. She'd inherited her mother's headstrong attitude, and she'd want to witness what had happened to her beloved pet.

They'd bought the dog when Daisy was four years old. Dom had held out for a year or so, fending off her pleading *Can we have a puppy?* moments with talk of how expensive they were, how they needed a lot of exercise, and what a tie it would be. A four year old didn't care about these things or understand them, and when Emma's allegiances on the matter shifted from Dom to Daisy, the decision was effectively made. She'd grown up with dogs in the house, and although all he said was true, the idea had started to appeal to her more and more.

Dom had been the one most smitten when the Labrador puppy had arrived.

'Oh, Jazz,' she whispered, voice breaking.

'Who would do this?' Daisy asked.

'I don't know.'

'I'll kill them.'

'Now, Daisy, you've got to—'

'I'll *kill* them!' Her voice was louder, and with a twist and a shove she broke free of Emma's arms. She didn't go far. Four steps towards the dog's corpse, she half knelt, then stood and backed away again. There was nothing left to stroke that wasn't corrupted with blood. No soft fur to bury her face in, no warm muzzle, no living, loving eyes.

Emma glanced at the back door. It had been forced open, the uPVC framing around the handle and lock cracked and crumbled.

Dom had always said that Jazz would be useless as a guard dog, and that if they were burgled she'd lick them into submission. Emma wondered whether the dog had greeted the intruder, jumped around in excitement, and whether the attacker had petted her for a while before using the knife.

The gardens and houses around them were quiet, still. The myriad scents of summer hung on the air – cut grass, rose perfume, washing drying in the sun, the hint of an early barbecue. Their garden was quite secluded, but two neighbours' houses had windows looking down onto their lawn. They were silent and closed, reflecting sunlight and blue sky.

She looked at the back door again. It was only open an inch or so. Whoever had done this had pulled it closed as they left.

Or pushed it shut when they were inside.

'Daisy,' she whispered. 'Come on.'

Her daughter turned then, looking right at her. The grief was heartbreaking. Daisy didn't deserve it, Emma thought. She was a great kid, thoughtful and bright, relishing life and empathising with those around her. She lived for today and said she wanted to never have a real job. That annoyed Dom, unsettled him even though she was still so young. Emma thought part of that was fear that Daisy would have the same early experiences her mother had sought.

'Daisy, with me.' They backed towards the gate. Emma had her phone in her hand, and as they slipped out onto the driveway she swiped the screen to unlock it.

Daisy screamed.

Emma looked up, panicked.

Andy stood in their front garden, close to the drive gate twenty metres away.

'Em,' he said.

'Someone killed Jazz,' Daisy said. Andy didn't look at her. He was staring at Emma, glancing down at the phone in her hand. He shook his head.

'Em, don't.'

'Andy?'

'Dom's on his way.' His eyes flickered to the front door, first floor windows, back again. He swayed gently from foot to foot as if ready to run, seemingly unaware that he was doing it. Through the hedge that separated their front garden from the road, she saw the ghost red shape of Dom's Ford Focus.

'You're driving Dom's car?'

'I got the bump fixed for him.'

'Someone's stalking us,' Emma said. 'They killed our dog, Andy. I'm calling the police.'

'No,' he said. 'Not unless you want Dom to go to prison.'

'Prison?'

'Mum?' Daisy asked.

A car drove along the street, not slowing. Emma saw it pass by the end of their driveway, recognised it. Their friends Gill and Steve. Their families sometimes walked together, out into the countryside to a local pub. Once, it had started raining as they walked, and they'd all sheltered in a fisherman's hut until the summer storm blew over. Normal suddenly felt so far away, and she suddenly wanted to talk to them.

Not to Andy. Andy was frightening her.

'You'd better explain,' she said.

'Not here, and not now.'

'Andy, we can't leave Jazz,' Daisy said. 'Not like that.' Her voice was brittle, quiet.

'We need to go—'

'This is my *home*!' Emma snapped.

'I know, Em,' Andy said. 'And what happened to Jazz?'

Those bloody images were burned into Emma's mind, and Andy must have seen them as her expression started to crumple. His voice softened. 'Come with me. We'll wait for Dom, then go somewhere—'

'Safe?' Daisy asked.

'Safe.' He nodded.

Emma made her decision. But as she locked her phone and took her first step towards Andy, she saw in his eyes that safe didn't really exist.

Chapter Eleven

Carry On

Dom met them in the car park beside the hall where Daisy went to Scouts on a Monday. Andy had called him and arranged the meeting location, told him he had Emma and Daisy and that their dog had been killed. The hall was hidden from the road and not easy to find, unless you knew where it was. Dom knew that was why Andy had chosen it. That scared him.

What frightened him more was the fear on his family's faces as he parked the van. They were sitting on a bench in the shade of an old oak tree, at the edge of the park bordering the hall and car park. Daisy was huddled into Emma, sobbing and frightened, head resting on her shoulder. Emma was scared, too. But she was also angry.

Dom looked into his lap and fumbled with his keys before leaving the van, giving himself a few seconds to gather himself. *Has he told them already?* he wondered. Andy was standing beside his wife and daughter, a protective pose that flushed Dom with a cool fury. *He* should have been there.

But the feeling quickly subsided. As he approached them

across the dusty car park, he couldn't shake the feeling that everything had changed forever.

There was a children's playground directly beside the scout hall, deserted right now. A larger grassed area, shadowed with trees and a few areas of shrubs, provided shelter for a few parents with pushchairs. Toddlers toddled. A big dog sunbathed, panting. No one was looking their way.

'Someone killed Jazz,' Emma said as Dom entered the tree's shadow.

'Andy told me.'

'So *who* killed him?' she asked. 'Who would *do* that? And who's that spooky bastard following me?'

'I . . .' *Don't know*, he was going to say, but the rage in his wife's eyes told him that would be nowhere near enough. He looked at Andy, raised his eyebrows, wished they'd talked about what had already been said.

'Andy said you're going to prison,' Daisy said. She stood and came to Dom, hugged him. He was so glad. He looked at Emma over Daisy's head and wished that she'd hug him too. But everything was on pause until the truth was out. Her life, their lives, everything they knew and loved and took for granted. She seemed aware of that already, and seeing the knowledge in her eyes made him so ashamed.

'What have you done?' she asked, looking from Dom to Andy, back again. 'And don't tell me this is just some farmer who doesn't want to pay his bill.'

'It's complicated,' Andy said.

'So explain it to me in a nice simple way that I can understand.'

They sat on the park table and bench, Andy and Dom on one side, Emma and Daisy on the other. Dom's heart was thudding so hard he thought it might burst. He tried to breathe slowly, tried to calm himself, afraid that the palpitations would come again and never stop. He worried about that sometimes. He wasn't looking after himself quite as well as he should be, and something Emma had said a few years ago often hit home. *I want to be able to play with my grandchildren.* It had been one evening after she'd returned from a hard trail run along their local riverside, scratched by brambles, caked in mud up to her knees. He'd laughed and asked why she did that to herself. Her reply had been half-amused, but it had also carried a weight of admonishment, because she wanted him to play with their grandchildren, too.

He was trying. But he was also working hard to provide for their future in other ways.

'It was my fault,' Andy said. 'All mine. He was giving me a lift before work. I'd driven out to the White Hart for a drink with Claudette on Sunday evening, had a bit too much and got a taxi home. I needed my car, so I called Dom and asked him to drop me out there. It was sort of on his way to Monmouth.'

'Sort of,' Dom said. Because he had to say something. If he looked too surprised by the lie Andy was constructing, Emma would see right through him.

'We were on the way to the White Hart,' Andy continued. 'Through the lanes out past the old iron bridge, you know? I was larking around. I was in a good mood.'

'Because you'd seen Claudette the night before,' Dom said, smiling at Emma. She wasn't even looking at him. All her focus was on Andy.

'Yeah. So when the other car came around the corner, Dom didn't see it. Caught it a glancing blow. We stopped, so did they. There wasn't too much damage, at least I didn't think so. But it was . . . they weren't nice people.'

'What do you mean?' Emma asked.

'They're the ones who killed Jazz?' Daisy asked. 'Because Dad bumped their car?'

'It was a bit more than a bump,' Dom said. 'They came off worse, my car was just a bit scraped and—'

'You heard of the Hucknalls?' Andy pressed gently on Dom's foot under the bench, a silent *Shut the hell up.*

'Should I have?' Emma asked.

'Local rough family,' Andy said. 'They're quite spread out, live in Newport, Cardiff, Swansea.'

'Rough as in crime?' Emma asked.

'Well, yeah. Not nice people. There're parents, siblings, cousins. Couple of them have been inside for nasty stuff. Drugs, fraud, extortion, GBH.' He glanced at Daisy, shrugged at Emma, as if to say, *You don't want to hear any more.*

'One of them was in the car,' Emma said.

'We didn't know it at the time,' Andy said. 'Guy jumped out, a skinny runt but obviously a bruiser. Dom offered his insurance details, said he'd be in touch. The guy started getting feisty. I calmed him down.'

To Dom, it sounded ridiculous. It sounded like a scene from a Carry On film. *Carry On Robbing Post Offices.*

'Then what happened, Dom?' Emma asked.

He looked right at her. Looked into his wife's eyes and lied, and somehow, from somewhere, calmness settled over him. He didn't think about the money bag buried in the pill box outside of town. No images of the Looney Tunes gang flashed by. He didn't even consider the dead woman and child at the post office.

'Andy managed to sweet-talk him down, calm him a bit, and I apologised and we—'

'You apologised for crashing into him?' Emma asked.

'Well, yeah.'

'You should never do that!' she said, and that was when he believed she was going for the story. 'Apologise and you're as good as saying it's your fault.'

'It was.'

'Doesn't matter! That's for the insurance companies to decide.'

'There won't be insurance companies,' Andy said. 'And that's my fault too. The guy wanted money there and then. We didn't have any, so I said we'd deliver cash to him later that day, meet at a coffee shop in Newport.'

'And you didn't,' Emma said.

'I don't have five grand lying around,' Andy said. 'And Dom told me he didn't either.'

'Five thousand pounds?' Emma gasped.

'So they killed Jazz,' Daisy said. 'Because Dad bumped their car, they killed Jazz, cut her up and stabbed her.'

Dom could not answer. Somehow the lie made the bloody truth even more awful. This wasn't about a dented car and five grand. The reality was much, much grimmer. He wished he could believe his own lies and go on living that way.

'It was a Ferrari,' he said.

Emma rolled her eyes.

'We didn't show, so they got our attention,' Andy said. 'Now they'll ask for more money.'

'Police. Now.' Emma went to stand, and Andy held her arm. She glared at his hand and he let go.

'Em,' Dom said.

'This is ridiculous,' she said. 'Just *stupid*!'

'You've seen what they're capable of,' Andy said. 'Really, Emma, you don't want to involve the police now.'

'You can't be afraid of people like this,' she said.

'You can, and I *am*,' Andy said. 'Look, go to the police and, at the very least, Dom might go to prison. He left the scene of a crime.'

'What crime?'

'The guy's girlfriend was in the car. She was hurt. I got Claudette to ask around at A&E at the hospital for me, and a women came in that morning after a car crash. Whiplash, cuts from broken glass, broken nose. You've got to consider how the Hucknalls might react.'

'They've *already* reacted!' Emma said. She was raising her voice, Daisy was huddling into her, eyes watering. Dom wanted to end the conversation and take them home. Hide his head in the sand. If Andy wasn't here, he'd have told them everything.

'I'll sort this out,' Andy said. 'Really. I promise. I've still got this guy's number, I'll call him and sort it out.'

'You?' Emma asked. That one word carried a weight of inquiry. How would he sort it out? Where would the money come from? And how did he know how to deal with something like this?

'Just . . . trust me. I have some money saved, and you can pay me back.'

'We don't want to owe you, Andy,' Emma said. She turned away from them both and looked across the park. Dom glanced at Andy. His friend tapped his foot again.

Daisy sat staring at her hands. She'd lost her pet, Dom could see Jazz's blood on her fingernails. He felt a sudden, dizzying rush of terror the likes of which he'd never felt before, a fear of ultimate loss that made him want to hug his daughter to him, hold her so tightly that no one would ever be able to prise them apart.

'I want it all to go away,' he muttered.

Emma turned back to him, hearing his wretchedness. She held his hands across the table again. Stern, but loving, she gave him a cool smile.

'Dom should come with me,' Andy said. 'We'll call them and try to come to an agreement. It'll all be over by this time tomorrow.'

'This just all feels so unbelievable,' Emma said. 'This happens to other people. We're just normal!'

'They didn't have to kill Jazz,' Daisy said. Her voice was flat, furious. 'They didn't have to do that.'

'They know what they're doing,' Andy said. 'They know decent people like us fear them, and what they can get from us. It's the kind of people they are.' Dom remembered him saying, *I know their sort.* As soon as he and Andy were alone, he'd ask him how.

'So where do we go in the meantime?' Emma asked. 'I'm not staying home tonight. No way.'

'Mandy's?' Dom suggested.

Emma sighed heavily. 'I'll give her a call. Tell her we're . . . fumigating the house, or something.'

'This isn't fair,' Daisy said. 'It's just not fair! We should be able to go to the police without being scared. That's what the police are for.'

'Sometimes fair doesn't come into it,' Andy said. It sounded like he knew what he meant. *Something else for me to ask him,* Dom thought.

He felt sick at the lies they'd spun, wretched at the danger he had exposed his family to. Most of all, he felt a burning need to get Andy on his own and ask just what the fuck was going on.

'I'll come by Mandy's in an hour,' he said. 'I'll bring a Chinese.'

'Right,' Emma said. 'Because that'll make everything better.' She stood, waited for Daisy to join her, then the two of them walked back towards the car park.

Dom watched them go. They were the two people he loved most in this world. They'd been threatened, and he would do everything in his power to make that threat go away. He watched until they were in Emma's Corsa, and as it swung from the car park he waved. Sunlight glared from windows, and he wasn't sure if either of them waved back.

'We get the money,' Dom said, still staring after the car. 'We give it to them. And that's it.'

'It's not as simple as that.'

Dom sprang up from his seat and lunged for Andy. He grabbed his friend's shirt collar, his foot caught in between the bench's seat and table upright, and he went sprawling, pushing Andy down beneath him. They both hit hard. Andy gasped as he was winded, and Dom rolled aside. He sat up quickly, looking around. No one seemed to have seen.

He was breathing hard. So much was spinning in his head, so many possibilities and regrets. Were Emma and Daisy even safe? The very idea of not going to the police made him feel sick, but the prospect of prison made him cold. He couldn't do that. Not him.

'They're fucking murderers!' he said. He wanted to shout. Instead, he held out his hand and helped Andy up.

Andy sat on the table's edge and rubbed his back.

'Okay,' he said. He was looking at the ground at his feet, still rubbing. He seemed to be having some internal discussion. Dom had rarely seen him looking so vulnerable. 'Okay.'

'Okay what?' Dom asked. 'Andy, I'm going to sort this out. Get the money, wait for them to contact us, give it to them. Then they'll piss off, won't they? Leave us alone?'

Andy didn't seem to hear. He was still nodding slowly, then he looked up at Dom, and something about him had changed. It was as if a veil had lowered from his eyes, exposing something darker and grimmer beneath.

Chapter Twelve

Nothing Would Happen

Passing through the centre of town, Emma swung a left into the car park. It was hidden away behind the main street.

'Mum? Aren't we going to Mandy's?'

'Hang on,' Emma said. She parked in the far corner in the shade of some trees, reversing into a space so that she could see the rest of the car park. She was holding the steering wheel hard, knuckles white, fingers cramped.

'Mum,' Daisy said softly. She touched Emma's shoulder, and that simple contact broke a dam of emotion. Emma sobbed loudly, once and tearless, pressing her hands to her face.

'I'm okay,' she said quickly. She rubbed at her eyes, ran her hands through her hair and checked herself in the mirror. Every few seconds she scanned the car park. No white Jeeps. Plenty of people on their way home from work, picking up a bottle of wine for an evening in the garden or a bag of groceries. A flock of old women walked across the expanse of tarmac, all white hair and backpacks, finishing an afternoon hike with a coffee and cake in the museum cafe. No wild-haired men. No dog killers.

Emma had to be strong, for herself and for Daisy. Jazz had been part of the family, but her immediate fear was for themselves. Daisy's grief was plain and direct. Emma's was contoured with complexities. The family should be together now, not pulled apart by Andy and whatever he thought he could do to help them. And why *would* he? Was he really so guilty that he'd expose himself to such danger? She liked to think so but . . . she didn't really know Andy that well at all.

What she *did* know indicated that he was probably a bastard.

Dom had been terrified. She'd seen truth behind his eyes that craved release, but Andy had guided their conversation. She'd seen fear, too. He'd loved Jazz as much as the rest of them, but the terror she'd witnessed in him had transcended what had occurred, and she hated seeing such fear in the man she loved.

Dom might have been quiet, content without adventure in his life, but she had never considered him a coward. In business he stood up for himself, and he was not afraid to fight for what was right. Sometimes he even surprised her. Two years ago his company van had been stolen from outside a house he was working on. By lucky coincidence, their friend Mostyn had seen it parked outside a country pub a couple of miles outside Usk, and he'd driven Dom out there to confront the two young thieves. She still remembered Mostyn's delighted expression as he'd told her about Dom approaching the beer garden table were they sat, crowbar swinging casually from his hand.

Today, a different Dom had faced her across that park bench.

'We should bury Jazz,' Daisy said. 'She's just lying there and . . . there are flies. It's hot. What if the neighbours see her? What if they see the blood and that message?'

Then that makes what I need to do moot, Emma thought. If someone else called the police, the decision was taken from her.

'I just need to think,' she said. 'I just want to . . . hang on.' She opened her phone.

'Are you calling Mandy?'

'Not yet.' She opened her browser and entered *Hucknall family South Wales.* The search took a while, her connection poor, and its only results were to do with the band Simply Red. She tried something else, accessing the local newspaper's website and doing a targeted search. If any of the Hucknalls had made the news for any of the crimes Andy had listed, there'd be a report.

Again, nothing.

She closed her eyes and tried to take a step back, disassociate herself from what had happened. It was difficult, but it allowed a certain clarity of thought. A man had stalked her that morning. Someone had approached Daisy, threateningly. Their dog had been slashed to pieces.

'Fucking hell,' she muttered.

Daisy glanced at her, surprised by the foul language.

'This is just stupid. I'm calling the police.'

'Really?' Daisy sounded shocked.

'Yes. Really. It's what normal people would do, and we're normal people. Whatever happened with your dad and that car, it should be sorted out the right way.'

'Did you really believe Andy's story?' Daisy's surprise was obvious, her voice high. 'About Dad bumping a local bad family's Ferrari?'

Emma blinked at her daughter, and, of course, no, she didn't believe it. She hadn't believed it from the moment Andy started constructing the tale, butting in so that Dom couldn't talk. Lying to her face, and demanding that her husband go along with the lie.

'They've done something worse than bump a car,' Daisy said. She clenched her hands in her lap, staring from her side window into the hedge close by, seeing nothing. 'I've never liked Andy.'

It seemed like a random adult comment for a ten year old, Emma thought, but its simplicity illuminated the whole situation.

Emma started the car and pulled away.

She hadn't been sure about Andy since the moment they'd met two years before. He'd been biking with Dom. He'd nodded hello to Emma, smiling and comfortable in the same sort of kit that made Dom self-conscious and edgy. He'd seemed over-confident, even brash. She'd caught him eyeing her down and up again, annoying her and making her fold her arms across her chest. He'd seen that, and hadn't even looked away.

But Emma was the last to judge by first impressions, and over time Andy had become a fixture. He'd socialised with them, driving down to ride with Dom from Usk so that he could join them for a drink afterwards, and sometimes a meal. Dom liked him, though in private he was open about his new friend's perceived faults. *It's like he doesn't have a care in the world*, Dom would say. Andy was confident, but not quite pompous. Extremely clever, though not arrogant. Happy to take advantage of his good looks, physique, and charisma to charm his way in and out of a selection of beds. He kept his girlfriends at a distance, although Dom admitted to knowing that a couple had been married. Andy didn't seem to have any moral concerns about that.

Dom also seemed to know very little about him. There'd

been some vague talk about him living in London before moving to South Wales, but he rarely talked about background or family, and would avoid the subject when it was brought up. Emma wondered if he hid some family tragedy or rift, or whether he was simply someone who truly lived for the moment. Whatever it was, it gave him a shallowness that often made her suspicious.

Perhaps emphasising his faults, to Dom in her own mind, was a way of distracting herself about how she felt. Because she'd become drawn to him, and not in a way she was used to. She loved Dom for his mind, his humour, his love and sincerity. The physical side was strong too, and always had been. But she'd not experienced the base, animal attraction she felt for Andy since Max Mort.

He made her feel like a teenager again, and she'd enjoyed such naive sensations because she'd felt safe doing so. Nothing would happen. He was a casual friend, and even Dom had said that in reality he was more of an acquaintance. *He never opens himself up,* he'd once said. *I don't actually know him at all.*

Nothing would happen.

Until that one time.

Recalling that moment still inspired guilt and excitement, a flash of rainbow colours against a sepia background. A lazy Sunday afternoon, Daisy out with friends, Emma reading in the garden with hands still dirtied from planting some pots and hanging baskets. She found gardening therapeutic, whereas Dom just thought it boring. It was the perfect pastime for when he was out.

Around three o'clock, Dom and Andy rolled in from a forty-mile ride. Andy had driven down to their house to start the ride, so that he could eat with them afterwards. He always brought a kit bag with spare clothes. They were going to have a barbecue. Emma had prepared some kebabs, and Daisy was coming home in time to make her secret couscous recipe which Andy professed to love.

While the men disappeared upstairs to shower, Emma lit the barbecue. Jazz fussed around her, and she petted the dog before realising she had soot and soil still on her hands and clothes. Ensuring the barbecue was safe, she trotted upstairs to their bedroom. Andy was showering in the family bathroom, Dom in their en-suite shower room, as usual. Making sure the bedroom door was closed, she quickly stripped off her dirty shorts and underwear, and her vest top.

For a second as she opened the door to the en suite to take a wash, she thought everything was as it should be. Steam filled the room, and she wondered why Dom hadn't turned on the combined light and extractor fan. She enjoyed the waft of warm, damp air across her skin, the smell of Dom's minty shower gel. She was surprised that the shower was already turned off.

It wasn't Dom.

Andy stood on the bathmat beside the open shower cubicle, towel around his head and over his face as he dried his hair vigorously. His body glistened with water droplets. They speckled the hairs across his broad chest, dripped down his flat stomach, nestled on his closely trimmed crotch.

Emma held her breath in shock.

Andy lowered the towel and stared at her. He made no effort to cover himself. He wiped slowly from chest to waist, then dropped the towel at his feet. His eyes lingered on her breasts, drifted lower, then up again to her face. Once they locked eyes he didn't look away.

'He's in the bath,' he said. A statement, an explanation. An invitation.

It might have been only seconds, but it felt like minutes. Emma broke their gaze and looked down at him. She hadn't seen another naked man in the flesh in almost two decades. He was bigger than Dom—

Of course he is, she thought.

—and obviously enjoying her scrutiny. Her imagination was untethered, senses seeing and feeling and tasting things she only ever did with Dom.

If she'd covered herself up, things might have been different.

Andy took a step towards her, and without thinking Emma followed suit, so close now that she could smell him, feel the heat radiating from his scrubbed red skin.

He held her hip and pulled her closer. She felt him prod against her stomach and she reached down, brushing her hand against him. Andy drew in a sharp breath, and she was delighted at the effect she had on him.

He leaned close, inhaling her scent, his lips only touching her skin when he started biting, so gently, beneath her left ear.

Emma's knees weakened, her eyes closed, and she leaned against him. It was as if he knew her so well, and this moment was simply a confirmation of everything that had already happened in both of their imaginations.

He chuckled softly.

He knew *exactly* what she liked.

Emma's eyes snapped open and she stepped back, pushing against his chest so that he didn't follow. *Dom must have told him I like being bitten there.* She knew that when men got together they talked about sex, but the idea of Dom talking to his friend about their love life enraged her. Andy's smile only made it worse.

'Emma,' he said, taking another step closer.

She was furious at Dom, but then Emma realised where she was, what she had done. Her anger flailed, then dissipated as quickly as it had arisen. She wanted to shout, cry, come.

Instead, she covered herself and turned around. 'Whoops,' she said. She grabbed the clothes she'd shed and left the bedroom, closing the door behind her, never once looking back at Andy. She hurried past the bathroom, hearing Dom humming to himself, the splash of bathwater. She still needed to wash. But she couldn't face him right then.

I need to speak to Andy, make it right, she thought. Guilt simmered hot and horrid. But she could not face him again, not alone. She could not bear to see his smile, knowing that he knew the effect he'd had upon her.

She washed in the kitchen and wore sooty clothes for the rest of the afternoon.

Neither of them ever mentioned that moment. To be fair to Andy, he never even offered her a knowing smile or a loaded comment. He could have made things so much more awkward between them, and over time she'd dulled the memory into a simple case of a foolish, private error. A one-time slip, that was really nothing more than a brief contact.

Only occasionally did her imagination untether itself again to consider what might have been.

She had been guarded ever since. Knowing that a man like him would fuck his friend's wife while his friend was in the next room . . . that made him no friend at all.

'I guess I don't like Andy either,' she said.

'So what do we do?' Daisy asked. 'If we can't call the police about these people, what do we do?'

'We get to Mandy's,' Emma said. 'Then I'm going to find out exactly what's going on.'

Chapter Thirteen

Bluebells

'I know the gang,' Andy said. 'I used to be a member.'

They'd been driving in silence for several minutes, and he'd chosen this moment – while Dom was paused at a junction, negotiating busy traffic – to drop this bombshell.

Dom was stunned silent. Someone flashed and waved him on, but he sat staring through the windscreen, unable to react.

'Dom, they're letting you go.'

'You? In a gang?' He still couldn't look at his friend beside him. The car flashed again, tooted, and Dom pulled out, raising a hand in thanks without even thinking about it.

'I know it's probably a lot to take in.'

'No,' Dom said. 'Not a surprise at all.' He said it sarcastically, but he felt the revelation instantly drive a thick wedge between them. The suspicion that he'd had all through their friendship that he didn't truly know Andy became concrete, hitting hard as if falling from a height. His friend had turned into a stranger in the space of a minute. 'Fucking prick.'

'Sorry, mate.'

'So tell me.' Dom waved his hand beyond the car, as if

everyone and everything out there was out to get them. 'Explain all this.'

'I left them years ago. Long story. Then I heard whispers about their upcoming hit on the post office. I have . . . scores to settle with them, and I thought stealing the cash without them knowing who'd done it seemed a good way of doing that. But the information I received wasn't precise; I should have known that, should have seen it. I thought they were doing it next week.'

Dom blinked quickly as if to clear dust from his eyes. He was driving on autopilot, functioning in the same way, seeing only Emma's and Daisy's hurt, frightened expressions.

'All your fault,' he muttered.

'Mate, I made a mistake and—'

Dom had held up one hand, and Andy fell silent. His immediate reaction was to stop the car and smash Andy in the face. But he was not a man of violence, and had not punched anyone since he was thirteen years old.

Instead, he continued driving.

'So where are we going?' Andy asked.

'To get the money. To give it back to them.'

Andy didn't argue. They left the village in simmering silence, Dom absorbing what he had been told and trying to make these new facts fit in with current events and knowledge. It left more holes and mysteries than solutions. But it also joined dots that he had previously been unable to connect. Dots about Andy, the history he never talked about, and how such a garrulous type had so few friends.

He'd make him pay. When all this was over, he'd never let him forget.

'Fucking prick!'

'Yeah. So you said.'

It was almost six in the evening, still unbearably hot, roads busy with people driving home from work to their normal homes and contented families. Dom felt jealous of every one of them.

As he turned off the main road and headed up the winding lane towards the pillbox, he glanced in his mirror at the cars passing behind him. Mothers and fathers, sometimes with kids in the back, they all had concerns he didn't know about. Perhaps some of them were deep worries – *What is that lump in my left breast? Is she really sleeping with Steve? I wonder how long Dad has left?* But he doubted any of them equated to his. The sense of dread combined with an intense feeling of unfairness, even though he'd believed that he'd entered into this of his own free will.

But he really hadn't.

'You steered it all from the start,' he said. 'Took us out that way on the bikes, parked across the square from the post office. Planted the seed.'

'Yes,' Andy said. 'First time we did that route four months ago, I'd just heard that they'd scoped the place. There was a good chance nothing would come of it, I knew that. But there was a small chance something would.'

'And it was that long ago you thought about you and me robbing it before them?'

'No, I didn't know *what* I might do. Just leave them alone, maybe. Or perhaps leave an anonymous tip with the police, get them caught.'

'So why didn't you do that?'

'I know them too well. I was afraid if they were cornered, people might get hurt.'

Dom coughed a laugh, hard and false. 'Oh, and we wouldn't want that, would we?'

'That was my fault,' Andy said. 'I got the wrong week. If I'd been more thorough, we'd have hit it seven days before them, and they'd have lost their chance.'

'Instead of five minutes before them.'

Andy nodded.

They drove up the hillside, passing beneath the shade of overhanging trees. The road surface became pocked and uneven, and Dom slowed as they approached the pillbox. He glanced in his mirrors frequently, just to make sure no other vehicle was behind them. They seemed to be alone.

Parking just off the road, he turned off the engine and slammed the door as he got out. Hard.

'You stay with the car,' Andy said. 'I'll get the bag.'

'Yeah, right. Good plan, fuck-face!' Dom leaned against his side of the car, back turned to Andy. He glanced up and down the road. If anyone came he'd hold his phone to his ear, pretend he'd stopped to make a phone call. Maybe he'd even try to smile.

He heard Andy open the boot and root around for the shovel they'd used the day before. He looked across the road into the woods that continued up the hillside and over the brow, networked with rarely trodden paths and alive with memories. He and Emma had walked in there during their first year living in the town, sitting on a fallen tree with shoulder and legs touching, talking about their future. They were already engaged then, and later that month it emerged that Daisy was already a part of them. Dom frequently thought back to that long afternoon. It had become one of those perfect moments in life that are barely recognised when they're actually happening, but which later take on an almost mystical sheen.

The woodland seemed like a strange place now. It felt unwelcoming, as if it knew him and had excluded him.

116

'Were you like them?' Dom asked. He didn't turn around, because he didn't want to look at Andy. But he did want answers.

'For a while,' Andy said. 'But never . . . no one ever died. Not until the end of my time with them. That's why I left.'

'What do you mean?'

'I could see the way things were going. Someone new joined, and he was bad news. Steering things closer towards violence. That was never what we were about, not in the beginning, and it certainly wasn't me. I didn't want any part of that, so I left.'

'As simple as that?'

'Not simple at all. I quit with seventy grand in the bank, when it should have been half a million. I was given a choice – go with that, or stay and make more. They screwed me out of—'

'Good,' Dom said. He turned and looked across the car roof at Andy. Heat haze shimmered from the metal, making his friend's face fluid. 'I'm glad they screwed you out of your dirty criminal money. How many people's lives did you ruin? How many did you terrify?'

Andy's face hardened for a moment, then he looked down at his feet, shaking his head.

'They've killed an old lady and a young girl,' Dom said. '*We* caused that.' He felt a heavy pressure behind his face, and a deep, cold dread in his heart. However hard he tried, he was unable to deny the conviction that their actions had resulted in those murders. It was sickening.

'You don't need to remind me.'

'They've killed my dog. Threatened my wife and daughter.'

'I know.'

'Can you contact them?'

'Haven't tried in years.'

117

'But you knew they were planning on doing that post office.'

'I learned how to keep track of them online, follow their web access, track some of their texting. It was more to protect myself than anything else. To hide, and make sure they hadn't found me. But I won't need to contact them. They obviously saw us. Maybe you weren't thorough enough muddying up your number plates, they'd get everything from that – your name, where you live, phone numbers. They'll be in touch soon enough, then I'll give the cash back to them. After that they'll piss off, and so will I.'

He looked at Dom as if expecting some comment, perhaps even a plea to stay. But Dom only nodded.

Andy climbed the gate and waded through ferns, approaching the pill box at the edge of the field. He pushed through the brambles, unconcerned when they snagged his clothing and skin. Soon he was inside and out of sight, and Dom was glad.

He closed his eyes and breathed in the hot evening air. He felt like such a fool. Andy had used him, probably from the moment they'd met, and he'd seen nothing but a confident, slightly lonely man seeking only friendship.

His eyes snapped open. 'Were we ever friends?' he called out.

'Dom,' Andy said, voice muffled from inside the old, smothered building. 'Of course. You're the best part of my new life, mate. I never meant for you to meet my old life.'

'Which is why you lied about it all this time.'

'I didn't lie. I just didn't tell you.'

Dom did not reply. Andy was right. He'd kept himself something of an enigma, though one with a friendly face and who was always good company.

He heard the sound of Andy scraping at the soil inside

the pillbox. He almost asked more about the money, but he didn't really want to know. All the pints Andy had bought him, the bottles of wine when he joined him and Emma for dinner, the meals, the coffee shop breaks when they were out biking, he just did not want to think about how they were bought with stolen cash.

'For fuck's sake,' Dom said quietly. A bird in the nearby hedge seemed to take offence, chirping and flying away. He couldn't kid himself. Now that he knew some of the truth, he needed more. He might have been steered and coerced, but he had still put that Hulk mask on of his own volition.

'Maybe I'm as bad as you,' he said, not intending Andy to hear. Andy was just pushing his way from the pillbox, face scratched, hands muddied, shoving the money bag before him.

'You're a good bloke. You don't deserve any of this.'

'Don't try to sound like you're sorry.'

'I am.'

'Bullshit!'

Dom's phone rang. He jumped. Andy's eyes went wide.

Dom glanced at the screen and saw Emma's picture, and for a terrible, unreal, panic-filled moment he imagined that they had her, tied up and sweating and terrified, and that they were calling to demand the money as a ransom. It was ridiculous, but then so was this turn his life had taken.

He answered. 'Em?'

'Dom, where are you?'

He sighed in relief, and Andy's shoulders seemed to slump as well. He was as frightened for Emma and Daisy as Dom was.

'I'm with Andy, we're going to—'

'That bastard,' Emma said.

'Em, are you and Daisy okay?'

'Yes, just dandy. Why shouldn't we be? We've rocked up at Mandy's unannounced, she's gone out with that arsehole boyfriend of hers, we can't go home in case South Wales's worst crime gang come looking, and then I get a call from a mad old bitch threatening us. So yes, we're fine. What haven't you told me, Dom? What's going on?'

'What mad old bitch?' Dom asked. Andy froze where he was climbing over the field gate, like a rabbit in headlights. *He knows*, Dom thought. *Maybe I'll just ask him.*

'I had an unlisted call on my mobile. When I answered, a woman asked if I was Emma. I thought it was someone trying to sell something to begin with. She sounded like anyone's grandmother, sweet and polite. Then she asked for what she was owed. Just like that. "I want what I'm owed." I waited for a bit, then . . . I couldn't just say nothing. I told her it was only a bump, it was an accident, and that we'd pay for the damage willingly.'

Andy was still astride the gate, staring at Dom expectantly. Dom put the phone on loudspeaker and touched his finger to his lips.

'What did she say to that?' he asked his wife. He wished he could reach through the phone to touch her, comfort her, but he doubted she'd welcome that.

'She laughed,' Emma said. 'Then she said, "Tell your stupid husband and his friend, if we don't get what we're owed, we'll let Lip do his stuff".'

Andy hadn't changed position on the gate. It was as if he was waiting for something else.

'I felt like I was a kid being talked to. I didn't know

anything and she knew everything, and I couldn't even reply. There was nothing for me to say.'

'She say anything else?' Dom asked.

'She left me a number. Read it out twice, slowly, so I had time to write it down.' She read it out. Sitting astride the gate, Andy tapped it into his phone. 'After that she just hung up. What haven't you told me, Dom? What are you and Andy doing? And if you mention a bumped Ferrari, I'll . . . I'll fucking divorce you. Don't treat me like an idiot.'

'I know you're not that, babe,' he said, and he felt so wretched. He switched the loudspeaker off and pressed the phone back to his ear, turning his back on Andy, the car, the pill box and the bag of money. He looked across at the woodland rising up the slope before him and wished he could be there with Emma again, the two of them alone in love and planning a safe, happy future.

'Is it the post office in Upper Mill?' she asked.

He wasn't surprised. His wife was far from stupid. But he was not ready for such an admission, and everything that would come with it. He didn't have the time, but neither did he have the emotional resilience to enter into that conversation just now. Later, perhaps. When he knew that it was over and they were all safe.

'It's nothing that bad,' he said, not really a denial. 'It'll all be over this evening, and we'll be back to Mandy's in a couple of hours.'

'Not "we". I don't want Andy here. That woman knows him, I could tell.'

He listened to her breathing, faster and heavier than usual, loaded with fear. He felt intensely ashamed. But somewhere beneath the shame and fear there was a spark of excitement, and a sense that at least he had tried. The gang had made their demands, and soon they would be met. After that he could return to his family a changed man. It was how he handled that change that would define his future self.

'Right,' he said. 'Just me. And a Chinese.'

'You'd better not do anything to hurt my family,' she said, voice flat and without intonation. The sense that she was excluding him from the comment was threat enough.

'We're going to be fine,' Dom said. 'I'd do anything to protect you and Daisy.'

'Including going to jail?'

'It won't come to that. Listen, I've made a stupid mistake, but I'm going to put things right. Just hang in there a while longer and I'll be there. I love you, Em.' He looked into the woods and imagined those same words mingling in there from years before, bouncing from tree to tree and never likely to completely fade away.

'You too. Be careful.' She hung up.

Dom turned back to Andy, who was at the car's open boot.

'That was Sonja Scott,' Andy said, dropping the shovel inside and slamming the boot. He kept the bag over his shoulder. 'Gang's leader. Evil old bitch.'

'How old?'

'She must be . . . seventy-four now.'

'A seventy-four year old woman leads a gang of bank robbers?'

'They don't all play bowls and go to afternoon tea, you know,' Andy said, smiling.

Dom didn't smile back.

'Look, Dom, it wasn't always bank robbery, I left when—'

'Who's Lip?'

'Philip Beck. He's the reason I left. Nasty piece of work.'

'The one who's been following my wife?'

Andy nodded.

'You think you can handle all this, don't you?' Dom asked. 'There's nothing at stake here for you. You can't understand the threat, the danger my family is in.'

'I understand,' Andy said quietly. 'Now let me call the old bitch and we can put an end to it.' Andy dialled.

Dom moved closer to listen. He heard the phone picked up after two rings and Andy said, 'It's me.'

The old woman's voice was distorted, but the evening air was still, hot and heavy, no breath of sound from elsewhere. Dom heard her reply just fine.

'Hello, son,' she said.

Chapter Fourteen

Little Things

By eight o'clock that evening, Rose knew that she was leaving France and returning to the UK. It was the little things that had finally made up her mind. Small mistakes on Holt's part, combining to make her worry and be concerned about his well-being. But mainly it was because of her sense of duty.

She didn't have much, but she owed Holt everything. She quickly brushed aside the thought that he'd deliberately left without her, because it didn't matter. They were as close to each other as either of them had been to anyone in years, but their relationship was complex, deep, and probably as dysfunctional as they came. She didn't even know his given name, only his surname. He'd told her that the last person to call him by his first name had been his wife.

It could have been that he had left her behind for her own safety. Or perhaps it was because this was such a personal journey to him – it had taken him far back, shedding everything he had done in the past decade, the people that he'd met.

After all, Holt had been waiting for almost ten years to kill the man who'd murdered his sister in such a brutal manner.

Either way, three things made up Rose's mind to follow.

First, he'd left his laptop behind unlocked and with search histories not wiped, both of which should have been as habitual as breathing. The history showed the browsing he'd done over the past twenty-four hours, including news sites, local town websites, and transport routes and ticketing information. Everything was connected to the murders at the South Wales post office. That he had forgotten to delete the search meant that his mind was clouded and elsewhere, not in the now. He'd told her so many times that living in the moment was the best way of ensuring you made it to the next one. Holt had let his mind drift, and that had already sown seeds of danger on his journey.

The second mistake was the identity he'd used to book a ferry crossing for his car. It was the same name and passport information he'd used fourteen months before, when the two of them had travelled to Spain to help a farmer and his family being threatened by a local gang. She was surprised that he hadn't discarded and destroyed the identity, and even more surprised that he'd dared use it again. They each had at least two unused names and sets of documents for emergency travel.

But the third fact that convinced her to follow was what he'd taken with him. She knew several places around the caravan and its field where he hid weapons, and there were probably as many again that she didn't know. Every place she knew was empty. He'd also taken what he called his box of tricks. Old mobile phones, GPS units, circuit boards, microphones, listening devices and trackers; Holt often spent

125

time experimenting and refining gadgetry that could help him track, follow and kill a target.

The caravan felt empty of him and his things, and she wondered whether he'd ever planned on returning. But she doubted he was even thinking that far ahead.

Rose quickly erased Holt's history on the computer, going in deep to make sure there was nothing left to find. She performed a sweep of the caravan, ensuring there were no other signs that might point the way. No notepads, scribbled scraps of paper, maps, anything else that might put someone on their track. Taking one last look around, she wondered whether she'd see this place again. There was no nostalgia or sadness to her thoughts. Just a knowledge that their brief time at rest was probably over, and that their lives were shifting once again.

It didn't matter. It would have happened sooner or later, and part of her felt a quickening at the prospect. She didn't like feeling too comfortable, calm, or even experiencing a shred of being at peace. It felt like a betrayal of her murdered family.

She cycled home quickly, pushing herself hard and feeling the burn. By the time she arrived back at the gîte she was streaming with sweat, throat burning and lungs heaving. It felt good. It felt like being alive.

She hurried inside, stripped her kit and stepped into the shower. After drying and dressing she made her travel arrangements, reading her name from the new passport just to make sure she was letter-perfect. Then she started packing a bag.

There wasn't much to take. All the clothes she owned, washing and personal hygiene stuff, a couple of books left behind by tourists in the local cafe, training kit, they all fit into the same big holdall. Her whole life in one bag, and when she zipped it closed she was hidden away from the world once more.

Rose liked it that way. It was easy to move, and easier still to leave everything else behind.

She scoured the gîte for half an hour, making sure she'd left no sign of ever having been there. Gathering all the weapons in the kitchen, she felt a pang of regret at having to lose most of them. She kept only the Glock, five spare magazines, the combat knife and the grenade. Wrapping them in oil cloth, she hid the package in her car, tucked into a space beside the catalytic converter.

The last time she'd left for a couple of days she had hidden the weapons in the septic tank. But now she felt certain that she would not be returning. It took fifteen minutes to walk down to the lake, where she opened the rucksack and threw the remaining hardware as far out as she could. The ripples of each heavy splash merged and then quickly faded away.

Ready to leave at last, Rose made a strong coffee and sat out on the lawn. The countryside around her was mostly quiet, only the sound of distant farm equipment serenading the silence.

Molly runs onto the lawn from another woodland far away and a long time ago, waving a handful of dandelions and trailing seeds behind her like mid-summer snows.

Rose drank her coffee. The sun beat down on the back of her neck. A bird of prey circled on thermals high above.

Chapter Fifteen

Windy Miller

Andy had never frightened him. He had a confidence which Dom sometimes lacked, a self-assured swagger that stopped short of arrogance, a natural grace, and fitness easily maintained. He seemed to be once of life's champions, while Dom worked hard for everything he had, and struggled to maintain it.

But now for the first time, Andy actually scared him.

Dom had a stranger in his car. Andy's voice was still the same, but his presence and bearing had changed. Maybe it was only in Dom's perception, knowing what he knew.

The gang was Andy's *family*! Family, with a capital "F". Dom shouldn't have been surprised, really. And he supposed it didn't really make much difference.

'So your mother's a murderous crime lord and bank robber,' Dom said. 'Who else should I know about? Uncle Corleone in Sicily? Grandfather Capone?'

'I guess you *should* know, if we're going to meet them,' Andy said.

'Yeah, why don't you fill me in on who's likely to stab me or bury me in a motorway parapet.'

'They're not like . . .' Andy started to protest, but he trailed off, glancing across at Dom. 'They weren't, anyway. Until he came.'

'Lip. So who's he, long lost brother?'

'No. He's seeing my half-sister, Mary. Sonja had her after Dad died. Heart attack while he was fishing. He was a good guy. I was nine. Mum went off the rails a bit after that, booze and drugs and a string of boyfriends, then she got pregnant. Mary and I never really hit it off. She didn't know her father. Me neither; he ran off before she was even born. She's ten years younger than me and she's always had a violent streak. When Lip appeared on the scene she changed, became even more brutal. He influenced everyone but me. He's weird. I wouldn't call him charismatic, but . . . powerful.'

'Who else?'

'Frank, a cousin from my dad's side who was always close to Sonja. We were like friends, really. He's a big guy, steroid junkie, body building, all that. A rough sort, but he's bright with it.'

'That's it?'

'Sonja, Frank, Mary. And Lip.'

'And you,' Dom said.

'I told you, not any more.'

'But old habits die hard.'

They'd be there in five minutes. Sonja had told Andy to meet them out at the old windmill. It was known locally as Windy Miller's, although Dom was sure Andy's estranged family wouldn't know the name. That simple fact made him feel a little more confident. This was his place, his town, and he knew it like the back of his hand. They were the invaders, outsiders come here to steal and ending up committing murder. Soon they would be gone.

When that happened there was so much more he'd have to go through. Secrets he'd have to keep, live with, sleep with if he could. A deep injustice in the murderers of an old woman and a teenage girl still walking free, while he knew who they were. Also the chasm that he'd already felt opening between him and Emma and Daisy. That gap could be bridged, he was confident, but it would always be there, a dangerous drop into dark knowledge and violent history that might doom him at any moment. He'd always have to walk that bridge carefully.

The ragged sails of Windy Miller's appeared in the distance.

'Let me do the talking,' Andy said. 'I'm the one they'll be interested in.'

'This is a bad idea,' Dom said. He eased back on the gas and the car slowed. Cruising it to a halt in a field gateway, the top of the windmill was just visible half a mile away. 'Four of them, and they have guns. What's to stop them just shooting us and running? That place is abandoned and deserted. We'll lie there dead for weeks.' His stomach felt low and heavy, filled with dread. His limbs were lead. His hands on the steering wheel felt like someone else's.

'They won't all be here,' Andy said.

'How do you know?'

'Well . . .' Andy frowned uncomfortably. 'One of them, maybe Lip, will be looking for Emma and Daisy.'

'But they're safe!'

'They are, don't worry. He won't find them at Mandy's. And Sonja will likely be holed up somewhere, guiding things. Probably not that close.'

'I should warn Emma,' Dom said, but he had no idea what to say.

130

'And say what? Dom, she'll be safe. They don't know everything. They got your address, names and Em's phone number from your car registration, but they don't have a clue about your friends, or where Mandy lives. Come on. No point in being late, that'll only antagonise them more.'

Dom drove to the narrow turning leading towards the windmill. There had been talk for years about developing the old mill and associated land into business units, and one time a famous footballer was rumoured to have bought it intending to turn it into a luxury home. He sold it on again, and year by year it had become more dilapidated. Dom had cycled out there with Daisy the year before, parking their bikes against the fence surrounding the mill and going exploring. They'd looked for a way in but the lower doorways and windows were closed up with steel sheeting, the two upper balconies out of reach. The sails were skeletal and locked, never moving even in the highest winds.

There was talk of ghosts, of course. Dom quite liked that. It gave the sad old building a new character after losing its old purpose.

They bounced along the dry, rutted track, raising a cloud of dust behind them. As they approached the windmill it looked as still and silent as ever, and just as lifeless. It was the corpse of something once alive, a rotten thing whose life had been shed, leaving behind a hollow shell.

'No cars,' Dom said.

'They'll have parked out of sight.'

Dom looked in the rear-view mirror and saw almost nothing because of the dust. They were hardly keeping their presence a secret.

'This is going to be fine, isn't it?' he asked.

'Of course. No problem.'

131

Dom wanted to speak with Emma, hug Daisy. He didn't want to be here. But this was facing up to what he and Andy had done. Not quite making things right, but putting things behind them.

He parked and turned off the engine. With their windows down the sudden, complete silence was disconcerting. Dom could not even hear birdsong. Perhaps the sound of the engine had startled them silent, or maybe it was the potential violence in the air.

'Remember, I do the talking,' Andy said. 'You okay, mate?'

'Fucking dandy.' Dom opened the door and jumped out. After the air-conditioned car, the evening heat took his breath away. Dust drifted slowly across the unsurfaced area around the mill's base. A pair of buzzards circled high up.

Attached to one side of the circular mill was a small single-storey building. Just past that, Dom could see the nose of a blue car.

The metal sheeting over the entrance door in the mill's wall had been prised aside. The triangular gap was dark.

'You've lost weight,' a woman's voice said. Dom shielded his eyes and looked up. The windmill had two external balconies, the first ten feet above the ground, the second fifteen feet higher. The woman stood on the highest balcony.

'You haven't,' Andy said.

'Thanks,' Mary, his half-sister said. 'You don't write, you don't call, and the first thing you do after not seeing me for three years is call me fat.'

She didn't look fat to Dom. Tall, slim, dark-skinned, her long hair was tied in two plaits, which hung over each shoulder as she leaned on the balustrade. She looked striking, wearing khaki shorts and a white vest. The sun was low now, sinking to their right, interrupting his vision. But he thought that Mary was smiling.

'How's that charming boyfriend of yours?' Andy asked.

'Still my boyfriend.'

'Wow. I thought you'd have tied the knot by now, nice guy like that.'

'Just because you want to be best man.'

'Nah, not when you've got Frank. Hey, Frank, you still got bigger tits than Mary?'

Dom glanced at Andy. What the hell was he doing? They'd come here to hand over the bag and settle things, not antagonise. But he was starting to realise very quickly that the complexities of family must stand in the way of this being anything approaching easy.

No one answered. If Frank was here, he was keeping quiet and out of sight.

'Aren't you going to ask after your mother?' Mary asked.

'No.'

She seemed to shrug. Or maybe she just stood up straight. Dom couldn't quite tell, the sun was hurting his eyes.

'Come on up,' Mary said. 'Both of you. Bring the bag.' Then she disappeared inside the windmill.

Dom took a step closer to Andy. 'So where's Frank?'

'Keeping an eye on us, I expect,' Andy said. 'Come on.'

'You're just going in there?'

'No choice,' Andy said. 'They've got the upper hand here.'

'Let me call Emma, see if—'

'We just need to get this finished with,' Andy said. 'Trust me.'

Dom raised his eyebrows, but Andy was already walking towards the windmill. He could only follow.

They squeezed through the gap between steel door and wall.

Inside it smelled of age. Damp and musty, but also a tinge of neglect, as if the building, untouched and unloved, was slowly going to rot. The air was as heavy and warm as outside, laden with disturbed dust and narrow spears of low sunlight filtered through openings in the walls. Lower windows were roughly covered with timber boarding, some of those further up left open and bearing the dust and bird shit of decades. It was surprisingly bright, mainly because much of the internal structure had been stripped away. There were thick, heavy beams spanning the space above them, but floor boarding and ceilings were largely missing.

Sunlight touched upon loose piles of timber, bags of cement gone solid over time, and the workings of the old mill still in place. Big cogs, wheels and axles were rusted a dark, common colour. The massive grinding stones on the ground floor were honeycombed with bolt holes, edges worn down from past decades of constant use.

Daisy would love this, Dom thought.

'Come on,' he said. He shoved past Andy and headed up the timber staircase. The first flight followed the wall a half-circle before reaching the first floor level. A doorway led to the balcony outside. It was closed, bolted and padlocked. He stepped across exposed joists and started up the second, longer flight of stairs. The tower was narrowing, the stairs becoming steeper and not quite as wide.

Dom glanced around as he climbed, keeping tight to the wall. Andy followed close behind. The stairs had a timber balustrade, but it looked weak and old, and the drop back down to the first floor almost seemed to lure him close. He wasn't afraid of heights, but he had a healthy respect for them.

He passed two windows as he climbed, squinting in the sunlight. The glass was dusty, but looked to have been recently wiped in several places. *Might be fingerprints there,* he thought. *And on the metal doors downstairs, the bolts.* He was already thinking ahead, even though the present was still uncertain and promising danger.

An anonymous call, a few names, a place where the killers had hidden . . . Maybe there *was* a way to bring justice, without the law also falling onto his shoulders.

Dom reached the second floor level, Andy right behind him. The tower had narrowed considerably, the space only about twelve feet across. The flooring was more complete up here, and scattered with the pale grey bodies of dead pigeons. Bird shit speckled the dusty timber like old acne. The smell was worse, as if the stench of neglect rose with time.

The door to the higher balcony was open.

'Nice views out here,' Mary said. 'Come on out.'

Dom and Andy exchanged a look between them. Andy looked calm and confident, and he nodded, mouthing, *It's all fine.*

Dom believed him. Just for a few seconds, he actually believed what the man who'd been his friend said. Then they stepped outside onto the balcony, Andy holding Dom back so that he could go first.

As Andy went, he pulled something from his pocket.

Mary stood to the right, one hand on the railing, the other resting on her hip, ankles crossed. She nodded Andy a greeting.

Her eyes switched to Dom, and then over his shoulder and along the balcony past the doorway.

The sun was behind him, and Dom saw the shadow cast past his feet. A huge shadow that moved, flowed, as it pointed something their way.

'Andy!' he shouted. An instinct fed by tension and fear took hold. Without turning, he folded his knees and fell back through the doorway.

A loud blast followed him. Someone screamed. Dom realised it was him.

Chapter Sixteen

Splinters

Emma's friend kept such a clean house that Emma was almost afraid to sit.

Childless, Mandy's place could almost have been a show-home for the new estate she lived on. Cream carpets, a cream leather suite, shelving without a speck of dust, and a kitchen that gleamed like new, Emma often took the piss out of her.

Mandy would shrug and smile, content in her own existence. Most of the time Emma wondered if Mandy really wanted kids and a husband as she professed. But just occasionally, she felt a pang of irrational jealousy.

Now she was pacing the house, carrying her fourth cup of coffee and checking that doors were locked, wooden blinds half-closed, and that her phone had a signal anywhere inside.

In contrast to how she lived, Mandy was absent-minded and just a bit mad. As Emma and Daisy had arrived she'd been dashing around the house readying to leave. She was late for a date with her boyfriend, and she hated being late, though somehow her frantic dashing seemed to leave no messy wake. She'd thought nothing of Emma asking if she and Daisy could spend a couple of hours there. Her expression had said, *Argument with Dom?*, and Emma had done nothing to disabuse her of the notion.

'How long do we have to stay here?' Daisy asked again.

'Until Dad gets here. He's bringing a Chinese.'

Daisy was sprawled on the sofa, phone glued to her hand. Dom and Emma had debated their daughter having a smartphone at almost eleven years old, but the 'all my friends have got one' argument had trumped any concerns either of them had. She had a good set of friends and they were constantly in touch, Snapchatting or tweeting or whatever the hell-ing else kids did nowadays.

'So what do you think he's really done, Mum?'

Emma paused in her slow pacing, leaning against the living room door frame. Daisy had connected her phone to the sound system and Mumford & Sons pounded and strummed, volume low.

'Something stupid,' Emma said.

'We'll look after each other. I know karate.'

'You do,' Emma said, smiling. Her daughter was a purple belt, and she'd seen her put a teenaged girl heavier and harder than her onto the floor in five seconds flat. Daisy was a sweet kid, but she could pack a punch.

'I miss Jazz,' she said. Tears fell.

Emma went to her and sat beside her, reaching out and grasping her hand.

'We all do, sweetie.'

'I still think . . .' Daisy said, holding up her phone.

'No!' Emma said. 'I told you, don't tell even your friends where we are, honey. Just for now we'll be here on our own. Only Dom and us know where we are, not the rest of the world.'

'Like a secret?'

'A secret.'

'Johnny English secret?'

'But not so much face-pulling.'

Emma kept thinking of the police. She lived a normal, mostly conventional life, and such a reaction to current events was automatic. But the assurances given her by Dom and, through him, Andy, echoed in her mind. That, and the threats from the old woman.

She'd found Emma's number. The freak in the Jeep knew where they lived. It was terrifying, and one thing Emma and Dom shared was their fear of bad people. Unreasonableness. Violence. It was what made them such a good team looking after Daisy and themselves, any other differences aside. Now that she knew Andy was embroiled deeper in this than she really understood, her love for Dom, and her concern for him, had grown.

Not just yet, she thought. *But the minute something else goes wrong, that'll be the time to call them.*

With Daisy slumped on the sofa, Emma padded across the hallway to the dining room. It opened onto the kitchen at the back of the house, but the front windows looked out over the main road running east out of Usk.

She sipped her coffee and watched the world go by. It was gone eight o'clock, and though growing dim inside, she didn't want to turn on any lights. The timber blinds would keep her shielded from view.

Emma blinked and experienced a sudden memory of Andy standing naked in their en suite. The rush of emotion she now felt was hatred, not lust. He was a bastard. 'What the fuck have you got my husband into?' she muttered.

A white Jeep passed slowly along the main road.

Emma held her breath. Squinted. She almost parted the blinds to get a better view, then held back. It was moving on. White, dirtied, tinted windows, it looked so familiar. As it moved away she sighed heavily, not even realising that she'd been holding her breath.

Its brake lights flashed red.

Several cars slowed, overtook, then the Jeep reversed back along the road until it was directly opposite the entrance to Mandy's short driveway.

I parked the car in the driveway, she thought. *Bloody idiot!*

'Mum?'

'Stay back and keep still.'

'Is that him?' Daisy appeared beside her, staring through the blinds. She raised her phone and touched the screen, then started snapping pictures.

'Just keep still!' Emma said.

The Jeep's driver's window powered down. He stared at the house. A van passed between them, then a heavier lorry from the other direction. The man's focus and expression did not change.

'I don't like him,' Daisy said. 'He's spooky.'

He's worse than that, Emma thought.

Daisy took more pictures. 'If he killed Jazz, I want the police to be able to catch him.'

The vehicle reversed a little, mounting the kerb slightly and coming to a halt. The window remained lowered, and the man sat back in his seat as if getting himself comfortable.

Emma backed away from the window but didn't take her eyes off the Jeep.

140

Daisy took one last snap. 'Got him,' she said. 'Wanted, for crimes against hairstyles.' She was joking, but Emma could hear the fear underlying her daughter's quips.

She picked up her own phone and dialled Dom.

Dom fell back through the open door into the windmill, splinters peppering his exposed left arm and neck. Landing on his hands he kicked forward, diving for the head of the staircase, knowing he should stand but fearing that to pause would doom him. He rolled instead, tipping over the first stair and clasping his arms around his head, turning onto his back and drawing his knees in to his stomach, catching one quick glimpse behind him before he bounced from one timber tread to the next.

The doorway was empty, but shadows flitted back and forth across it.

Dom was winded. He tried to stretch out his legs to arrest his fall, but one foot snagged between balusters, twisted, then flipped free with a soft wooden snap. He hoped the snap was the bannister, not his ankle.

He rolled twice more then struck a joist, feeling himself starting to drop through the floor. He panicked, stretching out his arms and legs. One arm curled over a joist and his legs, held straight, bridged him over the gap. He looked down. Dust drifted below him, and a shard of broken timber bounced from the floor below. His phone slipped from his pocket and fell, case cracking, battery bouncing free.

Another gunshot blasted from above.

Dom rolled onto his back and stood shakily, stepping sideways and tight against the wall, feet planted firmly on joists.

Someone shouted. A male voice, a roar. The roar turned into a shout, startled and high. A pause, during which the silence seemed to stretch forever. Disturbed dust danced in the air. Pain sang in from his leg, his arm, his neck and scalp.

From outside and below Dom heard a heavy, sickening impact. A wet crack. He knew immediately that someone had fallen from above, and that he was now in the vicinity of death.

A shape appeared in the doorway above and swung around. It was Mary, running so quickly down the stairs that she almost stumbled the whole way, left hand hugging the post office bag to her hip, right hand clasped around the handle of a knife. Both hand and blade were red with blood.

Dom pressed himself back against the wall, breath held. He froze. He could have run, he could have kicked out to keep her away from him. He might even have been able to scream for help. But for the seconds it took for Mary to pass him by with hardly a glance, he was like a butterfly pinned to the wall, waiting to die.

He watched her descend to the ground floor and then slip outside. Her scream was short and wretched, filled with grief.

From above came another blast, and he heard Mary grunt. Then fast, light footsteps.

'Dom, stop her!'

Oh, God, oh, God, it wasn't Andy, was all Dom could think.

Andy pounded down the stairs. He was holding a short-barrelled shotgun in his right hand. 'You okay?' Dom nodded. Andy ran on, leaping down the stairs to the ground floor then out through the boarded up doorway.

Dom followed on shaky legs. Emerging into evening sunlight, his life changed.

He'd only ever seen two dead bodies. His mother dead

in a hospital bed, then his father at the undertaker's seven years before. Neither of them had looked anything like this. The one he saw now, its state, its mess, was testament to the fragility of the human form.

Frank was twisted on the gravel, a big shape made small by death. His head was misshapen and leaking blood and a thicker, darker fluid into the gravel. His limbs were askew, one leg turned beneath his body, one arm almost vertical from elbow to hand and pointing an accusing finger to the sky.

Dom felt sick.

'We've got to stop her!' Andy said. 'Where is she? Which way did she go?'

'You killed him,' Dom said.

'I think I winged her, but from a distance. This thing . . .' He hefted the shotgun. It was shorter than others Dom had seen, pump-action.

Dom looked from Andy to the body, back again. 'You killed him.'

'He was trying to kill *us*! Come on, help me, if we don't find her quickly—'

'We're killing people.'

'She'll skirt around the building and run directly away from the other side. We'll run faster.' Andy darted across the forecourt, shielding his eyes and peering across the fields.

'But it's over,' Dom said. Confusion fogged his brain. He stared down at the splinters stuck in his arm, planted in bubbles of blood. Sweat stuck his T-shirt to his back.

'Not when she opens the bag,' Andy said. And he actually laughed.

'What?'

'I left the money buried. She's got a load of those rotting clothes from the pillbox.'

Dom tried to work out what this meant, how Andy had assumed this meeting would work, even if his cousin Frank *hadn't* started shooting. His brain was sluggish with pain and the sight of a dead man.

'That was your knife she was carrying.'

'No, that was hers. This is what I was going to use.' He pulled a small handgun from his pocket.

'What the fuck were you going to do with that?'

'What the fuck do you think?' He pointed at the sky and pulled the trigger. Nothing happened. 'Piece of shit.'

'*You're* the piece of—'

A phone rang. Dom reached for his pocket, but remembered that his phone had tumbled to the floor, broken.

Andy looked down at the body. 'Paging Frank,' he muttered.

'What's that supposed to mean?'

Andy frowned at the body. Then he glared at Dom. 'Call Emma. Now!'

'My phone's screwed.'

Andy pulled out his, and even before the dead man's phone had stopped ringing he had dialled and was handing it to Dom. 'She'll listen more if it comes from you.'

'If *what* comes from me?'

'Tell her to run.'

Just as Emma was about to try Dom's number again, her phone rang. Andy's face popped up on the screen.

'Is that Dad?' Daisy asked.

Emma shook her head and accepted the call. A cold flush went through her. *Something wrong.*

'Em, it's me.'

'Dom?'

'My phone's broken, I'm on Andy's.'

144

'What's happening? Is it all sorted?'

Dom did not reply for a moment or two, and she heard his breathing, fast and sharp. A voice in the background. Andy.

'Dom?'

'You're still at Mandy's?'

'Yeah.'

'Em, you've got to get away from there. Get in the car, you and Daisy, and meet us . . . I don't know. But just leave.'

'You're scaring me,' she said. Daisy glanced up from her phone, eyes wide. 'What's happened?'

'Something went wrong,' Dom said, and his voice sounded ready to break.

'The Jeep's here,' she said. 'Parked out front. He cruised by slowly fifteen minutes ago, then braked and backed up. Must have been looking for my car . . . so stupid leaving it in the driveway like that. Now he's just watching the house.'

'He's on his phone again,' Daisy said. She had moved closer to the blinds, still far enough back to avoid being seen.

Emma frowned, hearing a ringing from somewhere remote. She had her phone, Daisy held hers. Mandy's landline was on the coffee table, silent and unlit.

'Lip's there,' she heard Dom say, and she heard the ringing in the background below his voice. There was muffled movement, a brief exchange she couldn't hear, and then Andy came on the line.

'Emma, you and Daisy need to get out of there.'

'Hairy man's getting out of the car,' Daisy said.

'I heard that,' Andy said. 'Emma, you need to—'

'You should be here!' she said. '*You*, not us. This is all your fault!'

'Fault doesn't matter right now,' Andy said. 'Listen, Emma. This guy, Lip, he's dangerous. A really nasty piece of work.'

Emma moved closer to the window beside Daisy and looked through the blinds. Lip was standing outside the Jeep, driver's door still open. He had his phone pressed to his ear and was talking, all his attention on the house. Tall, thin, he wore jeans and a black T-shirt, arms landscaped with muscles and blurred tattoos.

'You can't let Lip near you. You can't let him catch you.'

'Mum, he's crossing the road,' Daisy whispered.

'He's coming,' Emma said.

'Out the back way,' Andy said. 'You know the town, get away on foot. Where shall we meet you?'

'Castle Woods,' she said.

Andy repeated the name, and Dom must have nodded. 'Right. Go.'

'You'll pay for this,' she said. She hung up before Andy had a chance to reply. 'Daisy. We need to leave, now.' The fear must have come out in her voice. She could not remember the last time she'd seen Daisy so scared.

She took one more glance through the dining room window. Lip was standing at the end of the driveway, half-hidden behind the high hedge that bordered next door's garden. His wild hair and beard seemed almost to blend in. But whatever was causing him to hesitate would not last long. He'd seen her car, he knew they were there, and he was coming for them.

'Mum . . .' her daughter said, not needing to say any more.

'We'll be fine, honey. Just follow me. Quickly and quietly. We're going to meet Dad.'

A rush of possibilities flickered in her mind, each of them considered and discounted in the blink of an eye. Leave the back door unlocked, wait until he's in, then run out the front door. Hide under the stairs and rush out when he's looking elsewhere. Sneak out the back door and try to get in the car before he sees them or reaches them. But every idea depended on Lip taking a certain action or route, and she knew she could only rely on herself. Requiring him to do something specific to enable them to run would doom their escape. This was all down to them.

She rushed through the kitchen to the back door, glancing at the knife block as she went. But she would not arm herself. The very idea felt foolish, almost melodramatic. *But what the hell have they done?* she thought, thinking of Andy and Dom. She was more convinced than ever that the post office murders were connected to current events. But that way lay horrific thoughts about her husband.

She could not distract herself with that now. She had to focus.

She opened the back door.

'Over there,' she said, pointing to the bottom left corner of the garden. It wasn't a huge plot, but it was enclosed, its only gate leading onto the driveway. Mandy had built a barbecue out of breeze blocks and bricks, and it would provide an easy way over the fence. 'Go.'

She made sure that Daisy ran before her, climbing onto the barbecue and leaning across, lifting her right leg over the fence, balancing for a moment, then dropping down the other side. Emma did the same, pausing on the fence to check out Mandy's house. There was no one in the windows, no movement, no sign that he was inside.

As she let herself slip into the neighbour's garden, the side gate opened and Lip appeared.

He looked right at her.

She landed in a flower bed. Daisy was standing on the lawn, shifting from foot to foot.

'He saw me,' Emma whispered. 'There, quick.' This house also had an enclosed garden, but there was a side entrance leading towards the front. She took one step that way, then changed her mind. 'No. This way.' She dashed across the lawn to the rear fence, rose bushes pricking at her legs, jumping at the same time as Daisy, swinging a leg over, dropping into another garden. If he followed them, he'd assume they'd take the easiest route. Or maybe he'd double back and be waiting for them out on the road.

'Mum,' Daisy said, pointing.

A family was sitting on their patio eating tea. A half-empty bottle of wine rested on the table, surrounded by salad bowl, bread board, and a plate of meats and olives. The man and woman stared open-mouthed, while two young children pointed and giggled.

'Please,' Emma whispered, pressing her finger to her lips.

The man's attention shifted to their feet, and Emma looked down.

'Get off my veg!' he said, not quite shouting, but loud enough.

Emma grabbed Daisy's hand and ran for the side of the house. 'Sorry, sorry,' she said as they passed within six feet of the shocked family. The woman had said nothing, the kids were now huddled together. Emma pulled a face and they laughed again.

Down the side of the house was a tall gate, bolted, and as they approached she so hoped it was not locked. There was a padlock, but it hung free. She worked at the bolt. It was stiff, squealing as it slid halfway back, then from behind them she heard a shout.

'Hey, get out of my garden! What the hell do you—' A heavy, meaty thud ended the man's protestations, and then the bolt slid back and she tugged the gate open, hauling Daisy after her as they emerged into the end of the cul-de-sac next to Mandy's road.

Emma knew these streets. She had to hold onto that, use her knowledge to help them escape.

'He's close!' Daisy said, voice high, and Emma squeezed her hand and saved her breath.

They ran, passing three houses on their left and right before turning right. There was a snaking path leading from this new estate to one a little older. Kids called it the cutting, adults knew it as dog-shit alley. If they could exit its far end before Lip, there'd be a larger choice of escape routes.

They darted between houses and into the cutting. Garages on either side shaded it from the evening heat, but the air hung still and humid, redolent with the smell of cut grass and old dog shit. They ran fast. Emma felt the scratch of brambles and the kiss of nettles across her legs, but she did her best to ignore them. The path was so narrow that she had to let go of Daisy's hand, but she was pleased to hear her daughter's footsteps close behind, her breathing fast and deep.

'I'm scared,' Daisy said.

'Me too. But we can run fast.'

As the path jigged to the right she risked a glance behind them. Lip was standing back in the street, and at that moment he caught sight of them and started running.

They turned the corner. Emma figured they had about twenty seconds' head start. They passed though the old kissing gate left over from when the site of the new estate had been overgrown fields, and she grabbed a long, heavy stick leaning against the gate's far side.

'Go!' she said, and Daisy ran on. She was silently counting in her head.

Five . . . six . . . seven . . .

She rammed the stick behind the metal upright and wedged it against the framed wooden gate.

Nine . . . ten . . . eleven.

Daisy was ahead, but only jogging now. Emma sprinted to catch up. Garden fences and hedgerows hemmed them in, and with every step she looked for somewhere to squeeze through. But unless an easy opening presented itself, she knew they'd be better making it out the other end.

Fifteen . . . sixteen . . . seventeen.

They turned another corner and she risked a glance back. There was no sign of Lip at the kissing gate.

A few seconds later they emerged onto a road. Right took them towards home, left led eventually to Usk's main street. They went left.

An old couple she knew from her visits to the local butcher were working in their front garden, and Emma raised a hand in greeting. It would have felt ridiculous if she wasn't so scared.

What will he do if he catches us? The idea plagued her. But if he did somehow draw close, they were surrounded by houses, and soon they'd be on the main street with shops, pubs, restaurants. They should have been safe, even now.

'Mum, this way to Castle Woods,' Daisy said, pointing.

'I was thinking the main street.'

'This way's quicker. And as long as he doesn't see us take the path . . .'

Emma nodded. Daisy was right. With a quick glance back the way they'd come, they headed along the narrow lane. There was no sign of Lip. With every road they took, every turning, they lost him some more.

Castle Woods was maybe half a mile away. But once there, what then? She tried not to worry about that.

Tried not to stress about how much their present had been fractured, their future made more uncertain than ever before.

Hello, police? My husband and his friend are murderers.

The lane curved slightly uphill and to the left. It passed between old houses, the original buildings around which much of the small town had been built. One even had a blue plaque on the wall. She'd read it once, taking a walk with Dom and Daisy in her pushchair. She could no longer remember which literary or famous figure it celebrated.

Just a mother and daughter out for a jog, she thought. She wore summery sandals. Daisy was slapping the ground in flip-flops.

They passed a couple out with their three young kids, and Emma coveted their normality. She knew the woman vaguely from a keep-fit class she attended through the winter. They nodded a greeting and the woman said, 'Keeping it up I see, Emma.'

'You didn't see us,' Emma said, surprised at her own breathlessness. 'Hide and seek.' The woman's expression slipped and then they were past, following a lane lined with blooming rose bushes and rhododendron spilling over garden fences. They saw no one else, and a couple of minutes later they reached the lane's far end.

They were on the edge of Usk now, and across the road and up a steep hill sat the remains of an old, small castle. It was privately owned, not monopolised for tourism like many other castles in the area. An occasional wedding was held there, and those in the know sometimes picnicked in its open grounds if they wanted somewhere quiet and atmospheric to spend their time.

It was perfect.

'Go!' Emma said. Daisy crossed the road; she followed. They could not rest. They had to get out of sight, up through the small castle grounds and beyond, into the woods where it would now be dusk beneath the trees.

She was sweating. She needed a drink, water or something stronger.

'You okay, Mum?' Daisy asked.

'I'm fine.'

'Good. Me too.'

Holding hands again, Emma and her daughter ran towards Usk's oldest building and the shadowy woodland beyond.

Chapter Seventeen

Jane Smith

'We have to go!' Dom said.

'I winged her. I *know* I did!' Andy was standing beyond the windmill staring out across the fields, shotgun hanging from his right hand.

'And now you want to chase her down to finish the job.' Dom was finding it difficult to speak. Not when there was a dead man close by. He tried not to look at the fallen Frank, but a sick fascination drew his attention again and again. Blood was pooling in the gravel from his broken head making islands of stone, a map of red and grey.

Andy came back to Dom. His left arm was slashed, a four inch cut pouting wetly across his forearm. He held his fingers splayed, dripping blood. Dom hadn't noticed before, or perhaps the wound simply had not registered.

Andy didn't raise the gun, but that didn't make Dom any less afraid of him. *I'm a witness. I've seen what he's done. I'm part of it.* He took one step back.

Andy froze, held out his bloody hand. 'Woah, Dom. Mate. You don't have to be afraid of me.'

'You just threw your cousin from a windmill and killed him.'

'He tried to kill you!'

'You're not bothered by what you did.'

Andy looked down at the body lying between them. His expression barely changed, but he glanced aside and blinked quickly, as if to clear dust from his eye or an image from his mind.

'You brought a gun!'

'Piece of shit didn't work.'

'You took it out even before Frank was on us.'

'I was going to threaten Mary. Insurance.'

'Just threaten her, Andy?'

'We don't have time for this!' Andy snapped. 'Mary's gone. We have to meet your family. That phone call was probably Sonja checking in, or maybe Lip. Either way, they'll know what's happened. Mary would have told them by now.'

'Maybe if you'd blown her head off, we'd still have more time.'

'It is what it is, Dom.' Andy stepped around the cooling corpse and approached his friend.

This time Dom did not step back. 'You've *made* it what it is. What would have happened if this had gone better and they'd opened the bag?'

'It didn't go better.'

'But if it had?'

'Then I'd have started negotiating.'

'For what? Forty grand? Seriously?'

Andy didn't reply. He grabbed Dom's hand and pulled him towards their car.

'If my family . . .' But Dom could not finish the sentence or thought. Its implications were too horrendous, and contemplating them would cloud his mind. He needed to be clear-headed.

They reached the car, Andy checking behind them frequently, as if expecting Mary to return.

'What about him?' Dom asked, nodding at Frank's corpse.

'Broke in, trespassed, fell.' Andy slapped his hand on the car's roof. 'Dom! Keys.'

Dom opened the car and dropped into the driver's seat. If he'd been quicker, perhaps he could have locked the doors and left Andy behind. But he was already in the car, shotgun resting across his lap.

It was an oven. The windows had closed automatically when Dom locked the car. As he grabbed the wheel his hands started to shake. He held on hard, took a deep breath, trying to calm himself. Glancing sideways, he saw that Andy's hand was shaking too. He held onto the shotgun but his injured arm quivered.

'Never killed anyone,' Andy muttered, almost to himself.

'Life's full of these little milestones,' Dom said. He started the car and spun it around, heading back towards the road into town.

It was almost 8.30. He nursed Andy's phone in his lap, willing Emma to call and tell him that everything was all right. But it remained silent.

It was a ten-minute drive to Castle Woods.

'It's all getting worse,' Dom said. His shock persisted, but behind it was a dawning realisation about what had happened. 'It was supposed to be settled, but now it's even worse than it was before. We're murderers.'

'You didn't do a thing.'

'But I was there.'

Andy gasped. He was inspecting the cut on his arm, and one quick look made Dom feel sick. He could see the flesh, the insides of Andy's arm as he tried to squeeze the wound together.

'First-aid kit in the glove compartment,' Dom said.

'Needs stitching.'

'Want to walk to hospital?'

Andy shook his head and reached for the first-aid kit. He wound a small bandage around his wound, pulling tight and groaning. The bandage was nowhere near up to the task, and quickly soaked through with blood. But it was all they had got.

'Emma knows some first aid,' Dom said. She'd once put butterfly stitches onto a cut on his finger. He'd fallen in the garden. They'd been out late, lying on Daisy's trampoline and drinking wine in the darkness, watching the Perseid meteor shower and sharing each other's warmth. 'She'll fix you.'

If Lip hasn't already got to them.

He felt sick with shock and fear, but suddenly focussed and sharp, his senses keen. He could smell Andy's blood and the rich odour of his own sweat. He could hear the evening song of birds in the hedgerows they sped past. He saw the shadows and shades of dusk splayed across the low hillsides above Usk, a full palette of fiery colours that should bode well for the next day. He only hoped that old rhyme held some truth today.

'So what now?' he asked.

'I'm not sure.'

'What now for my family, Andy? They've killed our dog, is it us next?'

'Of course not. No. Not if I can help it.'

'And can you?'

Andy leaned back in his seat, head against headrest. He looked pale and vulnerable. 'One shell left,' he said.

'That's not an answer.'

They passed the big houses on the edge of town, following the river that led eventually to the large stone bridge. Dom turned left before then, taking a lane that led to the car park just up the wooded hillside from the ruined castle. They were close. It was growing dark. He had to switch on his headlights, and he imagined Emma and Daisy hiding somewhere beneath the trees, listening to every sound, every flutter of leaves in the evening breeze, and wondering if it was someone coming to hurt them.

'What now?' he asked again. 'Do we contact them? Negotiate?'

'After this, people like that won't negotiate.' Andy was agitated, fingers drumming against the shotgun's stock, knee lifting and falling as he tapped his foot. He did not look at all like a man in control. His gaze was distant, as if fighting with a decision. Any suspicion Dom had that Andy had engineered events to this stage took a hit. But his friend became more of a stranger with every moment that passed.

'It's a mess,' Andy said softly. 'But I know someone who might help.'

'Who? What's his name?'

'It's a her. And her name's Jane Smith.'

Jane Smith met John Williams on the ferry at Cherbourg. He was sitting on the open deck at the huge boat's stern, in an area where several other smokers had congregated. A gentle sea breeze carried their smoke away from the ferry, but even so other travellers kept away from them, as if they were diseased rather than people who enjoyed a cigarette. Even if she hadn't seen him, Rose would have been able to smell his rank brand of tobacco from a distance.

Families and couples milled on deck. Children scampered back and forth, tanned from their recent holiday, wearing "I(heart)France" T-shirts and exuding excitement. Parents stood at the handrail, tired and eager to reach home. Rose watched these happy families for a while, trying not to be too obvious in her observations, smiling even though it was the last thing she felt like doing. Tears would make her stand out in the crowd.

'You must have driven quickly,' he said when she pulled up a plastic chair and sat next to him.

'You must have driven slowly.'

'Speeding attracts attention.'

'You really smoke those shitty-smelling things in public?'

Holt took a deep drag on his cigarette. 'Don't need your help here, Jane,' he said.

'I'm not offering it. Really, did you have to leave without telling me?'

'It was a snap decision,' he said.

'Bullshit. You never make snap decisions.'

He glanced at her, cigarette in the corner of his mouth, smoke caressing his face before the breeze snatched it away. 'Normally true. But in this case, I did. A decision of the heart.'

She wasn't sure what to say to that. There was so much to Holt that she did not know, and so much of what she did know, she did not understand. He had a past rich in blood, so deep that its histories and origins seemed lost. She knew little about him before his life of violence, and there were also sorrows that he rarely spoke about. She didn't think it was because he did not trust her, but because they had grown too close. Such sorrows might solidify between them and drive them apart. Her own were enough for both of them.

At least, that was what she suspected. Holt rarely revealed anything that might make her sure, or otherwise.

All she knew was how Holt's sister had died.

He had told her soon after the Trail hunt in Wales had ended and they spent a couple of months moving around some of the smaller Greek islands. Rose had been nursing her wounds, both physical and mental, trying to perceive just how much revenge might have helped her.

Holt had helped her through this period as he had through her alcoholism, though at the time she hadn't realised what he was doing. She had believed herself to be the stronger one then, able to look back and define her revenge, embrace it, welcome it into her life. She still hadn't realised how it would only serve to complicate things even more.

One evening, they'd sat on the beach and built a fire, cooking fish on the hot rocks surrounding the flames. He drank water; she drank coffee. Smoke hung in the air, from the fire and his cigarettes. She berated him for smoking. He agreed with a rare smile that it was bad for his health. And later that evening, something Rose still did not understand prompted Holt to open up.

'There's something about revenge that's life-giving,' Holt had said. 'The need for vengeance, the lust, keeps you grounded and level and straight. It feeds you. I've done what I do for a long time – so long that I can hardly recall when it all began – but it's not what's kept me alive. I'm older than you think I am. I've seen and done more than I'll ever tell you. But it's a hunger for retribution that drives me forward now.'

'Retribution for what?' It was the most Holt had said about himself since the first time they'd met in that Italian bar, and Rose was nervous, terrified that he'd clam up and smoke and stare once more into the flames.

'I'll tell you,' he said, and then he *did* stare for a long while. The flames danced in his eyes and flickered in the plastic water bottle in his lap. She did not prompt him. After a few minutes he started again.

'Her name was Adele.' He looked away from the flames, as if they showed him too much. He stared out over the ocean instead, at the palette of blood-colours on the dusky horizon. 'She was my sister. A good person, not like me. She had a husband, Alain, and a young daughter. I've never met my niece. I only met Alain twice, and he's the only man who's ever hit me and not had worse back. Adele loved me, I think, but she was aware of the sort of man I'd become. She didn't know details. You know more about me than anyone else alive, Rose. But Adele . . . she was sensitive, and fragile, and too beautiful to have me in her life.

'I did my best to remove myself. We lost contact eventually, and I never tried to get in touch. She'd never have been able to find me, of course, though I don't know whether she tried. Part of me likes to think she did, but another part of me hopes she lived the last few years of her life not thinking about me at all. She'd never have been at peace with who and what I am, so I hoped she'd manage to cast me from her life. But for Adele, family was sacrosanct. I fear that our estrangement probably upset her more than the knowledge of who I'd become.'

He went to drink and found that his bottle was empty. He glanced back at the small beach hut they were sharing, where there was a small fridge with more water. But he made no move to fetch it, and Rose would not help. This was the most he'd ever said in one go, and she didn't want to do anything to break his flow. She remained motionless, staring at the sand, trying not to be there at all.

'One day, a man looking for me found out where Adele lived. It was a small village in Switzerland, close to the French border. Alain's work had taken them there. You know me, Rose. I knew all about where they lived and what Alain and Adele did for a living. I didn't intrude, but I kept track of their lives. It was my way of being close, perhaps. Even now I'm not sure why I kept tabs on them, having no intention of ever intruding again. My life had its own ruinous terrain; I had no intention of damaging what they had made for themselves. It turned out to be my greatest mistake.

'He called himself Monk. I was hired by a crime family in New York to kill him, because he'd killed three of their number over the previous few years. I suppose he was a hitman of sorts, but in truth he was simply a man who loved killing. He'd have continued doing so even if he wasn't paid for it. Rival families were using him, and this family had been unable to track him down.

'But the politics of violence don't matter here. The sordid story behind why I went after him . . . that doesn't matter. What matters is that from the very first moment Monk knew that I was on his trail, he was planning his escape. I don't think I scared him. I think the opposite is true, and he saw my involvement as something that might provide him with excitement for years to come. But before he went, he wanted to give me a real reason to follow.

'He traced my own investigations into my sister's life and location. I haven't seen my wife and daughter in almost thirty years, and I've let them go. I suspect they have new lives, a new husband. Perhaps I'm even a grandfather now. But I couldn't let my sister go, and my persistence doomed her. Following trails I had uncovered, Monk found out where she lived, and by the time I discovered that he had a day's head start.'

Holt sighed and picked up a big stick to poke the fire. Logs turned and spat, flinging sparks at the sky. The fire flared, expanding the circle of light around them and catching the white foam of breaking waves. It was dark now, the time of day Rose hated least. The dark held possibilities, and sometimes she imagined how her life might have been different.

'You didn't get there in time,' she said. She knew it was the truth, but Holt looked suddenly startled, as if he was living ten years ago and he'd discovered the scene all over again.

'He'd taken her to an old house on the outskirts of the village. One of those places left behind after the owner dies, no next of kin, just frozen in time under a layer of dust. She was cold by the time I got there, even though I went as quickly as I could. She was the only new thing there. He'd beaten her, tied her to a chair, superglued her mouth closed and then her nostrils. She'd suffocated. And . . .' He looked away from Rose and the fire, seeking darkness that would not reflect his moist eyes. 'I think she was probably cursing me as she died.'

'I'm sure that's not true.'

'What do you know?' His voice was harsh, and he was right, she couldn't know. It was a platitude, and she more than anyone should know the brutal truth.

'She'd have known that Monk was there because of me. He probably told her. And she knew she was going to die, horribly, and that Alain and her daughter would grow older without her. Because of me. We hadn't spoken for years, but still the choices I made in life ended up killing her.'

162

They sat in silence for a while. The fire crackled, the sea *shushed* onto the beach. The tides of life pulsed around them, indifferent to their fleeting existence.

'I'm afraid,' he said. 'If I finally track down and kill Monk for what he did, perhaps my life will be over. Revenge has become the sustenance for my anger, and that keeps me alive. What comes after? What life do I really have?'

If he was questioning her, Rose still did not answer, because she knew exactly what he meant. Revenge against the people who had murdered her own family had been a hollow victory, leaving her feeling empty and sad. It was as if they'd died all over again.

Now, on the deck of a ferry crossing a dark sea towards a place that had once been home, Rose remembered that conversation, and wondered just how lost she had become.

But she was not Holt. Revenge might have left her aimless and adrift, but she still had her family to cling on to. Dead though they were, she had a history that defined her, and which was the one solid rock around which the rest of her sad life could ebb and flow.

And she had found a way to carry on. She helped people in difficult situations. Not bad people, like Holt sometimes chose to work for. But good people who had become embroiled in bad events. Sometimes she offered advice; more often she used her continually developing IT skills to guide them towards a new life, a fresh identity, and freedom from who- or whatever it was that ailed them. She was Jane Smith, the do-over woman. She could never pretend that she was a good person, but she had found a route on from the hollowness of revenge. Most of the time, she didn't wallow in hopelessness.

'If it's a decision of the heart, you have to follow it,' she said. The ferry's engines had powered up and they were starting to move. The sea breeze was already bracing, and she liked the fact that it had driven some of the people inside.

'You sound like a self-help book.'

'Maybe I'll write one.'

'With your spelling?'

She smiled. 'I'll get an editor.'

'Jane Smith's Guide to False Identity and Bloody Vengeance.'

'There's a market. I'll dedicate it to you.'

They sat in silence for a while longer. He rolled another cigarette, she raised her hood and snuggled down in the seat. She browsed her phone, jumping onto the ship's WiFi to check various email accounts, news sites, and then clicking through to Twitter. She followed hundreds, but there were only a few accounts she checked semi-regularly. One of them was owned by a man she had helped three years ago. He'd found a new home quite close to where the post office murders had happened, and that troubled her so much that she'd checked six times already that day.

'Really, Rose,' Holt said, using her name in public without thinking, a clumsy mistake that displayed his distracted state of mind. 'This is all my business.'

'Ah, shit.' Rose sat up in her seat and held the phone out towards him. 'Not any more,' she said.

The account name was AndyMan.

The latest post read, *Jane Smith was born in Sorrento.*

It was a call for help.

Chapter Eighteen

Rocks

As soon as Dom parked the car, Emma and Daisy emerged from beneath the trees, pushing through ferns and brambles to reach the small car park. He turned off the ignition, pocketed the keys and jumped from the car, running to meet his family.

They embraced. Emma felt good in his arms, warm and damp with perspiration. Daisy joined in and hugged them both. He pulled back and looked into his wife's eyes, and though he knew there was so much anger and resentment there for the danger they were in, for a while they were simply glad to be together again.

He said nothing, hoping that the moment might go on, and on.

'What happened to your arm?' Daisy asked.

Emma pulled away and looked past Dom at Andy.

'What's happened?' she asked.

'You first,' Dom said. 'You're both okay?'

'We lost him in the town. He was coming towards the house, Dom. What would he have done?'

'I don't—'

'Same as he did to those people at the post office?' she asked.

Dom saw Daisy's eyes go wide, and he wanted to say, *Not in front of her.* But he had no right to say anything of the sort. He couldn't keep anything from Emma any more. Not if they were going to remain a team, a family unit, and pull through this.

He already had an idea about how this might all end.

'They're Andy's family,' he said. 'Andy and I took money from the post office. They turned up right afterwards and carried out the murders.'

Emma put one protective arm around her daughter.

'You're bank robbers?' Daisy asked. The fear he saw in her expression, the shock in her voice, made him more ashamed than he ever had been of anything before in his life. To see her scared of him drove a knife into his heart.

'I don't understand,' Emma said. The light was fading, but out in the open of the car park the setting sun reflected in her eyes.

'How close behind you is he?' Andy asked.

'We lost him.'

'He's not stupid.'

'I don't understand,' Emma said again. 'Your family, Andy? Why are they threatening us? Why did they kill Jazz? Did you plan all this?'

'No time now,' Andy said. 'And not in front of Daisy.'

'This concerns her too!' Emma said. They'd always been honest and open with their daughter, never condescending to her. *That lamb on your plate was running around a field yesterday . . . Some people believe in God but I don't . . . I know you know "bastard" and "fuck", but I never want to hear you using them.* But Dom hated the look in her face right then. She was a child again.

'Please, Em,' he said.

'Why couldn't you have just stayed boring,' his wife said. He wasn't sure she could have come up with anything more cutting. But he deserved it.

'Dom, we need to stay quiet and get away,' Andy said. 'I've already asked for help.'

'And who is this mysterious Jane Smith?' Dom asked, spinning and putting himself between Andy and his family. He saw that Andy had left the shotgun in the car, and he was grateful for that.

'Someone who's helped me before,' Andy said. 'I can explain everything. But now's not the time or place.'

'What happened?' Emma asked. 'Your arm's bleeding. You both look scared.'

'Please,' Andy said. He was backing towards the car. 'Come on!' Talking quieter, more urgently.

Emma's phone rang.

'Don't answer it,' Dom said.

But she already had. The light from the phone's screen lit her face, her wide eyes, the sheen of sweat across her nose and upper lip. Daisy pressed close to her mother, still staring in fear at the father she'd thought she knew. Dom smiled in an attempt to reassure her.

'Don't,' Daisy said, looking away. Dom felt bereft.

Emma threw the phone to Dom. He caught it automatically and held it down by his side.

'It's her,' Emma said.

Dom wanted to hang up, throw the phone away, discard and deny everything that had happened. But he also knew that he had to take responsibility. More than that, he had to take control. Andy had coerced him up to now, steered his actions and anticipated his reactions. But the man who'd been his friend had let control slip away. That had resulted in murder.

I can make all this end, he thought. A call to the police would put himself and his family under their protection. He would tell his story and submit himself to whatever punishment that would entail. His wife's and daughter's safety were paramount, and he could no longer avoid responsibility for what he had done.

He put the phone to his ear and said, 'I'm calling the police.'

'Hello, Dom,' the voice said. 'I'm Sonja. It's nice to talk to you at last. Let's discuss how we can end all this nastiness without resorting to that, shall we?' This was Sonja Scott, Andy's mother and leader of the family gang. If what Andy had told him was true – if even a small amount of what he said could be taken as genuine – she was a violent, evil woman. But she sounded calm and intelligent, completely in control. She reminded him of the headmistress at Daisy's school, whose gentle voice was also assured.

'If there's a way, I'm ready to hear it,' he said. He was looking at Emma and Daisy, but also aware of Andy shaking his head in his peripheral vision.

'Of course,' Sonja said. 'I've already taken steps to ensure this is over quickly and quietly. Much against my family's recommendations, I've already called in help. And with that help we're going to find you, your wife and daughter, and that murdering bastard of a son of mine, and we're going to kill you all.'

Dom's next breath was a soft gasp. He could not speak. Shock winded him.

'You killed Frank,' she said, her voice now rough with grief.

'Not our fault,' Dom said. But it sounded hopeless. It sounded like begging.

'You won't die as quickly as him,' the woman continued. 'It'll be slow. Lip likes it slow, and the people I've called *love* killing. Luckily for me, the job is their reward, and that's reflected in their nominal fee.' It sounded like she was relaying a favourite recipe rather than a death sentence.

'You don't need to do this,' Dom said. He felt sick and removed from the world. He wished everything would go away, leaving him in safe, insulated blackness, an isolation in which there was only him and his mistakes forever. No repercussions. No pain inflicted on others.

'You can beg if you want,' she said. 'But that's unseemly. Not very manly. And I'll bet you feel *very* manly right now, Dom?'

'Please,' he whispered.

'Andy's forced me into this, and you're his partner.'

'No, really, I didn't know what he was doing, I had no idea.' Andy was walking towards him, hand held out for the phone. 'I'll get you the money. Then it's done.'

Sonja did not reply. Dom thought he heard whispers, but perhaps it was a breeze in the trees, or Andy's shoes brushing across the rough gravel surface.

'Are you there?' he asked.

'Yes, I'm still listening. Just keep begging. It's funny. Let's see where it gets you.'

Dom lowered the phone slowly, looking around at their surroundings. The car park was small and rutted, surrounded by ferns and banks of brambles. Thirty feet away the trees began. *Just keep begging . . .*

He disconnected and whispered, 'He's here!' He waved Emma and Daisy towards the car. 'She wanted me to keep talking,' he said to Andy. He'd reveal what else she'd said later, but first they had to leave. Danger stalked the shadows beneath the trees.

'Dad?' Daisy said. 'We're going to call the police, right?'

'I will,' he said. 'Jump into the car with your mum.'

He followed, wincing when Emma opened the door and the internal light came on. Andy was around the other side, snatching the shotgun from the passenger footwell and slinking away again.

'Andy!' Dom whispered.

'Drive,' Andy said. He was already lost to the shadows, down amongst the undergrowth.

Dom had no time to argue. And besides, maybe this was how he would escape Andy's deadly influence. It was not a selfish thought. It was all about protecting his family as best as he could. He dropped into the driver's seat.

'Stay down,' he said, and glancing in the rear-view mirror he locked eyes with Emma as the internal light faded away. Then her shadow disappeared down behind the seats to shield Daisy from harm.

Dom reached for the keys. They weren't there. He'd pocketed them. Digging into his jeans pocket, trying not to panic, he snagged the key ring Daisy had made for him in school three years before. Tugging, keys catching on threads in his jeans pocket, every moment stretched out in painful slow motion.

'Dom!' Emma said.

He didn't reply. The keys sprang free and he slipped the ignition key home. Pressing on the clutch, slipping into first gear, he turned the ignition.

The engine grumbled to life and the automatic headlamps splashed on. He held his breath, expecting to see Lip standing before them, a monster caught in the beams. But there was only the car park's churned gravel and a bank of ferns and brambles, stark in the sudden light, solid shadows behind them.

He wondered where Andy was.

Dom saw the fleeting movement and had time to think, *Bird? Bat? Moth?* before the rock struck the windscreen. It was big and had been thrown hard. The windscreen smashed. The rock fell through, bounced from the steering wheel and struck his left arm.

Dom's foot slipped from the clutch. The car jerked forward and stalled.

The windscreen had cracked in thousands of staggered lines, safety glass mostly holding in place but now obscured.

'Punch it out!' Emma said. 'Go, Dom! You need to go, you haven't *seen* him!'

Dom pressed the clutch and started the car again, and the second rock smashed through the weakened glass and struck his face.

Everything went away, consumed in the blaze of shock and pain. Perhaps he groaned, or maybe he shouted. His face felt wet and hot. The agony was centred around his nose, a blinding fire radiating outwards behind his cheekbones, circling his eye sockets, pulsing in his teeth and jaw.

Unable to see, hear or sense what was happening, Dom slammed his foot on the gas and shifted his left foot from the clutch.

The car surged forward.

Emma lunged between the seats and grabbed the wheel.

'Keep your foot on the gas!' she said, close to Dom's left ear. He was groaning, his face glimmering with blood and speckled with knots of glass from the shattered windscreen. He leaned his head against her arm and it felt wet.

She stretched further, both hands clasping the wheel. She leaned to the left, struggling to turn before they ploughed into an overgrown area and stalled again. Emma knew this car park from a few previous visits, thought that the entrance lane was to the left, but she couldn't be sure.

The engine roared, labouring high and fast. Wheels span, gravel spat behind them.

Something pale appeared from the right, standing, and Lip hefted another rock.

Emma jigged the car to the right. She didn't have time to consider what she was doing. If she had, she might have wondered why he'd made himself such an easy target.

The car struck the heavy concrete post buried beneath creeping plants. It was a glancing blow, and she fell to the left with both hands on the wheel, tugging it down and back onto the gravelled surface. The post scraped across the car's right side.

Daisy was screaming in the back seat, desperate for it to all end. It was her cries more than anything else that terrified Emma. She'd never heard her daughter like that before, and every single parental instinct prickled.

Something hit the left rear window. It smashed. Emma felt stinging impacts across her left thigh and hip, but she ignored it, heaving herself upright again and concentrating on steering.

Dom grunted and rested his hands on the wheel, both of them over hers. Together, they aimed the car at the lane leading back towards the main road.

'Daisy?' Emma shouted.

'Mum! Mummy!'

'Daisy, are you okay?'

'I . . . yeah. I think Andy shot the car.'

'But you're okay?'

'Yes, Mum. Just go. Please, the man's gone, but just go.'

'Dom, second gear,' Emma said, and Dom did so, slowly, deliberately. 'When we reach the road—'

Andy appeared in the headlights. *Keep going*, Emma thought, and she was about to say it when Dom pressed the clutch and released pressure on the gas. The car slowed, drifted, and while it was still moving Andy opened the front door and dropped into the seat.

'Go,' he said. He glanced at Dom, then at Emma stretched between the front seats, still steering for her husband. He reached for the wheel. 'I've got it.'

'I've got it!' Emma shouted, and she wanted to smash Andy in the face. But she needed both hands.

'Mum?' Daisy said from behind her. 'I'm fine, really, it's just a sting, but . . . I think Andy shot me.'

'Just keep going,' she said to her husband, and she caught sight of his face in the rear-view mirror, ghostly in the dashboard lighting, glimmering with blood. She hardly recognised him, but at that moment she hated him and loved him more than she ever had before. He'd been such a fool, but now he was doing his best to put things right.

She risked a quick glance back. Daisy was holding her hand up, turning it this way and that. 'Bleeding?' Emma asked.

'No, it's just like a big bruise.'

Emma checked her daughter's hand quickly and saw that the skin was not broken. She wanted to kiss her fingers. *Special Mummy medicine*, she used to say.

'Turn left here,' Andy said as they approached the junction out onto the main road. Emma had moments to think about it. Left would take them back into town, and with a smashed windscreen and a driver covered with blood, hiding would be impossible.

Partly because of that, but mostly to act contrary to Andy's instruction, she tugged the wheel around and to the right. 'Let me take over now, babe,' she said, and Dom gratefully eased back on the gas and knocked the car out of gear. They drifted to a halt.

'Emma, we need to—'

'Why are you even still with us?' she shouted at Andy. 'You're not part of this family!'

'I'm trying to help.'

'Look at him, see where your help's got us!' She dropped back into the rear seat and went to check Daisy.

'Dom, tell her.'

'Just shut the fuck up,' Emma said. Daisy laughed, and she felt a rush of love for her daughter. Even under these circumstances, Daisy could find humour in a swear word.

Emma reached for the door.

'Mum!' Daisy said.

'I've got to drive. Your dad's bleeding and he can't see that well.'

'Is he okay?'

Emma didn't know. Maybe it was just a cut and bruised face, or a broken nose. Or perhaps the impact had cracked his skull. He hadn't said much. 'I don't know,' she said. Now was not the time to lie to Daisy, or anyone. There had been too many lies.

She jumped from the car. The road was quiet. Night had fallen, a soft summer night when shreds of sunlight lingered in sparse clouds high in the sky, and the landscape was silvered by moonlight. It was still warm and humid.

Dom's car was a mess. The front wing was dented and torn, and all along the driver's side the metal was deeply scraped. The shattered windscreen was even more obvious, and she knew they wouldn't be able to drive it for long.

Her car was back at Mandy's house. She realised with a sick, sinking feeling that they couldn't return there, and neither could they go home. *We're being hunted,* she thought, and though a horrible idea, it was probably quite accurate.

Dom might need a doctor's help. Daisy was running on pure adrenalin, but inside she'd be petrified. Andy was still with them. Andy, who had caused all of this.

She helped Dom from the car. He stood upright, leaning against the back door.

'Hurry,' Andy said from inside. While she didn't reply, she did feel his urgency.

'I'm okay,' Dom said. He didn't look okay. His nose was still pouring blood, it coated his face and T-shirt. But she knew it might appear worse than it was.

'Sure?'

'Yeah. For now. Just drive, we'll go somewhere safe.'

'Where's safe, Dom? Where can I go where Daisy won't be in danger from some fucking madman?'

'Andy. He knows.'

'Andy!' She snorted.

'Em . . . just drive.' Dom sat in the back. Emma closed the door behind him, seeing Daisy snuggle up next to her dad and hand him a wad of tissues from her pocket.

She sat in the driver's seat and started driving.

'So talk,' she said.

*

Dom listened to Andy telling his wife what had happened. Daisy sat beside him, trying to hug him better, as he had cuddled her all those times she'd been sick. He could tell that she was listening intently, but she said nothing. He knew that she was scared, but she was also taking everything in. Often quiet, she was also sharp as a knife.

His face throbbed. His nose hurt every time he breathed, and his eyes watered. Blood was sticky and thick across his lower face, and fresh blood flowed. But though the pain pulsed like the worst hangover, he waved away any concern. The time to tend his injuries was not now.

They all had to raise their voices. Andy had smashed out the rest of the shattered windscreen, and even with Emma driving slowly the breeze was loud, whistling around the metal doorposts and making them squint.

Andy told Emma about his family the Scotts, and Philip Beck, the man known as Lip. He relayed what had happened at Windy Miller's, taking only a few sentences to do so. He did not hold back on the awful details.

'And now they want revenge,' Emma said. 'Because of your squabblings with your scumbag family, *my* family is in danger.'

'They only want me,' Andy said.

'No,' Dom said. His voice felt weak, but it was still loud enough to silence the others. Daisy sat back a little, wanting to look at him as he spoke.

'What did she say?' Emma asked.

'That she's called in help to hunt us all down and . . .' He closed his eyes and reached for Daisy's hand.

'And kill us?' Daisy asked. Dom had never heard her saying anything so serious, so unbelievable and out of the norm. He hated hearing those words in her voice. It made the pain in his face feel like nothing.

'What help?' Emma asked.

'Sonja knows some nasty people,' Andy said.

'Your family aren't nasty enough?'

'Not like the ones she'll call. It all changed when Lip hooked up with Mary.'

'I don't care about your family history or problems,' Emma said. 'I care about mine.'

'I've called in help too,' Andy said. 'She's already acknow-ledged that she's coming.' He held up his phone.

'Jane Smith,' Dom said. 'So who is she? How can she help?'

Several sets of headlights approached from the opposite direction. Dom felt incredibly exposed with their windscreen gone. Emma slowed to a crawl, and the cars passed without slowing. They were following a curving road out into the countryside, and Emma took the next turning, dipping down a steep hill and then around to the left. It was the access to two fields, and she reversed the car behind a high hedge that shielded it from the road.

The engine fell quiet, darkness closed in. The sudden silence was shocking. Dom heard his own laboured breathing, and when he moved pain pulsed behind his eyes.

'We need to change cars,' Andy said.

'We need to know more about Jane Smith,' Emma said.

'But Mum, the police?' Daisy asked.

A loaded silence. *I'm a murderer*, Dom thought. Even though he had not harmed the woman and girl in the post office, or pushed Frank from the windmill's balcony, he felt the awful weight of their demise like a pressure around his heart. The Dom of a couple of days ago now seemed like a naive figure, with a life the Dom of now would give almost anything to regain.

'You know that's not the way to go, right?' Andy asked. He was talking directly to Emma.

'Just tell us about Jane Smith,' Emma said. 'Then I'll decide.'

Dom closed his eyes, and Daisy snuggled close to him again. It wasn't for warmth. He tried to put his arm around her, but the movement made his head swim. He was the one needing comfort.

The darkness felt safe, and for the first time in a while he wanted to rest.

'I only met her once,' Andy said. 'Three years ago. I'd left my family under strained circumstances.'

'You mean they didn't give you as much blood money as you thought you were due,' Dom said.

'Yeah. I was after a fresh start to set up legit. Wanted to go straight, and I'd already seen what Lip was doing to the family. Mary had gone that way already, and fast. She fell for him hard, and dropped into his ways almost without blinking. He's strange. You can't say charismatic, because there's really not that much to him, no glint, no obvious personality. But he does have a presence. There's a real power to him'.

'I tried to find out who he really was, where he'd come from, but it was as if he hadn't existed before the day he met Mary. So I left, but I knew they'd come looking. If not Frank or Mary, then Lip. Because I knew them all too well, knew too much. I didn't for a minute believe he was the sort of guy to hang around for long, and he's already surprised me on that. But I also knew that however long he *did* stay for, he'd want to feel safe. With me out there somewhere, he'd feel exposed.'

'So he was the only one you were worried about?' Emma asked.

'Well . . . not really. I've already told Dom, the others screwed me out of money when I left. Money that was mine, that I'd earned.'

'By robbing?'

'We weren't common thieves,' he said. He paused, as if seeking a way to explain. Then he sighed heavily and continued. 'Look, I can't expect you to understand. But the moment Sonja knew I was going, she shut me out completely. Gave me a token amount, sent me on my way. So one of my main aims was ensuring I was provided for. I set up a system that would bleed funds to me from the family, hopefully without them knowing. Sonja controlled the finances, and she moved money around Europe and the US to exchange—'

'Don't need to know that,' Dom said. He sounded bunged up, his nose filled with blood and pain. 'Don't care. Just tell us about her.'

'Right. Yeah. Jane Smith. I'd heard about her, the do-over woman. Dig deep enough on the net and you find traces of her. She's less than a shadow. But for the right people, she'll help you start a new life. You know, background stuff, a new location, traceable history online, all that sort of stuff. She did that for me.'

'That's how you ended up in Abergavenny,' Dom said. 'A technical writer? Really?'

'Why not?'

'We don't want new lives,' Emma said. 'We were happy with our old life.'

'Were you?'

'Fuck you, Andy!'

Andy remained silent. Dom breathed through his mouth, bloodied face pulsing with every breath.

'So you've asked her for help,' Dom said.

'And she's coming.'

'Why?'

'Because she helps good people. That's what she told me. She said, "I was a good person once, and I like to help people who were like me".'

'What does she mean by that?' Daisy asked.

'No idea. I don't know much about her, other than what she did for me, and what she told me the last time we communicated. She said that she knows computers, but knows guns more. When it was finished and she left, she told me how to contact her if I ever needed her.'

'So how much will this cost?' Dom asked.

'I don't know.'

Silence hung as heavy as the heat. There were no whispers, no breeze to blow it away.

'It's her or the police,' Andy said at last.

'Great,' Emma said. No one said anything else. 'Great. The law, or a mercenary.' She started the car.

'No, stay here,' Andy said. 'She'll tell us where to meet her.' He reached for the wheel.

Emma shoved his hand away and slipped into gear, moving off, hitting the road and heading away from town. 'You can sit there waiting if you like,' she said. 'I'm getting my family somewhere safe.'

Dom caught his wife glancing at him in the rear-view mirror. In the darkness he saw what he hoped was a smile.

Chapter Nineteen

Cat

Lip had once killed a man with a cat.

He'd had to kill the cat first, which had been a disappointment, because this method of murder had struck him as beautifully creative, taking a life with a hissing, snarling life. But the little bastard had squirmed and thrashed, lashed with claws and teeth, opening his arm in a dozen places. He'd thought that holding it by the tail would be enough. But the animal was incredibly flexible, arching its back, twisting, an ever-changing knot of muscle and sharp edges. Two swings against a wall and it had fallen quiet. The old man hadn't. His screams had increased, terror now tinged with grief. It had been his pet.

That had amused Lip. He'd even broken the ghost of a smile the nineteenth time he pummelled the dead creature into the old man's face.

It had taken forty-seven more impacts before he was certain the old bastard was dead. He'd obviously fed the feline too much; it was fat and soft. If it had been skinnier, less insulated, harder, his suffering might not have persisted for so long.

Lip didn't lose any sleep over it. To cause suffering was never his prime aim. It was a by-product of his fascination. A result of his interests. If a victim slipped away quickly, that did not concern him. Similarly, an intense and drawn-out death troubled him little.

It was the method that mattered.

A rock was not very imaginative, but it was all he'd been left with. Now, out in the darkness with the car vanished in the distance, making his way back towards the town, he was not at all disappointed. Sonja would be. She'd call soon, ask him what was happening and whether he had them. He'd have to tell her that they had escaped. But that only meant he would have to find them again, and again, and it was in the search that he often gained most satisfaction. It gave him time to think, and plan his next lesson. And if it went well, it also offered the opportunity to steer the search's end. His mind was awash with possibilities. Taking time to find Andy and those others again would enable him to take the outcome, and their demise, more under his control than ever.

Under a bridge with fire, he thought. *Flames casting shadows across the mossy brick arch. Screams echoing down into fast-flowing waters.*

It was the art.

In a manhole, tied up and gagged, left to die over several days beneath a thousand unknowing feet. Hearing children's laughter. Feeling the patient caress of rats' whiskers on exposed, cold skin.

Every moment was an oil painting, each image a memory to cherish.

Head caved in with a full bottle of wine that I'll open and drink afterwards.

182

He stepped in a hole and went sprawling, hands held out to break his fall. Brambles bit into his palms, seeding pain. He felt them beneath his skin. He'd have to pick them out. Or perhaps Mary would do it, if she could dry her eyes.

Frank was dead. Mary was upset, so was Sonja. But he'd been a big, overweight prick, with little going for him beyond the family, and the intelligence of a squirrel. No great loss.

Lying in the undergrowth with something soft and sly creeping across his hand, Lip attempted to see Frank's demise from Mary's point of view. It was difficult. Just another random death amongst many, but Mary would be sad that Frank had gone. He had to allow for that when he saw her again soon. Maybe he'd spend some time alone first, give the others time to grieve. It was easier than being with them and pretending.

He stood and breathed in the warm night air, relishing the darkness beneath the trees. He liked these peaceful places away from other people. It was where he felt most comfortable, honest, and less alone. In places like this he could concentrate on himself.

Every sensation became a potential focal point, and it was the prickling pain in his hands that drew him. The pain should not be there. The likelihood of that pain ever existing, signalling a brain, featuring in a conscious thought, was so remote that he revelled in it. The chance of *him* existing was so ridiculously remote that he sometimes got lost in trying to consider it.

He was born and grew and learned, and was still learning. How to use things. How to wield different objects as tools. The wonder of connecting with his surroundings never ceased to amaze him.

Once, he had killed a woman with a pint of gravel.

He started walking back through the woods towards the town, and the points of pain in his hands were like stars blooming and dying across the galaxies of his skin.

His phone vibrated in his pocket. He sighed, thought of ignoring it, then decided it would be best to answer. The pursuit was on, and he wanted to be at the forefront. Sonja had suggested she might call in help. Although he'd objected, she had sounded quite insistent. If that was the case, he'd have to ensure whoever she used did not intrude on his enjoyment.

He answered the phone and held it to his ear.

'Lip?' Sonja asked when he said nothing.

'Uh-huh.'

'Where are they?'

'Gone.'

'Gone where? You're telling me they slipped away?'

He said nothing. Creatures rustled in the trees and under-growth, startled by the phone's light and his gentle, low voice.

'They won't get far,' Sonja said. 'They're not going to run, not yet. Not with the woman and girl still with them. We'll have time to find them, and we'll have help.'

Lip closed his eyes and sighed.

'Lip? You're there?'

'I don't need help.'

'It doesn't sound like it. ' The old woman's voice lowered. In its softness, its gentleness, he could hear every shred of the inimical bitch she was. She hated him as much as she hated everyone else who wasn't family. 'Lip, Mary's really cut up about Frank. She needs you here.'

'Right.'

'Now, Lip.'

'I'll be there. Give me . . . an hour. I have to steal a vehicle.'

'No. Wait in the village square. I'll have you picked up.'

'By who?'

'It's up to them to tell you their names.'

'They're here already?'

'They're from Cardiff. It's a small world, Lip.' She disconnected.

Lip locked his phone and pocketed it, enjoying the absence of light once again. But the woods around him were aware of his presence, and he walked back to the ruined castle in a bubble of silence.

The village was busy with the evening crowd. Couples strolled hand in hand, families hurried to or from takeaways or restaurants. A pub on the square's corner spilled laughter and light across the pavement.

Three small dogs on leads started yapping at him, and he looked down at them as he walked by. Their owner glanced away from the cashpoint machine she was using and saw a tall man with a wild halo of unkempt greying hair, casually dressed, athletically built. She saw him pause and kneel, holding out his hand to the dogs. She might have seen the speckles of blood and the dark spines of thorns across his palm, but probably not. She would have seen the man tickling the dogs' necks, and then she would notice nothing more. Just a nice stranger who stroked her pets.

In the square, a car was already waiting. It was one of many, but Lip knew this one was for him. A man sat in the driver's seat with both hands on the wheel, and when he rounded the corner the man spoke to the car's interior. He was alone. But across the square outside the closed butcher's shop, another figure lifted a phone to its ear.

Lip raised a hand and waved. The two men looked at each other, surprised.

Fucking amateurs.

He sighed and walked around the square, keeping to the pavement until he reached the car. He climbed into the passenger seat and sat there, silent until the driver started speaking.

'Shut up and drive,' Lip said.

He leaned back and closed his eyes. His expression did not change, but everything felt a little lighter this evening, a little more alive. He could still smell the final breath of the last person he had killed, and he knew there was more to come.

Chapter Twenty

The Team

Isaac runs into their bedroom wearing the Buzz Lightyear outfit they bought for his birthday. He glances at his parents, sees that they're awake, grins, and runs back out. He wants to be an astronaut. What kid doesn't?

Rose breathed against the car window and drew in the condensation. A rocket, with flames blasting from its back end. It soon faded away.

She watched through the windscreen as Holt waited by the harbour. He could have been an old fisherman, short and thin, denuded by time and the sea. His straggly hair flickered in the breeze, and she saw him shrug the coat higher around his shoulders. Even at midnight the air was still warm, but the sea breathed cold.

The marina was filled with hundreds of yachts, ranging from small hire craft for cruising back and forth along the coast to a few big, multi-million pound vessels owned by businessmen or celebrities. Lights bobbed on some of the boats, dancing like fireflies in the night. Many more were dark. It would be a good place to hide, and Rose filed it away.

They'd taken his car, an old Renault that he'd bought with cash from a French farmer a few months before. It was rusted in places and scarred with dents and scratches. But he'd spent days installing a new engine, along with new suspension, brakes, exhaust system and electronics. It might look old and decrepit, but underneath it was almost as good as new. She'd left her own car in long-term parking at the Portsmouth ferry port. Holt had leaned casually against the bonnet as she reached underneath to retrieve her Glock, knife and grenade, which she'd hidden in the vehicle's chassis.

She wound down the window. His car stank of stale cigarette smoke. She'd rather have the cold than the smell. Once back inside he'd insist on the windows being raised before lighting up again.

Rose used her phone to check various online resources. All was quiet, even AndyMan's Twitter account. She'd told him to wait for her to suggest a place to meet, and she'd decide on that the closer she got to South Wales. The email address she'd passed on to him had no new mails. That was strange. By now she would have hoped for some clearer indication of what his problem entailed.

But she felt reasonably safe putting two and two together. AndyMan asked for her help three years ago in escaping the clutches of his criminal family. Close to where she had established him with a new life, a post office had been robbed and two people horribly murdered. Now he wanted her help once again. His family were back, and one of them committed murder in the same way as Monk, the killer of Holt's sister.

Her money was on the man calling himself Philip Beck. He'd been Andy's main reason for leaving his criminal family. Rose had tried to pry into his past but found only a blank.

That was unusual, and it troubled her, because only certain people could appear and disappear again like that.

She wasn't one for regrets, not any more. But perhaps if she'd persisted in her background research on Lip, she might have found something more.

Light played across the car and she glanced up. Holt was silhouetted in the beam of a boat's light as it drifted in towards the harbour wall. He raised one hand and the searchlight powered off.

Rose straightened in her seat. The weight of the Glock was a warm comfort in her belt. But Holt seemed unconcerned. One pull on his rollie and his face briefly flared a pale orange.

The boat nudged the harbour wall and Holt caught a thrown mooring line, dropping it around a metal pin. Shapes moved on the motor boat's deck. A bag was passed up, an envelope handed down. Then Holt strolled back to the Renault, dropping the bag into the back before relaxing into the driver's seat.

'Risky,' Rose said.

'I've used Billy before, few years ago. He's trustworthy.'

'With guns?'

'People.' Holt started the engine and they pulled off.

Rose looked back at the bag. It was wound tight, straps tied around the contents. It was not as big as she'd expected.

'Where'd you dump the rest?'

'Local river.'

'What have you got?'

'Glock, shotgun, ammo and my box of tricks.'

'Do you think that's enough?' There had been no more discussion about whether or not she was going with him. If he really hadn't wanted her along he would have insisted.

'If it's not, we're not doing things right,' he said. He glanced across at her, one eyebrow raised. 'You really smuggled a grenade next to your exhaust?'

'No one would think of looking there.'

'Right.'

'You're worried I might have blown myself up?'

'Worried you might have sunk a ferry while I was on it.'

Rose put the seat back down a little and adjusted position, trying to get comfortable. 'Bloody French cars,' she muttered.

Holt hit a pothole. The whole car juddered and pain ghosted through her hip. He'd probably aimed for it.

'Wine gum?' She offered a bag across to Holt.

'Really?'

'Yeah. Picked them up on the ferry. There are *some* things I miss from my homeland, you know.'

'Sweets that taste of wine?'

'They don't taste of wine. They taste of sugar.'

'So why are they called Wine Gums?'

'Because . . .' She held up the bag, tried to read it in the flash of passing street lamps. 'Because they taste nice and are addictive.'

'Should I consider weaning you off them?'

'You're worried because I'm eating sweets with "wine" in the name?'

'Slippery slope. Next thing you'll be cuddling a vodka bottle, soiling yourself and sleeping in random car parks.'

'Ah, the good old days.' She popped three sweets into her mouth and chewed. The rush of sugar almost lit up her vision.

'What else do you miss?' Holt asked. This was positively chatty for him, and Rose wanted to take advantage of his rare loquaciousness.

190

'Fish and chips. Pasties. Chocolate.'

'We have good chocolate in France.'

'Not Mars Bars. Not in many places, anyway. Mars Bars are the best. Although they were much bigger when I was a kid.'

'Roast beef?' Holt's English was almost perfect, but he exaggerated his French accent.

'I'm sorry?' She sounded mock-offended.

'You miss it?'

'Always preferred pork.'

'Uh. Pigs.'

Holt had taught her to shoot in Italy a few years before. Once, he'd used a pig's corpse for her to practise on.

'You can use every part of them, you know,' she said. 'Adam always said . . .'

She drifted off. She never talked about her dead family in front of Holt. Ever. Maybe coming back to Britain had jarred some of the defences that she'd built, the moat of denial that separated her from the awful landscape of her past.

'Said what?' Holt prompted, gently.

'That a pig was the definitive proof of the existence of God.'

'No,' he said. 'That's coffee. Talking of which?'

Rose reached down between her feet for the big flask still half-filled with coffee.

Adam fries bacon, slabs of bread laid out ready for Sunday morning sandwiches, the kettle boiling and cafetière ready for their first coffee of the day.

Rose poured and handed Holt the mug. She'd make do with the plastic cup. He insisted that coffee should never be drunk from any plastic or cardboard container.

191

In truth, she missed nothing of home. Nostalgia hurt. Memories of the past were always sheened with the smell of her husband's breath, the sound of her children's laughter or tears, the feel of his hand on her hip, their small hands in hers. The false memories she had built and subsequently tried to shed of their murders when she wasn't there to help.

No, she missed nothing.

'Maybe two hours to Wales,' Holt said.

'Land of my fathers.'

'Your father's what?'

She laughed softly. 'Doesn't matter.' Her last time in Wales had ended with a trail of blood and bodies. With Holt coming for his own reasons, she feared the same thing was about to happen.

At least this time she was properly prepared.

She closed her eyes, and headlights danced shadow and light across her eyelids.

With the windscreen gone the breeze was cold, even though the night air was still warm. Dom sat awkwardly in the back seat, Daisy huddled into him, his head held forward to try and avoid shuddering impacts from the headrest. Emma was worried that his injury really was worse than it looked.

Andy had promised that the mysterious Jane Smith would help them, but this concerned Emma as much as those bastards already chasing them. You didn't fight fire with fire, you fought it with water. Trouble was, she had no idea where the water might come from.

She had been driving in circles, keeping to the country lanes and avoiding any main roads, with no real aim in sight. It was close to midnight when she realised that they were nearing her place of work. The narrow lane twisted over a low hill, and from the brow she could see the college campus laid out down the slope.

'Somewhere safe,' she said.

'Security staff?' Andy asked.

'Only one old guy,' she said. 'Brian's usually asleep in the entrance lobby. My card will get us inside.'

She parked out of sight of the buildings and the main road, backing in between two big-wheeled bins beside the brick-walled bin store. Turning the engine off woke up Daisy, and she yawned and stretched her arms. Emma heard her daughter's sad sigh as sleep melted away, and awareness of what had happened closed in.

'Where are we, Mum?'

'The college. We'll go to my office, wait there for a bit.'

'Talk things through,' Andy said.

'I'm not sure you'll have any say in what we decide,' Emma said. 'Come on. Dom, you okay?'

'I'm good.'

'Daisy, help your dad.'

They crossed the car park, taking almost five minutes to reach the main building. Dom walked slowly, holding Daisy's hand. Andy walked slightly apart from them, the dark shape of the shotgun swinging from one hand. He'd told Emma that it was now empty, but she still hated the sight of it.

She'd been into work during the night several times before, usually when there was a student emergency on campus. She had always been expected, but though she wracked her brains she could not remember whether the parking areas, or paved areas around the buildings, had automatic lighting. It niggled her until they drew close. The lights remained off. She breathed a sigh of relief.

Her card worked for every door, and once inside her small office she drew the blinds before switching on the table lamp. The lighting was low but sufficient, and she didn't want anything brighter. They were already taking a big risk.

'Toilets are three doors along on the left,' she said.

'Anything to eat or drink?' Andy asked.

'Vending machines, just down the corridor. But let's just do one trip.'

'Right.' Andy stood by the door, looking embarrassed.

Emma pulled a drawer open on her desk and scooped up a handful of pound coins. She wanted to throw them at him. 'Water, chocolate, crisps,' she said. He nodded, and she was glad when he left.

Dom had settled into one of the comfortable chairs, easing himself down slowly, closing his eyes. Daisy sat on the seat beside him. They still held hands.

Emma sat on the coffee table and leaned close. 'How are you?' she asked.

'Feeling like a real idiot.'

'That goes without saying. I mean that.' She pointed at his bloodied face.

'Honestly, it feels like the worst hangover ever.'

'Daisy, top right drawer of my desk there should be some painkillers.' While Daisy went to search, Emma leaned in close to examine Dom's face. She moved slightly to the side so that her shadow did not dull her view.

It wasn't nice. The rock had hit the right side of his face, cutting his nose, puffing his eye, bruising and grazing his cheek. His eye wasn't completely shut, and the eyeball appeared undamaged. Most of the blood had come from a gash in his lower eyelid and his mashed nose. Its flow had ceased, but his face was a mask of dried blood.

'Here, Dad,' Daisy said. She dropped two tablets into his hand and he nodded his thanks, dry-swallowing.

'You need stitches,' Emma said.

'I need kicking.'

She sat back and sighed. She didn't realise how tired she was. Every instinct was to be raging at Dom now that they'd reached somewhere relatively safe. But letting rip her anger wouldn't help their predicament at all, and making a noise would be foolish. Besides, he was hurt. He knew what he'd done was stupid, and now he was paying the price.

She only hoped it was the most any of them had to pay.

'We'll be fine,' she said.

'Em, I've been thinking. We should call the law. It's not about me and prison, never should have been. It's about you and Daisy. That's *all* it's about. You have to be safe, and if something happened . . . if anything . . .' He turned away, a bloody tear leaking from his damaged eye.

'Just keep still and quiet,' she said. 'Let the painkillers take effect. I've been doing some thinking too, and I'm afraid.'

''Course you are.'

'No. I'm afraid that if we call the police now, that won't be the end of it. They arrest you and Andy. Question you, put you on trial, you both go to jail. Maybe I go as well, for aiding and abetting a bank robber.'

'Mum, it was a post office,' Daisy said, rolling her eyes.

'Of course it was. So, you two go to jail. Maybe me too, leaving Daisy with who? My father?'

'God forbid.'

'Right. And what about Andy's family?'

'We tell the police.'

'And what? They catch them?'

Dom frowned, wincing as the cut beneath his eye pouted.

'I get it,' Daisy said. 'Mum's right. We don't know where they are, and if they're as bad as Andy says, you know, always doing stuff like this, they'll be hiding.'

'They're *always* hiding,' Emma said. 'That's how they live. They'll just melt away.'

'For a while,' Dom said, and she saw realisation dawn. She hated how it made him look, because she saw her own terror in his eyes. He glanced at Daisy.

'They're inhuman,' Emma said. 'What they did to that postmistress, her granddaughter. Horrible.'

Daisy was quiet. She looked back and forth between them, eyes wide and desperate as if her parents were already being dragged away from her.

'I'm only ten and eleven months,' she said. 'I know what'll happen to me. Foster home, or adopted, or something. I don't want to lose either of you. We're a team, right, Dad? That's what you always tell me.'

'We're a team,' he said, nodding through the pain. He held out his hands. Daisy took one and Emma took the other, squeezing tight.

'We've got to see what this Jane Smith woman suggests,' Emma said. 'She might have an idea. A plan that doesn't just involve running.'

'Yeah.'

'And Dom . . .' She waited until he looked her in the eye, focussed, all his attention on her. 'Andy doesn't factor in our future. We're what matters. Daisy, me, you. Our team. You understand?'

'Way ahead of you there, babe,' he said.

'Where is he?' Daisy said. 'I'm starving.'

Emma leaned in and kissed Dom, then gave Daisy a hug. 'Check in my desk where you found the painkillers. Should be some wet wipes in there. Give your dad's face a wash, but be gentle.'

'Wet wipes are for babies' bums!'

'Well, your dad is an arse.'

Daisy giggled while she searched, and Emma went to the door, opened it carefully, and peered out into the dark corridor. She couldn't see much. On the ceiling, two smoke alarms emitted very faint glows that gave the corridor a bluish haze. It was just enough by which to see, and she left her door ajar so that some of the lamplight spilled out.

'Andy?' she whispered. She headed along the corridor, and at the first junction she peered around at the bank of vending machines further along. Andy stood there, the glow of his mobile phone lighting his face. He looked up and caught her eye.

'Jane Smith,' he said. He pocketed the phone and scooped chocolate bars and crisps from the vending machine's well. 'Give me a hand?' He nudged at the plastic bottles and cans lined at his feet.

Emma helped him carry the food and drinks back to the office. Their footsteps sounded too loud in the darkness, the rustle of crisp bags and tink of tin cans echoing along corridors more used to bustle and chatter. It was a strange, haunted place at night.

'Well?' she asked as they entered her office.

'She'll be here soon, couple of hours,' Andy said. He smiled as he popped the ring on a can of Coke. 'Don't worry, Em. You'll like Jane Smith. She's hard too.'

Emma turned her back on him and sat on the coffee table again. As Daisy dabbed dried blood from Dom's face, Emma ate a bar of chocolate, trying to forget that Andy was even there.

Chapter Twenty-One

Hired Help

'You're kidding.'

'Kidding how?' Sonja asked. She was sitting on the car bonnet, smoking, wrapped in a heavy ski jacket. She always appeared to feel the cold, even on nights like this.

Lip nodded at the two men who'd brought him here. Well, one man and a kid. He can't have been more than twenty. With youth came attitude, and he was the one to step forward, chin jutting.

'Roman, don't be a prick,' Sonja said. 'He'd have you for breakfast.'

'Not hungry,' Lip said. 'Where's Mary?'

'Here.' She emerged from the shadows.

They were parked beside an old stone barn, walls standing strong but roof holed and rotted away. The road leading past the barn was narrow and rough, rarely used, but even so they'd parked out of sight. Starlight silvered the rolling landscape beyond, a gentle hillside sloping down into a wide valley. A few lights sparked here and there, distant and flickering in the heat. All was quiet.

'Okay?' Lip asked.

'No,' she said.

She wore shorts and a vest top, and its left strap was torn and speckled with dried blood. Her shoulder and upper arm were bandaged. But he knew it wasn't the pain dealt by shotgun pellets that was upsetting her. He saw no self-pity in her eyes, only rage. They glimmered. But he had never seen Mary cry, and she did not break that habit now.

She stood close and leaned against him, and Lip held her around the waist. She was hot and tough, coiled like a wild animal. To him, she always felt like violence ready to explode. He guessed that was why he'd stayed with her far longer than he'd ever intended.

'So they got away from you?' the other hired help asked. After ten minutes in their souped-up Subaru – about as inconspicuous as a hard-on in a nudist colony – Lip already knew far more about this streak of piss than he wanted. His name was Callum, he was originally from Edinburgh, he was thirty-four and claimed to have murdered four men, the first when he was seventeen. His wife killed herself seven years ago when he was inside for aggravated assault. They'd had a kid together when they were in their twenties, but she'd been removed by social services. He had no interest in tracking her down. He loved Scotland, hated England, and liked hurting people for money. He didn't drink or smoke, but he enjoyed recreational drugs.

He'd worked with Sonja several times before, the last time five years ago when the Scott gang turned over a security van in Melton Mowbray. He enjoyed heavy metal, but not American music. He liked raw burgers. Blah blah. Lip had tried to shut out the continuous chatter but it had filtered through, subliminal bullshit.

'So you're a murdering child-abusing junkie who can't keep his mouth shut,' Lip had said, the only words he spoke during that ten minute journey. He hadn't even opened his eyes. Callum had fumed in the driver's seat, but nothing had happened.

'They got away from me,' Lip confirmed, speaking slowly. He stared Callum down. It was easy. He'd never met anyone who could meet his gaze for long.

'They'll have gone to ground,' Sonja says. 'But they'll still be close. Andy won't run, not yet. He hit the post office because he knew we were looking at it. Somehow.'

'Fucking weasel,' Mary said.

'He did this?' Lip asked, touching her shoulder. She flinched.

'Who else?' she said.

'Not a very good shot,' Lip said.

'Only broke the skin in a couple of places. He'll regret missing.'

'So how did he know?' Lip asked. 'He's been gone three years. Strange that he pops up now.'

'Someone fucked up,' Sonja said. 'Sent an email, did a web search, something like that.' She looked at Mary. Then Lip. She grunted. 'Probably Frank. Never the brightest flower in the bunch, bless him.'

They were silent for a while. Sonja smoked, lighting a new cigarette with the butt of the old. She might have been in her seventies but she was still sharp and strong, and Lip held a grudging respect for her. In some regards, at least. She knew how to run what they did, keeping them below the radar. She even thought she was in charge. But Sonja was no fool, and he knew that she understood his place with them. He was there because it suited him. Mary was a nice distraction, but little more than that. He's shown them the

200

landscape of his true desires, mostly in isolated incidents since just before Andy had fled.

At the post office he had let that landscape erupt, bloom, and reveal itself in its full glory.

By then, he knew that Mary, Frank and Sonja would barely blink. He had been right. Mary especially had revelled in the act, wielding the brick with glee.

'So why these two?' he asked.

'I've worked with Cal and Roman before,' Sonja said. 'They enjoy what we have to do. They're good at it, and trustworthy.'

'And cheap,' Roman said. Lip guessed he was Greek, though his English was good. He must have been living in the UK for some time. They came as a double act, and that worried him already. He saw no talent in them, little style or pride, only bluff and bluster. The fact that he'd spotted them in seconds in the town square only displayed their carelessness.

'Cheap,' Lip said, nodding slowly.

'Lip, this is what's happening,' Sonja said. 'Just until we get Andy. He can't be left now, not after what he's done. You know that.'

'He's really your son?' Cal asked. His smile was ugly.

'He's really my son.' Sonja went to draw on her cigarette, looked at it, flicked it away with a sigh. 'Fruit of my loins.'

'Nice family dynamic,' Roman said. Cal nudged him, but the Scot was still grinning.

'We should be away from here,' Mary said. That surprised Lip. He thought she'd be burning to avenge Frank. He'd never liked the big man, thought him stupid and aimless, but Mary had a soft spot for him.

'We will be soon,' Sonja said. 'Just as soon as my Andy's dead.'

'And the others,' Lip said. Even thinking of them excited him. The man, his face darkened by the rock Lip had heaved. The girl, all limbs and youth. The woman. She was strong; he had almost smelled the motherly instinct seeping from her as he'd chased them through the streets. They had become a challenge. He had never backed down from a challenge.

'So what's the plan?' Cal asked. Eager to go, Lip saw. Itching to move. No caution, only impulsiveness and hunger for the hunt. He was probably the stupidest of the two. Roman was quieter, and that meant he saw more, didn't cloud his judgement with unnecessary chatter. They made a strange team. Maybe they were lovers.

'I can find out where they are,' Lip said. He stared at Sonja, and it was a full ten seconds until she glanced away.

'Okay,' she said. 'Mary, you stay with me. We'll scan the police channels, try and pick up any sign of them. If they keep driving around in a car like that, they'll soon be reported. You two, walk the streets.'

'Walk?' Cal asked.

'Stay in the town. Leave the car, it's a fucking eyesore. Keep an eye on their house, just in case they're stupid enough to come back. Check in with me every thirty minutes.'

'All our weapons are in the car.'

'Idiots,' Lip muttered. They heard; Cal stared at him. He didn't care.

'Come here,' Mary said. She grabbed his hand and pulled him after her, heading around the parked car and towards the darkness inside the dilapidated barn. They passed under the heavy lintel and inside. Creatures scurried away, rustling through the brambles and undergrowth clogging the building's interior. Mary pulled out her phone and used it to guide their way.

Lip let her lead him. But he was eager to go, keen to pursue what he knew was a remote chance at best. Because it held the promise of pleasure. His life consisted of blank periods filled with the white noise of existence, when mundanity ruled and he did little more than exist. Wake, eat, move through the day, drink, fuck, sleep, repeat. But sometimes, opportunity called and he truly lived. At the post office he had come alive, and he was hungry for what the immediate future might bring.

Mary stopped, turned around and embraced him. She rested her head on his shoulder, squeezing tight.

'I can't believe Frank's gone,' she said.

'I can't believe you both let Andy get the better of you.'

She pulled away. In moonlight, he saw the true landscape of grief on her face and realised why she'd brought him here. She didn't want to be seen as weak.

'You're not at all sad about Frank, are you?' she asked.

'I'm crying on the inside.'

'How would I ever know? You wear a mask. You're face-less. You don't even have a come-face. What guy doesn't have a come-face? If I didn't like it on my belly, I'd never even know when you were done.'

He tried to care, tried to figure out how he could say something to please her so they could be on their way. But he was a man of few words, and those he did share were rarely false. Life was as he wanted it; he saw no need to lie.

'Jesus, Lip.'

'I need to go,' he said. 'Time's ticking. Sonja might be wrong, they might be running.'

'You don't believe that.'

Lip shrugged.

'Jesus.'

He said no more. Mary pushed past him and walked back to Sonja and the hired help. Lip remained there for a while, looking up at the stars through holes in the roof. He really didn't care about Frank, but he did welcome the consequences of his death. The fury and grief felt by Sonja and Mary.

The need to deal more death in return.

It sounded like they were screwing. Animal grunting sounds, small cries from her, the rhythmic creaking of bed springs. It would have been better if they were asleep, but Lip didn't really care. At least their mutual rutting sounds covered any creaking stairs or rustle of clothing as he climbed the staircase towards them.

The family's car was still in the driveway. He'd taken a cursory look inside, then circled around to the rear of the house once again. He'd already crossed that garden once, only several hours before. It had taken him two minutes to lift one of the patio doors out of its track and snip its locking mechanism. No dogs barked. No lights flickered on.

On his way through the dark house he had looked for weapons. He carried what he had chosen in his right hand.

He paused on the landing and listened to the sound of flesh on flesh, the man's whispering, urgent and sibilant, too quiet to make out. The woman's frequent cries, high and sharp. Bed springs creaked, and a heavier knocking sound matched their rhythm.

Lip was not at all aroused by the sounds of sex, nor the anticipation of seeing these strangers coupling. His excitement came from the promise of violence.

He slipped into the room and quickly assessed the situation. The bed was against the left wall, offering him a side view of the couple. She was face down, looking away from the door. He was hunched over her, sheet still covering his rump.

Lip stood close to the bed and held the sheet, whipping it smartly away.

They continued for a while, lost in what they were doing, or perhaps both thinking the other one had pulled the sheet aside. It was hot, after all. The room was heavy with musty sweat.

Lip hefted the object in his hand, then swung it hard at the man's head. The man grunted and fell to the side. The woman looked at him, turning on her side, perhaps thinking he had finished or wanted to change position.

Lip used their momentary confusion to walk around the end of the bed and strike the man again. The hardback book he'd chosen was heavy and thick, and after several impacts he felt the front cover tear away. The man grunted with each strike, so shocked that he didn't even bring his hands up to protect his face or head.

Lip stepped back, book raised ready to strike again.

'Who are you?' the woman shrieked. One hand sought the sheet to cover herself, but it was on the floor. She sat up against the headboard, knees drawn up and one arm across her breasts. Lip didn't care. He wasn't looking at her.

'I need to know where Emma and her family are.'

'Emma? What? Who are you?'

'What's your name?' Lip asked.

The woman shook her head.

Lip struck the man again, aiming for his crotch this time with the edge of the heavy book. The man gasped, curled into a ball, and it took a few seconds for him to start groaning again. Strange, how ecstasy and agony could sound so similar.

The room stank of sex and alcohol, fear and sweat. For Lip, his focus was the moment, every sense absorbing the here and now. Beyond this darkened room where frightened shadows writhed there was nothing. Outside the walls, reality had faded away. The book was a solid thing, slick with sweat or blood. Every breath, every heartbeat, fed him.

'Mandy,' the woman said.

'Mandy. I need to know where Emma and her family are. Your friend Emma was here earlier with her daughter. I want to speak with them.'

'I don't . . . I came home and . . .'

Lip went at the man again. Head, shoulders, crotch, stomach, the book thudded and slapped down. This time, the man made some effort to protect himself. He tried to kneel, and Lip smacked the book into his throat. He threw a punch, and Lip swung the book up and connected with his wrist, hearing the delicate crack.

'Please!' Mandy said.

'Please what?' Lip's voice was soft. He never got out of breath. He was too much in control for that.

'Please, stop,' she said.

'Then tell me. If you don't know where they are, tell me where they might be. If not home, where would they go? Somewhere safe. Somewhere close where they might spend the night if they can't stay at home.'

'Why can't they stay at home? What's happening?'

'I'm asking the questions,' Lip said. He hefted the book. The cover had fallen off, and as he held it up the pages slumped open, making a gentle whisper as they fanned. He turned it towards the weak starlight streaming through open curtains, squinting. '*Lord of the Rings.* Good book.'

'I . . . haven't read it.'

Lip considered this for a moment and decided it didn't matter.

'Please don't hurt Paul any more.'

'If you don't start telling me what I need, I'll beat his brains out with this book you haven't read.'

The woman, Mandy, didn't answer.

'Last chance,' Lip said. He lifted the book. The man was curled on the edge of the bed, hands drawn up to cover his head.

'Maybe . . . her parents'? They live in Nottingham, I think.'

'Closer,' Lip said. 'Like I said, somewhere nearby.'

'Um . . .'

He hit the man. Hard. He could smell blood. Page edges were sharp, the corners of the remaining back cover mean.

'I don't know!' Mandy said, voice distorted by tears. 'I really don't, I don't understand why you're here or what's happening, we haven't done anything, I don't know—'

Lip's phone rang. He held up his free hand until the woman stopped talking, then pulled the phone from his pocket and looked at the screen. Sonja.

He sighed, then connected. He said nothing.

'Lip, I know where they might be. At least I have three options, and between us we can cover them.'

The man crawled up the bed and Mandy held him. He bled onto her.

'You're sure?' Lip asked.

'Yes.'

'How do you know?'

'New information,' Sonja said. 'You get anything?'

'No,' Lip said. He stared at the pale shapes on the bed, wretched creatures whimpering instead of roaring, submitting instead of fighting. His focus had been broken. The outside world had intruded. 'I'm just picking up my car.' He let the book slip from his hand.

'Meet us in the town's main car park. You know it?'

'Yes. I'll be there in five minutes.' He disconnected before Sonja could say anything else and pocketed the phone.

Mandy and the man were making sounds. He recognised these noises because he had heard them so many times before. Similar to the involuntary sounds they had made whilst fucking, these were instinctive, animal whimpers of pain and fear, groans or subtle cries of dreadful anticipation as they balanced between this moment and whatever might come next.

But for Lip, the moment was broken. He looked down at the book on the floor, little more than a shadow in the poor light. Touched it with his boot, moved it across the carpet. Gone from his hand, it no longer resembled a weapon.

'I'm going,' he said. He turned for the door and heard the sound of sudden movement on the bed.

The man rested one knee on the bed, his other foot on the floor. Coming for him. He was shaking. His face glimmered, blood black in moonlight.

Lip pinned him in place with his stare.

'If you contact your friend, I'll come back. I'll do you first.' He pointed at the man. Then at Mandy. 'After him, you. Slowly.'

They probably wanted to say more, beg, assure him of their silence. But Lip left them, walking calmly downstairs and exiting through the removed patio door.

His Jeep was still parked across the street on the opposite pavement. As he climbed inside and started the engine, he glanced up at the woman's house. The lights remained off. He had left darkness in their lives. His expression did not change, but inside he allowed himself a small smile.

Chapter Twenty-Two

Night Watch

Dom swallowed a couple more painkillers. It felt like they were working. Either that or he was becoming used to the discomfort, and Daisy cleaning his face had eased the pain somewhat. He wasn't sure whether or not his nose was broken, but his head throbbed, a pulsing discomfort behind his eyes. He could still see from both eyes, though the right was puffy and swollen half-shut.

None of this mattered. Pain would go away, and a broken nose would heal. All that mattered was his family. He had to concentrate on the present and the future, not the past he had messed up so comprehensively. Blame and shame could come later.

Daisy sat on the comfortable chair beside him, nibbling on another bar of chocolate. She was very quiet, but alert, eyes wide and startled. Emma was behind her desk with her feet up. She looked at Dom without expression, seeing something more distant. They had opened the blinds to allow moon- and starlight inside, but other than that there were no lights. Andy had insisted they turn off the lamp. Dom only knew Emma was awake because of the faint glimmer of her eyes.

Andy stood close to the door. They'd left it ajar, and he was keeping watch.

None of them had spoken for ten minutes. They were waiting for Jane Smith, who Andy said would be with them soon. What happened then, Dom had no idea.

He remembered the sickening impact of Frank falling from the windmill. The weight of the rock parting the smashed windscreen and impacting his face. Daisy's expression when she saw her dad bloodied and in pain.

'I need to pee,' Daisy said.

Dom took a deep breath and stood, groaning as his head thumped, but determined to move on his own. It wasn't as bad as he'd feared. No dizziness, and the pain was no worse than a monster hangover. Mind over matter.

'I'll go with you,' he said.

'I'll go,' Emma said. 'I need one too.'

'You sure?' Dom wanted to do something, to act in defence of his family. He'd been sitting down nursing his wounds for too long, allowing Daisy to clean his face and Emma to feed him painkillers. Perhaps it was nothing more than misplaced ego, but he wanted to take charge.

Emma was already up and heading for the door. Andy stepped aside. She didn't even look at him.

'We'll have to be quiet,' she said to Daisy. 'Brian isn't always sleeping on his shift. We'll hear him if he's doing the rounds, he breathes like an asthmatic buffalo.'

Daisy did an impression, but did not laugh.

'Where's the toilet?' Dom asked.

'Past the vending machines. We won't be long.'

He grabbed her hand, and they shared a squeeze.

'Dad, we're fine,' Daisy said. 'I know karate.'

'Be quick,' he said. Emma and Daisy both looked at him,

a moment paused. It was the phrase they used to urge Jazz out of the house to pee.

Andy checked both ways along the corridor, then stood aside to let them pass.

'*Any* sign of something wrong, call my phone.'

Emma looked at Dom, eyebrow raised.

'Mine broke,' he said.

Emma nodded, and she and Daisy left. Andy pushed the door to behind them, leaving an inch gap. He leaned against the wall and watched them go.

'How're you feeling?' he asked without looking at Dom.

'Like I was hit in the face with a brick.' Dom picked up a bar of chocolate from Emma's desk. It hurt to bite and chew, but it tasted good. 'Where's the money?'

'What? Seriously?'

'You brought a bag full of mouldy clothes to give to your family. I can't believe you left the cash where it was.'

'You're really concerned about your share, now?' Andy asked.

Dom took a step towards him. Andy was bigger and stronger and, as was becoming clear, far more used to dealing and witnessing violence. But still he tensed against the wall.

'I don't give a fuck about share,' Dom said. 'But if your Jane Smith wants paying, I need to know we can afford her.'

'Sure, Dom,' Andy said. 'I'm not that bad. I tucked it in the spare wheel well of your car when I was putting the bag in the boot.'

'We can't use our car again.'

'Already thought about that. I saw a white van out front, maybe it belongs to the security guard. If we can't get the keys I can hot wire it.'

'Then we're driving around in a stolen vehicle.'

'What else do you suggest?'

'Where's your car?'

'Abergavenny.'

'Maybe we should drive the van there when the time comes, take your car. Unless they know where you live.'

'They won't,' Andy said. He sounded confident.

'Can't risk it. Park in Waitrose car park, walk through the woods above the new housing estate, get to your place that way. We can suss out if they're watching, then get in across your apartment block's back garden.'

'Sounds like a plan.'

Dom sat down again. He didn't like not having Emma and Daisy here with him. He should have gone with them.

'I don't know you at all,' Dom said. He looked at the man by the door, this person who pretended to be his friend, and in the darkness Andy could have been anyone, thinking anything. A shadow was an accurate representation of who and what he was.

'You know me better than anyone has for years,' Andy said.

'Maybe that doesn't say much,' Dom said. 'You're more like them than you are like me.'

'It's peace and quiet I wanted,' Andy said. 'I intended to be a loner, comfortable in my own company. And the company of an occasional woman. But we met and got on well, and became closer than I wanted to allow. That's the truth.'

'You killed your cousin today. You don't seem cut up about it.'

'He tried to kill us, Dom. When we were there to put things right—'

212

'You pulled a gun to try and put things right?'

'Yeah. Well. We never got that far.'

'Where did you even get it?'

'There are places, if you know where to look.'

'So all these trips you take, the mountain climbing, parachute jumping. That time last year you went for three weeks to climb Kilimanjaro. All those times, were you off around the country robbing places?' Dom didn't really believe that. He couldn't, because that would mean he'd been even more of a fool than he feared. But equally, he had no idea how much of the Andy he thought he knew was still there. Maybe he was no more real than a shadow-man.

'No, they were all genuine. I'll admit maybe they're attempts to get the adrenalin flowing. I left my family with every intention of going straight, living a normal life. I paid Jane Smith to help me do that. But when I figured out they were going to hit the post office . . .' The shadow moved. A shrug.

'Temptation was too great,' Dom said.

'Yeah.'

'So what did Lip do that made you leave?'

Andy turned to look at him. Something happened with the light. Maybe clouds cleared from the sun, because his face was a pale oval, stern and almost inhuman.

'He's a monster,' Andy said. 'Soon after he and Mary hooked up, Sonja brought him into the fold. I was against that from the start. He was a stranger, but I guess Sonja saw a like mind.'

'You call your mother by her name?'

'The word mother implies love. Anyway, we were planning on turning over a holiday park in Cumbria. You know, caravans, tents, clubhouse. The amount of cash that passes through those places in one weekend, you wouldn't believe. Lip was invited along for the ride and he accepted. Couldn't tell if he was excited or confident. You can't tell anything with him, most expressionless bastard I've ever met.' Andy trailed off, looking along the corridor again. He glanced at his phone.

'So what happened?' Dom prompted.

'Plan worked well,' Andy said. 'We broke in at night, raided the office, got the safe into our van without anyone noticing. It was all going smoothly. Then a cleaner appeared from out of nowhere, wheeled bucket and mop, the full works. She clocked us, turned around, tried to walk away.'

'She saw your faces?'

'No. We wore masks. But before anyone could speak, Lip had shoved her through a door into a store room.' Andy sighed heavily. If he was faking his unease at these memories he was a great actor. 'There was no call for what he did. None at all. She'd almost shrugged when she saw us; she wasn't worried about us robbing the place. She'd probably still get paid. She was casual about walking away, as if it was the most normal . . .'

Andy checked his phone again. The brief flare of the screen lit his features. Stern, grim.

'Lip picked up the dropped mop, smacked her around the head, and shoved the handle end into her eye. I heard the pop. The squelch. It was . . . horrible. I've never heard anything like it before or since. He leaned on it, all his weight, pushed it down into her brain. She died pretty quickly, I guess. She was the first person I ever saw die. After that—'

Someone screamed.

Dom leapt up, tugged the door open and pushed past a surprised Andy. Maybe telling the story had taken Andy from the moment, stolen his alertness. Dom was ahead of him along the hallway, moving as quickly and quietly as he could.

Maybe I imagined it, he thought. *My head's taken a knock, maybe my skull is fractured after all—*

Another short scream, followed by a shout from Emma. 'Leave her alone!'

'Where is he?' A man's voice, accented, perhaps Scottish.

'Don't hurt her, don't hurt—'

'Where is he?'

'I don't know!'

Dom reached the corner and swung around, dashing past vending machines towards a half-open door on the left. Someone had turned the bathroom light on. He knew Emma would not have done that. He could hear footsteps behind him, and Andy hissing something at him, but he couldn't hear the words, and he'd take no notice anyway. Every moment felt like an eternity, each breath forever. So much could happen in an instant.

Lip picked up the dropped mop and shoved the handle end into her eye.

'Where is he, where is he, where is he?'

'Please, my office, I'll take you just don't—'

Dom hit the door at a run.

In the split second he had to observe, he understood what was going on, and instinct took over.

Emma was standing with her back against a row of three sinks on the left, hands held out beseechingly. To the right, past a spine wall built to hide the bathroom interior from outside, was Daisy. A man was holding her, one arm around

215

her waist, the other pressing a gun barrel into her cheek. They had their backs to a line of five toilet cubicles.

Everything became clear in Dom's mind, a series of thoughts that probably lasted less than a second but which flowed with a startling clarity.

I might slip on the floor.

He has a gun.

If I stop, I lose the surprise.

If I run, he might pull the trigger.

Is this Lip?

That last thought almost hobbled him. But Dom was driven by a momentum both physical and mental, a pure, unadulterated fury at what this man was doing to his daughter.

He took one more long step and then jumped.

Daisy grasped the man's arm, levered it away, and dropped.

The gun fired. It was incredibly loud in the large tiled room, but Dom barely noticed.

His right hand caught the man's collar, his left grasped his wrist and flung it back, lifting the gun high as the second shot blasted out. A mirror smashed. His momentum drove the man back against a cubicle door. It swung open and they fell inside, Dom kicking with his legs to drive the man down before him. The pan struck the stranger in the back and his eyes widened in surprise and pain. But they were also hard and cold, and his sneering grin convinced Dom that this was not someone who gave in easily.

The man's head snapped forward and up, connecting squarely with Dom's nose. Pain roared. A flare was ignited behind his eyes. But instinct kept him there, and he brought up his right knee, driving it hard between the man's legs.

He cried out, then groaned.

Behind him, Dom heard shouting and the sounds of a

struggle – raised voices, an impact, a pained cry. But he could not risk turning around. Blood was flowing from his nose, and he pushed forward and up, snorting and splashing blood into the man's face and eyes.

The gun fired again, so close to his ear that it felt like a solid punch. The man thrashed and struggled, writhing so much that he wriggled out from beneath Dom and started sliding upright against the cubicle wall.

Dom refused to let go of his gun hand, rising with him, half-blinded by pain and blood.

The man head-butted him again. He laughed. 'Fucker. Like that, do ya?' *Glasgow kiss*, Dom thought, and even through the pain and confusion he managed a laugh. The man's left hand rooted between them, swung free again, and Dom heard Daisy shout, 'Dad!'

If he'd turned to look at Daisy, he might have died. But he recognised the urgent warning in his daughter's voice. Left hand still clasping the Scot's gun hand, Dom released his collar and fell against him, crushing him against the cubicle wall and swinging his right hand down, blocking the knife blow that might otherwise have gutted him.

The man grunted, swung his hand back for another stab, and Dom bit into his face. He clamped his teeth as hard as he could, feeding off the image of the man holding Daisy with a gun to her head, and the knowledge that he had already pulled the trigger.

The man squealed. Dom tasted sour skin and blood, and felt the knotted hardness of gristle.

Pain sliced across Dom's right arm. Teeth still clamped, he ripped his head to the side. He still had something in his mouth. The man screamed, Dom spat, and then something hard struck him across the face.

Stars bloomed, darkness loomed, as he slid against the cubicle wall.

'Dad, no!' Daisy shouted.

I let him go, Dom thought. *I had him and I let him go, and now Daisy and Emma are just standing there and—*

He lashed out with both hands. His left hand struck cool metal which instantly flared hot as the man fired the gun again. The porcelain toilet bowl shattered, shards scattering like ice rain. Dom drove up with his head lowered and felt it connect squarely with the man's face, forcing him back against the wall.

He heard a metallic *clunk!* as the gun dropped to the floor. Risking a glance to the right he saw Emma and Daisy crouched against the sinks, watching him, glancing to their right, back again. There was no sign of Andy, but shadows fought beyond the open bathroom door.

The man punched him in the gut.

Dom gasped, winded, and saw the cruel serrated blade swinging in for his stomach. He slammed his arm down and the blade kissed across his forearm, parting skin and flesh.

They grappled. Dom turned sideways and pressed against the man, using both hands now to grasp at his knife hand. His hands were slick with blood. The man drove a fist into his back, a shockingly painful impact against his kidneys, again and again.

Three rapid gunshots came from elsewhere, beyond the bathroom.

Andy! Dom thought, and he slipped. Blood or water, he didn't know, but his feet went from under him and he half-fell, hanging onto his enemy and pulling him down.

The man swung the knife around as he came. Face a mask of blood, nose torn and tattered, Dom had never been so afraid of anyone in his life.

He was ready to shoot my daughter, he thought, and past the man's bloody visage, past the arcing knife, he saw his wife appear in the cubicle doorway, the dropped gun held out in both hands.

Dom caught the man's wrist as the knife's blade was a hand's width from his face. He winced, pushed up as hard as he could, while the man lifted himself ready to drop all his weight through his left arm.

Emma's hands were shaking.

Dom felt around and found a chunk of the shattered toilet pan. He grasped it and slammed it into the side of the man's head, twice, three times. It was only as he struck the fourth time that he realised it was more of a shard than a chunk.

The man's right eye flooded red. He looked surprised, and then confused. His strength seemed to bleed away as blood flowed from the puncture wounds in his temple.

Dom heaved him aside and stood shakily. Emma helped him up, still clasping the gun in her left hand, lowered now and aimed towards the man.

He was moving slowly in the cubicle, legs pushing through blood and water, right hand touching the ruined mess at the side of his head. His hair was clotted and wet, and blood and a clearer fluid pulsed from the wound. His mouth opened and closed, but only a quiet clicking noise emerged.

'Dad!' Daisy said, and she ran to him, embraced him, turning him away from the sight of the man he might have just killed and smothering his bloody face with kisses.

A shape shadowed the bathroom doorway. Emma span around and raised the gun, but Andy held up his hands. He also carried a pistol. He looked from Emma, to Dom and Daisy, then down at the man's feet protruding from the toilet cubicle.

Dom could not read his expression.

'What happened?' Dom asked. 'Is this Lip?'

Andy looked past him. 'No. There were two of them. I don't know them, Sonja must have called in freelancers. You okay?'

Dom nodded, then actually smiled at the surreality of the moment. No, he wasn't okay. He glanced back and the man had mostly stopped moving, only his mouth opening and closing, that clicking sound quieter and quieter. No, he wasn't okay at all.

'They killed the security guy,' Andy said.

'Brian?' Emma asked, one hand going to her mouth.

'Cut his throat. I grappled with the other guy, he dropped his gun, ran.'

'We heard shots,' Dom said.

'I missed. Chased, lost him, then came back, I thought I might be able to . . .' He nodded past Dom.

'What, help?'

They stood silently for a moment, none of them knowing what to say. Dom felt sick. But he thought it was from the pain more than shock of what he had done. His right forearm was bleeding badly and the wound looked horrific.

He looked down at the dying man and felt nothing.

'I couldn't let him . . .' he said.

'You saved Daisy,' Emma whispered into his ear, and she gently touched his cheek and turned his face to hers. 'You were brave.'

In the stink of blood, consumed by pain, slick with sweat, those words meant the world.

They left the bathroom with Emma on one side of him and Daisy on the other. Daisy was shaking as if cold, though her skin felt hot. He was worried for her; she had seen everything. But now was not the time.

Andy went ahead. He hefted the gun he'd taken from the other man, shoved the one Emma gave him into his pocket. There was no discussion, no plan. Simply an unspoken urgency to leave as quickly as possible.

Andy did not have to hot-wire Brian's white van. He simply took the keys from the dead man's pocket.

'I killed a man,' Dom said. He was in the back of the small van on a rough wooden bench, Emma beside him, Daisy huddled into his other side. Contact was very important to him right then. He hoped all his family felt the same way. Emma clasped a sock around the wound in his arm. It needed stitching.

Andy drove, alone in the front. He carried injuries but did not mention them.

'You stabbed him with a toilet,' Daisy said.

Emma snorted laughter. She shook next to him, shoulders moving. She laughed out loud, and then Dom joined in. Daisy looked back in surprise, also smiling.

We need this, Dom thought. Despite his wounds and how much they hurt, despite the cold, stark truth of what he had done, he found himself laughing. He knew it was a form of hysteria, loss of control, but that did nothing to quieten them or lessen the need.

Also in the van's dark interior was the plastic bag they'd retrieved from Dom's wrecked car. Andy had stood guard, all of them nervous that the other attacker would be hiding in the darkness with another weapon. But they'd escaped undisturbed. Inside the bag were wads of money. He hadn't even wanted to look at it. Its allure was long gone. Now it was purely a way to help them out of this mess.

But nothing could ever be the same again. Behind the laughter his thoughts were serious and leaden. He hugged

221

Daisy tight, wondering how her young mind could process what she had seen and how much damage had already been done. She was quiet and seemed in control. Shouldn't she be crying? Shouldn't she be more afraid? Emma leaned into him, her own laughter fresh in his ear, her breath an endless kiss.

Dom had always sworn to Emma that he would be able to kill someone threatening his family. She had always agreed that she could, too. It was never a heavy conversation, more of a matter-of-fact statement from both of them. It almost went without saying.

But the truth could never be so simple. He had started the chain of events leading to this. He was responsible, and guilty.

Their manic laughter soon subsided, and Andy steered them onto the main road leading towards Abergavenny. The phone in his lap lit up and chimed, and he glanced at the screen.

'She's an hour away,' he said. 'But I don't think we should wait for her. We need to keep moving. I'll arrange somewhere to meet.'

None of them replied. *Maybe Jane Smith is already too late*, Dom thought. *Maybe I'm beyond saving.*

'I killed a man,' he said. This time there was no laughter, and his words hung in the dark silence.

Chapter Twenty-Three

Gone

When Emma's mother had died several years before, the world went away for a while. She'd had her family around her offering support. Dom held her and loved her, she and her father gave each other strength, and Daisy was a dancing fairy of concern for her sad mummy.

But for just a few days reality had fallen heavy and full, its awful truth smothering most of what she had once deemed essential. Small concerns faded to nothing. Routine continued – sleeping, cleaning of teeth, drinking of coffee, fending of phone calls – but her life, and grief, became very focussed on the staggering hole her mother's death had left behind.

Nothing else had seemed to matter. For a while, not even love. Death had washed across her like a tsunami, and in its wake it had taken her some time to retrieve everything that made her feel alive.

She felt like that now. Watching through the van's windscreen as the headlights lit the empty road, she tried to make sense of things. But she felt brain dead. Everything she knew, all that she had taken for granted for years, had been ripped away.

I saw Dom murder a man, brutally, bloodily.

Daisy is adrift, and I don't know if we're the islands she's hanging onto, or if it's the other way around.

Andy is a stranger who might mean us harm.

Her mind flashed back to that moment in their en-suite bathroom, their nakedness, Andy's arousal. If that moment had continued differently, would they be less strangers now? She thought not. The idea of not stepping away from him had used to make her feel guilty. But guilt had no place in this new, awful reality. Guilt was for the blessed, not the cursed.

She was lost in the darkness, and boredom now felt like heaven.

Emma understood that every effort to extricate themselves from this mess was only digging them deeper. Perhaps that was human nature. It was always the next moment that would make things better, the next action that would turn things around. As the situation worsened, the certainty that they should have gone to the police straight away grew.

But even then, things might not have ended. Andy knew more about these people, his gang, his family, than he was letting on. She was sure of it.

Now they had left the scene of a double murder. Dom's blood was mixed with the dead guy's on the toilet floor of her place of work. They had stolen Brian's van, Dom's and Andy's blood no doubt speckling its interior. Poor Brian, who used to talk to anyone who'd listen about his pet dog, Lady, and who'd never once denied the fact that he often slept on his job. No one seemed to mind. Brian was like that. A sweet old guy, whiling away the years to retirement in a safe, quiet job.

Emma had not wanted to approach his body, but she couldn't avoid seeing. They'd cut his throat and then pushed him to the floor, hidden behind the reception desk so that he wasn't visible from outside the building's main doors. The pool of blood was huge. Against the pale porcelain floor tiles, it was black.

Neither attacker had been Lip, the beast who had chased her and Daisy through Usk. She'd seen him clearly, his cold and detached expression. He'd reminded her of a shark or a crocodile, those dark expressionless eyes, that determination when he was on their trail. Even when she'd seen him from—

'Oh, my God,' she whispered. Her voice was loud in the silent van.

'What?' Daisy said. 'Mum?'

'Mandy,' Emma said. 'Lip found us at her place. Maybe he went back.' She caught Andy's eyes in the rear-view mirror as she said this. She didn't like his expression.

Emma dug out her phone and checked for texts or calls. There was nothing.

'Emma, maybe you shouldn't,' Andy said.

'Don't be ridiculous,' she said. She thought of adding, *You know nothing about friends.* But by then she'd tapped Mandy's contact, and Andy had no say in this at all.

The phone rang and then went to voicemail. It was almost two in the morning, so that was hardly a surprise. She almost left a message, then hung up. She texted instead: *Hi Mandy, all OK there? Sorry we had to leave in a rush. Catch up soon.* It felt strange trying to sound so matter-of-fact, but she didn't want to panic Mandy.

All OK there?

What if everything wasn't all okay? What if Lip had gone to visit and added Mandy and Paul to his monstrous tally?

Her blood ran cold. She felt dizzy.

'I'm sure she's fine,' Dom said.

'You can't say that. What a *stupid* thing to say! After all this, Dom? Really?'

He touched her leg, tried to offer comfort. She could see his own pain, both physical and psychological.

She dialled Mandy's landline. It rang, and rang, and then it almost shocked her when it was picked up. *Please let me recognise this voice*, she thought, closing her eyes.

'Yeah?' A man's voice. Paul.

'Paul? Hi, it's Emma. I was just wondering—'

'What the fuck do *you* want?'

'I'm sorry?' Emma heard a fumbling sound and muted voices, then the line crackled. Someone breathed.

'Emma,' Mandy said.

'Mandy. Hi, I was . . . I just called to see . . .'

'I can't talk to you,' Mandy said. 'Someone came—'

'Who?'

'A man. A terrible man.'

'Is he still there?'

'No, no, he's gone. But we can't talk. Emma, sorry. I hope you're okay. Paul wanted to call the police but I said no.'

'No police,' Emma said. 'I'm in a mess, Mandy. But please, whatever you hear, you have to know it's all about protecting my family.'

'What am I going to hear?'

More fumbling sounds, and then Paul came on again. His voice sounded strange.

'Look after yourself, Emma,' he said. Then he disconnected.

'They're okay?' Andy asked.

'He's been and gone.' The implications were obvious. Been, gone, and they were still alive. But he must have warned

226

them off calling the police, and talking with Emma. At least now she knew how those two guys had known to go to the college.

Emma started shaking. She'd feared her friend was dead. *I've got to pull myself together*, she thought. *Got to feel strong, carry on.* The idea was like a revelation. She'd hauled herself from the pits of despair over her mother's death due to something the sick woman had said to her days before she'd died. She could do the same now.

Her mother had known she was going and had been very brave about it. One day when they were on their own in her parents' house, her mother in bed, Emma sitting in the chair beside her, her mother surprised her by talking of death.

'I'll be gone soon,' she said. 'And I know you'll be sad. I'm lucky enough to love my family, and to be loved in return. But promise me that you'll get on with things. At the same time you're grieving, you'll remember that you have a good man in Dominic, and a beautiful little angel in Daisy. Your life goes on. That's the best thing I'm leaving behind.'

Life goes on, Emma thought. She felt the heat of Dom's body next to her on the wooden bench, saw Daisy on his other side. The people she loved were with her, and she would do anything to protect them.

Dom already had.

'We'll be fine,' she said, more to herself than anyone else. But they all heard, and though they did not reply, the atmosphere in the van seemed to lift.

They entered Abergavenny through a back road and parked on a small wooded rise above a building site. A new housing estate was being constructed, and for now the area was a fenced-off wasteland of trenches, drainage pits, storage compound, and office units. There were lights on across the site and a couple of the units were lit. Security guards watched against vandals or those out to steal materials.

But for their purposes, the site was perfect.

Emma and Andy left the van. Dom and Daisy remained behind, outside the van and sitting under the cover of nearby trees. Andy left one of the guns with Dom, after giving him a brief lesson in how to keep it safe, and also how to shoot. Emma watched, feeling a swell of pride in her husband. After what he'd just been through he seemed attentive and alert. The gun troubled him, but he didn't for a minute consider not keeping it.

They moved quickly, down through the woods and past the eastern extreme of the building site. Andy did not speak, and Emma was grateful for his silence. She had plenty to say to him, but none of it was good, and none of it for now.

The site was surrounded by a high timber hoarding, and they hugged its shadows until they reached one of the main roads leading into town. Here they could not avoid the intermittent glare of street lamps. Emma tied her hair in a bun, Andy made sure the gun was tucked into his belt and hidden by his loose shirt. And though it made her skin crawl, she saw the sense when he took her hand. They headed into town like carefree lovers walking home way past midnight.

After crossing a river bridge they approached the small apartment building where Andy lived. It was a grand old place, and had once been a hotel. Now it was home to six apartments occupied by a mix of young professional couples and single people, a small parking area at the back, a shared landscaped garden at the front and side.

They stopped at the edge of the park opposite, shadowed by trees looming out over the pavement.

'Car's around the back,' Andy said.

'You got the keys?'

'No. I'll have to go inside.'

'Great.'

'I think you should stay here.'

He sounded sincere. Nervous. She could not bring herself to trust a thing he did or said, but right now they had the same aims.

'I'll wait,' she said. 'But after five minutes I'm heading back to the van.'

'Plenty of time.' He smiled. She did not smile back. She was painfully aware of how close they were, and that he carried the other gun. Even though she did not trust him, she had put herself at his mercy.

Andy crossed the road and approached the gate.

There were a couple of lights on in the large building, and occasional cars passed by. But Emma saw no signs of movement elsewhere, and no indication that the apartment was being watched. If there was someone keeping watch, would they we waiting inside? She thought it likely. If they did know where Andy lived, they might think it so unlikely that he'd come back that they'd want to wait in comfort.

She'd find out soon.

Another car came. She held her breath. It swept past her, past Andy, and kept going. He glanced back towards her, waving. She did not wave back. He wouldn't have been able to see her anyway.

He entered the old hotel's front garden and used his entry card to open the main doors.

Emma looked at her watch, ready to give him five minutes. For every one of those five minutes, she wondered what she and her family would do if they had to leave Andy behind.

He was the main cause of the terrible mess they were in, but he also appeared to be their best chance to get out of it.

No new light came on inside the building. But three minutes later she heard a car engine start nearby, and then Andy's car emerged from the car park behind the apartment block. He pulled over for her. She jumped in and breathed a sigh of relief.

'No sign of anyone being inside?' she asked.

'No reason there should have been. I don't use my real second name, there's no way they could track me. Jane Smith is very good at covering tracks.'

'I hope she's good at more than that,' Emma said.

Andy didn't reply. As they drove back towards where they'd parked the van, Emma tried not to consider just what might be needed to save them all.

Things that Jane Smith would have to do, and she and her family might yet be forced to face.

Chapter Twenty-Four

On the Move

'Time to split up,' Holt said. They'd been driving in silence for the last hour, and since crossing the Severn Bridge into Wales Rose had known this moment was coming. It made sense. Andy had called for her help, not her and someone else. She had not initially embarked on this journey in answer to his request, but when it had appeared en route she had not been surprised. Besides, Holt was not here for Andy.

Although she was almost certain that their paths here would cross again soon, she and Holt would approach from different directions.

'Service station in two miles, drop me there,' Rose said.

'I'm happy to leave you with the car.'

'This heap of shit? I'd rather walk.'

Holt tapped the wheel as if comforting his old Renault. He was probably secretly glad she had not taken up his offer. She suspected that he was pleased that she had come. There was something about when they were close that kept the world at bay.

Holt was taciturn as usual, but over the few years she'd known him Rose had gone some way to understanding

Holt's language. It had taken her a while to realise it was more in what he did not say or do than what he did. A man who had seen so much death and horror, and who had dealt some of it himself, could never communicate in any normal, even rational way. But there were instincts he could not hide.

Rose believed that he had come closer to her than anyone else since leaving his wife and child almost two decades before. He'd never told her that directly, and their relationship had never become physical. At least, not in the sexual sense. She believed they were *very* physical with each other, even though they rarely touched. They could communicate with a look, a shrug, the way they held their bodies, and whenever they were close she was aware of his presence with a warm clarity. It did not require contact for them to touch each other.

At times, she was afraid that he had become her safety buffer against the horrors of the world. She was even more afraid that after he had spent so long killing for cash, she had become his.

Rose had never wanted to discuss this aspect of their relationship. She feared that if either of them analysed it too much, it might set a seed of ruin into whatever it was they had. So she and Holt did what they always had. They continued. They persisted. And, sometimes, they worked together.

Their work was something she found much easier to analyse. Rose had acquired a new set of skills, tutored by Holt and progressively more self-taught. They ranged from electronic surveillance, to covert observation, to diverse methods of killing. She used these skills to help people she believed deserved her help, and sometimes in return she was paid.

Holt sometimes still killed for money because he still enjoyed it.

Their purposes and reasons were clear, but such truths troubled her. She had never felt that Holt was trying to draw her into his own clouded world, and she was glad. But she also did not have the right to try and lure him out towards hers. After what she had done, Rose was the last person in the world to distinguish between good and bad.

He pulled off the motorway into the service station. The satnav on his phone indicated that there was less than twenty miles to go before Abergavenny.

It was almost two in the morning, and this time of night the roads were mostly deserted. Overnight freight lorries, night workers, a couple of coaches, the service station car park was relatively quiet.

'There,' Rose said, pointing across at a Travel Lodge. Holt turned off the car lights and parked a hundred metres away, drifting to a halt close to a parked van. They waited in the darkened car for several minutes in case anyone was watching them. Peoples' attention quickly drifted.

While they waited, Rose checked the small rucksack she'd brought with her. It was a runner's backpack, fitted with hip pockets, water bladder and straps that would ensure it moulded closely to her body. She'd spent a long time adjusting these straps' placing and length, and now it hardly felt like she was wearing it. Inside were a few spare clothes, money, the grenade, knife, and her Glock and spare magazines. She carried her phone in her shorts pocket, and in the rucksack were two cloned SIM cards.

There was also an old iPad, intricately locked, containing information that she would never show anyone else, not even Holt. Over the years she had constructed her own network of useful contacts, faceless social media outlets and information.

In a hidden pocket there was also a whole new identity, including passport, National Insurance card, driver's licence and other documentation that would give her access to a sleeping bank account and online presence. The identity she'd used to enter the country was already cast aside. Now she was Jane Smith once more. She liked it better that way.

'I have the feeling we'll be seeing each other again soon,' Holt said.

'We should stay in touch,' Rose said. 'We can help each other.'

'Don't we always?'

Rose left the car and closed the door behind her. No goodbyes. No good lucks. As always, they acted as if this was merely a pause in their lives together.

Yet Rose felt a tug at her heart when Holt drove away. One day he'd turn his back on her and she would never see him again. Either he'd end up dead in a shallow grave, or she would.

She did not watch his car leave. A woman standing motionless in a dark car park would look suspicious. She strolled towards the hotel, rucksack slung over her shoulder, and all the while she was checking out the few cars in the hotel's dedicated car park.

All the usual were there. Fords, Mazdas, a few BMWs, a sporty Mercedes, a couple of Vauxhalls. She ignored the cars parked in the row directly next to the hotel, because some people tried to park as close to their room as possible. Last thing she needed was a curtain twitching at the sound of a car engine. By the time she reached the wide path to the hotel's main entrance, she'd singled out a Renault Megane. Several years old, easy to steal, and not a vehicle likely to dear a second glance.

She left the path and headed across a grassed area towards the corner of the car park. All was quiet. She took a tool from one of her rucksack's shoulder straps, a stiff metal band that was hooked at the end.

It took almost a minute to pop the car's lock and open the door. She waited anxiously for the scream of an alarm. If one came, she'd walk casually away. No one took much notice of car alarms, but if they saw someone running at the same time, she might be in trouble.

No alarm. It was a messy car inside, passenger seat scattered with fast food wrappers, a jacket hanging in the back. Probably a businessman's vehicle. It made her feel less guilty than if she'd been stealing a family car.

Three minutes later she was driving from the service station, sun visor down and baseball cap on in case any CCTV cameras caught an image. Britain was the most watched country on earth, making much of what she did more hazardous than usual. Perhaps that was why she'd only been back once since her experiences with the Trail.

That visit had been three years ago to help Andy Scott escape the clutches of his family. He'd seemed like a good guy at the time. He'd got in touch through convoluted channels, and she'd spent several weeks researching his story and assessing his needs before even replying. Everything he'd told her panned out. The Scott gang were very good at remaining hidden, and they had been avoiding the law for almost a decade. She suspected they had an internet wizard at their disposal to help facilitate this. But Rose had her ways and means, and while she'd found it difficult to pin down their exact location or responsibility for various crimes, Andy's stories had merged perfectly with what she had been able to discover.

They had met once. She always met her clients. Experienced though she was at all manner of electronic communication and research, nothing beat meeting face to face. She'd liked him. He'd seem honest, for a criminal, at least. But he had never been a man of violence. His reasons for wishing to establish a new identity were sound, and she could understand. His family gang had perpetrated a sudden rash of increasingly violent crimes, led by the man called Lip who had come into their midst, and who had driven them quickly to murder. The man who she suspected was Monk, the killer Holt now pursued.

Andy had wanted out.

Since then, her work had kept her overseas. There had been two requests from Britain, but both she had turned down, burning all communication channels and ensuring that the people she'd shunned had no way of holding a grudge.

Rose had travelled to Turkey, Egypt, Moldova, Portugal and Sweden. Holt had gone with her most of the time. Sometimes the jobs were simple and clean. Sometimes they were not. She had killed again, as had Holt. She made no effort to keep count, and the faces of those she had murdered made no appearances in her dreams. The weight of guilt she bore was reserved only for her dead family, and there was no room for more.

Only bad people died at her hand. It was no justification, and certainly no defence. But she ensured that remained the case nonetheless.

The fine lines, the grey areas between good and bad, were places Rose did her best not to travel.

Turning from the motorway and heading north towards Abergavenny, her phone chimed as a Twitter message came in from an account for which she'd set up notifications. AndyMan: *We're on the move.*

Chapter Twenty-Five

Amateurs

Even before he stopped the Jeep halfway along the driveway, Lip knew they weren't there.

The place might have been a rich family's summer home, and this summer they were elsewhere. Or maybe it was a holiday let that had not been booked for this week. Either way the converted barn looked deserted, locked up tight and lifeless.

Lip exited the Jeep to get a better look. He was used to trusting his hunches, and he had a strong feeling that Andy and the others were not here, and never had been. Curtains were too neatly tied back each side of the windows; if someone was hiding inside, the curtains would have been disturbed, maybe even drawn. A burglar alarm high on the front wall blinked, still armed. Through one of the tall windows beside the front door he could see the faint blue glow of the alarm control panel.

He walked slowly along the gravel driveway. There was no sign of movement anywhere. This was not the place,h he was almost certain of that now, but he'd have to check.

It was a shame. He was looking forward to some more fun.

The couple he'd caught fucking in their bed had got off lightly, and he was already regretting leaving them so soon. Maybe he should have stayed a while longer. The book he'd been using was torn and slick with blood, but he had already spotted the man's belt over the back of a chair, a reading lamp, a pint glass of water beside the bed. There were countless ways to hurt and kill, and that was why he so rarely used knives or guns. His was a whole world of weapons.

He scooped up some gravel and threw it at the building. Most of it clicked dully from the stone facade, but a few chunks clunked from glass. Nothing broke, but the sound was loud enough to alert anyone inside.

No movement. Nothing. This was a waste of his time.

Lip turned his back on the empty barn, and as he reached the Jeep his phone vibrated. It was Sonja.

'Nothing here,' he said.

'Nor here,' she said. 'I can't contact Cal and Roman.'

'Ask me if I'm surprised.'

'They went to the college, we'll meet you there.'

Lip disconnected and jumped into the Jeep. He'd known from the beginning that the hired help were amateurs. If they'd lost Andy and the others, encouraged them to flee, he'd have words with them himself.

Somewhere quiet, and without Sonja to mother over them both.

'Still nothing?' Lip asked.

'I've been inside,' Mary said. 'Security guard's throat's cut, and I found the Scot dead in a toilet.'

'Best place for him,' Lip said.

'But there's no sign of Roman,' Sonja said. 'His phone's going to voicemail.'

'We'd best not hang around here,' Lip said.

'Where else do we go?' Mary asked.

'Mary, you need to do your thing,' Sonja said. 'They were hiding here, but now they're on the run. We need to know where they'll be going. Any holiday places the family might have, relatives, anything like that. You know what to do.'

'And any place Andy might have, too,' Lip said. 'A bolthole or safe house.'

'He's not so easy to find,' Mary said.

'We know who his friends are now. You'll find where he lives.' Lip scanned the car park, alert for dangers. They shouldn't stay this close to two bodies. There might have been shooting. Police might already be on the way, and they spent a lot of time and effort doing their best to avoid any contact with the law, accidental or not.

But it was still heavy and hot, even the air itself feeling lethargic and exhausted. Lip was tired. He had not slept for over twenty-four hours. He wanted this over soon, and Andy and the family in their grasp.

Then perhaps he'd rest before the real fun began.

Sonja lit a cigarette, breathed in and sighed heavily. The smoke hung around her head, ghostly in the moonlight.

'Mary can come with me,' Lip said. 'We'll head out of town in a different direction, but not too far. Stay in touch. Either we'll hear from Roman, or more likely Mary will find us something useful.'

'I don't like the thought of Andy getting away,' Sonja said. 'After all this, I don't like the idea of him still being out there.'

'He isn't out there,' Lip said. He held out his hand, palm up. 'He's here, with me. We're just letting him have a final run on his last day.' He looked up at the sky. The few sparse clouds were streaked silver, and those higher up were already tinged pink.

Sonja left in her BMW, and Mary jumped into the front of the Jeep. As Lip pulled out of the college grounds she opened her rucksack and took out her laptop, phone and tablet.

After she'd connected her phone, she flipped open her laptop and the current webpage faded in. Lip caught a glimpse of movement as a frozen image flowed into a film clip. The pale flash of bare skin. A tuft of pubic hair, a flurry of movement, a close-up of a flaccid penis. The sound of a scream. Blood on skin, and then the deeper, more intimate colours of opened flesh.

Mary tapped a few keys and the image froze, then closed down. She didn't even glance at Lip, nor did her face betray embarrassment or shame. He'd seen her watching such images before, fascinated, totally absorbed, and shameless. He knew her predilections, far better than she knew his.

Sometimes, she played videos while they were fucking. She seemed to get off on it, and he didn't mind. But they did nothing for him, these frantic images of naked flesh, frightened faces, and eventually a blood-red climax to match her own. He could watch them with no reaction either way. They were unimaginative and boring. 'If only you could see some of the things *I've* done,' he'd said to her more than once. Over the past couple of years she *had* seen a few things. But now he believed she would see so much more.

He might even let her film some of what happened. The thought of that struck him, and he jerked the steering wheel. She glanced up, but said nothing.

That would be something to watch while we're fucking, he thought. He imagined Andy's face melting with acid . . . Dom's stomach open and squirming with rats . . .

'We'll get them,' he said quietly.

'Sure we will. Now let me work.' Mary began her thing.

As Lip drove, he glanced across at the open laptop now and then. This part of her life was a mystery to him. He'd never been one for technology. Just as his weapons were usually improvised, so his technological know-how was similarly basic. He found no need for social media or internet, and he used his phone sparingly. While faces shone with the reflected glare of computer screens, his awareness of his surroundings remained sharp, and he saw so much more.

That didn't detract from Mary's abilities. He respected what she could do, and sometimes it proved useful. He hoped that now was one of those times.

'Digging,' she said. She often muttered to herself when she worked. She knew that Lip was not really interested, but still she spoke, and he'd never told her to be quiet. In truth he quite enjoyed hearing her voice like this. Distracted, almost innocent, shorn of the need for acceptance that often strained her words. Especially when she spoke to him, he heard a desperation in her voice. It was almost as if she knew he would leave her eventually.

'He's a slippery fucker,' she said, tapping keys. 'Always knew he'd had some help to disappear. I've spent a long time over the past three years looking for him, here and there. But when you've had a good job done, it's almost impossible. He's like a different person now.'

'He's still the same smug bastard.'

'You know what I mean.'

Lip drove slowly and with no real aim in mind. He glanced frequently across at the screen. He made little sense of what he saw, but it was still intriguing.

'But now I know where he lives,' she said. 'The area, anyway. So I can check local directories. Filter out the Andys. Still a few hundred in the county. Check which are married, which have kids.' She hummed softly, scrolled her phone while a coloured wheel span at the centre of the laptop screen. 'Narrowed it down, but could be he's married on paper anyway.'

'What about the other one. Dom.'

'Yeah, already working on that.' She propped her tablet against the dashboard and the screen lit up. 'He's far easier, especially as we have the address. Dominic Morgan. Electrician. Wife is Emma, student liaison at the college. The kid's called Daisy. Dog's Jazz. Frank made a mess of that one.'

They passed through the square. It was deserted. Lip knew they should park up soon; any vehicle prowling the streets at this time of night might draw attention they didn't want. But with the windows down and Mary thinking aloud, he was almost enjoying the journey. Even though as yet they had no destination, it felt like they were going somewhere.

'Dom runs his own electrical firm. Small office and yard, got the address. List of clients and recent jobs. Reviews of his work. Mentions in local press. He's a school governor. No criminal record, not even points on his licence. Boring fucker.'

Lip's cheek twitched. It was as close as he ever came to a smile.

They approached a bridge across the road, beyond which was a lay-by beside the river. He pulled in and killed the engine. Mary hardly seemed to notice that they'd stopped.

'They play squash together,' she said.

'How do you know that?'

'Debit card details. Hang on.' She scrolled, tapped, swept one screen onto the next. 'Here we go. Clumsy. Dom registers both names sometimes when he's booking a squash court. He's calling himself Andy Holson now.'

'So you can get an address?'

'Probably. Give me five minutes.'

Lip tipped the seat back a little, eager for a brief rest. Two minutes later, his phone rang. Sonja.

'Roman's following them,' she said. 'He's only just managed to get through on the phone. They've gone to Abergavenny in the dead guard's van, dumped it, picked up a car, and they're heading west.'

'Why hasn't he stopped them?' Lip asked.

'He says he was jumped at the college, Andy almost shot him. He doesn't have a weapon.'

'He's got a car, hasn't he?'

'He hot-wired their old one, the red Focus. Pretty smashed up.'

'Fucking amateur. I told you that, Sonja.'

'Whatever. Lip, we're close to getting them now. Where are you?'

'Just outside town. Mary's got a name, Andy Holson.'

'Doesn't matter. So long as Roman doesn't lose them, we can catch them up.'

'I can get a three-way Skype going,' Mary said. She'd been leaning in listening to the conversation, and Lip saw her eyes glitter with excitement. He was excited too. But he never gave anything away.

'Yes,' Lip said. 'Whatever that is, do it.'

Mary used her own phone, and soon she had it propped on the dashboard, Sonja's face on the screen ghosted by dashboard light, Roman's car interior unclear. They were both driving fast, Sonja with a cigarette hazing her image. Reception flickered in and out. Roman's voice cut in with directions, shouted above the scream of air through the Focus's smashed windscreen.

The chase was on.

Chapter Twenty-Six

Tumble

'We're being followed,' Andy said.

'How do you know?' Dom asked.

'Trust me on this.' Andy was driving, maintaining a sensible speed. His sporty Seat Leon was a refreshing change from the bumpy van.

'Jane Smith?'

'I doubt it. She'll let me know when she's close so we can arrange a meet.'

'They're pretty far back,' Daisy said. She and Emma had turned in their seats to look out the back window. 'Looks like a motorbike.'

'It's a car with one light working,' Andy said. 'I spotted it just as we left town. Been behind us for the last few minutes.'

'This is a main road,' Dom said.

'And there's been three junctions and roundabouts,' Andy said. 'Plenty of places for them to turn off. I'll try something.' Two minutes later he took the first turning at the next roundabout, a dogleg that virtually turned back on themselves.

'It was speeding up as you turned off,' Emma said.

Andy slowed the car to a crawl, looking in the rear-view mirror. The view of the road they'd left was obscured by a high bank.

'What if it's them?' Dom asked.

'Then we don't let them catch up. And we know the area. I'll head back through the lanes, take the Tumble, plenty of turnings, and this car will purr up there.'

Dom and Andy had ridden the Tumble before on their bike rides, a five-kilometre climb averaging ten per cent gradient. It was a tough ride, and well known amongst cyclists. It was also barren, leading up and over one of the highest local mountains, moorland on either side, gravelly car parks, windswept hillsides and lakes and nowhere to go for help. All things considered, he knew it was the right choice.

'There it is,' Daisy said. 'Dad, I think it's your car! I think the windscreen's smashed!'

'The other guy at the college?' Emma said.

'Looks like it,' Dom said. 'Everyone strapped in?' Emma and Daisy sat facing front again, and he caught his wife's eye. She was scared but determined. *Good*, he thought. *No point looking back now. We've got to look forward.*

They drove for a mile or so, then turned onto the road that led eventually to the mountain climb. They cleared a small built-up area and swerved around to the left, the first steep climb.

'He's getting closer!' Daisy said.

'Andy?' Dom asked.

Andy held the wheel with both hands, guiding them around a tight bend and then powering up the steepening slope. There was no street lighting here at all, and the head-lamps lit some way ahead. To their right were trees and a slope, beyond which the wild landscape lay like a darkened blanket. To their left the hillside sloped steeply upwards, interrupted only by occasional pull-ins.

'I know what I'm doing,' he said.

'Andy, we can get away from him, especially going uphill. Your car's much faster than the Focus.'

'Not *much* faster. A bit. Maybe not enough.'

'Closer,' Daisy said. 'Much closer than he was before.'

Dom looked back. His battered, smashed-up Focus was less than a hundred metres behind them, the one functioning headlamp obscuring most of the view inside. But he could imagine the man behind the wheel, focussed on the car that contained the person who'd killed his friend. He could almost feel the hatred radiating through the darkness.

'If he gets too close he'll start shooting,' Dom said.

'I got his gun.'

'He might have another one!' Daisy said.

'Dom, start shooting.'

'What? No. What if it's not him? I've never shot a gun—'

'Then leave this to me! I know what I'm doing. Shut the fuck up and let me concentrate.'

The battered Focus was so close now that its single head-lamp illuminated the Seat's interior. Rather than dipping the mirror to shield his eyes Andy kept glancing into it, squinting to see ahead.

'Dad, he's going to—'

The car jolted forward. Andy gripped the wheel and kept them straight, knocking down a gear and giving it gas.

'Still not convinced it's him?' he asked.

Dom felt the gun in his lap. It was warm from being nestled between his thighs.

'Don't bother,' Andy said. 'Chance of you hitting anything important is remote. I've got this.'

The car slowed and Andy straddled the white line. They crossed a cattle grid with a brief vibration, then the steep bank to their left fell back a little. They were up on open moorland now, the drop to their right less drastic and no longer obscured with trees. Looking past Andy, Dom could see the night-time landscape laid out for miles.

'Coming again,' Emma said.

'Hold on tight,' Andy said. He slammed on the brakes and veered to the left, dropping into second and gunning it instantly. The pursuing car had swerved to the right and come almost level with them, its nose edging past the back door. It shifted left and hit the car. Dom felt a sickening lurch as wheels skidded and gripped again, a jolt translated right up through the suspension. His stomach rolled. It reminded him of being on a roller coaster, something that Emma loved and he hated.

The Focus's engine screamed as the driver dropped a gear and surged forward. Andy was careful to follow the road, checking in his side mirror. They took a sharp bend to the left, and at the last moment Andy swung out to the right.

Dom braced himself against the dashboard as he saw only darkness ahead, empty air that swallowed the car's lights.

The screech of metal on metal was horrific, a teeth-grinding tear. The air stank of straining clutch and burning rubber. Glass smashed.

Andy swung sharply left again and pulled them back onto the road, and when Dom looked back he saw the Focus's headlamp spinning wildly, waving at the sky like a frantic searchlight as it rolled and dropped from view.

'Got him!' Daisy screamed.

'He's gone,' Emma said. She looked at Dom, face grim. He nodded. *We might have just seen someone else die.*

'Shouldn't we stop?' Dom asked.

Andy nodded down at the gun. '*Coup de grâce?*'

'No!' Dom shouted. 'To see if he's still alive, not to make sure he's dead! What the hell do you think I am?'

'Okay, okay.' Andy's door window had smashed and he held his face, right hand over his eye.

'You hurt?' Dom asked. Andy only shrugged.

'We don't stop,' Emma said. 'Keep driving, Andy. If he was following, he'd have told the others he was on our tail. They might be right behind.'

'My thoughts exactly,' Andy said.

Dom stared ahead, frowning, trying to figure out exactly where they had got to on the climb. Was where the Focus had gone over a long drop? There were a few farm tracks leading down the hillside that way, he might have just flipped onto his roof and come to a stop. Or he might still be rolling.

Andy drove fast, still pressing his right hand to his face. When he needed to change gear he did so quickly, on a relatively straight stretch of road. He was confident and relaxed, wheel vibrating beneath his hand as he powered them around corners.

Two minutes from the top of the hill, as they took a corner in the middle of the road, there was a vehicle coming from the other direction. It skidded out of their way as Andy fought with the wheel, and a moment after they passed, the strobe of silver-blue lights filled the car.

'You're shitting me,' Andy said. He was slowing down.

'What are you doing?' Dom asked. *I have a dead man's blood on my hands*, he thought.

'Yay, police!' Daisy said. 'Now we can tell them everything that's happened.'

250

Andy pursed his lips and shook his head, then slammed on the brakes. He had two hands on the wheel now. His right eye was closed, blood speckling the eyelid and skin around his eyebrow.

The police car had spun around and given chase, and was so close behind them that it almost smashed into the car's rear. It stopped a couple of feet short.

'You all know I have to do this,' Andy said. 'Dom's covered in blood, some of it not his. I'm smashed up. There are two bodies in your place of work, Emma. And maybe a dead guy back down the hill.'

Dom nodded.

'You all know.'

'Yes,' Emma said, barely a breath.

'Oh, no,' Daisy whispered. 'Please don't hurt them.'

Andy dropped into reverse and floored it. The impact against the police car was slight, but the sound of wheels spinning on tarmac, then gravel, almost deafening. Andy pushed the advantage, tweaking the wheel to the right and edging the other car towards the drop-off.

The police car's engine roared, wheels burning on tarmac as it countered the movement.

'Don't look back!' Dom said. He didn't want his wife and daughter being seen, perhaps recognised. He knew nothing about modern policing. Was there a camera on the police car? Was their number plate even now being transmitted to control? Would their images be splashed all over police channels?

'There you go,' Andy said, easing off the accelerator, changing gear and surging forward.

Dom looked back. The police car's headlamps were pointing up at forty-five degrees, the car having rolled backwards from the road. It looked stuck, but not badly damaged.

Dom eased back in his seat. His heart was hammering, he was nauseous, and every moment felt like one he wanted to wish away. But they were on a course now, and their momentum seemed to be growing. The further they went, the harder it would be to stop.

'You're a good driver,' Daisy said.

'Thanks.'

'That's because he's a getaway driver for bank robbers,' Emma said.

Dom watched Andy driving. Even with one eye bloodied and closed he looked calm and in control. But he was not in control. None of them were. If they were, they wouldn't have been fleeing into the night.

'Call her,' Dom said. 'We can't keep driving, not after what we've just done. The law will have *everyone* out looking for us. Get off this road and call her now. She has to help us.'

'I don't have her real number,' Andy said. He looked across at Dom, who gave him only a cool gaze. 'Yeah, right, I'll sort something. And maybe you can drive for a bit. I've got glass in my eye.'

Down the other side of the mountain he took several turnings, passing through a housing estate and heading across the valley and up the next hillside. It was even more desolate and remote here, the landscape scattered with sad remnants of a long-dead coal mining industry.

Andy parked behind a derelict brick building and sent a Twitter message to Jane Smith.

Chapter Twenty-Seven

Superglue

As Rose drove into Usk just past three o'clock in the morning, something about the small town didn't feel right. It was off-kilter, unnaturally quiet, like a place where something violent had happened and then ceased. The town felt shocked. She was used to such scenes, such places. She had grown to trust her feelings.

Parking in a side street, her phone chimed as a tweet came in. AndyMan had sent her a message, and it was not as obscure as usual. *Need to talk.*

Rose lowered the window a crack and breathed in the warm night air. She caught the faint whiff of fresh bread. Somewhere in the village, the baker was awake.

She dialled Andy's number. It was picked up on the first ring.

'Jane Smith?'

Rose said nothing, listening to the sounds coming down the line. Andy's voice was tense but not stressed. It sounded like he was in a moving vehicle. There were no whispered threats, no signs that he was being coerced.

'You alone?' she asked.

'Oh, it is you. Where are you?'

'I ask the questions,' Rose said. 'That's how this works. You tell me what I need to know, and nothing else. Got it?'

'Got it,' Andy said.

'Good. There's no such thing as a secure line. Now, are you alone?'

'No. There's a family with me.'

A family, Rose thought.

Alex runs into her bedroom with a badly glued Airfix model, making machine-gun sounds and knowing he can fly.

'How many?'

'Husband, wife, daughter.'

'Are you all okay?'

'Well . . .'

'None of you are dying?'

'No. Few bumps and bruises. They're chasing us.'

'How many?'

'Two less than there were a few hours ago.'

Rose let that sink in. Andy had sounded almost pleased, as if he was trying to impress a teacher. She wondered if the two he referred to were dead but decided it didn't matter.

'One of them's the superglue fan?' she asked.

'One of those chasing, yeah.'

'Tell me more.'

'How much?'

'All you know of him.' Rose didn't care if this part was overheard by anyone listening in. The chances were slight. But if someone did hear, they'd know only that her knowledge was growing.

'It's the one I told you about before. The reason I left. His name's Philip Beck, everyone calls him Lip. He hates Phil. He's maybe early fifties, mean motherfucker. *Really* mean.

254

There's nothing else to him. No empathy, no emotion. As I told you before, I don't know anything about his past. He's driving a white Jeep at the moment, although that might change. And yeah, he's the one who killed the people in the post office.' Andy paused. 'Why are you asking about him?'

'Where are you now?' she asked, ignoring his question.

'I thought you said this wasn't a secure line.'

'If you want me to help, that's a risk you have to take.'

'We're heading west, along the Heads of the Valleys road. We're going . . . How can I send you a map? A location?'

She knew that Andy was a keen cyclist. She knew a lot about him. 'Do you have Strava on your phone?'

'Yeah.'

'Manually input a journey, with a stop-off point where you're going.' If he did this quickly enough, and she followed him and downloaded, she could have their destination in under a minute. 'Do that, then in two minutes delete it.'

'How will I know you'll get it?'

'Andy. Listen to me. I can help, but you have to trust me. Don't question what I say, just do it. Understand?'

'Yeah,' he said. He sounded like a petulant kid.

'Really?'

'I understand.'

'Because Lip isn't someone who just wandered into your life. I know more about him than you. He's been doing this for decades, under different names, and he'll do anything he can so that he can continue. You get it?'

'You know more than me?' Andy asked.

'Of course I do. I know more than anyone.' Rose disconnected and accessed Strava. It took two minutes to follow Andy, find his new trip details, and download the map. Then she unfollowed and deleted her false account.

Dialling another number, she looked along the quiet street. A light had come on in one of the houses, and from somewhere farther away she heard a motorbike engine sputter to life. She much preferred work like this to be done in the dark, but she could not hold back time. The world was waking up.

'Good morning, darling,' Holt said.

'Hello, sweetie. Monk's going under the name Philip Beck now. People call him Lip.'

'Right.' His voice was cool, flat, tempered by bad memories.

'Maybe we should have stayed together. They're on the Heads of the Valleys road, heading west. Lip's probably after them.'

'Hmm,' Holt said.

'What does that mean?'

'It means the lead I'm following has just got much warmer.'

'What lead?'

'I've been snooping police channels. A police car was run off the road less than half an hour ago. I'm heading that way.'

'Where?'

He told her the road number.

'I'll meet you there.'

'Drive safe. Pick up some doughnuts and muffins.' He hung up.

Rose was worried. Holt sounded too hurried, too impulsive. He was chasing ghosts, and with the past on his mind he might become careless.

Now that the police were involved things would become far more dangerous. But as Holt liked to quip on occasion, a little danger was good for the soul.

Sonja was staying on Andy's and the family's tail. Still miles behind their quarry by Lip's reckoning, she was keen to continue, and he suspected she had some inkling of where Andy was going. He hadn't asked, and she had not yet volunteered the information. He was fine with that for now. The time would come.

She asked him and Mary to see if Roman was still alive, and he was fine with that, too.

Roman had been relaying road numbers, and before the Skype audio connection was lost, they had heard his scream. There was always the chance that he was still alive.

Lip drove quickly. Mary had packed away her gadgets, and she stretched in her seat, searching the road for signs of Roman. As they headed uphill they both saw several sets of skid marks, and a couple of hundred metres further on the grassy verge was churned up. Lip pulled over, craning to see down the slope.

'There's a car.'

'Could be it,' Mary said. 'Let's—'

'Wait,' Lip said. He stared into the rear-view mirror. The road behind was deserted, but he was sure he'd seen an unwelcome flash of light. He was about to reach for the door handle when it came again.

Blue light, flashing through the trees far back down the hillside.

'Got your gun?' he asked.

Mary lifted her rump from the seat and took the pistol from her belt. Then she froze as she looked into her side mirror.

'Cops? Really?'

Lip said nothing. Mary knew the score. They could not be caught.

'Put your window down ready,' Lip said. 'Pretend you're on the phone.'

Mary did as he said. The police vehicle powered up the road behind them, lights flashing, sirens silent. It did not appear to be slowing down. It passed them so quickly that Lip had no chance to see who was inside, or whether they even spared his Jeep a glance.

'Maybe we should follow, Andy might have crashed.'

'Maybe,' Lip said. He thought it through. 'We're here now. Wherever they're going to isn't that close. If Andy had crashed, it would have been here.'

'And Roman might still be alive,' Mary said.

'He might,' Lip said. He jumped from the car, slammed the door behind him, and stared down the slope.

The battered Focus was visible in the trees below, lying on its side with its underside showing. It had flattened a few bushes, scraped past a rocky outcropping, and come to rest thirty metres down the slope. There was no sign of movement, but it would only take a few minutes to check.

Lip closed his eyes and breathed slowly. *Fucking amateur*, he thought. He'd never liked the idea of Sonja bringing in help. Maybe Mary knew what he was thinking, maybe not. Whatever the case, she would see things his way in the end. She always did.

They worked their way down the slope. Lip went first, moving cautiously but quickly, holding onto rocks and small trees when he could. He smelled petrol and the heat of hot brakes, the tang of burned rubber. Dawn smeared the horizon, and already the sky was lightening. The road above would soon start to grow busier. He had to be quick.

A few metres up the slope from the car he paused. Mary was just behind him, edging towards the car's rear. Lip held up his hand and signalled her to stop. The car's underside faced them. Petrol dripped.

Someone was breathing. It was fast and light, punctuated with an intermittent groan.

'Alive,' Mary said.

'Hello?' Roman said. 'Someone there?' His voice was muffled and weak.

Lip nodded at Mary, then worked around the front of the battered vehicle. It had come to rest against a rocky outcropping, and he had to ease himself over the rock to drop down beyond the mangled bonnet.

'Oh, thank God!' Roman said. 'I'm trapped, something's on my legs. I tried to release the seatbelt but my arm—'

'Quiet,' Lip said. Mary appeared from behind the tilted car, and they knelt together and looked inside.

Roman was lying on his side against the smashed driver's door, ferns half-obscuring his face. They were spattered with blood. His right arm appeared to be trapped, and his left arm flailed like a landed fish. Lip wasn't sure how badly he was hurt, but it didn't really matter.

'You messed up,' he said. 'You and that prick Cal.'

'Hey, *he* fucked up. I tried to put things right.'

'And yet here you are,' Lip said. He sat on the ground and examined the vehicle. It had come to rest on its side with the bonnet leaning on a rock, a thin tree bending beneath the weight of its rear end. Some of the tree's branches were bent, others had snapped off and fallen beside the car.

'You have to get me out,' Roman said. 'I smell petrol.'

'Me too,' Lip said. 'You're lucky I don't smoke. Lucky it's not Sonja come to rescue you.'

Roman smiled, but his expression quickly dropped again. He could sense something. Lip liked that, when they knew.

'Hey, you need to get me out,' he said.

'Lip?' Mary asked.

He looked at her. She already knew, he was sure, but that single glance told her everything. She smiled. *I've been with her too long,* Lip thought. *She's starting to enjoy it. That's not right. It's my thing, not hers.*

'Hand me that branch,' he said. Mary did as he asked. He checked the snapped end. It was the thickness of his thumb, frayed where the living wood had been ripped from the tree's narrow trunk. It was still moist.

'What are you doing?' Roman said. 'My legs. My arm's trapped, too. You'll need something stronger than that.'

'No,' Lip said, plucking away some of the frayed splinters. 'No, this'll do fine.'

He leaned towards the smashed windscreen, branch held out before him. He could hear Mary's breath increasing. Her phone chimed as she started recording, light illuminating the scene. He didn't care. Maybe they'd watch it together later, or maybe he'd wipe her whole phone when the time soon came to leave. Perhaps he'd wipe her, too. On that matter, he'd made no decision one way or the other.

'Wait,' Roman said. 'Wait, what do you—'

Lip jabbed. It was a clumsy first shot, catching the corner of Roman's mouth and flexing his cheek, scraping his gums and tongue.

The trapped man cried out in shock, surprise.

Lip changed position slightly so that he could grip the branch with both hands. He waited, breathing slowly, watching Roman try to jerk his head aside. But he was pressed to the ground on his right side, and there was little scope for movement.

The next jab was aimed better. Roman screamed as the branch's ragged end pierced his left eye. He shuddered in his seat, head shaking from left to right.

'Keep still,' Lip said. His voice had barely changed.

As if compelled by some idea that Lip really was trying to help, Roman became suddenly motionless.

Lip placed one hand flat against the branch's other end and pushed.

'I got it all,' Mary said. 'All of it.' She showed him the phone, eyes wide and excited, pupils dilated. It looked like she'd just had sex, not watched a man die.

Lip nodded but said nothing. These were private moments for him, and he craved peace and solitude to process them. So he climbed up towards the Jeep, leaving Mary to follow behind. She knew him well enough by now to remain silent and give him space. He was glad.

He moved quickly. They had to be away from here as soon as possible. Roman had been an unexpected distraction, but the main fun was still to be had. All they had to do was catch them.

As usual following a killing, the world opened up around him, his senses sharpened, everything fresher and louder, more colourful and fragrant. It was as if murder gave him a new lease of life, temporarily seeing away age and ills and resetting him to a stronger, younger self. His painful left knee was comfortable once again, the failing sight in his left eye no longer a problem. He climbed that hill as a younger man, but still retaining the knowledge and experience of someone older.

It was like a drug, and it coursed through his veins and sparked his synapses. If he could bottle it he would be rich. But Lip did not care about money or perceived wealth. *This* was what he lived for. It was very much his own special narcotic, and it was not for sharing with anyone.

He heard the car before he saw it. The engine sound did not seem to match the battered old vehicle that pulled up thirty metres behind the Jeep. He froze and crouched, glancing back at Mary. She was down the slope from him and slightly to the left. He gestured for her to move further away, and she scampered through ferns until she was hidden within a clump of trees.

He'd heard no doors opening or closing. The engine still turned over, headlights illuminating the Jeep. Dawn was close.

He headed up the slope at a crouch, eyes still on the banged up old car. The engine sounded too powerful and well-tuned for the vehicle. What sort of person took care of an engine and not the chassis?

A car enthusiast. Or someone trying to hide.

Lip paused. He was ten metres from the Jeep. The slope was still too steep for him to see inside the other car, but he was sure the driver had not exited. At times like this, forward motion was often the best course of action. Holding back, staying down, meant losing control of the situation. Lip was someone very much used to control.

He scrambled up the slope towards the front of the Jeep, and as he reached for the door he strained to see past the glare of the other car's headlights.

'Right there's fine,' a voice said from behind him. 'One hand on the handle. You can raise the other one.'

Lip froze.

'I said raise it. Higher.'

A hard voice, with a subtle French accent. That tweaked his memories, but he could not sort through them. The present was still drowning the past with its wash of recent sensations. When he blinked, he saw Roman's punctured eye oozing around the splintered end of the stick. The

Frenchman's voice was only a vague echo against that. A whisper from the past.

The fact that he knew the voice meant trouble. Soon he would place it, and the trouble would find form.

Lip kept his right hand on the door and raised his left.

'And a little higher.'

He stretched.

'Where's the other one?' the man asked.

'What other one?' Lip replied. There was a good chance the man had not seen Mary and was simply fishing. The pause confirmed this.

'Okay. Right hand up too, then turn around slowly.'

'I know you,' Lip said before he turned.

'You'll know me a lot better when I can see your face,' the man said. His voice had dropped and grown quieter, and Lip felt a rush of something he was unused to. Fear.

The man was waiting for him to turn around before he shot him.

Lip raised his right hand. He risked a glance down the slope towards where Mary had fallen into the shadowy embrace of the trees. He could not see her. She was quick and silent when she wanted to be. Mentally damaged, but effective at what she did. Maybe she'd already had long enough. Maybe she needed a little longer.

'We can work this out,' Lip said.

'There's nothing to work out,' the man said. He sounded surprised. 'Turn around or I'll shoot out your left knee.'

Lip turned slowly.

'Monk,' the man said.

Lip blinked in surprise. He hadn't heard that name spoken in some years. But coming from this man, it instantly placed him in Lip's past, illuminating a history he had mostly forgotten. Of course. The man was from a past life. It was not often that Lip, né Monk, né many other identities, allowed his new and old lives to cross over, not even in memory. It was why he had survived so long.

This was not the first time he had stared into the barrel of a gun. But it must have been the closest he had ever been to dying.

'I killed your sister,' Lip said.

'You tortured her, then you killed her.'

'And you're going to do the same to me.'

The man did not reply.

'Holt. That's your name. I remember it now. You were sent to kill me, and . . .' Lip's right shoulder twitched half an inch higher. His version of a shrug.

'I've been torturing you in my imagination for a decade,' Holt said. 'Now I have you, killing you will be enough.'

'Then you'd better—'

The gunshot shattered the morning silence. Lip dropped to the side, breath knocked from him, and rolled across the verge and down the slope. He came to rest on his front, flattened against the sheep-shit-covered incline and looking up, expecting a bullet in his face.

Holt was leaning against the front of the Jeep, sliding slowly down. He still held his gun, but it looked as if he'd forgotten what he had come here for. His face was slack with confusion. He looked down at his front, and at the bloom of blood appearing across his left hip.

Mary skipped around the front of the Jeep and pressed her gun against Holt's neck. She snatched his weapon away from him, looking up and down the road, then down at Lip.

'Who the hell's this?' she asked, eyes wide. 'Shall I do it? Let me do it.'

'No,' Lip said. He stood and walked back up the slope, pausing in front of Holt and looking him up and down. His dark, wrinkled skin was greying, and his eyes swam. It must be hurting a lot.

'Fuck you,' Holt said.

'Your sister knew you were the reason I was killing her, because I told her.'

Holt came for him, pushing himself from the Jeep, left hand clawing for Lip's throat.

Lip simply stepped aside. One hard nudge sent Holt to the road's gravelly edge. One solid kick against the gunshot wound in his side made him scream, and then pass out. He moaned groggily. His hands scratched at the road, and perhaps he was torturing Lip in his mind's eye once more.

'Help me,' Lip said, reaching for Holt's legs.

'Thanks would be nice,' Mary said.

'Thank you.'

They bundled Holt into the Jeep's spacious boot. He wasn't very heavy. 'There's rope under the back seat,' Lip said.

'Can't you get it?' Mary was pissed that he hadn't let her kill the older guy, but Lip didn't care. Why Holt was here, how, and who might have come with him were problems for later. This was another unexpected bonus, and one he could have never imagined landing in his lap. It looked like today was going to be a good day.

'No,' Lip said. 'I'm getting the glue.'

Chapter Twenty-Eight

The Hottest Day

Andy had scratches on his eye. Emma fished out a shard of glass from the shattered window, and plucked several more gravelly glass bits from his eyelid and surrounding skin. She could do no more than that. Andy could see only watery images, so he kept his eye closed against the slicing pain. Perhaps the damage was permanent, but he seemed unconcerned. Though injured and in pain, he was the only one who could steal another car.

Dawn was breaking and the roads were coming to life. They chose a small valley town with a main car park already half full. Dom parked against the side wall of a derelict building at one edge of the car park, shielding the battered wings and smashed window of the Leon from casual view. He tucked the pistol into his waistband and made sure his shirt covered it before leaving the car. He took the bag of cash with him.

Andy rooted around in the boot and took out a small tool roll. He plucked a couple of items from it, slammed the boot shut, and threw the roll at Daisy. She caught it easily.

Andy took just over two minutes to break into an old-style Mazda 6 estate and get it started. He shuffled over, Dom jumped into the driver's seat, and five minutes after entering the car park they were away again.

'So where exactly are we going?' Dom asked.

'Back to the Heads of the Valleys road and head west,' Andy said. 'I have a place near the coast close to Aberaeron, a getaway. I go there sometimes, haven't even told you about it. I train for some of my trips there, relax, spend time alone. It's somewhere safe.'

'You're sure?' Dom asked.

'Sure what?'

'That it's safe. Because everything we've done up to now has ended up far from safe.'

'Dom, I'm in this with you.'

'No. You're really not. You're in this with *you*. I'm in this with my family.' He looked in the mirror and saw Emma and Daisy huddled together, Daisy's head on her mother's shoulder. Emma stared back. She looked grim, but she spared him a smile.

'Jane Smith will help,' Andy said. He drew in a breath, knocked down the sun visor and opened the little mirror. He groaned as he opened his eye and tried to examine it.

'You need a hospital,' Emma said. 'So does Dom.'

'Jane knows people,' Andy said. 'By the end of today we'll be fine, and we'll get stitched up.'

'Then what?' Dom asked. 'Everything back to normal?'

'What, you enjoyed normal?' Andy's voice was almost mocking. Dom felt like punching him. But he stretched back in his seat instead, trying to shake the aches and pains.

'Normal is a wife and daughter who love me, and who I'd die protecting,' Dom said. 'So yes, I like it.'

Andy fell silent. In the back seat Daisy was doing the nodding dog, but Emma stared ahead, catching Dom's eye in the mirror now and then. Events had reduced them to their basic selves. Whosever fault it had been, however much blame Dom had to shoulder, this was purely about survival. He and his family were in terrible danger. Andy might have put them there, and Dom had started to suspect he might even be keeping them there. But they had to do whatever was necessary to extricate themselves as much as they could from this mess.

Once the Scott family were no longer hunting them, then that might mean giving himself up to the police.

As he drove, Dom scraped flakes of drying blood from the creases on his knuckles.

The radio told them it was going to be the hottest day of the year.

By eight o'clock the sun was glaring and the outside temperature was already twenty-three degrees. It was set to reach thirty by two that afternoon.

They travelled in the clothes they'd fled in. Dom's shorts and T-shirt were stained with dried blood, and the over-shirt he'd slung into the back seat was torn and similarly stained. He smelled of stale sweat. He wasn't used to stinking like that, even when exercising he was fastidious about his cleanliness, and his sweat was usually an honest smell. This was the odour of fear and guilt.

Daisy's long hair was knotted. Andy stank worse than Dom. To make matters worse, the car they'd stolen had no functioning air conditioning. They drove with the windows down, even when they eventually hit the motorway, and that comforted Dom. It ensured that he remained awake even though exhaustion was threatening to smother him. And it meant that they could not talk.

There were only bad things to say.

Dom realised he was hungry. At the thought of food, his stomach rumbled and his vision blurred. When was the last time he'd eaten? More important, when was the last time he'd even had a drink?

'Anyone got money?' he asked, shouting against the noise from the open windows.

'Really?' Emma asked.

Dom laughed. It was a wretched sound. Thinking of the cash hidden in the bag in the boot brought everything back into sharp focus.

Five people are dead, he thought. *Maybe six, if the guy in the car bought it. Andy killed one of them. And I killed one. Stabbed him in the head with a shard of a smashed toilet. Destroyed his brain. Wiped out all his memories, his story, everything he'd been and done ended at that moment, by my hand.*

But curiously, his guilt did not stretch as far as the murder he had perpetrated. He viewed it dispassionately, like an observer watching a movie, or someone reading an account of the event. Considering it objectively was not a pleasant process, but neither did it make him want to vomit. He had ended a man's life because that man was threatening to murder his family. In everything that had happened, with all the complexities and coincidences he was still trying to fathom, that was the simplest equation of all.

'Food and drink,' Andy said.

Dom used the master window control to raise the windows so they could talk.

'And clothes, for you two especially,' Emma said. 'If we're ever going to be seen in public again, that is.' She'd meant it as a quip, but there was no humour there.

'We'll stop at the next services,' Dom said.

'No,' Andy said. 'Quick pit stop, that's all. We don't know how close they are behind us.'

'We've changed cars!' Emma said.

'More reason not to stop,' Andy replied. 'There are cameras everywhere nowadays. Petrol stations are dripping with them. Police will be looking for us, and this stolen car. We'll find a local shop and stock up.'

'How long to your place from here?' Dom asked. They'd left the motorway behind and were negotiating A roads, busy with rush hour at this time of the morning.

'Lots of slow winding roads now,' Andy said. 'Another couple of hours.'

'And we'll meet Jane Smith there?' Emma asked.

'Yes, I sent her a map.'

'What then?' Daisy asked. 'I should be in school. Miss was going to test us on long division today, but instead I've been in a car crash and I've got blood on me.'

Dom glanced back, surprised that she was awake and listening. He'd hoped she might have a rest, retreat from this madness for a while into dreams. She looked tired and heavy-eyed.

'Yeah,' Dom said. 'What then?'

'Then she helps us out of this mess.'

'How?' Daisy asked. 'I don't want us to be like you. I don't want her to give us a new life and new names, so we spend our lives lying. I want to go home.'

'That'll all depend,' Andy said.

'On your family,' Emma said.

'Maybe.'

'And how reasonable they can be?' Emma asked.

Andy did not reply to that. He sighed heavily, reclined his seat a little and leaned back. 'Just keep driving,' he said. 'I'll give you directions.'

Dom drove. Daisy leaned into Emma again, eyes closed. Emma seemed alert, even twitchy, and Dom could not blame her. He searched the mirrors for pursuing police cars, and he knew that if they were pulled over, that was it. He was driving now. There would be no more car wrecks, no shunting police vehicles over the sides of mountains. He didn't want to be caught, but if it happened, they could only tell their story.

Emma and Daisy were innocent. His guilt hardly mattered at all.

The roads grew quieter, and soon they were crossing the Carmarthenshire countryside. It was hilly and beautiful, heavily farmed but with frequent patches of woodland swathed across the hillsides. Evidence of the scorching summer was everywhere, and Dom didn't think he'd ever seen the British landscape looking so parched.

Emma appeared between the front seats, resting her hand softly on Dom's arm. In the mirror, he saw her pressing a finger to her lips.

Andy had nodded off, head resting on the window frame. She reached down into his lap and picked up his phone.

What? Dom mouthed.

Keep driving.

Emma sat back down. Daisy grumbled and rested her head on her shoulder again. This felt bad. However angry she was at Andy, whatever she suspected him of, it was invasion of privacy. But he had invaded *their* privacy, entering their lives and turning them upside down.

She opened his phone, relieved to see the screen had not yet locked. The background image was of wild countryside on the top of a local mountain, and she recognised Abergavenny nestled down in the wide valley. She touched the "Messages" button and a list of his text messages appeared.

Dom was there, and JS which must have been Jane Smith. There were a few threads to Claudette, the nurse he was seeing. But the most recent message was to neither of these.

It was to someone called Bitch.

Emma held her breath, glanced at Andy, saw that he had not moved. Dom's eyes were flickering back and forth to her in the mirror. She frowned at him.

One touch opened the "Bitch" message thread. She read the latest message. It said, *I look forward to it.*

She scrolled up. With two movements of her thumb and a quick read, she realised that her vague suspicions had been true.

Emma closed her eyes and gripped the phone.

Maybe I can change things, she thought. *Perhaps seeing this gives my family an edge.*

When she opened her eyes again, Dom shrugged and mouthed, *What?* to her.

'Just a minute,' she mouthed back. And she started typing.

This is Emma. Dom's wife. I assume by "Bitch" Andy means Sonja, his mother? If that's the case, you have to know that he's lied to us all along. He's led us on. Even my husband, Dom, was coerced by your son. This is nothing to do with us.
She thought for a while, wondering what this Sonja was like. What sort of mother was she if she wanted her son dead?

Emma continued writing. *This isn't our world. You're not the sort of people we know. I don't care about Andy, but please let my family walk. Nothing will be said, no fingers pointed.*

She hovered her thumb over the "send" button, agonising, wondering whether she was doing the right thing. Was begging the way to go? Would Andy's mother empathise at all?

Then the car hit a pothole in the rural road, her thumb brushed the screen, and fate carried her message away.

'Oh my God,' Emma whispered.

'What is it?' Dom said.

Andy stirred, shifted position, and groaned a little in his sleep. The groan of someone finding a moment of comfort.

'Him,' she said. 'That bastard. He's been leading them along all the time. He gave them three places to look, and the college was one of them. And he's *taunting* them now. Making sure they follow.'

'Why would he do that?'

'Because he's sick. And we're nothing to him, Dom. Nothing. He'll see us dead and hardly break pace. You see that, don't you? Stop, kick him out, and then we'll figure out what to do.' She looked down at the phone as a plan began to form. 'We'll give him to them.'

'We can't do that!'

'Why not?' She was almost shouting. Daisy woke. Andy stirred again, then sat upright in his seat, looking around at their surroundings. He searched for his phone, quickly becoming frantic. He glared across at Dom.

'Looking for this?' Emma asked. As she held up the phone, it buzzed as a message arrived.

'Give it to me,' Andy said.

'Fuck you, Andy,' Emma said mildly. 'Bitch is replying to my message.'

273

'What? Emma, you have no idea—'

'Hang on.' Emma read the message. The breath was punched from her.

Be seeing you soon.

'Give me the phone,' Andy said again, turning in his seat and reaching back for her.

'Or what?' Emma shouted. 'You'll kill me?'

'Mum,' Daisy said, hunkering back against the door.

Dom pulled into a field gateway.

Emma slammed the phone against Andy's hand, knocking it aside, leaning forward and smacking it against his face, aiming for the bloodied area around his eye. He grabbed her wrist and squeezed, and she was amazed at his strength.

'Fuck you!' she shouted into his face.

'Yeah, you nearly did,' he said. He spoke softly, but his words stilled the car's interior, defused the violence. He prised the phone from her hand and turned forwards again, swiping the screen to read what she had written.

'What did you say?' Dom asked.

'Nothing,' Andy said. 'Why are we stopping? We can't afford to stop.'

Dom turned off the engine and pocketed the keys.

'Have you been leading your family to us?' he asked.

'Dom—'

'Simple question. One word answer.'

'Yeah.'

Dom nodded. He was sweating. His forehead was beaded, and a drop ran down his temple. He grabbed the door catch and shoved it open, leaping from the car, rushing around the front and meeting Andy as he did the same.

'Dom,' Emma said.

'Mum, what's Dad doing?' Daisy asked.

274

'Something stupid.' She opened her own door as she heard the sound of the first punch.

This was Dom's second fight of the day. The first one had ended with a man dead. Before that, he guessed his last scrap was when he was in his early teens. He had never been a fighter.

And he had never realised that punching someone in the face could feel so satisfying.

His fist caught Andy on the cheek as he was standing from the car. He fell back against the door pillar and Dom pushed forward, the door between them, shoving it so that it pinned Andy against the vehicle. He swung again, catching him a glancing blow across the forehead.

'Dom, you don't want to do this!' Andy shouted.

Dom punched again, and this time Andy ducked the blow, reaching up and grabbing Dom's wrist with his left hand, standing, shoving his arm high and punching him in the face with his right.

Pain flared in Dom's injured nose and ignited behind his eyes. He staggered back a few paces. His heels hit a mud-hardened tractor track and he stumbled, reaching back to break his fall. Nettles brushed his bare arms and they immediately began to tingle.

Andy stood before him, blocking out the sun. He reached down for Dom.

Dom took his hand, using his weight to stand on unsteady legs. The pain was so intense that he gasped, trying to spit it out, but it had settled like fire into his skull. He could barely see. When he fell against Andy and started punching again, he relied on blind luck.

His fists connected and Andy fell back, unsteadied by the

assault. They went down with Dom on top, but he was too close in now, unable to punch.

'Bastard!' he hissed.

Andy head-butted him in the face.

Dom was vaguely aware of being rolled aside and someone holding his head, making sure it didn't hit the ground. He reached for his face but didn't quite touch it, afraid that to do so would only hurt more.

'Stop it, Dom,' Emma said, and he thought she might be crying.

Fuck you! she'd shouted at Andy.

Yeah, you nearly did.

'What happened?' Dom asked of the pain, never expecting it to reply.

'We can't do this,' Emma said. 'He'll hurt you more, Dom. That's the sort of person he is. He's lied to us all along.'

'I haven't,' Andy said from somewhere, but Dom didn't care about him now. Emma helped him sit up, then he leaned forward with his head between his knees. He felt more hands on his arm and Daisy was there. She'd seen more than any girl her age should ever see, and his prime motivation now should be to make her safe.

But not like this. This wasn't safe.

'You can get lost,' he said. He looked up at Andy, shielding his eyes against the sun. 'Take the car. Go. Play with your family, kill and get killed, I don't care. Just leave us out of it.'

'It's not that simple, mate,' Andy said.

'Don't ever call me "mate" again. And yes, it really is. I killed a man today, Andy.' Dom snorted, blood and snot running from his damaged nose. 'If I see you again, I'll do that to you, too.'

'You can try,' Andy muttered.

'What? Seriously?'

Andy shook his head and kicked at the dusty ground. 'You'll never be safe again,' he said. 'Not from them. If we follow my plan, *maybe* you will. But are you willing to risk that?'

'Risk what?'

'Being out there on your own when they find you?'

Dom stood. He leaned into Emma, his rock, his support, even after all he'd done.

'Jane Smith is your only hope as much as she is mine,' Andy said. 'Stay with me, meet her, and you've got a chance of getting your life back.'

'Liar.'

Andy shrugged. He touched his damaged eye, wincing as his fingertips brushed the bruised eyelid. 'You're hurt as bad as me. Think you can help your family protect itself?' He nodded at Daisy. 'Will she shoot the gun for you?'

'This is so messed up,' Dom whispered.

'So don't mess it up any more.'

'You've been luring them in.'

'Yeah.'

'What, to kill them all?'

Andy looked away.

'Why?'

'Cos of what they did to me.'

'And what was that? Stole some cash?'

'No,' Andy said, looking down at Dom's feet but seeing something more distant. 'That's not all.'

Dom turned to Emma, and she pressed her face against his. 'Maybe we should listen,' she said into his ear.

'In the car, what did he mean?' Dom asked.

Emma blinked at him, unable to speak.

'Maybe that's for later,' Dom muttered.

'We should move,' Andy said.

'You need to tell us what's happening,' Dom said. 'Your reasons. I don't trust you, and never will. But I want to know why you're doing this to us.'

'When we're on the move,' Andy said. 'I'll tell you everything. But we need to go.'

Dom nodded slowly. *Where else do we have to go?* he thought. *What else can I do?* But he felt stronger. The pain was fading a little, and he thought perhaps it was because he'd tried to take control. He'd asserted himself.

They got back into the car. Emma drove. Dom sat in the back seat behind Andy. He nursed the gun between his thighs.

He spotted Daisy looking down at what he was doing. He felt an initial rush of pride, and then a growing sense of disgust in himself when he saw her approval.

Chapter Twenty-Nine

One More Scar

Rose drove the stolen Megane far quicker than was safe. But it was not her safety she was worried about now. It was Holt's. She'd found his car abandoned by the roadside, engine still running. There was a crashed car further down the hill with a dead man inside. There was blood on the road, sticky in the morning heat.

Holt had been taken or killed, and now her job was many times harder.

She'd snatched the box of tricks and weapons from his car's boot, noticing that the pistol was absent, then turned off the engine and pocketed the keys. Remaining there any longer than necessary was a big risk, but she'd paused anyway, examining the scene again and trying to make sense of what had happened. The bloodstains were thirty feet along the road from his car. Maybe there'd been another vehicle there.

Maybe it had been a Jeep.

The dead man had not been killed in the crash. He was mutilated, a thick branch shoved through his left eye socket and into his brain. Rose had seen many dead bodies, and been the cause of quite a few, but this one disgusted her. It spoke of intense enjoyment in the act of killing. A sick delight in inflicting horrendous pain.

Monk had been here, the man now calling himself Lip. Somehow, he had taken Holt.

She thought of trying his phone but decided against it. Lip might still believe that Holt had come alone. If that were the case, then in such dire circumstances she might still retain a slight advantage of surprise. Although with someone like Lip she wasn't sure that was really much of an advantage at all.

Watching Holt's old Renault in her wing mirror, sad at leaving something of him behind, she'd continued up the steep road. A couple of miles further on she'd passed several police cars, a recovery vehicle, and an ambulance. She'd slowed as she passed, offering a concerned smile to the officer who waved her past, and noticing the nose of a police car protruding just above road level.

If they had yet to discover the crashed car and signs of a bloody fight just two miles back, this must all have happened very recently.

Since then, she'd driven hard for the place Andy had told her about. A quick couple of texts to him had confirmed that they were still untouched.

We need to meet before we get there, she'd texted. She couldn't afford to trust him. Meeting somewhere neutral was the only way to begin this. She'd googled and found somewhere appropriate. *There's a pub a few miles before Aberaeron, the Helmsman. Midday. Be careful. They're ahead of me.*

I think we've lost them, Andy had replied. She did not trust that, either. People like Lip and the Scott family did not leave things to chance. She knew that from the research she'd carried out into them three years ago, although Lip had been a blank. Now that she knew more about who and what Lip was, she could not underestimate them for an instant. Neither should Andy.

Holt had been shot before. She'd seen his scars. They were both marked by their pasts, physical wounds the least painful.

'One more scar, you clumsy bastard,' she said as she drove. She only wished he could offer one of his terse responses.

Rose had never learned the levels of control and detachment that Holt possessed. Her hunt of the Trail had been driven by chaos and randomness, and she had maintained a state of restrained panic all through that pursuit, and beyond. It had settled somewhat during the years after, and in subsequent violent confrontations, with or without Holt by her side, she had reined it in. Learning to control the heart-thumping panic had turned it to her advantage. Indeed, it had lowered from panic to an alertness, adrenalin-driven and sense-sharpening.

Holt seemed to stroll through these encounters, while she sprinted.

Now, she felt less in control than she had in a very long time. Since the Trail, nothing she had embarked upon had been personal. There had always been a sense of justice at play in the contracts she accepted, something else that set her and Holt apart. But she could never call it personal. There was no catharsis in her actions, and no sense that by helping them she might help herself. She was not that foolish. Nothing could change what had happened to her family, and nothing she ever did could lessen the horror. Even killing Grin, the bitch directly responsible for their deaths, had done little to fill the emptiness.

But Holt was her friend. He pinned her to the world to stop her being blown away. Now with him in danger, perhaps even dead, she felt the storms closing in once more.

'Keep control,' she muttered to herself. 'Take it easy, don't get too . . .'

Adam stands before her in their kitchen, rubbing her earlobes and whispering 'Ooooo-saaaaahhh', smiling away the stresses of a hard day at home with the kids.

Rose accelerated to overtake a slow-moving tractor.

Events were rolling fast, and now that the police were involved, things would quickly come to a head.

Perhaps she should have brought bigger guns.

The Helmsman was a large roadside pub with a spacious car park, a grassed picnic and play area for kids, and a block of four independent retailers alongside selling clothing, crafts and confectionery. It was very obviously aimed at the tourist market. The pub itself was an old building that had been extended several times over the years, an expansive two-storey structure with four large bay windows on each level facing out onto the car park. Tastefully done, its facade promised more than a basic chain pub's fayre.

Dom circled the car park once, searching for any CCTV cameras. Seeing none, he reversed the Mazda estate into a space close to the main building, turned off the engine and sighed heavily.

'So she's here?' Emma asked.

'If she is, she'll be watching us,' Andy said. 'Come on, let's go inside.'

'I'll check it out first,' Dom said.

'I think we should—' Andy began, but Dom cut him off.

'I'll check it out.' He slammed the car door behind him

and walked quickly to the main entrance, looking around, trying not to seem twitchy. They'd stopped half an hour earlier to buy some new T-shirts for him and Andy, but there was no hiding his injuries. Conscious of his swollen eye and puffy red nose, he opened the door and paused in the large glassed-in foyer. There was a cash machine on the left, and beside the tall windows viewing into the pub's interior were two long tables of tourist information leaflets and posters. He pretended to browse the leaflets whilst scoping the interior.

It was a large open space. Pillars were set at regular intervals, and tables and chairs were placed almost at random. Some were dining sets, others more comfortable sofas and seats. Several island units housed condiment stations and collection points for trays of dirty crockery, and the bar was large and U-shaped, protruding into the pub at the rear. Lines of real ale pumps glimmered gold in the sunlight streaming in the south-facing windows. Staff bustled behind the bar and delivered food around the pub, all dressed in dark-blue uniforms. There was a dedicated coffee bar in an extension to the main building on the right, open to the bar. The whole place was bustling.

Fire escapes were prominent in every wall.

Dom smiled grimly. Usually the first thing he'd look at in a place like this would be whether they were serving real ale, and then he'd peruse the menu boards to see what daily specials might be on. Now, he was looking for points of escape and areas where danger might be hiding.

He moved along the leaflet displays and plucked up a few at random. Beyond the large entrance hallway, he could see no signs of Lip inside. An older woman sitting in a comfortable chair in the coffee bar might easily have been Sonja, because he'd never seen her. A younger woman ushering a couple of kids along *could* have been Mary. He'd only caught a quick glimpse of her. She held her arm awkwardly, maybe from a gunshot wound. But why would she have kids? And this woman was black, whereas Mary was mixed race.

Another woman was looking directly at him. She sat at a two-seater table on her own, a mug and plate before her. As he caught her eye she looked away, brushing her phone screen with her thumb and taking a sip from her mug.

Dom waited to see if she looked again. Maybe this was Jane Smith. Or perhaps it was just someone who'd glanced his way and seen a battered and bruised man loitering in the pub's entrance lobby. Anyone would stare. Wouldn't they?

She did not look again.

As he turned around to go back outside, Emma and Daisy entered, followed by Andy.

'We need the loo,' Emma said. She paused and glanced past him.

'Is that her?' he asked Andy. 'Behind me, sitting at a small table by the red pillar?'

Andy looked and shook his head.

'I'll get drinks,' he said to Emma. She came close and kissed his cheek, and he felt ridiculously grateful. He watched Andy over her shoulder. He seemed nervous.

'Come on,' Emma said to Daisy. They entered the pub, and as Dom went to follow, he felt the gun tugged from his belt.

He span around. Andy was already tucking the weapon into his own belt and ensuring his T-shirt covered the butt.

'We can't afford to make a scene,' Andy said.

'So what are you going to do with that?'

'A lot more good than you, should the shit hit the fan.'

Dom turned his back on his ex-friend and entered the pub. Noise swept over them, a comfortable, carefree hubbub. He walked past tables, skirted a large comfortable seating area, and headed for the coffee bar to the right. He waited in the queue to order drinks. Andy stood beside him.

'Get me a cappuccino?' Andy asked. 'Probably best we don't stand together, we look like extras from a war film.'

'Sure,' Dom said. As Andy went to leave, he grabbed his arm. 'What you said, about Emma. About how she almost fucked you.'

'That was nothing,' Andy said. He lowered his voice, although music played through ceiling speakers and dozens of conversations provided a stew of noise. 'That was all me. She loves you, mate, and she's a good woman.'

'You tried to screw my wife?' Dom asked.

'I made the offer,' he said. 'She declined. Without a moment's thought.'

Dom thought of punching him again, how good it had felt. Confusion stirred his thoughts, tiredness made his limbs heavy. Yet he could not do anything like that here. The violence that had so recently made him feel good had left behind a sense of nausea.

'Yeah,' Andy said. 'I'm a bastard. I'll find us somewhere to sit.' He nodded at the coffee bar, behind which the barista was now waiting for Dom's order. 'Extra shot.'

Mary's phone shrilled, and when she glanced at the screen and put it on loudspeaker, Lip immediately knew who it was.

'I have them,' Sonja said. 'But it's delicate.'

'Where?' Lip asked.

'A pub called the Helmsman. I've sent the postcode to Mary's phone.'

'Already plotted it,' Mary said. 'We're five minutes away! Don't let them leave.'

'Why's it delicate?' Lip asked.

'They're in a pub, Lip. It's big. Lots of people here.'

'You're waiting for us?'

'In the car park, by the kids' playground to the left of the main building. I'm wandering around between parked cars. Can't do this too long or I'll start looking suspicious.'

'Try to get closer,' Lip said. 'Leave the line open. See what you can see.'

It was usually Sonja giving orders, but she didn't object. She knew that this was more his sort of world. The hunt, the kill. She'd been drawn in, just like Mary and Frank. But Lip was the one who lived and breathed this sort of work.

'What about . . .?' Mary asked, glancing back.

The man in the back of the Jeep was bound up tight, arms and legs secured. He could not shout. But Lip knew it would be a risk, leaving him there while they parked in a public place.

Maybe I should just stop and kill him now, Lip thought. The idea brought a thrill of anticipation, but also the disappointment of an opportunity lost. He didn't like to rush these things unless he absolutely had to. And with Holt, he didn't want to.

He watched for an opportunity, and only a minute later fate smiled. He pulled off left onto a narrow lane, winding down a steep slope towards the sea in the distance.

'You're going to do him now?' Mary asked excitedly.

'No.'

'Then what?'

'Just shut up, Mary.'

She fidgeted angrily but said no more.

The building Lip had seen signposted from the coast road appeared a couple of minutes later. It was an old, run-down church. Slates were missing from the roof, ivy smothered the tower and spire, and if it had stained glass windows they were hidden away behind purpose-cut timber boarding.

'Let us pray,' Mary said, giggling.

'Stay here, keep watch.' Lip jumped from the Jeep and approached the rear hatch. He looked around quickly, ensuring they were alone. There was no sign of anyone else having parked here in a while – weeds populated the small parking area, and a silence heavier than the heat hung around the church. When he was sure they were alone, he lifted the door.

Holt squinted against the flood of light as the door and parcel shelf lifted up, then started squirming against his bonds. His wrists were already bleeding from where the rope had abraded his skin.

'I'll punch you in the nose,' Lip said. 'I'll keep doing it until it breaks. Then I'll leave you. Maybe you'll drown in your own blood. Or maybe you'll suffocate.'

Holt grew still, glaring at him. If hate could burn, Lip would have sizzled to a dried husk.

He assessed his prisoner. Ropes were still tight, and tighter every time Holt struggled against them. His left side was soaked with blood from his gunshot wound. So was Lip's Jeep, and he'd have to dump the vehicle very soon. But he was used to that. Material things mattered to him about as much as people. He grew attached to nothing.

He held Holt's face still and checked his mouth. It was still glued tight. If Holt had the use of his hands, maybe he'd be able to rip his lips apart, using fingers and fingernails to tear the skin. If he could handle the pain.

'My father raped me when I was a child,' Lip said. 'It started in secret, in the dark. When my mother found out she started to watch. She'd masturbate while he did it. During the day it was as if nothing had ever happened, and we played happy families. I was too young to understand. Then after a while they started inviting their friends to take part. Sometimes they paid, other times my parents gave me for free. There are probably still videos, somewhere. I grew up being subjected to that, and when I was too big and started resisting, they kicked me out. Disowned me and cast me out on the streets. Like it was my fault. So I wandered for a while, slept rough. Eventually found my calling.'

Holt's eyes betrayed no pity, and Lip was hardly surprised. This was a man with his own violent history, and no story would shock him.

'Actually, that's a lie,' Lip said. 'It's one I've told before. One of many. The truth is, I really like what I do. My parents were nice people. Normal, loving and devoted, unremarkable in every way. It was them I killed first. I've lost count of how many I've done since.'

Holt made a noise in his throat. A curse, or perhaps a promise. Whatever, they were words that would never find voice.

'Not long now,' Lip said. He delved behind Holt, brought out a tyre iron, and cracked him across the side of the head. Holt groaned and rolled onto his back, then his wounded side. Lip hit him again, across the back of the neck this time, and he stopped moving.

He might only be out for a few minutes, but it should be enough.

Lip heaved the unconscious man over his shoulder and headed for the abandoned church.

Chapter Thirty

Trouble

Emma was already thinking this was a mistake. Dom and Andy were drawing curious glances with their bruised and battered faces. Dom was worse off with his split nose and puffy eye, but Andy's right eye was still watering from where the glass had scratched it. He blinked quickly, and sometimes allowed his eyes to close altogether.

They were all exhausted. The coffee would only go some way to keeping them awake. They needed somewhere quiet and private to rest, not a public place like this. Families bustled, eating lunch on their way to or from holidays. Businessmen sipped beers, staring into computer or phone screens. Perhaps it was guilt, but Emma could not see any group that looked more out of place than them.

They'd managed to find comfortable seating close to the Helmsman's coffee bar, a couple of sofas and single seats, a table, and trellised plant pots with ivy and other climbers forming natural partitions. Andy had taken a seat affording him a good view of the entrance. He held his mug to his lips, sipping occasionally and watching through the steam.

Daisy and Dom sat close together on a sofa. He leaned back with his arm slung around her shoulder, holding her close. Emma knew what he was thinking. She knew without even asking, because she could see it in his expression, in every tense movement, every startled glance at a raised voice, a dropped glass, a slammed door.

Our lives have changed forever.

She leaned across from her chair and squeezed Daisy's leg. Her daughter smiled back. Dom reached for her hand, and for a moment the three of them were touching, forming a family circuit that gave them all strength.

Andy tensed in his seat and sat up straighter.

'She's here?' Emma asked.

But Andy only looked at her, Dom and Daisy, and Emma realised then just what a dangerous creature he really was. He was no friend. He never had been. This was all about him.

The old woman eased herself into the comfortable seat between her and Andy, across the low table from Dom's and Daisy's sofa. Emma realised straight away that this was Sonja, and as the woman groaned and made herself comfortable, Emma had a chance to size her up.

She sat down like an old person, pained and stiff, one hand pressing into the small of her back. But Emma didn't think for a minute that this was genuine. Sonja was thin and strong, and everything about her exuded strength, confidence and control.

She carried a small handbag. Grey, leather, it might have been owned by any older woman. But when she held it in her lap, and patted it when she caught Emma looking that way, Emma knew it contained more than purse, tissues and a packet of mints.

'Busy here today,' Sonja said. She was looking at Emma as she spoke, then she turned her head, nodding at Daisy and Dom before finally staring directly at Andy. 'Son.'

'Mother,' Andy said. His voice was flat and emotionless.

'Nice to see you've brought your friend and his two cunts.'

Emma caught her breath, and she saw Daisy twitch in her seat. To hear such language from an older woman – one who looked somewhat refined, intelligent and smart – was shock enough. But to hear it in such a place made it seem almost staged. Emma felt herself drawing in, their small group apart from the hustle and bustle, not part of it. This was a very private scenario. A brutal story being played out against a backdrop of normality.

'You killed Jazz,' Daisy said.

'Your poor pet,' Sonja replied.

'Fuck you,' Emma said softly, but loud enough for Sonja to hear. The woman didn't even blink. Emma caught Daisy's eye and shook her head.

Daisy pressed her lips together and glared at the woman.

'How have you been?' Andy asked.

'Oh, not too bad. My knees are giving me gip. I should probably wear glasses, but you know, an old woman's pride.' Sonja laughed and it lit up her face. She continued looking back and forth between them, making sure none of them made any foolish moves.

Where are the others? Emma thought.

'You've all been very stupid,' Sonja said.

'You're the stupid one!' Daisy said.

'Is that right, young lady?'

'The police are on their way right now! I have a phone; Mum and Dad don't know about it, and that prick certainly doesn't.' She nodded at Andy.

Emma and Dom exchanged a glance. *Does she really have a phone?* But Emma knew her daughter, sometimes better than she knew herself. She could tell that she was lying. Her voice was slightly higher than usual, her head was tilted subtly to the left. She would not have called the police. Not after what had happened, what she had seen her father doing.

'He is a prick, you're right about that,' Sonja said.

Emma scanned the pub, looking past a wall of potted plants towards the entrance. The place was so busy that the constant movement confused her.

'My daughter's behind you,' Sonja said. 'She's carrying a .44 Magnum. She gut-shot a man with that gun two years ago in Cumbria, blew out his spine and guts. Probably took him hours to die.'

Emma glanced over her shoulder. A young couple sat on the table directly behind her, eating bangers and mash and surfing their phones. Beyond them, an attractive woman sat alone. She had her hands crossed on the table before her, nothing to eat or drink. She wore a white vest speckled with dark spots, and several plasters were pasted onto her shoulder and upper arm. She was staring past Emma at Andy, and did not even acknowledge her gaze.

'Probably a couple of blades, too,' Sonja said. 'Mary always did like her blades.'

'Not always,' Andy said.

'Near enough always.' Sonja leaned over and picked up Dom's coffee. She didn't even glance at him when she took a slurp. 'Euch. Too much sugar. That's bad for your health. Sugar's addictive, and if you don't watch out you'll get diabetes. You look reasonably fit, I suppose. But not as fit as my son. Andy always did take his health and well-being seriously. Which is why I'm surprised at what he's doing now.'

'This is all about my well-being,' Andy said. 'My mental health, and my future safety, Mother.'

'Don't flatter yourself, boy. My one and only child is sitting over there with a gun warming against her thigh.'

'So I'm a bastard and she's a bitch. What does that make you?'

'In charge,' Sonja said. She tapped her chair. 'I'm in the seat, boy, because you made two big mistakes. You should never have been so clumsy. Should have killed us that first time. But your biggest mistake was resurfacing to finish the job.'

'What?' Dom sat forward. It was a sudden movement, and beyond him, just past the trellised plants, Emma saw another movement that mirrored his. And then she saw him, Lip, the man who'd chased her and Daisy through Usk, the one who'd heaved a rock at Dom's head. He was watching them from across the pub, little more than twenty feet away, and she had no idea how she hadn't seen him before.

Maybe because he's a blank, she thought. His face said nothing. He leaned against a column again, arms crossed, looking around as if waiting for someone. Yet all of his attention was on them.

'Oh, so what fairy tale did he tell you?' Sonja asked Dom, smiling. 'That we beat him? Were nasty to him?' She put on a faux-kid's voice. 'Poor little boy felt picked on by his family?'

'He said you got too cruel,' Dom said. 'So he stole money from you and left.'

'And so he did,' Sonja said. 'After trying to kill us all.'

'We don't care,' Emma said. 'About you, him, any of it.' She spoke louder than she'd intended, half-shouting to intrude into the conversation and make herself heard. For a couple of seconds the chatter on the tables and chairs around them faded out, then drifted back in again louder than before. No one wanted to hear an argument. 'None of it matters. He's no friend of ours, and he never was. Whatever sick history the two of you have, why can't you just take it away from us? We have the money in our car. Take it and go.'

Sonja smiled at her. It was not as complete as before, creasing her mouth but barely touching her eyes. It was probably her true smile.

'Too late,' she said. She looked at Daisy. 'Far too late.'

Emma slid forward in her seat, perching on the edge, less than two feet from Sonja now. She was aware of Lip moving closer, and Andy tensed, hand slipping down between his hip and the side of the leather armchair.

'If you even think about touching her, I will kill you,' Emma said.

Sonja raised her eyebrows, stared at Emma. Her smile slipped. 'Yes, I really believe you would.'

Emma felt a rush of something she didn't quite understand. It wasn't power, and she wasn't stupid enough to believe that she'd scared this woman. Maybe it was pride in herself.

'But let me fill you in on a few things,' Sonja said. 'This isn't only about what Andy tried to do to us back then. And it's certainly not about money. Hitting the post office before us, to spite us and goad us into coming after him . . . it's partly that. But it's *all* about Frank. My nephew. Your friend killed him.'

'Like Emma said, he's no friend,' Dom said.

'Yet you're still with him.'

'Not for long.' Dom looked around, spotting Lip behind him. Andy followed his gaze and gave Lip the finger. The man's expression did not flicker.

295

'Lip's a monster,' Emma said. 'What are you doing with him? How can a mother be happy that her daughter's with someone like him?'

'Don't try to engage her mothering sensibilities,' Andy said. 'She never had any.'

'So what is this?' Dom asked. He leaned forward, reaching for his coffee then changing his mind when he remembered she'd drunk from the mug. 'What do you want from us? Emma's right, we have the money, and you can take every penny. But what more?'

'You,' Sonja said. 'You helped my bastard son kill Frank.'

'No, I—'

'And from the looks of you, maybe it was you that did for Cal, too.'

'He was threatening my daughter,' Dom said quietly.

'Don't worry, I hardly knew him,' Sonja said. 'But did it feel *good*?'

'You're just *sick*!' Daisy shouted. She jumped up. 'My dad's good and you're a bitch, and I *hate* you!'

Stillness shifted quickly to movement. Emma panicked, heart hammering, but everything seemed to move very, very slowly.

Lip closed in, approaching Dom from behind. He was carrying something in his right hand.

Still seated, Andy lifted a gun from by his side. The gun Dom had been carrying. He looked around, eyes wide, and saw Lip coming for him. There was something about Andy's expression that chilled Emma. A cool, excited hunger.

She realised that this was what he'd wanted all along.

'Andy!'

The voice was loud, cheery, filled with delight. The woman who'd called out now stood directly behind Sonja, both hands resting on her shoulders. In her right hand, Emma saw a metallic glint.

Andy froze, gun held on his thigh. *Anyone can see that*, Emma thought. But people only saw what they want to see.

Daisy eased back down onto the sofa next to her father.

'Haven't seen you in ages!' the woman continued. 'And as for you . . .' She shook Sonja gently by the shoulders so that the blade scraped against the side of her neck, its handle hidden beneath her forearm. She leaned down, laughing, exuding bonhomie.

'Great to see you again,' Andy said, continuing the charade. His eyes were feral. Cold. Still gripping the gun, he went to stand.

Dom stood and stepped in front of him. Emma saw immediately what he was doing, and she felt winded, every instant the last before a gunshot blasted out. But it did not come. Whatever Andy had been about to do, Dom had prevented.

Lip paused where he was. Someone tried to get past him, muttered something, shoved. Emma was quite convinced that Lip was mad. But she also believed that he valued his health, and his freedom. His gaze didn't flicker away from this new arrival. He was assessing her, weighing the situation. In his hand were a knife and fork clasped together.

Jane Smith, Emma thought, and she had never been so pleased to see a stranger.

Of average height, middle-aged, with short, spiky blonde hair, she wore a stud in her nose and looked thin, wiry and fit. Her shorts-clad legs were landscaped with muscle, her arms the same. She was tanned but too thin and weathered to appear healthy. The smile did not sit well on her face.

'Who the fuck are you?' Sonja asked.

'Trouble,' the woman said. 'Tell your dogs to back down.'

'They're not doing anything.'

'The tall one with hair shaggier than an old man's ball sack is too close, and he's ready to come closer. He does, I'll stick that cutlery in his eyes. The woman has left her table and is trying to circle behind me. Neither of these situations makes me comfortable. When I'm not comfortable I tend to get nervous, and when I get nervous, I twitch.'

The movement was incredibly fast and almost unnoticeable, but Emma saw Sonja wince as the woman flicked at her neck. A spot of blood bloomed and dripped down to the collar of her blouse.

Sonja raised her hand, then dropped it again. Emma saw Lip blink and ease a step back, although he did not appear at all troubled by this new turn of events. Mary paused several feet behind Andy, close to a mirrored pillar, hand resting on a shelf stacked with used glasses. Both were now in the woman's line of sight, but probably still too far away in the noisy surroundings to hear any discussion.

'You two sit down,' the woman said to Dom and Andy. Dom sat and Daisy clasped his hand. Andy remained standing, glancing back and forth between Sonja and Jane Smith.

'But we can—' he started.

'Sit. Down.'

Andy eased back into his seat and slipped the gun down between his leg and the armchair's arm.

'You can all call me Jane.' She was a woman chatting to old friends. No one nearby could hear the discussion above the piped music, the hiss and pop of nearby coffee machines, the scrapes of cutlery and the raised voices of families, kids and businessmen making phone calls. 'I'm in charge. And to make you all certain of that, here's a little bit of psychology for you.'

298

She nodded at Emma. 'You, your husband and the girl have the most to lose here. You're the innocent ones. Though I see he's been in the wars.' She turned and looked at Andy. 'You're already neck-deep in shit. Including shit that sticks because, from what I just heard, you've already lied to me before today. But you still want to get out and away from this in one piece.' She nodded and smiled at Lip where he stood fifteen feet away, then glanced across at Mary. 'You three came here for something you won't get. You're professional. You've been doing this sort of thing for a long time; you know how to handle yourselves. Him especially.'

Lip lifted up and down almost imperceptibly on the balls of his feet, ready to pounce.

Jane Smith raised her voice so that Lip could hear. 'But even Lip doesn't want his coffee spilled. Because he likes this too much. He has plans, and he doesn't want things to end. Get caught, go to prison . . .' She shrugged. 'I guess he could do people in their cells. But it wouldn't be the same.'

'And the point of all this is?' Sonja asked.

'The point is, you've all got more to lose than me. I don't care what happens here. There's very little I *do* care about.' Emma watched the woman looking around, casually and carefully keeping an eye on the situation. 'And because I have nothing to lose, I'm the one who's now calling the shots. Agreed?' She shook Sonja slightly.

'Agreed,' Sonja said.

'Good,' the woman said. 'Now do as I say and call your dogs in closer.'

Rose exuded control. She was confident with that, and she felt reasonably certain that Sonja, Mary and Lip would understand the balance of things. They didn't know who she was or why she was here, but they would understand her expertise. It was plain to see. And they'd hopefully believe that everything she'd said was right – she really did have the least to lose.

Dom and his family would remain quiet and scared, and they'd do whatever she said. Andy had called for her help. She'd already heard details that suggested he'd lied to her the first time they'd met, but that was something to resolve later. For now, he was happy that she was here.

Mary was subdued. She could see her mother with a blade to her jugular.

But Lip was unknown territory. If something was going to go wrong here, Rose knew that he would be the most likely instigator. He was unreadable, and that worried her. His eyes seemed painted on, cool and cruel, and his messy hair and big beard hid any expression he might have. Knowing what he'd already done made him the centre of her attention.

She glanced around the large, open-plan pub. It was chaotic and noisy, but their apparent scene of calm did not seem so out of place. People moved left and right, carrying food and drinks or hauling toddlers, but there were also families and groups sitting and eating, and here and there simply chatting and having a drink. Two hundred witnesses, and several prominent CCTV cameras to back them up.

Sonja waved to Mary and Lip. Mary came first. Lip hesitated for a moment, then took a few steps forward. He still held the knife and fork. They were good weapons, because no one would give them a second glance. The Leatherneck knife Rose held was bulky, but for now she was hiding it well enough between her arm and Sonja's shoulder.

Lip and Mary stood beside the plant-smothered trellis, just behind the comfy sofa.

This was a loaded moment. Andy had already revealed the gun, and she couldn't keep her knife hidden forever. People took a while to see and understand something out of the norm. But once someone raised the alarm, things would start moving quickly.

If that happened, Andy and Lip would be the first to act.

'You and the girl, over with your wife,' Rose said to Dom. She really didn't want the two of them being so close to Lip. One quick move from him, a swing of the hand, and he could bury a fork in Dom's ear without anyone even noticing.

She kept her eyes on Lip. He was a cool customer, his eyes chilling. There really was nothing there, just black windows onto his darker soul. She'd met and tangled with some psychopaths, but he was something else. He glanced around at them all, placing everyone, assessing his options. Rose didn't like that. It was the sign of a man used to being in charge.

'Where's Holt?' Rose asked.

'Who's Holt?' Andy asked.

'I'm not asking you.'

Lip tilted his head slightly. Very little about his expression changed.

'Dead,' Mary said. 'I slit his throat.' She was talking too loud. A man walking by holding a toddler's hand glanced back at her, then across at Rose standing behind Sonja. He hurried on his way.

Rose knew that they didn't have long. Such pressure would never ease; it would always blow.

'Liar,' Rose said, without even looking at Mary.

'He's waiting for me,' Lip said. 'I'll be back to see him soon.'

Rose lowered her left hand from Sonja's shoulder, closer to the deep pocket containing her pistol. She kept the blade pressed against Sonja's neck. She could feel the blood there, sticky, cool.

'Where?'

Lip shrugged.

'Your Jeep's covered in blood,' she said. 'With the back doors open, it'll soon attract attention.'

Maybe Lip frowned, just a little and not for long.

'We're going,' Rose said. 'Me, Andy, and the family. You three are staying here.'

'Who the fuck *are* you?' Mary said.

'Like I told your mother. Trouble.'

Lip moved. Only slightly, but enough to draw her attention. At the same time Mary pulled a gun from her shorts pocket, tensing, ready to lift it and let loose in a crowded cafe, kids laughing and milling and eating, adults never realising what awful dangers existed in their midst.

There and then, Rose finally knew for sure how mad they all were.

She crouched a little, as if to whisper in Sonja's ear, and shoved the blade into her skin. She felt the slight give as it parted around the knife.

Sonja cried out, a small whine that she tried to turn into a cough. She knew that she would be the first to die. And mad or not, she obviously wanted to live.

Lip casually stepped sideways and gripped Mary's arm. He pulled her close so that the weapon was sandwiched between them.

To Rose's left, Andy was tensed in his seat. His own gun was visible again, held down by his knee. Past him, a couple of young men in shorts and T-shirts were looking their way,

frowning. One was leaning close to the other, saying something and pointing at Mary. They weren't talking about her good looks.

Rose knew that they had maybe seconds before the alarm was raised.

She smiled at the young men, rolled her eyes. They turned away, no longer chatting.

'Up,' she said to Emma. The woman stood with her husband and daughter. Andy also stood. He was still holding his weapon down by his leg. 'Put that away,' Rose said.

'You're joking!'

'You!' she said to Mary. 'Hide it.'

Mary exchanged a glance with Sonja. She seemed to slump, tension leaving her shoulders, and slid the gun into her belt, dropping her vest over the handle.

'Good,' Rose said. She withdrew the knife from Sonja's neck, tugging quickly. The older woman hissed and tensed, but did not cry out. Rose took a quick look. She'd been pretty careful about where she'd stabbed, and the knife had only entered half an inch.

'You'll live,' she said to Sonja, before starting to back away. She kept her left hand close to her pocket.

'You won't,' Sonja said, hand pressed to her neck as she turned to glare at Rose.

Emma held her daughter's hand and ushered Dom ahead of her, heading across the pub towards the main doors. Andy came to Rose, but she shook her head.

'But—'

'We need to move.'

'They're all there, together,' Andy said.

'You really want to start shooting in here?' Rose asked. He'd succeeded in surprising her, and she didn't like that.

She usually assessed her jobs carefully, learning about the client before taking them on. Andy had fooled her. Three years ago, it had never been about escaping his family gang's growing brutality. It had been about fleeing the results of his own.

He hesitated. But only for a moment.

'I won't let innocents get hurt,' Rose said, 'and you're far from innocent. Out.'

Andy followed Dom and his family towards the door.

Rose edged across the pub after them. She knew that this was the most dangerous moment. She had nothing on them now, no knife against a throat, and if they decided to start the fight here, they would.

Close up, she could often judge a person's intentions by their eyes. But she was now too far away to see clearly.

Sonja stood slowly, hand on her neck. Though wounded she looked furious. She said something. Lip and Mary both turned to her.

It was Mary who moved first. She stepped out from behind Lip, hand at her belt, and before Rose even had a chance to see what the woman was going to do, she had to make a split decision.

'Over there!' She pointed directly at Mary, Lip and Sonja, pausing for a second for people to turn and see. Then she shouted, 'She's got a gun!'

For a second, all conversation and noise ceased.

Mary's eyes opened wide. Rose realised that she was looking past her. She half-turned, saw Andy crouched in a shooting stance, then he fired, two shots in quick successions. One struck the trellis where they'd been sitting, plant leaves scattering. The second hit the mirrored pillar, shattering the mirror and smashing a dozen empty glasses across the floor.

Mary and the others had dropped. If Mary *had* been about to open fire she should have followed through with it, but now she was momentarily confused, crouching in the open, scrutinised by a hundred startled people. She held the pistol down by her leg.

Someone shouted. Someone else screamed. A glass arced through the air, spilling its contents and smashing at Mary's feet. From elsewhere a tray flipped end over end, connecting with Lip's upper arm.

Rose ran in a crouch and shouldered Andy in the stomach. He fell back into the doors and she drove with her feet, falling on him and both of them sliding across the tiled lobby floor. She pressed the knife against his neck and grabbed his hand, both of them making fists around the hot gun.

'Are you fucking stupid?' she hissed into his face.

'Are you? They're there, all three of them—'

'Up! Out!' She stood and pulled him up.

Inside, people were shouting and screaming. Glancing back she saw Mary and Sonja walking towards the bar, Mary holding her mother's arm. There would be a back way out through the kitchens.

But Lip was heading for Rose.

I could drop him now. One shot and he'll be down. She knew she could do it. Holt's tutelage had made her proficient with a gun, and with continuing practice she had become a crack shot. But there was a chance that Holt was still alive, wounded and bleeding. If she killed Lip now she might be wasting her one chance of finding him.

Besides, Holt had come here to kill Lip. She could not yet take that away from him. Shoving Andy ahead of her, they burst out from the air-conditioned pub into the humid summer day. The air closed in, oppressive and heavy.

They were waiting for her.

'Over there,' she said, pointing across the car park. She'd parked close to the exit, and now wished she hadn't. It was a long way to run whilst waiting for a bullet in the back.

'Their cars?' Dom asked.

'Taken care of.' She'd knifed the Jeep's tyres, but had not revealed its bloody interior like she'd said. She'd busted the vehicle open, then slammed the rear tailgate on the sight of more of Holt's spilled blood.

She hadn't known what Sonja was driving, but had taken a gamble and slashed tyres on the vehicles parked either side of the Jeep.

They ran. Rose made sure Andy was ahead of her.

'The Megane straight ahead,' she said.

'I'll get the money from—' Andy began.

'Forget it, just get in!' They piled into the vehicle, Rose in the driver's seat, Andy beside her, the family in the back. She risked a look back the way they'd come. People were pouring from the building, using several entrances and fire escapes.

Rose pressed her knife against Andy's gut. He gasped. 'Gun.'

'What?'

'Give me the gun. Slowly.'

'Hand it over, Andy,' Emma said from the back seat. She didn't sound scared. Rose was glad, and hoped it was because Emma knew what was good for her. Andy was the loose cannon here.

'One last chance,' Rose said.

'Fuck you.'

She shifted the blade from his gut to his crotch, pressing hard. 'Two seconds and I'll castrate you.'

Maybe it was her voice. She didn't sound angry, but she meant what she said.

'One . . .'

Andy dropped the gun in her lap.

Rose tucked it between her thighs and dropped the knife into the door pocket.

'We can't just run!' Andy said. 'They're all there. We have them! You and me together could—'

'I didn't come to help you kill your family,' she said.

'Then why *did* you come?'

'I was following a friend.'

Andy slammed the dashboard, then sat back, staring straight ahead.

Turning onto the main road, Rose knew that there must have been many sets of eyes watching them go. This was a marked car.

'So what now?' Dom asked. 'Thanks, but . . . you know.'

'Now we take a minute,' Rose said. 'Things have changed. I've got some thinking to do.'

Chapter Thirty-One

Armed Response

'They've gone,' Lip said. 'Let me drive. There's someone waiting for me.'

'They haven't gone!' Sonja said.

'You won't find them again. Whoever she was, she knew what she was doing.'

'Yeah, she was smart,' Sonja said. She chuckled.

Right now, Lip didn't really care about Andy and the family he'd hooked up with. Since the moment he'd left Holt behind he had been itching to return. Spend some time with him. That was unfinished business and he needed to finish the job, slowly, in comfort. Andy would always be there, and so long as he remained embroiled with the family, they'd be easy to track down. Their trail would not grow cold for some time. Blood could wait.

'I'm going to fucking kill him,' Mary said.

'If you don't get yourself killed,' Lip said.

'You *really* sound like you care.'

He said nothing. The silence was heavier than the heat inside the car.

Lip's Jeep's tyres had been slashed, and soon it would be

crawling with SOC officers. He suspected they would have no records of Holt's blood on their database. If he'd sliced off Holt's finger and left that, a perfect clue, they'd probably have no fingerprint match either. He and Holt were shadows. But it seemed that unlike him, someone would miss Holt when he died.

He didn't kid himself with Mary and Sonja, and neither did he care. He was a convenience for them. Mary might have been besotted, but he wasn't sure there was anything like love between them.

They still had Sonja's BMW. The woman had disabled the cars either side of his Jeep, but they had not been foolish enough to park close together.

They'd left the pub with everyone else. At first people had run from them, but by the time they'd reached the car park they had been part of the spreading panic, not its cause. Confusion had disguised their escape, and perhaps they were even lucky enough to have avoided direct views from the CCTV cameras.

Now they were back on the road again. Every minute that passed delayed Lip's final moments with Holt, and took them closer to a confrontation with the law. It was inevitable. Someone would have seen them get into the car, taken a note of its make and colour, and armed response units would be here soon.

Lip had to be finished and away before that happened, because the woman had been right. He never wanted this to end.

He glanced sidelong at Sonja in the driver's seat. He could kill her with his bare hands, and it would take only seconds.

But Mary was behind them, and she was still armed.

'We're wasting time,' Lip said.

'We're simply letting time catch up with us,' Sonja said.

'And what does that mean?'

'A bit of patience. Trust me.'

'I don't trust anyone,' Lip said.

Sonja chuckled again.

He looked at her. *Two hands, one quick twist,* he thought. He'd considered killing her many times. Most people he met found their way into his murderous fantasies, at one time or another.

This was the first time the idea felt serious.

Huddled in the back of the Megane with his wife and daughter, Dom could not help thinking that events were still being driven by anyone but them. The mysterious new woman, Jane Smith, had appeared on the scene just in time, defusing what might have been a violent end to their day.

Sonja had terrified Dom more than anyone. Lip looked like a psycho, and Mary had a wild look in her eyes . . . hunger for the kill. But Sonja could have been anyone's grandmother. Smart, fit, sharp, the truth behind her facade was horrifying.

She'd given them a glimpse, and then Jane Smith had taken over.

Dom had heard the gunshots and believed that the shooting had begun. But no more shots followed, and Jane Smith soon joined them outside, pushing Andy ahead of her and a panicking stream of people. He'd seen her determination then, and the cool calmness that hinted she was used to such situations. He could only wonder at her history.

She wore a T-shirt, her upper right arm displaying an ugly scar. There were scars on her face too, speckled around her

right cheek and jawline like sugar from a cake. She walked with a slight limp, carried a gun, used a knife with confidence.

The more he wondered, the less he wanted to know.

Andy's betrayal burned. Dom felt like such a fool. He had been lied to ever since the first time he and Andy had met. Yet he could not believe that every aspect of their friendship had been a sham. There was little that Andy could gain by befriending someone like him, other than friendship in return. He'd used him to rob the post office, yes, coercing him into crime to suit his own ends. But the couple of years before had been trouble-free. Fun days on the bike, pleasant evenings in the pub or at home—

Andy had tried to fuck Emma. *That* was the kind of man he was. Dom also had to wonder why Emma had never told him about that.

As Rose drove, she googled on her phone with her left hand. Dom tried to see what she was looking for, but the screens changed too quickly. She seemed calm and in control. Even Andy appeared subdued now, his initial anger having dissipated to the hot air.

'This might do,' Jane Smith said.

Dom leaned forward between the seats. 'What?'

'Somewhere to stop.'

'Already? But we have to get away! What if they're following us?'

'Listen, Dom. That's your name? Or are you a Dominic?'

'Only Emma calls me Dominic, and only when she's really pissed at me.'

'Then hopefully if you listen to me, and trust me, you'll always be Dom. And I'm Rose. Jane Smith works online, but face to face I like to have a name.'

'Nice to meet you, Rose.'

311

'No offence, but it really isn't. I'm here because you're in the shit up to your neck. I helped your friend here a while ago, I expect he's told you. Helped him break away from his family, establish himself on his own, invisible and untraceable. Although it seems he lied, to me as well as you, I guess. We'll get to that. But I came back partly because he asked for my help, said his family had found him and were closing in for the kill.'

'He lied about that, too.'

Andy was listening stony-faced. He didn't even look at them.

'In my line of work I don't like liars. They make things dangerous. I like a landscape I can see, not one filled with hidden places. Know what I mean?'

'Yeah.'

'Lucky for him I was on my way here anyway, with a friend. Lip has taken that friend.'

Rose trailed off for a moment, taking them around a roundabout and heading up a narrow road. As the road crested a hill and twisted down the other side, the sea appeared in the distance.

Dom felt a relaxing of his heart. He had always loved the sea, and connected it with family holidays, long hot days, fun.

'I had a family once,' Rose said. 'They died.'

'I'm sorry,' Dom said. He didn't know what else to say.

'You're the innocents in this,' Rose said. 'I help people like you, those who can't help themselves. So I'll do as much as I can.'

'Thank you,' Dom said. 'We . . . we had money. Left it in the car.'

'Don't worry about the money.'

'So where is your friend?'

'Don't know. But listen, all of you. Even you, Andy. You're in the same shit as Dom here, but yours is even deeper. Because now you're on my shit list, too.'

'Listening,' Andy said, still without looking.

'I am in charge. You trust my decisions. I know what I'm doing here. And right now, we're getting off the roads. Our little meeting back there will attract all the security forces in the area. Guns were involved, so anti-terror squads will be on the way, too. Armed response units, helicopters, maybe even Special Forces. The worst place we can be right now is on the road. And as beggars can't be choosers, the best place we can be . . .'

The car turned a bend and descended a steep slope, and at the bottom Rose turned into a gateway. The gate was closed and padlocked. A sign read 'Sandy Hills Holiday Park'.

'But it's all locked up,' Dom said. 'Even though it's summer.'

'Yep. Wait here.' She left the car running, rummaged in the boot, and emerged with a tyre iron. A few twists and the chain around the gatepost snapped.

Dom and the others sat silently, watching. There was too much he wanted to say to Andy to even begin now. Tension hung heavy. He glanced at Emma, and for the first time in a while he saw something he liked in her eyes. Rose had put it there. He prayed that her hope mirrored his own.

They drove into the park and Rose closed the gate behind them, draping the chain back around the post so that it appeared unbroken. She walked back past the car and looked around for a while. Dom guessed she was checking for CCTV cameras or perhaps signs of a caretaker. But the park seemed to be deserted.

It was a baking early September day, the tail end of a long, hot summer. Sandy Hills must have been closed for

refurbishment, but today the site was quiet. It looked tatty and run-down. With the help of modern technology, Rose might just have found them the perfect place to hide.

It was less a holiday park, more a forest. The road led past a small reception building that was little more than a large garden shed. It then curved around to the left and twisted into a wooded, hilly area. Dom could see the first couple of holiday lodges, but trees and folds in the land hid what might lie beyond.

Beside the reception shed was a noticeboard bearing a faded map of the park behind dusty glass. Dom squinted, tried to make it out.

'Looks like a dozen buildings,' Andy said. He'd lowered his front window and was close enough to see. 'The place is wooded, lodges are set back from the single road. Very secluded.'

'Very rundown,' Dom said.

'Ideal. No one else here.'

To their right a field sloped down towards the sea, ending in an overgrown hedge beyond which would be a sharp drop to the beach. The West Wales coast was invariably comprised of long sandy beaches and cliffs leading to the land above. It was rugged and harsh, and a favoured haunt of holiday-makers looking for a little more than sun, sand and ice cream. There were a few seating areas scattered around the field, and a sad children's play area a hundred metres away, with a rusted swing and see-saw apparatus and some tired-looking timber climbing frames. The grass in the field was long and sun-scorched. Wild flowers speckled a palette of colours, and beyond the hedge the sea was wide, grey and majestic. It was really rather beautiful.

'Will there be anything to eat or drink?' Daisy asked.

Rose jumped back into the driver's seat. 'Let's find a place and get settled first,' she said. 'We'll worry about food and drink afterwards.'

It was cooler amongst the trees. It was also just the sort of place Dom and Emma loved to visit on holiday. Quiet, secluded, peaceful, each lodge was well shielded from the others, with outdoor seating areas and a few with hot tubs. Daisy was just getting to the age when she wanted more lively holidays, but ever since she was born they'd had at least one holiday each year to somewhere similar to Sandy Hills. Dom and Emma sometimes admitted that it was more for them than Daisy, but they always made sure she had a great time.

Every family memory seemed suddenly more important to Dom. It felt like remembering a deceased relative, as if those times were now lost to them, each memory precious.

'We'll be okay,' Dom said. He was speaking to his wife and daughter, not caring that Andy and Rose also heard. They existed almost in another world to him.

'I can't see further ahead than this afternoon,' Emma said.

'He's right,' Rose said. 'You'll be okay. Let's park up, then we can talk. There. That one looks fine.'

The single gravelled track wound them through the trees, and Rose pulled up in front of a lodge that looked very much like several others they had passed. It was set a little further back from the road, but was made of the same dark red timber boarding, single storey, white windows and timber decking to the front and one side. The decking to the side was more extensive, containing seating, a hot tub and a barbecue area. It might once have been lovely. But the cladding needed a coat of paint, and shrubs planted along the borders had overgrown and swamped much of the raised decking.

'I'll get us inside,' Andy said.

'No, I'll do it,' Rose said. 'Better if we don't break the locks. I can pick them. Jump out, I'll hide the car around the back. The trees are good cover.'

Dom helped Daisy from the car. He felt dreadful. Maybe it was the prospect of getting inside the building and resting for the first time in what seemed like forever. His wounds were making a noise again, shouting to be heard. His eyes were heavy with exhaustion. Daisy ended up helping him towards the lodge, Emma following close behind.

'You smell, Dad,' Daisy said.

'Thank you.'

'You're welcome. It's important we're honest with each other. You're really sweaty, too. I'll keep my arm around you because you're my dad and I love you, but really. Euch.'

'Charming,' Dom said, and he was happy to hear Emma laughing softly behind them. Such sweet music.

Andy walked apart from them, and as they approached the lodge Dom became aware that he was looking across at them. Staring, trying to attract Dom's attention.

I'm just too damn tired, Dom thought, but he looked anyway.

'I'm sorry,' Andy said.

'What?' Emma gasped.

'Fuck off and leave my mum and dad alone,' Daisy said. 'Fuck off and leave us *all* alone.' It was the first time Dom had ever heard Daisy use that word. He was glad that she was using it right.

Andy looked away. Dom felt no pity for him. His betrayal had not only come as an emotional shock, but he'd also found it frightening. That someone could have used him in such a way, pulled the wool over his eyes, made him feel

like a child again. Though it exposed him to hurt, he still liked this aspect of himself. The innocence, the vulnerability, the trust and assumption that people were essentially good. What he didn't like was people taking advantage.

'What Daisy said,' Dom said.

Rose came around the lodge then, jumped up on the decking and approached the front door. She drew something from her small rucksack and bustled at the door, and within a minute she had it open.

'Home sweet home,' she said. She looked at Daisy, and for a moment Dom saw a shadow of sadness cross her feature. *She has a story to tell*, he thought.

'Come on,' Rose said, smiling at Daisy. 'Let's see if we can find some food.'

Chapter Thirty-Two

Option Three

Every fibre of her body was urging Rose to run. She sat at the dining table and looked at the strangers around her, and all she could think of was Holt. He had bled so much. Perhaps he was already dead. But that idea sent her cold, spinning once more into the chasm. If Holt was gone, then so too was she.

She closed her eyes and willed him to be alive.

'Green tea,' Andy said. 'It's all there was.' He placed the steaming mug before her, then brought more over for Dom and Emma. Daisy had a glass of water. There was no food. The lodge hadn't been used for a while, probably since last year's holiday season. They'd found a bottle of congealed ketchup, a bowl of shrivelled dried fruit, and a half-empty bag of soft, mouldy crisps.

Rose sipped. It burned her lip, but she didn't mind.

Daisy leaned into her father, grabbing his arm and hugging it tight.

Molly leans against her, constantly fidgeting as always, never still, always moving towards the next exciting moment.

Rose glanced to her left. There was no one there.

'So, we sit and drink tea,' Andy said.

'Just shut it!' Emma snapped. Andy sighed and sat at the table. He picked up a coaster between two fingers and turned it, tapped against the tabletop, turned and tapped again.

Rose so wanted to run, but she couldn't. Not when these people were in such danger. She would never forgive herself if the family suffered a grisly fate.

'Okay. I'm going to lay out your options as I see them,' Rose said. All eyes were on her. 'I've got to warn you, though, none of them are good.'

'Tell us something we don't know,' Emma said.

'There are three ways to go from here,' Rose said. 'First, we call the police. Tell them everything. Dom, you throw yourself at the mercy of the law.'

'Screw that!' Andy said.

'And *you* disappear,' Rose said to Andy. 'This time, without my help. Good luck with that.'

'I've killed someone,' Dom said. He stared at his hands, fingers splayed on the table before him. His fingernails and knuckles were dark with grime. Maybe it was dried blood.

'It was self defence,' Rose said. 'You were protecting your loved ones. You're a respectable family, a decent guy, they'll see that.' She shrugged. 'But then, you did rob a post office.'

'People died,' Emma said. 'Respectable or not, Dom would go to prison.'

'For a long time,' Rose agreed. She nodded at Daisy. 'She'd grow up without a dad.'

'If we call the law, Sonja and the others will melt away,' Andy said. 'That's what they do. That's how they survive.'

'Scared they'll creep up behind you one night?' Dom asked.

'Sure, and so should you be. They're animals.'

319

'Even worse than you?' Emma asked.

'Yes,' Andy said. His eyes clouded and he leaned back in his chair. 'What I did wasn't only for self-preservation. I didn't fit in with the new version of my family. Lip and I didn't get on from the first time we met, and they would have killed me in the end, so I tried to leave. They threatened the woman I loved. The *only* woman I've ever loved.'

Rose knew the look in his eyes. She saw it in her own each time she looked in a mirror.

'They killed her,' she said.

Shock seemed to silence their surroundings. The creaks of moving chairs, rustle of clothing, the sighs of tiredness and pain, all gave silent audience to what Andy said next.

'I stole money and ran away with Rachel, and I thought that would be enough. But she left me soon after. I was stupid enough to tell her the truth about them, about me, and she grew scared and left one night without even saying goodbye. I wanted to protect her. But I couldn't. I tried to find her, but they found her first. She had an accident. Fell down some stairs in a car park, broke her neck.'

'It doesn't matter,' Emma said after a brief pause. 'I'm not sure I even believe you, not after all the lies. I don't think any of us can believe you. Even if it *is* true, it doesn't excuse what you've done. And I don't care.'

Andy looked at her but said nothing.

'In answer to your question, Emma, yes,' Rose said. 'They're even worse than Andy. Although I'm not saying he's not a lying murdering scumbag.'

'Oh, thanks,' Andy muttered.

'If Dom *does* go to prison, when things have quietened down there's no saying they won't come after you and Daisy. Just to make a point.'

'And because Lip likes it,' Emma said.

Rose nodded. She thought of the dead guy in the car on the hillside, a branch shoved into his eye socket. The blood in the back of Lip's Jeep.

'They'll get to Dom in prison,' Andy said. 'Doesn't matter what sentence you get. You won't be coming out.'

'So I guess we rule out option one,' Dom said. 'What's number two?'

'I make you disappear.' Rose waited while Dom and Emma looked at each other, having a full conversation in silence. A married couple, people in love, could do that. She remembered communicating with Adam in that way. A smile or frown meant a thousand words.

'It's what I do,' Rose continued. 'I'm sure Andy will give you a reference.'

'So what does that mean, exactly?' Dom asked.

'It means today is your birthday. All three of you. Dom, what's your job?'

'I've got an electrical firm.'

'Not any more. Emma, your career ends here, too. Your families don't know what happened to you. You never see them or your friends again.' She glanced at Daisy. 'None of you. You'll go to live overseas, possibly Europe, more likely further afield. You've got debts? Good, they're written off. Savings? They're gone too. There'll be *nothing* to link you back to your life that's now ended.'

Emma was wide-eyed, trying to take in the implications. But Rose knew there were too many, and that they were too extensive. No one could really imagine everything they knew, all that they were, everything they had built themselves up to be coming to an end. It was like dying.

'Andy managed it,' Dom said.

'Andy *wanted* to do it,' Rose said. 'He was easy. He wanted to hide from his family, friends, associates, and he had the money.'

'But our families?' Dom asked. 'Really?'

'Once you're gone, you're gone,' Rose said. 'If this is the way we agree to do things, I push the reset button on your lives. It won't be quick, and for a while you'll have to retreat, lie low somewhere and not reveal yourselves at all. There are a few places I know. It'll take me some time to set things up for you. But for that period of time you're all as good as dead. Dom, Emma, Daisy, you'll be gone. When we're ready, you'll be born again as new people.'

'We don't have the money,' Dom said.

'Yeah, that is a problem,' Rose sighed.

'The money's in the Mazda back at the Helmsman car park,' Emma said. 'Could we . . .?'

'Don't be stupid,' Rose said. 'It'll be crawling with the law by now. How much was there?'

Dom blinked in surprise. 'We never actually counted it. We thought maybe forty grand.'

'Was it worth it?' Rose asked.

No one replied.

'There are ways and means,' Rose said. 'But it will take a good lump of money. If we go this route, for a lot of what is required I'm an enabler, not a doer. We'll need to pay for your new identities.'

'You mean passports, driving licences?'

'Not just that,' Rose said. 'It's not like the old days any more, Dom. Everything is recorded now, and anyone in the world, with the right know-how, can access everything about you on their phone. You'll each need a whole history constructed, from birth to present. Traceable, reliable.

That means employment and health records, bank accounts, social security details for whichever country you'll settle in, travel histories. It's a long, detailed, expensive process.'

'I'll pay,' Andy said.

'We don't want your—' Dom began, but Andy cut in.

'How much cash are you carrying, Dom? Cos that's all you have left.'

'It doesn't matter,' Emma said. 'We can't do that. Not to her.' She looked down at Daisy leaning against her arm. The girl was asleep, for which Rose was grateful. This wasn't the sort of thing a little kid should hear.

Though compared to what this child had seen, hearing things was nothing.

'I'd rather take the fall,' Dom said. 'Go to prison, ask for police protection from the Scotts. But leaving everything behind, no. I can't do that to Emma and Daisy.' Dom looked helpless, hopeless, and his love for his family was a physical thing. It warmed the room.

'So it's option three,' Emma said.

'You don't even know what it is yet.'

'I think I can guess.' Emma was glaring at Andy. He continued to turn the coaster, *tap, tap*, staring at it simply to avoid everyone's gaze. 'It's what he's wanted all along. The reason he lied to me and my husband, and drew my daughter into danger.'

'I didn't mean it to go this far,' Andy said.

'Really?' Emma was aghast. 'Is that meant to be some sort of apology?'

'No,' Andy said. 'Simple fact.'

'He wanted them all dead long before now,' Rose said.

Andy glanced up at her. She didn't look away.

'He doesn't realise that nothing like this ever goes to plan. There's always a wild card, and the closer to the beginning it's played, the more chaotic things become.'

'The wild card was getting his dates wrong,' Dom said.

'Yes,' Rose said. 'Meeting the Scotts at the post office instead of taunting them afterwards, drawing them after him, maybe picking them off one by one. From that moment on, everything he'd planned went wrong. That's why he called me to do his dirty work.'

'Not quite everything,' Andy said.

'No,' Dom said. 'Right. You threw Frank from the top of a windmill.'

'So option three is to kill them all,' Emma said. 'Sonja, Lip and Mary. Remove the problem.'

Rose was impressed at the steadiness of her voice. But then Emma had impressed her from the start and was continuing to do so, more and more.

'It's a different way of moving on,' Rose said. 'I have my own issue with the Scotts, now, and that might mean the same result. But for your sake, it's frankly the most likely way you can get out of this mess with anything like your old life left standing.'

'Really?' Emma asked. 'You think so? Anything like it?'

'There'll be a chance,' Rose said. 'We can make sure they're linked to the post office heist. Maybe the law will see what came after – the college, the chase across South Wales – as a beef within the gang.'

'That's exactly what it is!' Dom said. 'Maybe they should get him, too.' He nodded at Andy.

Andy froze in turning the placemat and stared at Dom. Rose saw something in his eyes that she hadn't seen before, and it was a look she knew all too well. Holt had it, she'd

seen it in the Trail, and when she looked in the mirror it was also there. He had the eyes of a killer.

'You threatening me?' Andy asked.

'Stating a fact,' Dom said. '*They're* your sort. Not us.'

Rose felt her senses calming and sharpening. Events slowed.

'Let me make this an easy decision,' Andy said. As he twirled the placemat to distract their attention, he reached into his shorts pocket with his other hand.

Rose had her pistol out and held across the table in a heartbeat.

Andy paused, still smiling. 'Quick on the draw, Rose.'

'Don't be stupid.'

'I'm far from that. But I'm about to speed things up.' He nodded down at his hand still in his pocket. 'Slow and easy, all right?'

'Slow and easy,' Rose said. She already had an inkling of what she might see.

He withdrew his hand and placed his phone on the table.

Rose lifted the pistol and pointed it at Andy's face. She could pull the trigger now and rid herself and this family of a constant wild card.

'How long?' she asked.

'I texted them about ten minutes ago.'

'Then they'll be here soon.' Rose hesitated for a moment more, then lowered the gun. An urgency prickled at her, the idea that the more time passed, the less likely it was that she'd see Holt alive again. She'd been wrestling with her conscience – go and attempt to save Holt; stay and help this family. Andy might just have settled her inner dispute for her.

'They won't come,' Emma said. 'They'll be expecting a trap.'

'They'll come,' Andy said.

'So what do we do?' Dom asked.

'We get ready.' Rose stood and pocketed her gun. 'Now listen to me, all of you. Here's what I want you to do.'

Chapter Thirty-Three

Stacked Odds

It was hot, still and sunny, the holiday park was deserted, and Dom was sure that they'd hear and see the Scotts coming. Rose had taken a few items from a box in her car and put together a sensor for the gate, which she said would tell her when it was opened. But he was still more afraid than he ever had been before. Scared for himself, and terrified for his family.

He had wanted Emma and Daisy to leave. There were other lodges, and they could hide in one and wait for everything to be over. But Emma had vehemently objected, and Rose had sided with her. They had two pistols and Holt's shotgun between them. Although Emma admitted that she was probably capable of handling a weapon – her father was a member of a shooting club, and her grandfather had been a farmer – it made no sense to split their defensive capabilities. To make this a success they needed to stay together.

Daisy had had the final say. 'I want to stay with you, Daddy.' That tugged at Dom's heart. He wasn't sure he could watch them walking away, knowing he might never see them again.

So they were together, and he was ready to protect them all against whatever was to come.

'It's so damn hot,' Emma said.

'Wish I was on a beach,' Dom replied.

'One far away from here.'

'Parasol.'

'Ice cream,' Daisy said.

'Good book.'

'Jug of Sangria,' Dom said. 'Watch the sunset, air-conditioned room with—

'Ice cream!' Daisy insisted. 'Chocolate flavour with—'

'What's that?' Emma leaned forward, closer to the bedroom window. Dom held her shoulder and eased her back.

'What'd you see?'

'Something moved. Over there, through the trees.'

'Rose!' Dom said. But she was already with them, slipping through the bedroom door and crossing the room almost soundlessly. She carried a pistol in one hand, shotgun in the other. She looked formidable.

'They came through the gate a few minutes ago,' she said. 'Must have left whatever vehicle they're using down by the entrance. Mary is approaching up the road, quite brazen. Trying to draw us out. Who did you see?'

'I'm not sure,' Emma said. 'It *might* have been Lip.'

'You trust Andy on his own?' Dom asked Rose.

'He wants the same as us,' she said. 'Don't worry. I'm keeping an eye on him.'

'What if he doesn't want any witnesses?' Emma asked, verbalising a fear that had been gnawing at Dom. He'd done his best to deny it, hating the images it presented. But nothing would have surprised him about Andy now.

'I've met a lot of bad people,' Rose said. 'He's not like that.'

'I can never trust him again,' Dom said.

'Good. Don't blame you. But I'm pretty sure he's not planning to put a bullet in the back of your head, Dom.'

'What about yours?' he asked.

Rose glanced at him strangely, then eased forward so she could see from the window.

'What do we do?' Emma asked.

'Look after your little girl. Can you handle this?' She offered Emma the shotgun.

Emma nodded and took the weapon. 'What now?'

Rose glanced from the window again. Lithe, tensed like a big cat about to strike, she grew incredibly still. 'They're coming. Hallway. Now.'

Dom grabbed Daisy's hand and followed Emma out of the room, just as the whole world exploded around them.

At first he thought they were going at the lodge with axes and sledgehammers. Holes were punched in walls, splintered wood and dust spat around, timber boarding split with a harsh *crack!* He soon realised they were gunshots. Behind the sounds of destruction around them he heard the *snap-snap* of gunfire, and he fell onto Daisy in the internal hallway, him and Emma huddling around her to protect her from the terrible violence.

The lodge was constructed in a block pattern, the central hallway feeding bedrooms and bathrooms on either side. They were lucky that they had an interior windowless space to hide in. But Dom had a feeling that luck would not last.

From close by he heard heavy gunshots as Rose returned fire. There were three, evenly spaced and very deliberate. He worried that she didn't have much ammunition. When she'd been explaining what she wanted of them, she'd seemed to avoid the subject of what weapons she carried.

She had given Andy his pistol back. For now it remained silent.

'Dad!' Daisy whispered. 'I'm scared!'

'Me too, honey.' He caught Emma's eye. They both grinned. It was at the ridiculousness of this, the sheer disbelief. Then a bullet shattered a framed print above them, showering them with glass, and the grins fell away.

More gunshots erupted from the room they'd just left, and then Rose fell back through the doorway. She crawled right over them, elbows and knees punching and prodding.

'What is it?' Dom asked.

'Lip coming around the back,' she said. 'They've got bigger artillery than us.'

'We've got shelter,' Emma said.

'Made of wood.' Rose crawled towards the bedroom at the end of the short hallway. As she shoved the door open she rolled onto her side, brought the gun up, and fired.

Rose had fought battles against the odds before. It made her sharper. But this time they were stacked, not just in numbers but in geography and weaponry. The lodge had at least ten windows in five or six rooms, too many for them to cover. The Scotts were using an assault shotgun, pistols and a Kalashnikov. Even Lip must have been wielding a gun, though she guessed he'd have preferred killing them all with a chunk of wood or a fucking squirrel.

Freak. Bastard. That's what kept her going, the idea that she was *not* a freak, *not* a bastard. She was doing her best for these people, mostly innocent, completely naive. She wasn't sure exactly what that made her.

As she shoved the bedroom door open with her left hand she saw the shadow at the window. The glass was shattered,

frame fractured, and Lip was already halfway inside. He was looking at her, expressionless in this cacophony of violence.

She dropped, rolled onto her right side, brought the gun up to bear and fired.

Lip fired at the same time. She hadn't noticed a weapon, and she cursed herself for that. She had trained herself to catch a snapshot of a scene and to then decode and understand everything it contained. On occasions such as this it had saved her life more than once.

Lips's lifeless eyes had drawn and distracted her.

The bullet parted her spiked hair and impacted the door frame above her head.

Lip shouted and fell back out.

Grenade! she thought. But she'd left it in the door pocket of the Megane. Stupid. It just showed how unprepared she was, and how rattled at Holt's disappearance.

Rose aimed at the wall below the window and fired three times. There were no more shouts, and she wasn't sure she'd hit him the first time. He might be lying there dead, or he might have crawled aside, looking for another way in. Either way, she had to push the advantage.

She scurried across the bedroom around the foot of the double bed, and sat against the wall to the left of the window.

More gunshots sounded from the front of the lodge. She heard Andy return fire, two careful shots. Good. He was conserving ammunition, and that would matter. If the Scotts knew how little ammunition she actually carried, they could simply hold back and shoot them into submission.

The clock was ticking. Deserted though the holiday park was, someone would hear the shooting. The police would come. Armed response would already be close following the shooting at the Helmsman, and then it would be over for

all of them. Any agonising with Dom and Emma about how to proceed would be decided for them.

As would Holt's fate.

Rose took a deep breath and looked through a bullet hole in the wall. The view was narrow, but she could see no movement, and no sign of anyone huddled against the other side.

He'd be going for another window.

Crouched, she ran back into the hallway.

Just in time to hear a sustained burst of gunfire, and look along the hallway to see the front door swing open.

'Kitchen!' Emma said to Dom. 'Units there, cooker, better protection.'

He nodded.

'And there are knives,' Daisy said.

The bullet impacts seemed to have lessened. As they crawled through into the open-plan living area, Dom saw Andy lying beside the sofa. For a moment he thought he was dead, but then Andy made a circle with his thumb and forefinger, smiling. *Smiling*. He was enjoying this.

Movement drew Dom's attention. A shadow shifted across a large window at one side of the living area. As he pointed, and Andy knelt to turn that way, Mary appeared in the window.

She was carrying an AK-47, easily recognisable from countless news reports. She opened up, spraying the room, twitching right as soon as she saw Dom and his family. The noise was awful.

Dom kicked, shoving his feet back and connecting with the wall, pushing Emma and Daisy ahead of him as hard as he could. The floor was cheap laminated wood, shiny and

smooth, and the units they slid behind absorbed most of the bullets. Crockery exploded inside, pans rang with the impacts.

Something hit Dom in the side. He grunted, winded, and pulled himself closer to Daisy, shielding her with his body. He quickly checked his side, terrified at what he'd find. But there was no blood.

A door was knocked from a base unit, swinging aside and spewing shattered chinaware across the floor. Emma thrust the shotgun into the cupboard and pulled the trigger, firing at Mary through the fractured wood. After one shot she tried again, but for some reason the shotgun was no longer working. Maybe it was jammed, or perhaps she wasn't as familiar with these weapons as she'd believed.

Dom grabbed her arm and pulled her away. She dropped the shotgun and they huddled together, instinctively ensuring that Daisy was sandwiched between them.

Someone screamed. The kitchen light, which Dom had intentionally left on, dimmed and flickered, and he knew that the front door had just been opened.

Using bits from what Rose had called her box of tricks, he had wired the metal handle directly into the fuse box, setting a rudimentary wire circuit connector that would work when the door was opened three inches, electrocuting whoever opened it.

The shooting ceased. The air was now filled with that awful, high scream.

Dom peered over the worktop.

The front door was half-open. Sonja held onto the handle, quivering as electricity pulsed through her. She stared at her hand as if willing it to let go, but it would not obey. Muscles in her neck and face stood out like cords. Her left eyeball began to smoke.

Mary was no longer at the window. Maybe she was taking advantage of the distraction to enter the lodge from elsewhere, but Dom thought not. Her mother was being cooked alive from the inside out.

'Where is she?' Emma asked from beside him. She snapped up the shotgun again and stretched it across the worktop, also looking at Sonja. 'Where's—?'

Andy knelt, aimed, and shot Sonja twice in the chest. The impact knocked her back off the timber-decked porch and onto the gravelled ground. The air smelled of burned hair and cooking meat.

Andy did not move. Dom saw him breathing hard and fast, but from the side he couldn't quite make out his expression.

He had just killed his own mother.

'Noooooo!' The scream was horrible, unrestrained, and Mary ran into view, kneeling beside Sonja and cradling her head. Dom saw burned skin slough from her face.

Andy aimed again. Dom heard the click of his empty gun. So did Mary.

'You fucking bastard!' she shouted, scooping up her assault rifle, leaping over their mother's body, and coming for them all.

From deeper in the lodge Dom heard a heavy impact and the sounds of a struggle. *Lip's in!* he thought. Help would not come from Rose.

He and Emma stood at the same time. Emma wielded the jammed shotgun as a club, Dom had snatched up a kitchen knife. As Mary reached the front doorway Emma threw the shotgun, hard. It span end over end and struck her on the left shoulder.

Mary gasped and tried to bring her gun up to bear, but the impact must have deadened her arm.

Andy launched himself at her, pistol raised in his hand. They met hard, breath knocked from bodies, fists flying, the violence shocking and confusing.

'Grab Daisy and get to the car!' Dom said to Emma, then dashed into the hall. He feared that Rose was already dead.

But if she was, there was no reason for Lip to be battering her like he was.

Rose had seen the door open and Sonja electrocuted. When the automatic fire ceased she knew what was coming, so she knelt and steadied her gun. Her right arm ached as it always did, reminding her of her battle in the mountains with the Trail. Her hip was sore. Other wounds fed her memories of other times, and that was good, it reminded her of who and what she was.

Andy shot Sonja, the woman fell back, and as Mary came into view Rose's finger squeezed on the trigger.

The impact on the side of her head was shocking, knocking her out of the world. She slumped down and hit the wall, and instinct clasped her hand around her gun. A weight dropped onto her and crushed her to the floor, and it took some time to realise that she was being beaten.

Her family watches her, silent, staring, not wanting her here. This is their place. Not hers. This is no memory, but the reality of what separates them. It is not her time.

She gathered herself, drawing inwards before bursting up and out again, struggling to survive and prevail because that was all that mattered. It was anger that brought her around. Anger at herself for forgetting about Lip, however briefly, and now he was in and beating her, killing her. If she died, so would everyone else here.

And Holt.

Rose slumped, lifeless, then willed strength into every part of herself, twisting, writhing, thrashing up off the floor.

Lip fell from where he sat astride her, tumbling to the side and striking his head on a door frame.

Rose took a moment to orientate herself. Blood clouded her vision, and pain thrummed in from around her neck and scalp. Whatever the damage, she could still function. Right now, that was all that mattered.

Lip came at her again, glass soap dish raised in his right hand.

Rose swung her pistol around and deflected the blow, squeezing the trigger three times. The bullets snagged Lip's shaggy hair but caused no injury.

He head-butted her. She drew back at the last moment and the impact was slight, but she could smell him. An animal scent, like rotten meat and death.

He pushed forward and bit her, grinding his teeth into her collarbone.

Rose screamed and pressed the gun into his side, pulling the trigger, even though some subconscious awareness had already told her she was out of bullets. She used it as a club instead, battering at the back of his head until he let go. Blood splashed. She saw shreds of her skin hanging from his reddened teeth.

A shadow fell over them and Rose knew this was it; if Mary had killed Andy then she was finished too.

A blade flashed. Lip saw it at the last moment and turned his head, and the knife tangled in his hair. He pulled back and shook his head. His cheek opened, his ear was sliced, blood spattered across the wall, and then Lip scurried back into the bathroom like a dog, kicking the door closed.

Rose sat up, panting, and Dom stepped over her, reaching for the knife that had dropped to the floor. From the bathroom came the sound of breaking glass.

She snatched a magazine from her pocket and quickly reloaded the pistol, firing six shots through the bathroom door before kicking it open.

The small room was empty. The window was smashed. Blood smeared the floor and wall.

'Emma!' Dom shouted.

'Hold on to me, tight!' Emma said, grasping Daisy's hand. She eased around the end of the kitchen unit and glanced back along the hallway. Dom was standing above where Rose and Lip fought on the floor. He had a knife raised in his hand.

In the living area, Andy and Mary rolled, punched, bit, kicked.

'We're going,' she said to Daisy.

They walked quickly towards the door, Emma remembering not to touch the handle in case the power was still on. Once outside she would run. Screw the car. As fast as she could, Daisy with her, she'd run in any direction that was away from here.

A hand closed around her ankle and she screamed.

Mary dragged herself closer, kicking Andy in the face as she did so, pulling herself upright.

Emma stumbled backwards into the corner TV cabinet, Daisy with her.

Mary advanced on her. She looked mad, blood smearing her face, sweat diluting it and dripping it down across her vest and shorts. Her hair hung free, clotted with blood. Emma didn't know whose it was.

Mary lunged, but tripped. Andy was behind her on the floor, reaching for her. It didn't look as though he could see. His face was scored with deep scratch marks and one of his eyes bled profusely, his lips were puffy and ripped. But he did not stop. He crawled on hands and knees and found Mary again, dropping onto her, pinning her down with his own body weight.

'Run!' he croaked, and Emma needed no more encouragement.

As she and Daisy burst through the front door and stepped around the dead woman splayed on the gravel, six gunshots sang out behind them. Emma screamed. But she did not fall. She smelled hot meat, shit, and sweat. The surroundings were beautiful, but around and behind her was violence that would forever mark this place.

It would mark her, also. And Daisy. However hard she ran now, however far, they could never fully escape.

She had only taken one step when Daisy shouted, 'Mummy!'

Something smashed into Emma's head and then she felt, and knew, no more.

Dom ran through the living area. Andy sat against one side wall, panting heavily, his face a bloody mess. Mary was splayed on the floor. There was blood everywhere. Dom didn't know whose it was, and he didn't care, because Emma and Daisy were gone. He could see Sonja's body outside the door, and trees, and gravel, but nothing else.

Outside, the air smelled of death.

Emma lay beside the gravelled road. He went to her, looking around for Daisy but not seeing her. Perhaps she'd run.

But no. Daisy would have never left her mother like this.

'Daisy!' he screamed as he knelt beside his wife, and he thought he heard an answering voice in the distance. But it might have been an echo.

Rose knelt beside him. She felt Emma's neck with bloody hands.

'She's alive,' she said. 'Lip took Daisy. We have to get her back.'

'Yes. Where? I can't see—'

Emma stirred, groaning and trying to roll onto her side. Her scalp was wet with blood, face smeared with it, and he had done this to her, to all of them.

'Baby,' he said. He reached for her face and her eyes snapped open, filled with pain. She grabbed his hand.

'Daisy!'

'He'll be going for his car,' Rose said. 'Come on, Dom.' She dashed around the lodge towards the Megane.

'I can't just leave you,' Dom said to his wife.

'You have to,' Emma said. 'I'm fine.' She didn't look fine. He thought she might have a fractured skull. But he knew there was no arguing. The monster had their daughter, and he had to get her back.

'Car's fucked.' Rose reappeared beside them. 'You have to get away from here, Emma. But first I need to know where Lip's going. Where he hid Holt. You need to find out from Mary. Can you?'

'If she's still alive,' Emma said.

'She is. For now. But Andy's in there with her.' Rose grabbed Emma and heaved her to her feet. Dom helped, holding his wife. He was amazed at the strength he felt in her limbs and torso. One of her eyes seemed lazy. She spat out a tooth shard.

'Go,' Emma said. 'I'll text Dom whatever I find out.'

'My phone's—'

'Get Andy to text it to me,' Rose said. 'And be quick. Every second we waste makes it more likely you'll never see Daisy again.'

Rose started running.

'Please come back,' Emma said to Dom, grabbing his arm. 'Nothing's more important than the three of us.'

'Nothing's more important than the two of you,' he said. He kissed her, then followed Rose.

Emma felt sick. A white-hot pain pounded in her head, one eye wasn't working properly, blood ran sticky and warm across her scalp, face and neck. But the greatest pain was inside.

Lip, with Daisy.

If she could have run, she would have chased him down to the ends of the earth. But she could hardly walk.

It took forever to edge around Sonja's corpse and climb the three steps to the decked area. She let go of the handrail and staggered to the front door, grabbing the frame for support. She knew that there was danger inside, but she had no time for caution.

Emma walked into the lodge.

Mary was on the floor, clawing her way slowly towards the sofa. A kitchen knife protruded from just above her left shoulder blade. She left a trail of blood on the laminate floor.

Andy was propped against the wall to Emma's left. He'd obviously sat there and slid down, slumped almost to the floor. She didn't think he could see her.

'I can't move,' he said. 'I'm weak. Feel sick. You need to take care of her.'

Emma looked at Mary again. Take care? He meant kill her. But she wouldn't do that. Not yet.

She looked around and saw Andy's discarded gun. She picked it up.

'Empty,' he said. 'Rose gave me . . . spare mag. Shorts pocket.'

Emma pushed from the wall and walked slowly, carefully, to Andy. She was worried that if she knelt she would not be able to stand again, but there was no other way. She held onto the low table beside him, taking her weight on her left arm, easing herself down.

'Don't get any ideas,' she said as she reached into his pocket.

Andy snorted blood. His laugh was like a series of small coughs, turning into a groan.

'Is that a magazine in your pocket?' Emma asked. She felt hysteria closing in, and wasn't sure she could control it.

'Don't!' Andy said, laughing again. 'It hurts. Too. Much. She broke something inside me, I think.'

'I know how you feel. Fucking bastard.' Emma drew the mag from his pocket and held it and the gun up before him.

'Hit that clip there.'

She did so and the empty magazine slipped halfway out. She extracted it, pushed the new mag into the pistol's handle.

'Click it home.'

She did. It lodged with a satisfying sound.

'You're ready,' he said. And she was. For a moment she stared at him, gun in her hand, and she was pleased to see the doubt, then the fear in his eyes. But she wasn't anything like him.

Rose went to Mary and crouched beside her. She was feeling better all the time. The pain in her head pulsed, but

341

she was taking action, protecting her family. Concentrating only on the present, not the possible, horrible future, Emma pressed the gun against Mary's neck.

'Where's Lip going?'

Mary halted her slow, pained crawl, relaxed onto her front, and laughed.

Emma tapped the blade in her back with the barrel of the gun. Mary's laugh turned into a long, low hiss.

'Where?'

'Fuck you.'

Emma showed Mary the gun.

'You won't shoot me. Soft white bitch. You have no idea—'

Emma pressed the gun against the side of Mary's left thigh and pulled the trigger.

The blast was deafening. Her hearing dulled, and it was Mary's scream that drew her back in.

'Holy shit,' Andy said from her right, but Emma did not look. Neither did she examine the damage she'd done to the woman's leg. She didn't want to see, and it did not matter.

Mary was writhing, sweating, bleeding.

'Where?'

The wounded woman spat across the floor. 'Fuck you. You won't kill me. Not while I know.'

'But I'll hurt you.'

'I like pain.'

Emma leaned down and whispered, 'I'll give you *real* pain, Mary. I'll do anything to protect my family. Will you?'

She rolled Mary onto her side and pressed the pistol low against her belly. It was a hunch. But Mary froze, even her breath stalling.

Emma knew that her hunch was right.

'A church. An old church, ruined, couple of miles along

the coast on a cliff overlooking the sea. Place called Wood Lane.' Mary stared wide-eyed, filled with terror for someone other than herself. Emma did not believe she was acting.

She eased back, stood up, and Mary pressed her hands against her stomach and curled into a protective ball. She might have been crying, but Emma didn't care.

'You need to get out of here,' Andy said.

'I know.'

'What about me?'

'Phone.' She held out her hand, and Andy dug his phone from his pocket.

Emma found Rose's latest text to him and replied with "Wood Lane, old church by the sea." Then she looked at Andy. Even wounded and in pain, he didn't look pathetic. He looked strong and capable, as he always had. She hated him more than she had hated anyone in her life before.

She pointed the gun at him. He stopped breathing.

'You're lucky I'm not like you,' she said. Then she threw his gun onto the sofa and left the lodge.

Outside it was still incredibly hot. She knew she could not run. She could hardly walk, but she had to. She heard what might have been a siren in the distance.

Deciding that moving downhill would be easier than up, she headed for the sea.

Five minutes later, as she crossed the park's picnic area and approached steps leading down to the beach, she heard a single gunshot.

Chapter Thirty-Four

The Beach

She knew they had only moments. It might already be too late. For Daisy, and Holt, and for Emma and Andy too.

Rose had to make every second count.

Lip didn't have much of a head start, and he was carrying Daisy. She'd be struggling, kicking, writhing in his grasp. *If he doesn't just kill her*, she thought, but she couldn't go there. She was the most innocent of them all, and it was the innocent who often suffered the most.

She ran, and Dom ran with her. They cut through the trees, shoving through undergrowth, brambles tearing at their bare legs. She was heading directly for the entrance where she hoped the Scotts had parked their car.

'Don't stop,' Rose said. She glanced back at Dom. He looked terrified but determined, and he reminded her of another man whose family had been in such peril. Chris Sheen had been capable and strong. Dom was not as fit as Chris has been, but the weight of guilt bore him forward and gave him strength. She only hoped she could predict the same positive outcome for him.

But current events felt much more out of her control. She was floundering, reacting instead of leading things.

They burst from the trees. Down the hillside she saw Lip arriving at a BMW. He flung open the door and threw the girl inside.

'Daisy!' Dom screamed.

Lip glanced up and saw them, then dropped into the driving seat.

Rose ran faster. Everything hurt. She fed on the pain.

When she was close enough she crouched into a shooting stance and aimed.

Dom knocked her from behind and sent her tumbling. 'You'll hit Daisy!'

'I'm aiming for the tyres!'

But it was too late. Lip wheel-span the car, rammed the gates, and screeched out onto the approach road.

'Oh my God,' Dom said.

'I could have stopped him!'

'He's got her. He's gone.'

'Hopefully not too far.' As Rose snatched her phone from her pocket it pinged. 'A ruined church, Wood Lane. Just along the coast.' She looked around, scanning the overgrown picnic and play area and the high hedge bordering the cliff top. 'There.'

'What?' Dom asked.

'A gate.' As she jogged she googled the church at Wood Lane, waiting for a map to load. She only hoped she was going the right way, that the beach was accessible, and that they might be able to reach the church before Lip.

There was so much left to chance.

Dom stayed with her. She could hear him panting as he tried to keep up.

As they reached the metal gate in the overgrown hedge, a partial map finally loaded onto her phone. She paused, checked it out, then showed it to Dom.

'Along the coast from here. If we run, we might even beat him there.'

'And then?'

'Don't know.' The gate squealed open. The steps down to the beach were steep, overgrown, and crumbling in places. 'Making this up as I go.'

The gentle sound of the sea drew them down.

He had left them behind. They couldn't follow in the woman's car because Lip had shot out its tyres. He had a good head start. It wasn't far to drive.

But he could not let himself relax. The police would be swarming across the whole area soon, and by the time they arrived he had to be finished and gone. No time to relish the moment, but still time to make the moment happen. He was still in control.

The lanes were narrow and twisting, the hedges high and overgrown. He had to concentrate on his driving, fast enough to give himself as much time as possible, not too fast to cause an accident.

Several minutes after leaving the holiday park the girl fixed her seatbelt, then reached over and scratched him across the face.

She surprised him, because she'd been quiet and easy to handle until then. The move was sudden, her little fist punching at the cut across his cheek, nails snagging in the flap of skin and tugging, setting fire to the wound.

Lip lashed out with his fist and felt it connect. The girl squealed.

Between one blink and the next the car bounced into a pothole, the wheel jumped from his hand and they struck a stone wall beside the road. Metal crumpled and the car dropped, steam surging from the damaged radiator. He jerked forward and the wheel punched his chest, winding him for a moment. If he'd been going much faster he might have broken ribs.

'Stupid girl!' he gasped.

She was curled on her seat, looking at the blood on her fisted hand, silent.

Lip tried the stalled engine. It started, but the car only crawled forward with a grinding of broken metal. It was crippled, one wheel damaged beyond repair.

He reached across and grabbed the girl by the arm. 'With me. Now.' He pulled and she followed, climbing over the front seats and scrambling from the driver's door. He knew that he had to get off the road, and thirty metres along the lane he found a gate into a wide, sloping field. The sea was visible beyond, and if he kept going that way he would arrive at the church.

He ran hard, clasping the girl tightly to his side. Sometimes she found her feet and ran with him, other times he dragged her along. She sobbed a little, and cried out when her feet slapped hard against the ground. But she wasn't snivelling like most kids would. He respected that.

Sonja was gone, fried alive. Mary was probably dead by now, too. He felt a pang at the thought, and it was a curious emotion. He could not identify it as regret or sadness. Not even shock at the loss of the pregnancy she had never found the courage to tell him about, even though he had known for a while. Maybe it was simply an awareness that time was moving on.

He had become far too comfortable with the Scotts. Now,

his future was the wide-open canvas of potential that he enjoyed so much. The next few minutes might be mapped out, but beyond that there was only mystery.

He would disappear again, find his way somewhere quiet and safe. Lick his wounds. Decide what the next portion of his life might bring.

He pushed through an overgrown kissing gate and headed across another field, the sea to his right at the bottom of a cliff, a gently rising slope to his left. Ahead he could see a busy copse of trees and wild hedgerow. Within, he could just make out the spire of the ruined church.

Close. Excitement built. He could almost smell Holt, waiting for the final touch. Lip loved the delicious irony of Holt's impending demise. Like sister, like brother.

'Hurry,' he said. The girl did not reply. Neither did she struggle against him, but he would not be lulled by that. She was a clever kid, and her parents had proved that they had fight in them. She'd scratch his eyes out as soon as look at him.

'Hurry,' he said again. 'We're almost there.'

The steps down to the beach were treacherous, and Rose descended them headlong, letting momentum carry her. She heard Dom behind her, sensed his panic and terror, and listened for a stumble. If he fell, she'd go too.

The steps had once been a pleasant descent to the beach for residents of the holiday park, but now they were overgrown and fallen into disrepair. Bushes snagged at her clothing, and several times the edges of concrete steps crumbled beneath her feet. They zigged and zagged down the cliff face, and a couple of minutes later they arrived at the beach. There was a timber gate, locked and bolted, but one kick sent it skittering across the pebbles.

Rose turned left and started running. There were a few people on the beach, so she tucked her pistol into her belt, making sure it was secure. She knew that she and Dom presented a strange sight, but she couldn't worry about that now. On her way down the steps she'd hoped for a sandy beach. Running on pebbles was hard. They made a noise, and faces turned their way.

'Didn't all these people hear?' Dom asked from close behind her.

'Probably didn't recognise it as gunfire,' she said. 'Save your breath. Run.'

Rose kept them close to the cliff. The tide was in, and closer to the sea there were a few families and lone dog walkers. The families splashed in the water or hung around base camp, spreads of beach chairs, towels, and wind breaks. Umbrellas were used as protection against the unrelenting sun. Most of the lone walkers were in their own world, staring out to sea, checking their footing, whistling if their dogs strayed too far. A few people glanced at Rose and Dom, but not for long.

Rose tried to regulate her pace. It would be too easy to sprint and wear herself out. Breathing deeply and evenly, she tried to settle into a rhythm. But it was difficult, leaping larger stones, dodging around rocks, slipping as pebbles slid against each other. She looked ahead along the long beach, scanning the clifftops for any signs of the church. There were none.

The cliff varied in height, protruding into a small headland maybe two miles along the coast. If the church was built there, it might be too far. Two miles running on a pebble beach would be at least twenty minutes, probably more. She'd never been fast, though she had built up an impressive endurance. Now, she craved speed.

'Where is it?' Dom called. He sounded further behind her, but Rose did not slow. She couldn't. Every second might count.

'Keep looking,' was all she said. She tried to check the small map she'd brought up on her phone but she had no reception. That was fine. She did not like relying too much on technology, because it could always fail.

It's all about this, Holt had told her once, tapping her head none too gently. *Not this*. He'd snatched at her phone and thrown it into a field. It had taken her ten minutes to find it, Holt sitting on a rock by that dusty Italian road, smiling and smoking.

'I'm coming for you,' she said, voice lost amidst the crack and snap of stones beneath their feet. The sea shushed to her right, mindless, careless. She'd spent long hours staring at the sea with Holt. He liked its timelessness.

The beach widened as they ran, cliff growing taller and retreating slightly inland. It was not sheer, and in several places steep paths and steps climbed towards its top. It reflected heat at them. Rose was sweating, a familiar feeling when she exercised, shedding weakness. She blinked it from her eyes, along with blood. Her hip ached, and her right arm. New wounds burned.

The gun was heavy in her belt.

She glanced back and saw that Dom was falling behind. He looked exhausted, desperate, but he waved her on. *He knows*, she thought. *He understands this is about every minute, every second. His little girl has been taken by a monster, and he knows I'm the best chance he has of ever seeing her again.*

She tried not to imagine what might happen if they were too late. To Holt. To Daisy. Lip would act quickly, but she

also knew that he would be cruel. It would be his final message to her.

An inlet opened on their left, a meagre stream winding down across the beach to the sea. Nestled in the craggy-walled inlet were a few buildings – a beach cafe, lifeguard station, and a couple of shops selling beachwear and touristy stuff. A few families sat outside the cafe, watching Rose and Dom run. Maybe some of them speculated. But none of them would ever know the truth. They'd sleep easy tonight.

Echoes of her own family, her children, skipped around her like whirling sand dervishes. Each time she looked they were gone. But not really.

Past the inlet, she climbed a rocky beach defence and dropped down the other side, relieved when she found hard-packed sand beyond. Her pace increased. She looked back to see Dom just mounting the rocky mound. He slipped and stumbled, scraping his bare legs on the rocks

She waved him on and shouted encouragement. He did not reply.

Rose checked out the clifftop, trying to assess how far they'd come. Perhaps a mile so far, maybe a little more, but there was still no sign of the church. She checked her phone again, still no reception.

Running on the hard sand was much easier, and she settled into more of a rhythm, speeding up and leaving Dom further behind.

Almost five minutes later, approaching the headland that marked the end of this part of the beach, she saw a smooth-lined structure within a mass of trees atop the cliff. It was a building of some sort. It might have been a spire.

She skirted left, scanning the cliffs for a route up. The gate was set up from the beach, several large rocks forming

a natural staircase to what she hoped was the start of a route to the top. The cliff was only around twenty metres high, and she could scramble and climb up it if she had to. But that would take time.

She pounded across the beach for the gate. As she reached it she glanced back and saw Dom a couple of hundred metres back, still trying to run. She made sure he'd seen her, then turned her attention to the gate.

It was made of rusted metal bars, heavy and solid, and was firmly chained and locked. Beyond she could see the steep staircase rising to the left and disappearing behind wild undergrowth. There were no ways to push through the bushes growing around it, so she started to climb.

Wounds old and new complained, but she cut out the pain. The gate scraped against her legs as she tipped over the top and went sprawling on the other side. With one glance back at Dom, still running towards her, she pulled her pistol and started up.

The stone staircase wound up the cliff face, and it had not been used in some time. Bushes crowded in from both sides, the treads were thick with last year's dried leaf fall, but she pushed through, hunching her head down and shoving past heavy brambles and roses gone wild. Thorns scratched at her skin and curled in, grabbing, barbed and cruel. She kept glancing up and ahead, the top of the cliff still out of sight. Trees grew close to the edge up there, those closest with roots exposed to the open air where constant erosion sought to undermine them. Perhaps that was why the church was abandoned. Maybe the congregation did not like the idea of time catching up with them.

The path jigged to the left again and she faced another barred metal gate. She had to climb this one too, and as she

swung her legs over the top, she wondered whether Dom would be able to do the same.

It took another five minutes to reach the head of the uneven staircase, and the final gate. Beyond was a mass of wild undergrowth, speckled with flowers and hanging heavy with green fruit that would make a fine haul of blackberries in a few weeks' time.

And beyond that, the church. It was quite small, surrounded by tall trees and undergrowth gone wild. Obviously abandoned, it still presented an impressive facade. Windows were boarded up, the main doorway hidden behind fitted metal sheeting, and a lush spread of ivy covered one side wall and reached for the spire.

There was no sign of Lip's car. It might have been parked around the other side. Rose paused and hunched low, listening. There was nothing out of the ordinary.

If he was already inside, she might already be too late.

If he had yet to arrive, she had to get inside before him.

Just as she was about to climb the final gate she heard Dom behind her, panting hard as he climbed the last few steps.

'Anything?' he gasped.

'No sign.' His effort was immense, and Rose knew it was all for his child. She had dreamed many times of saving her own, but she always had to wake up.

'There,' he said, pointing. 'To the left.'

Rose looked. A basement access stood open, the timber hatch set low beside the church's old stone wall.

Rose's blood ran cold. He was here already, inside, and she was so close to Holt and yet so far away.

She thought quickly. Dom gripped her arm and she turned, holding his hand and squeezing. She hoped he was more comforted from the contact than she felt.

'We can't both just rush in,' she said. 'We get one chance at this. Listen.'

For a terrible moment Lip worried that Holt had escaped, worked his way free somehow, wriggled away and hidden somewhere away from the church. But then he entered the building and smelled fresh urine, and he knew the man was still there.

On entering the church, the girl had started struggling more. He gripped her tighter. She swung for him and he absorbed the weak blow.

'Don't do that again. I have a knife.' He showed her the blade. Not a weapon of choice, but beggars could not be choosers. And once he'd done Holt there were rocks, and old door hinges, and other creative ways he could take on Dom and the woman close behind.

Holt was still tied up and hemmed in beneath the pile of old pews. He'd been struggling, but the knots were tight. He hadn't got far.

'So there you are!' Lip said. He hauled a pew aside, dropped it. The girl struggled again when she saw the bound man, and Lip had to squeeze her, hard. She grew still.

'I've been looking forward to this,' he said. 'Had to take care of something else first. Hope you're not too uncomfortable. I was worried you'd have snotted yourself and suffocated.'

Holt glared up at him, no fear in his eyes, only hate.

Lip released the girl and pulled her down before him, shoving her to the ground, knife pressed to her. He knelt on her. 'Don't move an inch.'

Holt looked at the girl and struggled against his bindings. His wrists were bleeding, ankles and thighs tied tightly. Blood

and snot smeared his mouth and chin. More blood stained the floor around him, and his side was darkened. Lip was glad he hadn't bled to death.

His mouth was still glued shut.

Lip leaned forward and pressed Holt's head back against a pew, placing most of his weight on the man. Holt tried to struggle but could barely move. Beneath his knees, Lip felt the girl writhing. He reached into his pocket and drew out the small tube of superglue.

'Bit of a rush,' he said. 'Both at the same time, I'm afraid.' He squeezed glue into Holt's nostrils, staring into his eyes as he did so. He saw no panic there, no terror at imminent death. Only a pure hatred.

'Big breath.' Holt sucked in his last lungful of glue-tainted air, then Lip squeezed the man's nostrils closed and held them tight. 'One . . . two . . . three . . .'

At ten he let go.

Holt started to shake, flexing his jaw and nose, stretching his face in an attempt to open an airway. But the glue was good. Lip knew that well enough.

'Goodnight,' he said. He stood, pulling the girl up by the hair. She screamed. He no longer cared. They would be here soon.

Rose tested the old wooden door. The latch was raised, there were no signs of any other locks, and when she pressed gently it shifted on its hinges. The small vestry was dank and dusty, little light finding its way through the boarded window. The door she had squeezed through was around a corner behind her.

She breathed deep and slow, trying to still her growing panic. Dom needed time to work his way through the door

they'd found leading into the chancel. To have any hope of success, they needed to approach Lip from two directions. With the girl he had a shield, but if they could confuse him—

'Goodnight,' she heard from beyond the door. And then a scream.

Rose took a deep breath, gripped the pistol, and pushed through into the light.

Dom knew that he should wait for Rose. But when he peered around a column, and saw the monster standing over a squirming, dying man, and saw Daisy pulled up by her hair, heard her scream, he could not hold himself back.

He grasped the object he had almost tripped over and darted forward.

Rose skidded on the dusty floor, and by the time she'd brought her gun to bear, Lip had hugged the girl to his body. He pressed the knife to her throat, breathing evenly. Everything was still in his control.

'Put her down!' Rose shouted. She was fifteen steps away. Even though she looked around for her friend Holt, hidden from her view beneath the pews and still writhing, the pistol barrel did not waver.

The girl bit into Lip's hand, startling him, and he thought, *Where's the father?*

The impact against his temple knocked him sideways, exploding his senses. He tensed his knife arm, ready to draw it across the girl's throat—

Pain exploded in his wrist as she bit him again. She stomped her foot down his shin. Confused, against every instinct he released her, and she scampered away to his left.

Lip pivoted as the first shot sang out. It punched into his right shoulder and sent him stumbling, and as he went he slashed the blade across Dom's throat.

He did not hear the next shot.

'Dom!' Rose shouted as Lip dropped to the ground. She took a few steps and put another bullet into the fallen man's head, just to be sure. Brains and a spray of shattered skull splashed across the dusty floor.

'Daddy!'

Dom had taken a couple of steps back and sat on an old pew, still grasping the wooden cross he'd used to smash Lip around the head. He raised a hand to his throat to stem the blood, but it was flowing freely now, the slash pouting as his panicked heart pumped blood from his body.

Daisy ran to him and reached him the same time as Rose. Dom looked at his little girl, eyes wide.

'Good . . . girl,' he rasped. Blood bubbled between his fingers.

Rose looked down at Holt. He glared back, imploring, rocking on his back, hands tied and trapped beneath him.

'Daddy!' Daisy shouted again. 'Help my daddy!'

Rose took one more look at Dom to confirm what she already knew. Time crushed her. There was a choice to be made, and she tried to consider who she had the best chance of saving. She really tried.

Kneeling beside Holt, she raised a hand and signalled him to be still.

His mouth was glued tight. His nose was misshapen, nostrils barely visible. She could slice off his nose, hack open his lips. But his throat might already be filled with blood, mucus, vomit. The time it would take to do that—

She scrambled to Lip's body and found the knife, a small blade but sharp. It dripped with Dom's blood.

She showed it to Holt and he closed his eyes.

His throat was slick with sweat. Rose had never done this before, but she'd read about it. She felt below his Adam's apple, placed the tip of the knife there, and pushed.

Holt whined and stiffened, shaking. She withdrew the knife and looked around, desperate, sensing him slipping away.

'My daddy!'

Dom was slumped to the side now, blood still gushing between his fingers clasped to his throat. His eyes were glazed. Daisy was crying, yelling, red.

Focus! Rose thought. *You've made your choice.* She spotted an old Bible, snatched it up, ripped off the cover, tore out the inner flyleaf, rolled it, and worked it into the incision in Holt's throat.

It hissed, bubbling blood and then air. His eyes opened again and he stared at her, blinking tears.

'Got you,' Rose said.

'Help my *daddy*!' Daisy screamed again. She was shoving at Dom, trying to make him move, denying his stillness like a baby animal prodding its fallen parent.

The girl's wretchedness, her impending loss, sank cool teeth into Rose's heart. She went to them on her knees, certain of what she would find. She was surprised. He was still alive.

But he only lasted for another two minutes.

Rose saw the moment when life left Dom's body. But Daisy kept nudging him, and she let the child do that for a little while longer.

Chapter Thirty-Five

The Hollow Woman

'He's going to be fine. It was touch and go, and for a while I was worried about brain damage. He lost a lot of blood. But he pulled through. I'll be going to see him soon.'

'Good,' Emma said. 'I'm glad. For you, and him.' The cafe was busy with holidaymakers, businessmen, and single travellers with their own unknown stories. Emma looked at these people and wondered about them. She never really had before, but now she knew that everyone had a story. Some were more interesting than others, some were sadder. Some, monstrous.

Rose sipped her coffee. 'And what about you?'

'Really? You'd ask that? My daughter witnessed my husband murder someone, then she saw someone kill him. She was covered in his blood and sometimes thinks she still is. I find her washing herself seven, eight times each day. She sneaks away to do it. She's seeing a child psychologist. My sweet daughter, in fucking *therapy*. There are people asking for our story. Offering money. Like it's an *entertainment*. What about me? I'm hollow. We both are.'

Rose glanced away, but she did not seem embarrassed.

Emma had always known she had a story, though she had never fully shared it. She was Jane Smith, the do-over woman, someone who knew how to fight and kill, but she must have been someone else before that. Emma could see it in her. A mother and wife, perhaps.

'Kids are resilient,' Rose said.

'How would you know?'

Rose did not reply. She drank more coffee, looking around. She always seemed on edge, wired, constantly expecting trouble. Emma guessed that was how she lived her life.

'What about your friends?' Rose asked.

'They've been priceless,' Emma said. 'Mandy and Paul got engaged. I think what happened to them made them realise how much they need each other. They used to argue about such stupid things.' Her voice faded a little, and she had a flash-memory of her and Dom, bickering over something foolish. 'They've been helping me so much. Me and Daisy. I honestly don't know what I'd have done without them. They're *good* people.'

She emphasised the "good". Rose nodded, gaze continuing to flit around the cafe.

'So what did you want to say to me that we couldn't do on the phone?' Emma asked. 'The police will want to know where I am.'

'Of course they will. Tell them you needed to get away.'

'I do.' Emma looked down at her hands again. She remembered shooting the gun into Mary's leg. She'd been found dead in the lodge, her brains blown out. Sonja was dead outside, eyeballs melted and skin blistered. There was other people's blood in the building, too, but no one else was found. *They took us*, Emma had told the police, and it was

the story she had to stick to. *They took me and Dom and Daisy, and threatened us, and I don't know why. But I think maybe Dom had something to do with the post office heist.*

That had been one of the hardest parts of constructing her story. Rose had helped her, of course, vision untainted by crippling grief and despair. Even though it was a version of the truth, blaming Dom had felt cruel, and it went against everything they had been fighting for. But as Rose had said, it wouldn't change anything for him. It was best to say that most of the truth had died with him. And now that he was gone, he would help them in any way he could.

'So?' Emma prompted.

'So . . . I don't want you to become like me.'

Emma snorted. But Rose stared at her, waiting until she caught her eye.

'I've suffered loss,' Rose said. 'Terrible loss. Much worse than you.'

'I don't think—'

'My husband and three children were murdered.'

Emma's breath caught in her throat.

'It almost consumed me,' Rose said. 'I know what being hollow feels like, Emma. I lost myself, and Holt found me again. That old bastard's the reason I'm still alive. Don't lose yourself. I've worked hard, and you have too, building a story that might just stick. You have a good chance to get through this and emerge out the other side. You won't be unscathed, and you'll both be changed forever. But it's up to you how that change affects your lives. You've survived too much to throw it all away now, and you have Daisy. She's your rock, your anchor to the real world. I know she needs you, but believe me, you'll end up needing her more.'

'She's the reason,' Emma muttered.

'Yes! She's the reason you did what you did. Remember that. Don't let rage swallow you up and blur the reason.'

'But *he's* still out there.' She sneered in disgust. 'Andy.' Saying his name, thinking about him, made her sick with hate. She blamed him for that, too – she had no room in her life for such feelings. It was as if even though absent, he was still playing her for a fool.

'Andy? You've nothing to be afraid of from him.'

'That bastard came into my family and destroyed it. Why should I not fear him?' Thinking of him always inspired a confusing rush of images and sensations – a laughing, confident man, sharing wine in their back garden on a hot day; he and her husband clad in Lycra astride their bikes; Andy bloodied and injured, waiting for her to leave so that he could spend a final moment with his sister.

A blazing summer afternoon in her and Dom's en suite, mint-scented steam caressing her body, Andy's heat as he pulled her close, the feel of him heavy and full in her hand.

She shivered, closed her eyes, tried to swallow the feeling of shame and disgust. That last memory was one that presented itself again and again. While she'd convinced herself that the moment was simply a foolish mistake, the memory felt like an ultimate betrayal. It was the guilt from this that she struggled with most, because she could never tell anyone about it. That was *her* dark memory.

'He's no threat to you and Daisy,' Rose said.

'You're sure? Do you know where he is?'

'I'm sure. And no, I don't know. I have had a look around, tried to trace him. His girlfriend Claudette hasn't seen him. Neither has anyone else. His trail's cold, but he was taught by the best.' She smiled. 'Maybe he'll go after his family's

assets, but I doubt that. I suspect Andy's vanished for good. Let your hate go, Emma. You both deserve more.'

The hatred was a fire, and perhaps over time she could douse its flames, let its heat bleed away. As for fearing Andy, she'd thought about that long and hard. She could conceive of no reason he might wish her and Daisy harm. Hearing it from Rose helped her in that. He might have been a lying, manipulative bastard, but he wasn't that sort of man. He wasn't another Lip.

'It's going to take me a long time,' Emma said. She'd cried too much already, and her tears seemed to have dried. But in their place was a deep, daunting nothing, a dark place inside that threatened to consume her every minute of the day. If she submitted to its lure she wasn't sure she would ever find her way back out.

'Let it,' Rose said. 'You can't fool grief. But remember your reason. However dark it is, she's your light.'

Emma saw sadness in Rose's eyes, a true, endless sadness that took her breath away. Rose glanced at the seat beside her as if looking for someone. Then her face hardened again, and the moment was gone.

'One thing.' Emma paused. 'I have to ask.'

'There was no helping him.'

'You're sure about that?' It had kept Emma awake at night, and it probably always would. 'You're *certain*? Because you chose to help Holt over Dom, and I don't know . . . I can never ask Daisy . . .' Her voice broke. There were no tears, but the darkness felt wider and deeper than ever.

'Certain as I can ever be,' Rose said.

Emma nodded. She felt a sudden, powerful urge to be away from this woman. 'I should be getting back. Daisy's at Mandy's, I'm due to pick her up.'

'Tell her I say hi.'

'I really don't think I will.'

Rose nodded. She understood. Emma thought she was probably used to being the woman who wasn't there.

'Listen, if you ever need me for anything, just go on Twitter and—'

'I'll never need help from the likes of you again,' Emma said. She cringed a little at how that had sounded. But she'd meant it.

'Good,' Rose said at last. She meant it too. She touched the back of Emma's hand on the table, a surprisingly intimate gesture. Then she stood and left, weaving through the busy cafe. Before she reached the door Emma looked down at her empty coffee cup. She never saw Jane Smith leave.

Five weeks later, Emma's life was starting to settle into its new shape. It was a shape she hated, because it was missing a vital part, and she and her daughter didn't fit. Daisy knew that too. But the little girl was strong, concerned for her mother, a whirlwind of activity.

Emma guessed she was holding much of her grief inside, and although the compulsive washing had ceased, at night the tears still came. But she'd been advised to be easy on Daisy. They spoke of Dom every day, and Daisy was very open about what had happened. The time she stopped wanting to talk about her dead dad would be the time for real concern.

The police still came around now and then. She'd given her account of events at least a dozen times to several different officers, and now there were national press agencies offering her stupid money for her story. The kidnapped family, the crime gang's internal feud, the killing spree across

South Wales. She was still declining, finding the whole idea repulsive. But she also knew that the money on offer would make the future easier for her and Daisy. Dom's electrical firm was in limbo. His apprentice Davey was keen to buy it, but her solicitors indicated that a sale would be a complex and time-consuming matter. Dom's life insurance firm was resisting paying out on his policy pending investigation into his criminal role in the carnage. Emma was on extended leave from the college, fully paid but with an undertone of disapproval from the management. She supposed that was fair enough. How could someone who had been through so much offer support to young, vulnerable minds? So the time might come when she would start serious talks with one of the newspapers, and everything would be on her terms.

She had briefly considered moving house. Everything at home reminded her of Dom, not only their belongings and the building itself, but the smell of cut grass, brewing coffee, and the strains of certain songs drifting from the radio. She'd realised that she could not run away from these memories. A couple of times she'd caught Daisy frozen in a moment, and watched without her knowing. She knew that her sweet daughter was remembering her father. So much had changed that Emma couldn't find it in her heart to change where they lived, as well.

Daisy had returned to school for the new year. Having her friends around her seemed to help, and she was doing well. As well as could be expected.

Emma wasn't.

The summer heat had broken a couple of weeks before, leaving scorched parkland and cracked reservoir beds a nightly image on the news. It had been the hottest British summer on record. Roads had melted, scrubland burned.

Emma would forever associate the smell of summer heat with death.

She was in the back garden, mug of tea cooling on the table beside her, book propped open and unread in her lap, when someone tapped gently at the gate.

'What?' she shouted, startled.

'Oh, sorry,' a man's voice said. 'I didn't mean to scare you. Is it okay if I enter?'

'The gate's unlocked,' Emma said after only a brief pause. She remained nervous. She carried a small paring knife in her jeans' pocket. It was sharper than it needed to be, and it went everywhere with her. She touched it, the metal handle cool and comforting.

The terrible thing was, she knew she could use it.

The man was tall and athletic. He wore chinos and a white linen shirt, tucked in and perfectly tailored to his physique. His shoes were good, hair neat, face cleanly shaved. He carried a hard laptop case. Emma supposed he was good-looking, but there was something about his manner that immediately put her on edge.

Not a cop, she thought. She'd met enough over the past few weeks to know them.

'Who are you?' she asked.

'I'm not here to trouble you,' the man said. He pulled out a seat across the patio from her and sat without asking. He seemed very assured, calm and in control. He placed the laptop case on the table and ignored it, crossing his legs, hands clasped around his knee.

'That's not an answer.'

'My name's Peter. I know you've been through a real ordeal, and I—'

'Where are you from? You're not a policeman.'

'No, I'm not.' He was smiling, but offering no answers.

'Press?'

'Far from it. I'm a friend of Rose's.'

Emma blinked, surprised. *Rose doesn't exist*, she thought. It was the most delicate part of the story they had created. Emma had never mentioned Rose's presence or existence, and she had impressed upon Daisy the need to do the same. So far as everyone was concerned, Daisy had no recollection of what had happened at the church. Events there remained a mystery. And even though several people on the beach had confused, conflicting memories of Dom chasing a woman, the story seemed to have held.

No one knew about Rose.

'Who?'

Peter stared at her. The smile remained. But there was something behind it she didn't like one little bit. Something about his eyes.

Emma had seen such a look before.

'I'd like to know where she is,' Peter said. 'I haven't seen her in years, and I'd love to catch up.'

'I don't know who you're talking about.'

Peter leaned forward. He touched the laptop case. 'I have enough on here to convince the police otherwise. I was convinced the moment I saw the first news reports. Such events, chaos like that . . . Rose's forte.' He tapped the laptop case with one finger, punctuating each sentence. 'Some deleted phone records. A couple of recorded conversations. Three blurred CCTV images. You know we're the most watched country in the world? Even a ghost gets seen sometimes.'

Emma did not reply.

'If the police received this information, I think they'd

become very interested in your story again. Especially the details you left out. You and Daisy.'

'I've nothing to hide,' Emma said.

'Maybe not.' He drummed his fingers on the case, then sat back again. 'I want Rose. I know she was here. Tell me what you know about where she is, and I'll leave, and you'll never see or hear from me again.'

Emma thought it through. This was not a man she wanted in her life. It seemed hopeless trying to maintain the lie, but at the same time she had nothing to tell him.

'Why do you want her?' she asked. 'You're no friend of hers. People like you don't have friends.'

'You're quick to judge.'

'I've seen your like before. So, why?'

'Because we have a history,' Peter said. 'She's the one that got away.'

Emma had no idea what he meant. But she decided to tell the truth.

'I don't know anything about her. When she left, she offered me a way to contact her. I didn't want it. I never want to see her again, and I have no idea where she went.'

Peter gazed at her, still smiling. His stare became uncomfortable.

'I believe you,' he said at last. 'It would be stupid to lie to me. I think you know that.'

Emma didn't trust herself to attempt a reply. She thought she might cry.

Peter stood, picked up the laptop, and left. He said no more, and as he closed the gate behind him he did not look back.

Emma took a few deep breaths, touching the knife in her pocket to ensure it was still there. Then she went inside to make some more coffee.

In the kitchen, she started shaking. The knife was a solid weight in her pocket. The grief flowed in, wave upon wave, and she experienced one of the familiar washes of memories involving Dom. They came frequently, unbidden but usually welcome. She was starting to wonder if it would always be like this.

Emma sobbed, grabbing hold of the kitchen worktop as she saw Dom at the sink, sitting at the table eating, laughing his way through the door with Daisy on his back. She gathered herself quickly, running her fingers through her hair. She felt the ridged line on her scalp. It was one of many scars, this one physical.

Taking the knife from her pocket and dropping it in the sink, wiping her eyes, she reached for the kettle.

Chapter Thirty-Six

Surprise

The farm was old and messy, the farmhouse a big stone affair, surrounded by several dilapidated barns and a couple of smaller buildings long since subsumed beneath undergrowth. There was a new tractor in the yard, and other pieces of machinery parked in one of the open-fronted barns. Chickens wandered the yard.

A dog watched her suspiciously as she approached. A farmer emerged from a building attached to one of the barns, nodded once, and pointed at a lean-to at the side of the farmhouse.

Rose headed that way. The dog watched her go. It was a working animal, not a pet. She whistled softly and its ears pricked up.

Even though it was nearing the end of one of the warmest, driest summers on record, still a chill breeze breathed in across the fields. She had been enjoying the wildness and remoteness of the Scottish Highlands. She'd always wanted to visit. Coming here alone, without her family, felt like something of a betrayal. But in a way she always carried them with her, and they were here too.

The lean-to housed a storage area, filled with bulging hessian bags and blue plastic containers. Through a doorway lined with a rotten frame, a smaller area contained an old mattress on the floor and a couple of kitchen units piled with mechanical parts.

Holt was sitting in a chair beside the mattress.

'Jesus,' Rose said. 'You stink.'

'We're on a farm.'

'Don't try to divert the blame. Have you showered? Do they have, you know, water?'

'Of course they do. Electricity, too. And they don't eat people up here any more.'

'Hmm.' She sized him up. He seemed thinner than the last time she'd seen him, if that was possible. A little greyer, too. But the Holt she knew was still very much there. Rose was glad. She'd really missed him.

She could never tell him that, of course.

'Gunshot wound?'

'It's good. Had to have the bullet dug out, but it hadn't splintered. No infection. I'm strong as an ox, apparently.'

'And the . . .' She touched her neck.

'Itchy. But the vet says it's healed well.'

Rose laughed.

'What?'

'A vet.' She smiled.

'I'm glad my discomfort and near-death experience amuses you.' That acknowledgement of what had almost happened hung between them.

She went to him and kissed his cheek, and Holt stood and embraced her. It was comfortable, a friendly contact. He felt warm to her, and Rose hoped she gave him warmth, too.

'Rose,' he said, pulling away, face serious. 'It's Benjamin.'

'What is?'

'My first name.'

'Really?' She stepped back, checking him out. He didn't seem to be joking. 'Fuck. Let's just leave it at Holt.'

He chuckled. 'Anyway, you know. Thank you.'

'For what?'

'Cutting my throat.'

'Don't mention it. So you're ready?'

'Where are we going?'

Rose pursed her lips and looked away. She'd been hoping he would not insist.

'Hell, don't worry,' Holt said. 'Surprise me.'

THE END